The
Ringing Bells
Inn

Daphne Neville

ISBN: 978-1-291-74212-1

PublishNation, London
www.publishnation.co.uk

Chapter One

1952

Throughout Paddington Station's vast structure, a muddled chorus of discordant sounds continually reverberated. High-pitched sharp whistles mingled with the loud echoing voices of the faceless crowds busily bustling to and fro, laden with bulging haversacks, brim-full holdalls, hand luggage and cumbersome suitcases. Yet, on platform one, undeterred by the endless din, two scrawny pigeons craftily concealed behind an overflowing litter bin, pecked hungrily at the discarded crusts of a potted meat sandwich deliberately dropped by a mischievous, blond haired boy of ten. He, unbeknown to his mother, had sneaked the crusts into the pocket of his duffle coat during his train journey to London, for fear there may be truth in his grandmother's claim regarding the ability of crusts to curl one's hair.

Food rationing meant the birds seldom enjoyed such a feast. Therefore, the untimely rhythmic clatter of fast approaching leather soles, sharply striking the hard surface of platform one, was without question, unwelcome, for it abruptly ended their modest lunch and sent them soaring high towards the station's grand arched roof in search of sanctuary.

Below, the young man responsible for the disruption, ran breathless and flustered along the near empty platform. In one hand he carried a large, brown leather suitcase: in the other, a briefcase. Tucked beneath his arm was a folded copy of the Daily Herald.

The guard was walking the length of the train systematically slamming shut the doors as the young man clambered on board and clumsily dropped his luggage onto the grimy floor. Pausing to catch his breath, he nodded politely to the only other passenger in the compartment.

"Sorry to burst in on you like this," he panted, wiping beads of perspiration from his damp brow. "I'm not usually this graceless or undignified."

From the back of the train, the guard's shrill whistle pierced through the thick, smoky atmosphere. The young man sighed with enormous relief and uttered thanks to the Almighty for sparing him the embarrassment of missing his train. With a renewed surge of energy, he then lifted his heavy suitcase onto the rack above and unbuttoned his overcoat. The train shuddered, creaked loudly and moved with a hefty jolt, causing the late arrival to stumble forwards and lose his balance.

The white haired stranger grinned. "Cut it a bit fine, didn't you?"

"Damn alarm clock," tutted the young man, as he regained his stature. "It didn't go off."

The stranger took out his pocket watch and looked at it with raised eyebrows.

"I know what you're thinking," the young man said, fully aware that it was fast approaching midday. "But I slept badly last night. Too much on my mind I suppose. It was four o'clock before I fell asleep properly."

Feeling overwarm due to his unplanned sprint, he removed his overcoat and trilby hat and placed both neatly overhead beside his luggage. While lowering himself onto the seating, he caught a glimpse of his untidy appearance in the mirror. Dismayed by the result of his missed ablutions, he roughly rubbed his hand across the stubble on his unshaven chin. Realising it was not possible to rectify his unkempt reflection completely, as a compromise, he took a comb from the breast pocket of his jacket, ran it through his wavy, russet brown hair and adjusted his tie. With half-hearted satisfaction he then sat down in the corner directly opposite the elderly man.

Discoloured, blackened buildings flashed past the windows through a haze of thick, swirling smoke as the train gathered speed. The young man watched until the view no longer appealed. He then picked up the newspaper which he'd previously dropped onto the seat.

The headline news, as on previous days, was dominated by the sudden death of King George VI, but now focused on Princess Elizabeth who had returned home prematurely from a holiday in Kenya as the new Queen. The country was in mourning and this mood was reflected throughout the entire paper. He read the Royal news and details of the forthcoming state funeral before thoughtfully folding the paper and laying it down on the seat.

"Sad time for the Windsors," he sighed, taking a cigarette from its packet and offering one to his travelling companion.

"Thanks," said the stranger, leaning forward and taking the proffered cigarette. "Sad time for us all, I reckon. It's not been an easy first half of the century has it? Two world wars, the abdication of Edward, the General Strike, the Depression, and now the untimely death of our King."

The young man nodded as he lit the cigarettes. "Perhaps a new monarch will be the beginning of happier and more peaceful times."

The older man sighed. "I hope so. I was just a lad when Queen Victoria died and it seems to have been doom and gloom ever since. Mind you," he added, with a twinkle in his eyes, "there were a lot of bright spots in between."

Grinning, the young man rose, lifted down his briefcase from the luggage rack above and placed the folded newspaper inside. As he lowered the lid, the words *STOP PRESS* caught his eye. Intrigued, he retrieved the paper and looked closely at the brief report.

'*Wagstaffe spotted in Rome,*' he read.

With a hearty laugh, he turned to his companion. "I see there's been another sighting of Willie Wagstaffe. Would you believe in Italy now?"

The stranger smiled. "He certainly gets around. I recall the Sketch claiming he was in Finland last week."

"Funny business all that," sighed the younger man, tossing the newspaper onto the seat as he sat down again. "Wagstaffe always seemed such a damn likable chap."

The older man nodded in agreement. "Quiet fellow so they say, but then the quiet ones are allegedly the worst."

The young man laid back his head and pondered over the ongoing saga of William Giles Wagstaffe, a successful, leading politician until New Year's Day 1950, when he and his housekeeper, Grace Bonnington, had both disappeared. Traces of blood had been found in Mrs. Bonnington's room at the Wagstaffe family home, along with a bloodstained silk scarf embroidered with the initials W.G.W. The top sheet was missing from her bed, and there were signs of a struggle. On the floor lay a tray on which sat the remains of her half eaten supper. A steak fork rested on the plate, but the knife was missing. According to associates of Mrs. Bonnington, a war widow, she and Mr. Wagstaffe had had a very *close* relationship, and because he was a married man with two children and his wife came from a wealthy, prominent family, the story inevitably caused a headline grabbing scandal when it first hit the news-stands during the early days of the new decade.

In spite of intense searching, Mrs. Bonnington's body had never been found. William Wagstaffe's car, however, was found abandoned in a disused factory yard a few days after his disappearance. Hence, two years on, sightings of him were still reported frequently in the press, stimulating rumours and beliefs that he was alive, well, and on the run.

A trolley rattled along the corridor startling both men. It stopped outside and a red faced, bright eyed youth slid back the compartment door.

"Light refreshments, gentlemen? Tea, coffee, sandwiches, rolls, cakes, pastries."

"Ah, tea please," said the younger man, eagerly eyeing the trolley, "and a current bun. I've not eaten anything yet today. Little wonder my stomach's rumbling."

"Yes, sir," replied the lad, eager to please.

The young man thrust his hand inside his jacket pocket and pulled out some change whilst the other passenger asked for a coffee.

"Going far?" the younger man asked, sipping his tea as the steward closed the door and left.

"Plymouth. I'm going to visit my daughter. The name's David by the way. David Braddley."

The two men leaned forward and shook hands.

"I'm Edward," said the younger man. "Edward Stanley, but everyone calls me Ned."

"How about you then, Ned," asked David, stirring two sugars into his coffee. "What's taking you to the West Country?"

"I'm going to Cornwall to convalesce. I've been knocked for six by wretched glandular fever and the doctor says I need some good, clean, sea air and plenty of rest. I thought Cornwall would be as good a place as any and I might even be able to do a bit of research into smuggling whilst there. I'm a teacher, you see, and I think it might capture the imagination of the youngsters when I return after Easter. Smuggling that is."

David nodded. "Hmm, should do the trick. I used to love stories of pirates, bandits and smugglers when I was a lad. Strange how young 'uns, especially boys, are drawn to such disreputable characters."

Ned laughed as he broke his bun in half. "Has your daughter lived in Plymouth long?" he asked, brushing crumbs from his lap.

"Three years. She's married to a boat builder and loves Devon very much. Funnily enough, she's a teacher too, at a primary school."

"Really! I teach first years at a secondary modern school in London. They're a smashing bunch of kids and I've really missed them during my illness."

"Do you have any of your own?" asked David, placing his empty coffee cup on the floor.

"What children? Good God, no! I'm not married. I hope to settle down one day, of course, when the right person comes along, but there's plenty of time for all that yet. I'll not be twenty-six 'til August."

David sighed. "I've been married for thirty-five years and I'd recommend it to anyone. Perhaps you'll meet Miss Right in Cornwall."

"Doubt it. I'm going to stay at an old inn located in a small village in the middle of nowhere on the Lizard Peninsula. I don't expect there will be any unattached females for miles around. Not ones that would interest me anyway."

David raised his hand and pressed it against his mouth to stifle a yawn. "Excuse me, Ned, it's not your company tiring me. It's just that I've been up since five this morning. I got up then to see my wife off to Scotland. She's gone up there to visit her sick, elderly mother, you see, and that's why I'm going to stay with my daughter in Devon." He chuckled. "Cynthia, my wife, says I'm not capable of looking after myself as I can't even boil an egg, and I'd be in the way if I went with her to stay with my mother-in-law. Anyway, it's too damn cold in Scotland this time of year. Give me Devon every time."

"Absolutely," Ned agreed. "But don't mind me, you have a nap and I'll make sure you don't miss your stop."

While David slept, Ned watched the bare hedgerows, leafless trees and endless fields pass by the window as the train steamed through the bleak, Somerset countryside. Dreamily, his thoughts drifted towards the idle weeks stretching out before him. Having never visited Cornwall before he was eagerly looking forward to the forthcoming experience and envisaging perpetual fresh air, walks over cliffs, strolls across beaches and rambles down winding, country lanes. He raised his arms and clasped his hands securely behind his head, a contented man, convinced the mere prospect of his expectations had a healing effect.

Glancing towards the window, Ned's gaze fell with approval on the contented, lined face of David Braddley as he snored gently in the corner seat. 'Fancy being married for thirty-five years,' Ned thought. It seemed an unimaginable scenario for himself. He had no intention of settling down for a while. He was able to cook, having learned the basics from books, and his father had made sure he was able to manage his finances.

"Pity he couldn't manage his marital problems," Ned mumbled, bitterly. For he had never fully come to terms with the separation and then divorce of his parents. Although he had to admit, they were, and always had been, chalk and cheese.

The train stopped. Several people climbed aboard and much to the disgust of Ned, two middle-aged women ambled into the compartment, shared until then only by David and himself. The loud, piercing voices of the new arrivals promptly woke David from his slumbers and their banal chat continued throughout the entire length of their short journey.

Ned heaved a sigh of relief when the women finally reached their destination and the train door slammed shut behind them. Half amused, he watched as still deep in conversation, they bustled along the busy platform carrying large baskets of shopping, oblivious of their surroundings.

"Talk about empty vessels," he muttered, as they disappeared down a flight of steps.

David laughed. He whole-heartedly agreed with Ned's sentiments.

As the train neared Plymouth, David Braddley gathered together his belongings ready for his departure. "Take care of yourself, lad," he said, buttoning up his thick overcoat. "Enjoy your rest, don't overdo it, and the very best of British luck with your research."

Ned stood and shook the hand of his travelling companion. "Thank you, and thank you for your company too."

David patted Ned's shoulder. "My pleasure. My pleasure indeed." He then lifted his suitcase and left the train.

Shortly after leaving Plymouth, the express steamed slowly over Isambard Kingdom Brunel's, Royal Albert Bridge. Ned, eager to see all, jumped from his seat, pushed down the window and gazed with awe onto the glistening River Tamar below, where grey Navy ships sat motionless on the still, distant waters, small boats bobbed at their moorings close to the shore, and midway between Devon and Cornwall, the Saltash Ferry, carrying a dozen cars, steamed across the estuary which separated the two counties.

When the river was no longer visible, Ned returned to his seat and from the window watched as the view reverted to houses, back gardens and the tedious, winter countryside. Feeling drowsy, he continuously drifted in and out of light sleep, but woke instantly when two stops before his own, a woman alone, climbed into his compartment. Ned sat up straight as her eyes looked him up and down before she gracefully placed herself in the corner diagonally opposite. Neither spoke, as from a large shopping basket by her feet, she took a magazine which she proceeded to read.

Ned peeped at her from the corner of his eye. She would be, he guessed, in her early thirties. Her bright auburn hair was obviously dyed and clashed dreadfully, in Ned's opinion, with her vivid, pillar box red lipstick and nail varnish. Her thin face was caked in make-up, her complexion looked tired and unhealthy. On her head she wore no hat and her body was completely enveloped in a voluminous fur coat.

Ned jumped when she abruptly closed her magazine and tossed it into her basket. She then sprang to her feet, removed her coat and looked into the mirror beneath the luggage rack. Reaching for her handbag, she took out her powder compact and dabbed yet another layer onto her pointed nose. To apply more lipstick, she steadied herself by lifting her right foot onto the seat. Her skirt slowly rose revealing the tops of her stockings. Ned, feeling a little hot under the collar, looked out of the window until she had finished her toiletries, brushed her hair, and replaced her coat.

The train jolted to a sudden halt. Ned had been so engrossed in the antics of his new travelling companion, he had reached his destination without realising.

The woman, however, was more organised. As the train stopped, she picked up her handbag and basket, opened the carriage door, and disappeared before Ned even had time to rise from his seat.

Chapter Two

Standing alone on the draughty platform of Gwinear Road Station, Ned watched his train steam off towards Penzance in a swirl of thick, grey smoke. With heart still thumping due to his unprepared, disorderly departure, he hastily staggered towards the waiting branch line train bound for the old market town of Helston.

The journey from Gwinear Road was less than nine miles and Ned was fully aware that Helston lay at the very end of the line. However, due to the unfamiliar Cornish landscape and unusual place names, he again failed to realise the approach of his destination and consequently was the last to leave the train.

Irritated to find all other passengers had already left the station, he made his way along the platform and out to the street where he hoped to find a taxi or a connecting bus link. To his dismay he found neither. The bus had already departed, the road was quiet, and in the taxi rank, a solitary car stood neglected and abandoned with a deflated front tyre.

Ned sighed deeply, and then from the corner of his eye he saw a telephone kiosk. Feeling a little optimistic he strolled towards it, pulled back the heavy red door and stepped inside. Frustrated that loitering had lost him both bus and taxi, he rummaged through the pockets of his jacket only to find he had no pennies amongst his change. Angrily, he swore beneath his breath. With no other option, he knew he would have to wait and hope a bus or taxi might soon return to the station.

Unaware how long his wait might be, he reluctantly lowered himself onto a garden wall and cast his eyes over the unfamiliar surroundings. Buildings and houses, large and small, in rows and detached, built of granite and darkened by dirt and age, lay nestled in a deep valley surrounded by hills.

Ned pulled up the collar of his overcoat as the sun and the little warmth it radiated rapidly disappeared beyond a distant hilltop. Murky clouds followed, each rolling swiftly across the dull sky and chased by a biting north westerly wind. Ned shivered. He felt fragile, vulnerable and downright miserable.

Ten minutes passed but still no bus or taxi arrived. Ned rose from the hard, cold wall and paced back and forth in an attempt to warm his numbed, frozen feet. With hands tucked deep inside the pockets of his overcoat, he wished his scarf and gloves were not still lying on the hall table of his Hammersmith flat.

The light was fast fading when Ned finally saw the welcome headlights of a car approaching. To his relief it was a taxi. With gratitude, he climbed inside, slammed shut the door and informed the driver of his destination.

Outside the Ringing Bells Inn, as the drone of the taxi's engine faded to a distant hum, Ned surveyed his new surroundings. It was almost dark but a warm feeling engulfed him as he viewed the outline of the large, old inn standing proudly against the moonless sky. Above its slate roof, the silhouette of tall trees waved eerily in the strengthening wind, each bare, twisted branch, partly obscuring four tapered pinnacles cornering the evenly spaced battlements crowning the church tower. While in their midst, the Union flag at half mast, flapped and fluttered in the breeze, a visual reminder to all of the late King's passing.

The front door of the Inn was also the entrance to the bar. Ned peered inside through a small, thick pane of glass, but no lights illuminated the room. He looked at his watch and on realising it was not yet opening time, walked around to a side alley where the bright light of a welcoming lamp shone above another door.

Ned put down his suitcase and pulled the worn rope dangling from an old brass bell. Inside, he heard the shrill call of a female voice, followed by the patter of approaching light footsteps. The large, green door opened and on the threshold stood a tall, slender woman in her mid to late thirties. Ned was speechless. She was elegantly dressed in a cream, fitted blouse and a pleated check skirt. Her shoulder length, chestnut brown hair, was parted on one side and swept back from her attractive face. On her feet she wore fine, brown leather, court shoes. But her legs! Ned could not recall having seen a more perfect pair in his life.

"Mr Stanley, I assume," she smiled, offering her petite, manicured hand.

"Yes," Ned croaked, shaking the proffered hand while cursing the fact he'd overslept thus leaving no time to shave.

"I'm Mrs Newton," she retorted, primly. "Please, do come in."

She stepped aside for him to cross the threshold and then abruptly closed the heavy door. Ned blinked to adjust his eyes to the light. He was in a spacious hallway, square in shape and bleak in décor. The floor was of slate flagstone, the walls part panelled in pitch-pine, and occupying the corner immediately opposite, a winding oak staircase turned and disappeared beneath a large oil painting of Saint Michael's Mount. He glanced around with a critical eye, doubting the hall had changed much since long before Victoria's reign, for it appeared to lack any of the modern features rapidly being introduced into post war London.

A middle aged man emerged from an adjoining passage. Mrs Newton turned to address him. "Frank, this is Mr Stanley," she said, as the two men shook hands. She turned again to face Ned. "My husband will show you your room."

She departed abruptly and walked off down the passage, leaving behind a waft of flowery perfume which reminded Ned of his mother.

Frank lifted Ned's suitcase. "Come this way, Mr Stanley," he ordered, walking towards the stairs. "I expect you're ready to put your feet up after your journey."

Clutching his briefcase, Ned obediently followed up the steep stairs and onto the landing where Frank pointed to a discoloured, white, half glazed door.

"That's the guests' bathroom," he recited. "There's usually plenty of hot water, so you can take a bath whenever you like."

Ned yawned. "Thank you," he said, as they turned right and walked along a dimly lit passage, lined on either side with panelled doors, numbered with polished, brass numerals.

"This'll be your room, Mr Stanley," said Frank, putting down the suitcase at the end of the passage. He opened the door and switched on the central, pendant light. The room struck cold and draughty. Ned immediately spotted the reason; above a small wicker ottoman, an ill-fitting sash window rattled noisily in its attempt to keep out the whistling, north wind.

Ned stepped inside the room and glanced around. In spite of its chill factor, it was neat, tidy and very spacious. Nodding his approval, he tossed his briefcase onto the double bed.

"I'll leave you to get settled in," said Frank, retreating towards the landing. "Dinner's at seven o'clock."

Ned hurriedly called after him, "If you don't mind, I'll skip dinner and go straight to bed. I really don't feel too good at the moment. I think it must have been hanging around waiting for the taxi."

Frank stepped back into the room and leaned against the old door frame. "Of course," he said, sympathetically, noting Ned's pale face. "You're here to convalesce, aren't you? I'd forgotten that. Come downstairs by the fire and at least have a bowl of nice, hot soup."

Ned agreed to Frank's suggestion with enthusiasm and carelessly slid his suitcase along the linoleum covered floor of his room, where it came to a standstill against the ottoman beneath the window. He then closed his door and followed Frank partway back along the passage. They stopped beside a small, unnumbered door. Frank lifted the latch, opened it and flicked on a brown Bakelite switch. From the ceiling, a shade-less, sixty watt bulb illuminated a musty, narrow back staircase. Ned closed the landing door and followed Frank down the steep, uncarpeted stairs.

"Mind your head, Mr Stanley," warned Frank, ducking, as he went through a door frame at the foot of the stairs. Ned obeyed and on raising his head found they were inside a large welcoming room which he assumed to be the Newton's living quarters.

"Here you are, sit down," ordered Frank, removing old newspapers from the padded seat of a dining chair, "and I'll just pop along to the kitchen to see Sylvia."

Ned sat on the appointed chair and surveyed the cluttered room with delight. Books were piled high on every surface, except the table. A treadle sewing machine stood in a corner, wedged between the wall and an old-fashioned sideboard whose surface was almost hidden beneath a large, wood cased wireless. In the recesses on either side of the fireplace, green cupboard doors stretched from floor to ceiling. In front of one stood a brown leather, wingback armchair. Beside the other, a three seater, brocade upholstered settee. And all around the room, partly obscuring the faded, floral wallpaper, hung paintings of fishing boats and seascapes, each bearing the artist's name, Josh Gilbert.

Ned was admiring the pictures when Frank returned holding a tin tray laden with a bowl of steaming soup, a wodge of white bread, and a thick slice of Victoria sponge cake. Close at heel was a huge, black cat.

"I've told the wife you're not feeling too good, Mr Stanley, and she quite understands, so she'll not be expecting you for dinner."

Carefully, he placed the steaming bowl and tea plate on the table.

"Thank you. I'm sorry to be such a nuisance."

"Nuisance! You're not a nuisance, Mr Stanley. You're no trouble at all. Now, come on lad, tuck in."

Ned grinned as he broke up a thick slice of bread and sprinkled it onto his soup. Frank's rustic charm gladdened him. He was clearly a caring man. When he laughed, his friendly eyes twinkled mischievously, lighting up the impish face part hidden beneath his neatly trimmed moustache and beard.

Whilst Ned devoured his soup, Frank pushed aside a fireguard and then stood in front of the hearth warming his back against the gentle, flickering flames of the small, log fire, until the smell of scorching caused him to move and sit in the leather armchair.

"You're a teacher, I hear, Mr Stanley?" he said, folding his arms.

"Yes, I teach eleven to twelve year olds. History's my subject, but please call me Ned."

Frank chuckled. "Of course. We run a friendly place here, no formalities and all that stuff. And you must call me Frank."

They chatted for twenty minutes until Frank hurriedly rose.

"Blimey, look at the clock. I best go and get spruced up, it's nearly time to open the boozer. Will you be joining us for a drink later?"

"No, no, not tonight," answered Ned, also rising. "I really must get some rest. It's been a very long day, travelling and all that, and I'm feeling extremely shattered. The soup was lovely though, so please thank Mrs Newton. It was much appreciated."

Frank lifted the fireguard and placed it back on the hearth. "Of course. We'll see you in the morning then, and I hope you sleep well."

As the two men prepared to leave the room, the cat, lying on the hearth rug, hurriedly leapt into the chair warmed by its master. Ned eyed it warily. He was not at all fond of cats and felt sure they viewed him with similar sentiments.

Ned shivered as he entered his chilly room and cursed the fact coal was still rationed. With teeth chattering he quickly pulled the flimsy curtains across the ill-fitting window and then searched through his suitcase. When he found his flannelette pyjamas he hastily removed his clothing and whilst holding his breath, leapt into the large, iron framed bed expecting the sheets to strike cold and unwelcoming. But much to his surprise, he found blissful warmth, for someone had tucked two hot water bottles inside his bed. Ned sighed, contented, as the soothing warmth spread through his tired limbs, and almost instantly he drifted off into a deep, uninterrupted sleep.

The following morning, Ned awoke to the monotonous sound of water dripping rapidly in the vicinity of his bedroom window and raindrops splashing relentlessly against the small panes of glass. At first he could not recall where he was, but as he rubbed sleep from his eyes, he remembered his brief encounters with the Newtons.

Ned sat up, pulled the eiderdown from the top of his bed, wrapped it snugly round his broad shoulders and surveyed the room. To his dismay, it looked no more comforting in the semi-light of a cold, wet, February morning, than it had the previous night. Certainly it was quaint, if you happened to like sloping walls and uneven floors. It was also clean. But cheerful, never.

He climbed out of bed with the eiderdown still wrapped around his shoulders, knelt on the ottoman and pulled back the curtains. The dripping water was directly outside his window. He fumbled with the catch, pushed up the rattling frame and looked heavenwards. A broken piece of guttering hung precariously overhead, allowing water to drip through with incessant haste. With a discontented groan, he closed the window and gathered up the clothes he'd strewn over the floor during their hasty removal the previous night.

"A bath." he muttered, "that's what I need to warm me up. A nice hot bath."

He tossed the eiderdown onto the bed, pulled his dressing gown from the suitcase and marched along the landing to the bathroom.

Feeling warmer once bathed and dressed, and presentable, once shaved, he returned to his room with appreciably more optimism. Seeing it was fully light, he opened the window to view his new surroundings. To his dismay the rain was still falling. Ned watched, mesmerised, as heavy raindrops gushed into the overflowing gutters of an out-building's corrugated tin roof, and then splashed unremittingly into a groaning, brim-full, water butt.

A sharp knock on the door caused him to jump. Quickly, he closed the window. On the landing stood Mrs Newton, a steaming cup and saucer in her hands. She smiled. "We don't usually wait on our guests like this, but as you were unwell last night I'm making an exception."

With eyebrows raised, Ned took the teacup from her hands. "Thank you, Mrs Newton."

"Please, call me Sylvia," she smiled. "And in case Frank didn't say, breakfast is at half past eight."

Ned watched her walk back towards the landing before closing the door of his room. With a satisfied grin, he sat in a threadbare armchair beside a bleak, empty grate and sipped his tea thoughtfully. When the cup was empty he placed it on the hearth slate and lit a cigarette.

"I think I'm going to like it here," he told the portrait of an old fisherman hanging on the wall.

The Inn's other guests were already seated in the dining room when Ned went downstairs for breakfast. On opposite sides of a small, square table, inside a south facing bay window, Mr and Mrs Johnson ate poached eggs, toast, and Spam fritters. Greg Johnson was an artist, who with his wife visited Cornwall every winter for inspiration to paint the sea in its roughest moods.

At the next table sat smartly dressed Charles Dunwoody, an insurance salesman, staying at the Inn for just a few days while he made business calls in the area. And tucked in the deep alcove to one side of the fireplace, a young couple on honeymoon, with eyes for no-one but each other, sat snugly side by side.

The only other guest was Major Smith, a well-bred man in his late forties, who having sold his Surrey home had moved to Cornwall and become a permanent resident at the Inn.

Ned eyed them all with curiosity as he sat at a table in the centre of the room. Once seated, he wished he'd chosen the unoccupied table in the other alcove, to allow subtle observation of his fellow guests.

From a door, which Ned assumed led to the kitchen, a petite blonde emerged and approached Ned's table. She asked his preference for breakfast after first reciting a brief choice. Ned ordered a lightly boiled egg, toast and plum jam: homemade, he was informed. As the girl returned to the kitchen, Ned wondered if she was the Newtons' daughter but instantly dismissed the idea for she had none of Sylvia's fine features or Frank's rugged good looks.

After breakfast, Ned returned to his room and unpacked the remaining items in his suitcase. With care, he hung his jackets and trousers in the large, double wardrobe; everything else he put in the chest of drawers by the door. Once the case was empty he slid it beneath his bed and looked from his window. To his delight, the rain had stopped and a patch of light blue sky cheekily peeked through the grey clouds. Without hesitation, he reached for his hat and coat, keen for a walk to the village post office to purchase a newspaper. During breakfast he'd observed a copy of the Daily Mail in the dining room for the use of guests, but Ned favoured the Daily Herald because one of its reporters was the friend of a friend.

Outside the Inn, Ned walked back along the road down which he had travelled the previous day in the taxi. By the church lichgate he stopped and gazed up at the tower. Gratifying stonework, entwined with the thick stems of a leafless creeper, covered the east facing side and through a gap peered the round, white face of a clock edged with black Roman numerals. As he turned to continue his journey, the clock struck ten.

The heart of Trengillion lay around the one main street, bordered on either side with houses and cottages. Ned took very little notice of his surroundings, but concentrated instead on avoiding the numerous puddles shimmering on the badly surfaced road.

He saw no-one until he reached a house standing back from the road with Ivy Cottage painted on a green, wooden gate. In the front garden, a grey haired woman wearing fingerless gloves, daintily picked a posy of pale yellow primroses. Ned greeted her pleasantly. Her response was an incoherent mumble. Feeling rebuffed, Ned walked on.

The post office lay towards the end of the village, opposite a primary school and next to a small development on which a row of new houses was under construction. To Ned's delight it sold a vast array of goods and he was even able to purchase a scarf and pair of warm gloves.

Walking back through the village he saw no-one as the unfriendly primrose picker had returned indoors. Work on the new houses seemed at a standstill. Ned put the lack of activity down to the wet morning.

Outside the Inn, the slowly brightening sky teasingly hinted at the possibility of sunshine, and so Ned continued to walk downhill, confident the sea must be very near. He was not disappointed. It lay beyond a few cottages, thus causing him to realise it would be visible from the upstairs, south facing windows of the Inn.

He crossed the wet shingle, walked down to the water's edge and took in a deep breath of the fresh, clean air. The sea was calm in the off shore wind. Ned watched as it tumbled and gently splashed close to his feet, bringing back memories of trips to the seaside when he was a boy.

The cove was moderate in size with high, impressive cliffs giving shelter to the east and the west. On top of the latter stood a fine looking detached house. Ned craned his neck to see more clearly. It was obvious the views from such a spot would be far reaching and breathtakingly beautiful.

The surface of the beach was predominantly shingle interspersed with patches of rippled sand. At the base of the cliffs, amongst huge boulders and craggy, weathered rock, lay small pools of water containing seaweed and tiny crustaceans. Further down the beach, surrounded by a flow of swirling water, a formation of gigantic rocks created a small island. Ned wished the tide was out, for he guessed at low water it would be accessible on foot and no doubt a favourite spot for sunbathers during the summer months.

As the first rays of sun peeped through the milky white clouds, Ned crossed the beach to a wooden bench. Close by, a steady trickle of fresh water ran in from a stream in the valley, bound for the sea.

Ned sat on the bench after first reading the inscription carved on the back.

In memory of Denzil Penhaligon - Fisherman -
Drowned off these shores, December 12th 1950.

Ned shuddered. He cared very little for water and the thought of drowning filled him with terror.

He opened up his newspaper and started to read, but soon his teeth began to chatter. Before the cold spread through his entire body, he decided to return to the Inn. On rising, he observed a small fishing boat chugging towards the cove. He watched as it reached the shore and the two fishermen on board went through a rigorous ritual of winching the boat up the beach.

Ned wondered if they had caught any fish but thought it impudent to ask. He left for the Inn and nodded to the two fishermen as he crossed the beach. They each nodded in return but neither smiled. Ned was beginning to think that apart from the Newtons all other inhabitants of the village were decidedly hostile.

After dark, Ned changed into his grey, flannel trousers and donned his favourite check, sports jacket. He then went downstairs for dinner.

Once again the other guests were already seated and at the same tables as for breakfast. Ned did likewise, but this time sat on the side of the table nearest the fireplace, where a one bar electric fire, almost threw out sufficient heat to warm the room.

For dinner there was no choice. Tomato soup was followed by shepherd's pie. The food, however, was excellent. Ned asked the unenthusiastic waitress, whose name he'd discovered, was Betty, who did the cooking. He was surprised the answer was Sylvia.

"She grows our vegetables too," said Betty, forcing a smile, seeing his raised eyebrows. "Frank reckons she saves a fortune on greengrocery bills."

Ned was most impressed. "Good-looking and practical," he mused, tucking into his Apple Charlotte. "Who'd have thought it?"

Last to leave the dining room, Ned made his way through to the bar where Major Smith was talking to a couple of men.

Charles Dunwoody sat not far away, perched on a stool, drinking whisky, as he wrote in a note book.

Through the open double doors of the snug bar, flickering flames in shades of red and orange, crackled around logs piled high in the inglenook fireplace. Above, ticked a large clock, its pendulum steadily swinging to and fro in a case of wood, cracked along the bottom due to the incessant heat of many years. And across the ceiling, supporting darkened floor boards, ran old wooden beams, each one almost hidden behind a vast collection of hanging, colourful plates.

Ned bought a pint of beer and then settled down on a large cushioned window seat in the snug within close proximity of the fire. The Johnsons came in and settled at the end of the public bar. There was no sign of the honeymoon couple. Ned finished his pint and bought a second. A few men came in from outside. He watched as they chatted and laughed amongst themselves. Judging by their dress, he concluded they were farmers.

Ned thought of David Braddley and wondered how he was enjoying Devon. He thought of his friends and work colleagues in London and wished they were with him for company. His eyelids began to feel heavy. The warmth of the fire, the sea air, his illness and the beer, all contributed to feelings of drowsiness. Through a muzzy haze, he saw Sylvia drift into the bar. She joined Frank who gave her a hug.

Ned watched. Suddenly, he felt very, very lonely. Quickly, he finished his drink, bade Frank and Sylvia goodnight, and then returned, with haste, to his cold, austere, inhospitable room.

Chapter Three

Ned awoke the following morning to hear irritating splashes of water dripping onto the window sill again. Swearing beneath his breath, he snatched the antimacassar from the back of the armchair, folded it into six and placed it on the window ledge outside to muffle the monotonous din. As he closed the window he angrily glared up at the miserable sky looming overhead like a coarse, grey blanket. What on earth was he to do if it was wet? He had not contemplated bad weather when he had first planned his stay in Cornwall. If asked, he would have assumed the rainfall on the Lizard Peninsula would be no more prevalent than in London.

"Drat the weather," he cursed, closing the door of his room and storming along the landing to the bathroom, only to find it engaged as someone whistled happily beyond the frosted glass. Feeling extremely disgruntled, he returned to his room and slammed shut the door so violently it caused the surrounding walls to shake.

When finally he went down to breakfast only the Johnsons were still seated in the dining room. Ned cast them a half-hearted smile as he unceremoniously sat at his table to await Betty's arrival. To his surprise, however, it was not Betty, but an appealing brunette, who approached his table with a wide, genuine smile, which perfectly framed her crooked, yet charming, white teeth.

"Morning, sir," she gabbled, brightly. "My name's Gertie, Gertie Penrose. I'm your waitress today. Now, what can I get you for breakfast?"

He chose the same as on the previous day.

"Certainly, sir," she smiled. "I'll be back in a jiffy."

With amusement, Ned watched her bustle off to the kitchen. He liked her instantly, sensing she had a warm personality and a keen sense of humour. Within minutes she returned, as promised, with his breakfast on a tray in her hands.

"Have you been here long?" Ned asked, promptly kicking himself for the trite content of his question, as she lowered the tray onto the table.

"What working? About, um, six months, I suppose," she mused, with hands on hips. "Yes, six months it'd be. I replaced Jane, you see, after she disappeared, and that was last summer."

"Disappeared," laughed Ned, niftily slicing off the top his egg. "What do you mean by disappeared?"

"Well, like I said, sir, she just sort of disappeared. Here one day gone the next. No-one knows where to. She never said a word to any of us, and we'd all been friends since we were kids."

"How strange. I take it she lives in the village."

"Yes, she does, sir. She lives with her Auntie Doris. Her mum died when she was a nipper, you see, and her poor old dad got killed at the beginning of the War, so she lives with her auntie at Ivy Cottage. And before you ask, her aunt's got no idea where she's gone to, either."

"Hmm, Ivy Cottage," repeated Ned.

"Yes, sir, it's along the main road by..."

"...I know," interrupted Ned, recalling the unpleasant primrose picker. "I saw it on my way to the post office yesterday morning."

The Johnsons finished their breakfast and rose to leave the dining room. Gertie wished them a pleasant day and then proceeded to clear their table.

"So what's your theory regarding this Jane's disappearance?" Ned called, across the room.

"Do you mean, what do I think's happened to her?"

Ned smiled. "Yes."

"Well, I really don't know." Gertie glanced around the empty room, placed her left hand in front of her mouth, and lowered her voice. "But there are rumours that she may have got herself into trouble, if you know what I mean." She winked her right eye repeatedly and patted her stomach. "And I'm not one to accuse them as isn't here to defend themselves, but she was very, very friendly with Percy Collins, sir."

"Percy Collins," repeated Ned, amused, "and who might he be?"

"He be a fisherman, sir. Fishes from the cove. He's a han'some fella who likes the ladies." She sighed, absent-mindedly. "Ah, dear Percy. He was potty about her and who can blame him, because Jane was, well, she was very beautiful."

"I see," mused Ned, as he finished his egg.

21

A dreamy eyed Gertie left the dining room with a tray of dirty dishes. Ned grinned. It was quite obvious the ladies were equally fond of Percy.

The rain continued to fall with no signs of easing, and so Ned reluctantly spent the morning in his room with just his newspaper to read, having at least ventured out to fetch it. He read the paper from cover to cover, including articles on football, even though he had no interest, whatsoever, in the game. Cricket was the only sport as far as Ned was concerned. Cricket, and the occasional game of tennis.

As the church clock struck midday, Ned, bored by his own company, popped down to the bar for a drink and something to eat. The bar was quiet. Ned asked Frank for a pint and one of the pasties on display in a dimly lit warming cabinet.

As he made himself comfortable on the same seat as the previous night, he noticed two trophies on the window sill behind. He lifted one and read the engraving. It was an award to Sylvia Newton, second prize for show jumping. He picked up the other. Again for show jumping, but this time first prize.

Ned caught Frank's eye through the open doors of the snug,

"Sylvia's a keen horsewoman, I see."

Frank nodded. "That's right, she has a couple of 'em. I bought her the first for a Christmas present, but by the end of February she was fretting old Winston was lonely out in the paddock all by himself, so I bought her another for her birthday."

"Winston," smiled Ned. "So is the second one called Churchill?"

Frank chuckled. "No, she christened him Brown Ale."

Ned took a bite from his pasty. "I suppose she makes these too."

Frank shook his head. "No, they're made by Flo Hughes. Good ol' Flo used to be cook here, you see, 'til she decided to retire, that is. Sylvia took over from her then, but she refused to make the pasties. She said they should always be made by a Cornish woman, and quite right too. So dear Flo makes 'em at home."

"They're delicious," said Ned, guiding falling crumbs onto his plate, "whoever makes them."

He continued to eat whilst Frank turned to serve an elderly couple busily removing their raincoats. He then bought a second pint to wash down his lunch. When plate and glass were both empty, he returned to his room.

Outside the rain continued to fall. With the knowledge he was confined indoors for the remainder of the day, Ned lay on his bed to rest and within minutes of his head hitting the pillow he was sound asleep.

When he awoke it was dark. He shivered, switched on the light and approached the window to draw the curtains. To his surprise his ears encountered silence. No water splashing against the window panes or thudding onto the old tin roof. Ned opened the window and looked outside. The rain had stopped, the air smelt fresh and the dark sky was clear.

"Typical," he muttered. "What a waste of a day!"

Much to Ned's delight, Gertie was waitress again at dinner.

"Evening, sir," she smiled, placing a bowl of celery soup on the table in front of him. "Are you enjoying your stay with us?"

Ned scowled. "Well hardly, it's damn near impossible with this wretched weather. You're the only bright spot at present, Gertie."

She wrinkled her nose, giggled, and returned to the kitchen. Ned sighed and supped his soup in silence.

With nothing else to do, he went into the bar again after dinner, where, except for a short balding man with tattoos on both his hands and around his neck, the only other drinkers were residents of the Inn.

Ned eyed the stranger as he talked surreptitiously to Major Smith. His appearance was reminiscent of an East End gangster, which started Ned fantasising about the nature of the conversation taking place. While deep in thought two men entered the bar. Ned turned as he heard the door close; he recognised them instantly as the two fishermen he had seen on the beach the previous day.

Frank greeted the fishermen as they approached the bar. "Evening Percy. Evening Peter. Your usual?"

"Yeah," they grunted in unison. Frank nodded and reached for two pewter tankards hanging with others from a wooden beam.

Ned leaned forward on the seat and watched with interest. It was easy to detect which of the two was the much admired Percy. He was taller and leaner than Peter. His dark, shoulder length hair was untidy and a combination of tight ringlets and loose, ruffled curls. His handsome face was brown due to exposure to the sun and sea breezes. He had a larger than average nose, rich, hazel brown eyes, long, thick, dark eyelashes and a pointed, stubbly chin. While Frank filled their tankards, Percy and Peter sat down on stools facing each other beside the bar.

A little later, as Ned waited at the bar for a refill, eavesdropping on Percy and Peter's conversation, a clean shaven man with thick, greying hair, rushed in and asked Frank for cigarettes.

Frank took a packet of twenty from the shelf. "Ned, this is someone you might like to meet." He gestured, with a nod, in the direction of the new arrival. "Reg, this is Ned Stanley, a school teacher from up London. And Ned, this is Reg Briers, headmaster of our school here in the village."

The two men shook hands firmly.

"Pleased to meet you," said Reg, handing Frank loose change. "But how come you're off school during term time?"

Ned briefly told of his illness. Reg listened with sympathy.

"Will you join me for a drink?" Ned asked, eager for company.

Reg sighed. "I'd love too, I really would, but I've a meeting to attend in ten minutes. I only popped in to get these for the wife."

He dropped the cigarettes into his pocket.

"Some other time then, perhaps?" said Ned, hopefully.

Reg kindly patted Ned's arm, and then turned towards the door. "Most definitely. I might be in at the weekend, but if not, then I'll certainly be in early next week."

Ned lifted his refilled glass as the Inn door closed. "He seems a nice chap. I would imagine he's popular with the kids."

"Hmm, he is," agreed Frank. "You'd have to go a long way to find a better and more dedicated headmaster than Reg Briers. Trengillion's very lucky to have him. Very lucky indeed."

Ned retired to bed more content and optimistic than on the two previous nights. He attributed this to his fortuitous meetings with Gertie and Reg, and eagerly looked forward to further conversations with them both. There was even the strong possibility of fine weather the following day, if the overheard, farmer's chat was to be relied on.

Ned slept soundly until the early hours when he woke suddenly feeling cold due to his bedclothes having slipped into a heap on the floor. Shivering, he sat up, yawned, and fumbled in the darkness for the bedside lamp switch. With the room illuminated, he jumped out of bed, quickly picked up the coarse blankets and tucked them back beneath the thick mattress. Once done, he spread the eiderdown neatly on top, climbed back into bed, switched off the lamp and snuggled down between the linen sheets. With eyes closed he attempted to sleep, but to his annoyance, sleep evaded him. The comfortable slumbers from which he had woken would not return. His bed felt hard and lumpy. His limbs heavy and awkward.

Ned cursed as he tossed and turned. In an attempt to distract his mind from the discomfort he was suffering, he directed his thoughts to the possibility of smuggling in the area, and then to the late King's State Funeral due to take place the following morning. He wondered if any of his friends would be amongst the crowds lining the streets of London to watch the cortège. Frank and Sylvia had invited the residents of the Inn to listen to the broadcast on the wireless. This pleased Ned. He respected the Royal family and the King in particular, for stepping, reluctantly, into the shoes of his brother, Edward in 1936, when Edward had abdicated, having chosen to marry his sweetheart, American divorcee, Wallis Simpson.

Eventually drowsiness slowly forced Ned's eyelids to flicker. The lumps in the bed dispersed and his body relaxed. Thankful that sleep was imminent, he snuggled his head deep into the soft feather pillow, closed his eyes and listened to the sweet sound of someone singing.

Singing! Promptly Ned opened his bleary eyes. Could he really hear singing or was he dreaming? He sat bolt upright, pinched his arm to make sure he was awake and strained his ears to listen.

Yes! Someone was singing, though it sounded distant and slightly muffled. He again switched on the light, climbed out of bed, opened the door and looked along the landing. It was eerily quiet with no evident sign of life, yet the voice could clearly be heard, singing sweetly and tunefully beyond the darkness of the night.

With curiosity raised, Ned reached for his dressing gown, slipped it on and took a torch from the pocket of his overcoat. After leaving his room, he quietly closed the door and crept along the dark landing, continually sweeping downward glances as he advanced, noting no glimmers of light shining from beneath any of the guests' doors.

Outside the last room, situated next to the bathroom, Ned stopped, aware of a repetitive noise. He smiled on realising it was nothing more than the quiet, rhythmical snoring of one of the residents. With relief, he turned the corner and tip-toed towards the staircase, flashing the dim light of his torch in the process at the now familiar surroundings.

At the top of the stairs Ned reached for the banisters, momentarily stopping to identify the song. He smiled with self-satisfaction when he resolved it was *Some Enchanted Evening* from his mother's favourite musical, *South Pacific*.

Casting a brief glance over his shoulder, he cautiously continued to descend the staircase, praying with each step that none would creak. They did not, and he reached the downstairs hallway safely. The voice, Ned realised, was coming from the dining room. He was surprised. It seemed a strange place in which anyone might sing, especially long after everyone had retired to bed.

Aware that the Newtons' living quarters were nearby, Ned was keen to ascertain the coast was clear in all directions before he proceeded along the dark passage. Cautiously he stepped backwards into the shadows, where to his horror something soft, warm and mobile brushed against his bare feet. The something yowled, spat and hissed. Ned's hair stood on end and his spine tingled. He regained his balance just in time to see the outline of the Newtons' cat, its tail huge and erect, as it disappeared along the passage encased in the quivering circle of his torch light.

"Ruddy, gormless animal," cursed Ned, his heart thumping wildly as he fell to his knees and crouched in the corner of the hallway; his body trembling as he hid amongst a vast array of hanging coats, praying the cat's untimely cry had woken no-one. For if he was discovered, explaining his reason for wandering around in the dark like an intruder would be very difficult and no doubt raise uncertainty as to the quality of his character.

Convinced after five minutes the rumpus had disturbed no-one, Ned emerged from his hiding place only to realise the singing had stopped. He was baffled, fully aware he'd seen no-one, other than the cat, in the passage. Not discouraged, however, he continued to make

26

his way towards the dining room. Outside the wide, panelled door he paused. All was quiet. He slid his hand over the brass knob and turned it gently. The door squeaked as he slowly pushed it open and beads of perspiration emerged on his forehead as he timorously peeped inside. To his dismay the room was dark, silent, cold and empty. Confused, Ned crossed the room and glanced through the connecting door to the kitchen, which stood ajar. He flashed his torch across the large Formica topped table, over the free-standing cupboards and towards the white Belfast sink. There was no sign of life. Utterly mystified, he retreated towards the dining room door and closed it quietly. He then fled down the passage and returned, with haste, up the stairs, two steps at a time, whilst keeping out a watchful eye for the cat.

Once back in the safety of his own room, he closed the door swiftly and stood, with heart thumping, beside his window and gazed out. The night sky was pitch black and starless. He could see nothing. Puzzled, he climbed back into his now cold bed, looked at his watch and switched off the bedside lamp.

"Who on earth," thought Ned, as he laid his head on the pillow, "would still be up, and singing, at three o'clock in the morning?

Chapter Four

The following morning, Ned joined the Inn's other residents inside the Newtons' living room to hear the BBC's coverage of the King's funeral on the wireless. And as a mark of respect, the Inn was to remain closed throughout the normal lunchtime opening hours.

No-one left the warm, cluttered room once the broadcast began, except Sylvia, who momentarily crept out to make a pot of tea and fetch a plate of cheese sandwiches, made earlier in the day.

The small group listened in silence. The sombre calm of the event was interrupted only occasionally by the gentle sobbing of Mrs. Johnson and the honeymoon wife. At two o'clock, the little party rose to their feet, bowed their heads, and joined in with the rest of Great Britain and fellow members of the Commonwealth, for two minutes' silence.

When the broadcast was over, Ned pensively walked down to the cove. He wanted to be alone to collect his thoughts. The emotion of the funeral had pushed to the back of his mind the events which had occurred during the night, but once outside in the dim light of a dull, February day, they came back to him fresh and clear.

Ned sat down on Denzil's bench and pondered over what significance, if any, the singing had. He then turned over in his mind the possibilities as to whom it might have been. As far as he was aware, there would have been only three females at the Inn during the night. Sylvia, Mrs Johnson, and the honeymoon wife, as he was sure neither Gertie nor Betty lived in.

Unable to reach any conclusions or satisfactory answers, Ned stretched out his long legs, closed his eyes and laid back his head against his cupped hands. The soothing, gentle whooshing of the tumbling waves falling gently onto the desolate shore, and the sharp rattling of small pebbles shifting beneath the rippling water, soothed his aching brow and within minutes, tired through the disturbances in the night, the sea's rhythmic lullaby lulled him into a welcome sleep.

Twenty minutes later he awoke, cold, stiff and uncomfortable. His arms were numb and his fingers dead. He stood, flapped his arms to revive his circulation and then huffed onto his fingers to retrieve their usual colour. Once near normality was restored, he decided, as the weather was fine, to take a walk in order to exercise his recovering limbs.

His preference would have been for a ramble over the cliffs and a closer look at the impressive house overlooking the village, but he concluded such a choice would be unwise. His strength had not yet returned sufficiently to risk venturing out of his depths. He settled, therefore, on a gentle stroll through the village and perhaps a little beyond.

He left the beach and walked along the main road, past the thatched cottages, the Inn and the church, and on towards the post office. Opposite the post office stood the village school, single storey and built of granite. Close by, peeping over the top of two tall privet hedges, peered the slate roof of a detached residence. Ned took a closer look; in between the neatly clipped hedges, hung a green, wooden gate, boldly engraved with The School House in capital letters. Ned smiled, it was no doubt the home of Headmaster, Reg Briers.

Between the school and The School House ran a narrow lane. Ned peered along it and contemplated whether or not to go down. It looked inviting. A sharp bend occurred less than thirty yards along and he felt curious as to what might lie beyond. Knowing time was plentiful, he made up his mind to explore and left the now familiar main road.

The lane was narrow, uneven and very winding. On either side, loomed high, dry stone walls, overgrown with twitch and the dead stems of wild flowers, grasses and underdeveloped wild shrubs, all knitted together, hiding the stonework and obstructing the view to the landscape beyond.

Ned walked on. The rugged lane twisted, turned and then gradually began to run downhill. Towards the bottom, the high hedgerows ended and the vista opened out to a valley where rows of leafless trees and a variety of bushes wound off in two opposite directions, clearly outlining the contours of a hidden stream. Ned stopped when he reached the very bottom of the hill. On either side of the road, small granite walls indicated there was a bridge below. He looked to his left. In the valley, above the emerging stream, a woodland stood dark and secretive. Beyond the bare, leafless branches of its countless trees, lay a seemingly large house, part-hidden; its roof was crowned with numerous tall chimneys, all but one devoid of smoke.

Ned wondered to whom the large house belonged for the smoke indicated it must be occupied. Guessing it was no-one with whom he had yet become acquainted, he peered thoughtfully over the bridge to the stream below, nestled between the muddy banks. On impulse he slid beneath a broken fence and down a well-worn path.

The stream was fast flowing from the direction of the house. He watched as the clear, bright water splashed and flowed over stones, dead branches and an old rusty paint tin. As it disappeared beneath the bridge, he realised it was, without doubt, be the same stream which flowed across the beach and into the sea beside Denzil Penhaligon's memorial bench.

A car passed slowly by in the direction from which Ned had been walking. Curious to know who the driver was, he raised his head to see but was too low down to even glimpse the vehicle's roof. Disappointed, he scrambled back up the bank, under the fence and onto the road to continue his walk.

Half way up the hill, Ned reached a row of four small cottages. In an untidy, overgrown front garden, littered with discarded broken furniture and rusty sheets of corrugated metal, a scruffy terrier whined as Ned passed by. He stopped and leaned over the fence to stroke the animal, but from the rear of the short terrace another dog responded with blood curdling growls. Ned straightened himself promptly and proceeded to walk considerably faster than before.

At the top of the hill, fatigue struck. Feeling weak and breathless, Ned stopped to rest on the grass verge. On the opposite side of the road a signpost indicated a bridle path lay in a southerly direction. Once refreshed, Ned climbed on top of a rickety five bar gate to see where it might lead. From it, beyond meadows and rolling hills lay a magnificent view of the sea. Awestruck, Ned drank in the beauty of the Cornish coastline; it was breathtaking even on a dull day when the sea was as grey as the sky and it was difficult to distinguish between the two.

Glancing further along the lane, Ned observed the buildings of a farm. However, feeling he had walked far enough, he turned and retraced his steps down the hill. At the bottom he stopped again. To get back his breath, he sat on the wall of the bridge to rest. Another car drove by, the driver of which was a thin faced, skeletal man. Ned watched as the black, mud splashed vehicle disappeared round the bend. He then continued back up the hill towards the village.

When Ned returned to the Inn, he found Sylvia in the hallway watering a plant on the window ledge at the bottom of the stairs. Rubbing around her legs was the cat. Ned scowled as Sylvia put down the can and picked up the black ball of fluff and claws. She smiled sweetly as he closed the door. "Ned, do come and meet Barley Wine."

He made a pathetic attempt to smile and forced himself to put forth his hand as though he had a desire to stroke the animal. However, his pretence was unnecessary, for the cat, with no desire to be petted by Ned, hissed wildly, jumped from Sylvia's arms and disappeared down the passage.

Sylvia tut-tutted, clearly amused, as it fled from view. "Silly puss."

Ned laughed falsely and then turned to climb the stairs. Half way up he remembered his quest for knowledge regarding smuggling.

"Smuggling," Sylvia smiled, when confronted with the enquiry. "I'm the last person to ask actually. I'm not a native to these parts, you see."

Surprised, Ned took two steps back towards the hallway. "Really! Which part of the country are you from then?"

"The Midlands. That's where I grew up, anyway."

"The Midlands. So what brought you all the way down here?"

She smiled and her eyes twinkled. "I came down for a break, ended up working here, married the landlord and I've never been back once."

"Good heavens! How odd. But surely you must miss your family."

Her smile faded. "What family? I was an only child, Ned. My poor mother died giving birth to me and my father died soon after of a broken heart. Neither of them had any siblings and so I was brought up in an orphanage. I have no family at all."

"Oh, I am sorry," mumbled Ned, foolishly. "Really, I'm very sorry."

Sylvia smiled. "Don't be. It all happened a very long time ago. It's history and best forgotten." She raised her hands to her mouth and thoughtfully stroked her bottom lip. "Anyway, in response to your question about smuggling, Frank might know a yarn or two, because he's been here a good few years now, and then of course, there's Farmer, Pat Dickens, and I mustn't forget Jim Hughes. Jim is a retired gamekeeper, you see, and he used to work on the Penwynton Estate. I know Pat and Jim have both lived in the area all their lives, but then so have a lot of other folks."

"The Penwynton Estate, that sounds impressive. Its boundaries wouldn't by any chance include a very large house with tall chimneys, would it? I ask because I saw such a place through the trees at the bottom of the hill which runs between the school and The School House."

Sylvia nodded. "Yes, that'd be Penwynton House, and the trees you speak of are known locally as Bluebell Woods. It, and many, many acres of land, several farms and some cottages, all belong to a crusty old bachelor called Charles Penwynton. I believe the estate has been home of the Penwyntons for donkey's years."

Ned raised his eyebrows. "Hmm, he's worth a bob or two then. Back on a more serious note though. You mentioned a Pat and a Jim. Do they drink here?"

Sylvia laughed. "Oh, yes. I'll get Frank to introduce you when next they're in. Meanwhile, I'm sure we must have a few books on smuggling, if you'd like to borrow some."

Ned rubbed his hands with delight. "I most certainly would. The more the merrier."

She led him back into the living room where they had all gathered only a few hours before and gestured towards the piles of books. "Help yourself, Ned. They're not in any order, I'm afraid, and I can't recommend any as I'm ashamed to say, I've not read even one. In fact there may be nothing there of any interest at all."

"That's alright, I'm sure I must be able to find something to satisfy my curiosity, and if not I'll make do with something completely different to pass away the time, if that's alright with you."

Sylvia stepped back and opened the door. "Of course. I'll leave you to it because I must go now and attend to things in the kitchen, otherwise dinner will be late and that would never do."

As she was leaving, Ned impulsively asked if she had been singing the previous night. Her reply was to throw back her head and laugh loudly. "Good heavens, no. Dear Frank banned me from singing when first we married. Don't even sing in the bath, he'd threatened. It might frighten away the guests."

Ned smiled and watched, as still giggling, she closed the door and left. She looked even more beautiful when she laughed.

When Ned went down to dinner, having eaten only a cheese sandwich since breakfast, he was ravenous. The walk had also contributed to his appetite, hence, for a change, he was not the last in the dining room, but the first.

A delightful smell escaped from the kitchen as Gertie opened the door and brought in a bowl of steaming vegetable soup.

"You've some colour in your cheeks tonight, sir," she commented. "Have you been out, or just sitting by the fire?"

Ned grinned, told her of his walk and his sighting of Penwynton House.

"Oh, had you gone just a little bit further you'd have reached our farm. Next time pop in for a cup of tea and introduce yourself. Mother makes excellent carrot cake and is always glad of a visitor."

Ned gobbled down his soup as quickly as the heat would permit. It was obviously homemade and no doubt concocted by Sylvia's own fair hands. The soup was followed by steak and kidney pie. Not Ned's favourite, the thought of kidney repulsed him, but he ate it all the same. Pudding was apple crumble and custard. Much to Gertie's surprise, Ned was the first to finish.

"Someone's got their appetite back," she commented, approvingly.

"I was starving," said Ned, as he rose from the table. "By the way, I keep meaning to ask you. Who lives in the big house on top of the cliffs overlooking the sea?"

"What? Oh, you must mean Chy-an-Gwyns. It belongs to some posh up-country bloke. He doesn't live there though, he just pops down from time to time, but he's ever so nice in spite of his silly name."

Ned grinned. "And what might his silly name be?"

"Willoughby," giggled Gertie, "Willoughby Castor-Hunt."

Ned laughed, amused by her cheerfulness and, feeling much better with a full stomach, he left the dining room for the bar.

The public bar was empty except for Frank changing the whisky optic and an elderly man with a black, Labrador dog which was lying at the man's feet.

Frank turned when he noticed Ned from the corner of his eye and gestured towards the lone drinker. "Ned, Sylvia told me you were asking about smuggling earlier. This here is Jim Hughes. He used to be game keeper on the Penwynton Estate. I'm sure he'd be able to spin you a yarn or two."

The two men shook hands. "Delighted to meet you," said Ned, enthusiastically. He knelt to stroke the dog's silky, black coat.

"He's called Don," grinned Jim, as the dog rolled over wagging its tail.

Ned laughed. "I like dogs," he said, turning his face to avoid a lick. "They're such loyal, friendly creatures. Unlike cats. I can't abide them, they make my flesh creep."

"Don't let Sylvia hear you say that," Frank chuckled. "She's got a cat, Barley Wine, and she's soppy about him."

Ned scowled as he stood. "I know, we've met."

Jim insisted on buying a drink for Ned, the two men then went through the double doors and into the snug, where they sat in the window seat near to the fire.

"So, you're interested in smuggling?" said Jim, removing his shabby coat and dropping it onto the floor.

"Yes, very much so, and I'm particularly keen to hear of goings on around here."

Jim laughed. "Well, there ain't bin no smuggling in my lifetime o' course, but my grandfather knew some descendants of them rogues. He always said they were a good, honest bunch of criminals, if you know what I mean."

"Honest criminals! That's got to be an oxymoron."

Jim's eyes glazed over as he gave a false, feeble laugh.

"Tell me about them," said Ned, realising his comment had fallen flat.

Jim scratched his head. "Well, I'll do me best, but you see, you gotta realise times were hard back then and they all had big families to feed. Smuggling was just another way of trying to make ends meet, a sorta job on the side like. Though o' course the chaps as was ring leaders became wealthy men on the strength of it all."

"Was the Inn used at all, do you know?" interrupted Ned, eagerly.

"Well, there's always been rumours that it was. There's lots o' caves along this 'ere coast and there's supposed to be a tunnel somewhere leading to the Inn."

"Really!" said Ned, fascinated, casting his eyes over his surroundings.

"Yes," chuckled Jim. "Me, and me mates often explored all the caves you can get to at low water when we were kids, but o' course we never found anything."

"How about this end?" Ned asked, excitedly. "Has anyone ever looked for a secret entrance in here?"

Jim laughed, revealing a mouth, half full of yellowing teeth. "I'll say. Just about everyone over the decades, I reckon. Every time the place is decorated folks hope to find something behind the panelling or old wallpaper, but I think the passage comes out somewhere else, in the grounds, the village, or even the churchyard maybe."

"Hmm, shame," said Ned, wrinkling his nose. "I might have to use a bit of poetic licence when I tell stories to the children back home."

After he had been up to the bar for a couple more pints, they chatted uninterrupted, and Ned listened intently as Jim told tales he had heard as a boy from his grandfather.

At nine o'clock, Jim glanced at the clock and hastily finished his drink, just as Frank had walked into the snug.

"Look at the time," said Jim. "I told the good lady I'd be home by eight."

"She'll be looking for lipstick on your collar," Frank teased, throwing more logs onto the fire.

"That'll be the day," said Jim, picking up his coat. "One woman's enough for any man, I reckon."

35

Don lifted his head from the hearth rug on the flagstones where he had slept with one eye open, and closely watched his master put on his coat and cap. Jim then bade everyone goodnight, and left for the lengthy walk home with his faithful friend to heel.

Ned was surprised to find the Inn relatively busy. He had been so engrossed in his conversation with Jim that he'd not noticed people coming in. Not even Sylvia, who was looking very glamorous, dressed in blue. Gertie was behind the bar also, cheerily serving drinks.

"Busy tonight," said Ned, to the major who was sitting in the corner.

"Always is on a Friday, although I did think it might be a little quieter this week on account of the funeral this morning."

"Wasn't it a splendid broadcast?" said Ned, stepping forward. "I thought it very moving."

"It most certainly was," agreed the major. "Fine establishment, the BBC. Makes one proud to be British."

He gestured towards the empty seat beside him. "Sit down, son. We've not been properly introduced yet. My name is Smith, Major Benjamin Smith."

The two men shook hands. "Edward Stanley," said Ned, taking a seat as instructed. "But everyone calls me Ned."

"I've heard on the grapevine you're here to convalesce," said the major. "Is Cornwall having a therapeutic effect?"

"It most certainly is and I've several more weeks to enjoy yet."

"Excellent, there's nothing to beat Cornish sea air. Now tell me a bit about yourself. That's if you don't mind. It's such a pleasant change to have some new blood about the place to liven things up."

Ned didn't think he had much to tell and so condensed his life into a brief five minutes. "What about you?" he asked, in return. "Am I right in thinking you're a permanent resident here?"

The major nodded. "That's correct, son. I've been here six years now. I came down to get away from old memories and start a new life." He shook his head and sighed deeply. "During the War I saw some terrible things, you know. Well, not just me of course; it was the same for all of us out there. Young men like yourself were gunned down or blown to bits before our very eyes. At times I wondered if I'd ever have the guts to carry on. But I did, and of course Churchill was great for morale. Damn fine fellow Winston, damn fine fellow."

Ned smiled. "You sound like my father."

The major took a sip of whisky. "I'm not surprised; his speeches were a wonderful source of inspiration to us all, Ned. And believe you me, we needed all the inspiration we could get." His voice lowered. "Especially after we'd lost family and friends back home. Losing my dear wife and beautiful children was the cruellest blow of all."

"Oh no, I'm so sorry," muttered Ned, shocked. "I didn't know."

The major shook his head. "Of course you didn't. Why should you?" He half smiled. "She was a lovely woman, my Violet. We had ten glorious years together. Ten glorious years. And our children, well, they were a couple of smashing kids. Little Catherine was just seven, and young Albert only five."

Ned felt light headed. "What happened?"

"They should have been safe," said the major, deep in thought. "We lived in a splendid house in a pretty Surrey village, and it was a great comfort to me knowing folks in rural England should've been untouched by the dreadful bombings and suchlike. Violet's mother lived in London, though. We told her she ought to leave the City but she wouldn't hear of it. She said, she'd lived there all her life and no-one was going make her leave, especially a tyrant like Adolph Hitler. Anyway, in 1940, Vi decided to go and stay with her mother for Christmas. She took the children up by train and planned to stay 'til the New Year. She wrote telling me of her plans, saying she was confident they'd be safe from air attacks, it being the season of goodwill and all that. She'd also heard, that some of the children who'd been evacuated to the country, were returning home to London to be with their families for Christmas. But how wrong she was. On the twenty ninth of December there was a most abominable air attack."

Ned gasped. His face dropped. "Oh no, the second Great Fire of London."

"You obviously know of it," said the major. He lowered his head and looked vacantly towards the hearth. "The Germans dropped thousands of incendiary devices on the City that night, causing hundreds of small fires. Once the City was ablaze they left, but not for long. They returned a few hours later after refuelling, only this time they were carrying damn, great bombs, which hit their targets because London was lit up by the lights of those wretched small fires."

Ned gulped. "My uncle's a fireman, and to this day he still talks about that night, how the wind got up, fanned the flames and caused a firestorm. Apparently, they fought really hard to put out the fires, and then the water ran out. But not to be outdone, they attempted to pump water from the Thames. Sadly though, the tide was at its lowest and the hoses got clogged up with wretched mud."

The major nodded. "That's right, the German's had planned it well, you have to grant them that. But not all was lost, because in spite of everything, many of those brave men managed to save Saint Paul's Cathedral. I'm told the sight of its dome towering above the flames was a magnificent and heart-warming sign of defiance."

"And your wife and family?" Ned nervously asked. "Did they perish in the carnage?"

The major nodded and pulled a large, white handkerchief from the breast pocket of his jacket. "Yes," he whispered, wiping his nose. "Mother-in-law's house took a direct hit. They didn't stand a chance." He tucked his handkerchief back inside his pocket. "I'm sorry to make a fool of myself like this, Ned, but it still hurts, even after all these years." His voice rose as he took control of his emotions. "Anyway, after the War I couldn't bear to live in my house any more. Too many painful memories. It broke my heart to sell the place though. To leave behind Vi's beautiful garden. Dear Vi, she did so love that garden."

From his wallet he took an old photograph. "That's the four of us taken in the summer of 1940 when I was home on leave."

Ned looked at the picture and the happy faces of the laughing children, their beautiful mother and the major.

"So much suffering," he said, with a lump in his throat. "There was so much suffering during the War. It's hard to imagine it now."

"And afterwards," added the major. "After the euphoria came the realisation that the country was bankrupt and the British Empire was no more. No, the misery didn't end on V.E. day, but then you'll know all about that living in London."

"I was a student up in Nottingham for much of the War. But after I returned to teach I was shocked and deeply saddened to see the extent of the destruction, which sadly is still ubiquitous even today."

"And will be for many years to come. Not just in London either. Coventry, Plymouth and other large cities all suffered badly too."

"So, what made you come to Cornwall?" Ned asked.

The major lifted his glass, took a large swig of whisky and grinned. "I invested most of my money into stocks and shares after selling the house. I didn't want to buy another place, you see. I didn't want to live alone. So I found a map of England, laid it out in front of me, closed my eyes and pierced it with Vi's hat pin. It stuck in here, Trengillion. So I packed my belongings into my car, and well, here I am. It's the best bit of luck I've ever had, next to marrying Violet and having the children, that is. The Newtons are like family to me. This is my home now, and I have the added bonus of people coming and going. I'm never lonely, not on the outside anyway, but sometimes, sometimes, on the inside, I do long for someone close."

"Sylvia's not from these parts either, I understand," said Ned.

The major nodded. "That's right, she's only been here a few years or so. Frank worships the ground she walks on. I wasn't too keen on her at first, I couldn't get her to talk. She had a tough childhood, you see. I think the world of her now though." He suddenly laughed. "And when she's had a glass or two of sherry, well, you can't shut her up."

Laughing and relieved the major was in a happier frame of mind, Ned glanced towards the bar. "Gertie's a real character too, isn't she? Such a bubbly, lively personality."

"Hmm, yes, she is," the major agreed, "but I truly miss dear Jane. She worked here, you know, and was a lovely girl. Nothing was too much trouble for her."

"Gertie told me about her," said Ned, "Apparently she was very beautiful."

"Yes, yes, she was very beautiful. Sensible too, although it wasn't unusual for us to witness the occasional bout of giddy behaviour. She had a lovely voice as well. Always singing she was. Especially songs from her much-loved *South Pacific*. Her favourite was, umm, oh yes, I remember, *Some Enchanted Evening*. Ah, sweet memories. Dear Jane, I can hear her singing it now."

Chapter Five

Ned lay awake in bed, confused, thoughts churning around in his head like bouncing balls in a tombola barrel. If it was Jane he had heard singing, then where was she? If she was in hiding, then surely she would never risk being heard by singing, especially at three o'clock in the morning. Perhaps it had not been Jane at all, but a gramophone record or the wireless. But that still didn't explain the time factor and the singing had definitely come from inside the dining room.

Ned turned onto his side. Perhaps, after all, he had dreamed the whole episode. Yet deep down he knew that that was not the case. Without doubt he had heard someone singing and he was utterly convinced it was Jane.

Angrily, he punched his pillow. There had to be a simple explanation, but try as he might he could not think of one. In fact there seemed only one plausible theory: that being that it was Jane's ghost he had heard and Jane was dead.

Ned laughed out loud, amused by the conclusion of his over active imagination. The idea of a ghost at the Inn was preposterous. Besides, he didn't believe in such things. Had he not had enough of that with his mother who claimed she had powers to make contact with the dead? Ned shuddered recalling his childhood, much of it marred by his mother's humiliating so-called gift - a dubious gift she claimed she'd inherited from her supposedly psychic mother: a claim both he and his father categorically refuted.

Ned opened his eyes and through the thin curtains watched the long shadows of trees waving in the light of a streetlamp. Was it possible she really did possess such skills, and through genetics, had passed them onto him? He winced at the idea, but had to concede it would explain why he evidently appeared to be the only person who had heard the singing.

Ned sat bolt upright and switched on the light. There was only one thing to do. He must to go down to the dining room. If Jane had been there before, she may well be there again.

Laughing at his own foolishness, Ned climbed from his warm bed, put on his dressing gown, slipped a half full packet of cigarettes into the deep pocket, picked up his torch and inserted new batteries. He then dropped the torch into his pocket alongside the cigarettes.

The wind had freshened considerably with the falling of darkness, its presence clearly audible, whistling without pause, down the dark chimney in Ned's bleak room. Undeterred, however, by its ghostly undertones, he opened the door and peeped into the long, dark passage. The coast was clear. Confident everyone was sleeping, for it was past two o'clock, he stepped from his room, quietly closed the door and then tiptoed along the dimly lit landing to the top of the stairs, where, contented none had creaked, he warily descended the staircase, avidly keeping out a watchful eye for Sylvia's cat.

At the foot of the stairs he crouched and hid in a dark corner, nervously listening to ascertain no other being was up and about. All was quiet. With fumbling fingers he switched on his torch and the bright beam of light instantly illuminated the dark hallway and lifted his spirits. With rejuvenated courage he confidently emerged from the shadows and wended his way along the passage towards the dining room.

Outside the door he stopped. No tuneful melody emanated from the room but all was not silent. Beyond the panelled door a rhythmic, repetitive creak disquieting his nerves, and sent an ice cold shiver deep down his already tingling spine. He paused, anxiously feeling a lump emerge in his dry throat. Warily he lowered his head and leaned his ear towards the polished brass keyhole. The mysterious noise abruptly stopped and only the sound of his deep, heavy breathing broke the silence. Boldly, he stood bolt upright. He had to go in. With forced determination he opened the door and slowly crept inside.

The heavy curtains were pulled back permitting a three quarter moon to shine through the large panes of glass, lighting the room sufficiently for Ned to see his surroundings. He switched off his torch and tiptoed towards the Johnsons' table in the bay window. As he laid it down on the linen cloth the creaking recommenced. Confused, Ned pulled aside the net curtains covering the lower half of the window and peered through the spotlessly clean glass. Above, swung the Ringing Bells Inn board, creaking noisily with each gust of howling wind. Ned laughed, and with relief heaved a mighty sigh. Anxiety quickly abated and he was able to relax. Calmly he pulled out a chair and sat down at the Johnsons' table, nervously hopeful of witnessing Jane's manifestation.

The room was cold. Ned contemplated switching on the electric fire but thought it would be impertinent to do so. Shivering, he reprimanded himself for not wearing slippers and wriggled his numbed toes, hoping to restore life into his ice cold limbs. From its packet he took a cigarette, slipped it between his lips, lit it and watched the smoke drift in moonlit circles above his head. Inside the room, deathly silence prevailed. Ned finished his cigarette and stubbed it out in the ashtray. Realising then confusion might be aroused if the ash were found in the morning, he tipped the ashtray's contents into his handkerchief and wiped out the glass with the cuff of his dressing gown. Not convinced, however, that it was thoroughly clean, and knowing the Johnsons were both non-smokers, he decided to swap the ashtray with the one on his table to avoid the detection of any smudges.

Ned rose and crossed the room. When returning towards the window, he felt a slight draught, as though something gentle had brushed past him. The room's temperature plummeted. Ned froze, his neck tingled, and goose pimples slowly crept the entire length of both arms. Carelessly, he flung the clean ashtray onto the Johnsons' table. Every sense in his shivering body warned of an invisible presence in the room. Ned gulped as courage deserted him. With blood chilled, he turned, praying fate would be kind. Seconds ticked by. He gained a little pluck and then spoke.

"Jane."

Not a sound was to be heard. The room was silent. Even the Inn's board had ceased its creaking, as though listening, in suspense.

"Jane," Ned whispered again, the pitch of his voice a little higher.

His eyes flashed as he sensed movement by the fireplace.

"Can you see me?" drawled a long, low, gentle, whisper.

Ned felt the hairs on the back of his neck rise as blood whooshed through his head causing him to feel giddy. Desperately he fumbled for support. His hands found the back of a chair. Gripping it tightly, he attempted to suppress the powerful desire to shout, and the strong urge to run.

"No," he eventually gulped. "No, I can't see you, but I can hear you and I feel your presence."

"You can? Who are you then and how do you know my name?"

His blood felt like ice. With heart pounding, he released his hand from the back of the chair and took a backwards step towards the closed door.

"Ned, my name is Ned," he gabbled, feeling extremely foolish, "and I know who you are because I heard you singing your favourite song in the middle of the night, last night, when everyone but me was in bed."

She laughed. "My favourite song?"

"Yes, the one from *South Pacific*. You know, *Some Enchanted Evening*."

"Hmm, I see."

"And if I might be permitted to say so, you have a very pretty voice."

"Thank you, but why are you here?"

"What! Do you mean, why am I at the Inn?"

"Of course."

"I see. Well, um, I'm staying here to find smugglers for the children, because I've been poorly and the doctor told me to get some clean air."

He cringed, aware nerves had reduced him to an incoherent, bumbling half-wit.

She gave a shallow, mournful laugh. "You must be careful then, Ned."

"Careful," he squeaked, nervously glancing over his shoulder.

"Yes, be careful what you see and be careful what you drink or you might be poorly again, Ned. Or worse still, you might find yourself dead."

"Eh?" he spluttered, puzzled. His voice sounded higher than he thought physically possible.

"I believe someone poisoned me," she whispered, close to his ear, "and that's why I'm still here. Hanging around in limbo, waiting for deliverance."

"What! Surely not. No, I mean, who, and...and...why?" burbled Ned, shocked, confused and wishing he was anywhere but in the dining room being quizzed by a paranoid, paranormal presence.

"I don't know who, but…,"

The sound of water gushing overhead through rattling pipes, indicated the bathroom toilet upstairs had been flushed. Someone was about. In panic Ned jumped, stumbled and clumsily knocked over the chair which had been his support.

"Jane," he pleaded, awkwardly grabbing the chair and pushing it back beneath the table. "Jane, don't go yet. I need to know who poisoned you."

As the sound of gushing water faded, the room reverted to eerie silence and only the sound of the Ringing Bells Inn board, creaking gently as it swayed to and fro in each intermittent gust of wind, broke the stillness of the chilly night.

Several hours later, Ned, with courage fully restored, sat bleary eyed at his table devoid of appetite, attempting to eat his breakfast, having already lit a cigarette and dropped ash into the smudged ashtray.

Aimlessly stirring his porridge, he turned over in his mind repeatedly what Jane had said, and asked himself the same, puzzling questions. Was she really poisoned and if she was, who on earth would want to poison her? Furthermore, whatever did she mean by, 'Be careful what you see'. Could there still be some sort of smuggling or other criminal activity going on? Surely not!

Gertie brought Ned his toast. "You alright, sir?" she asked. "You look as if you've been up half the night."

Ned responded with a feeble laugh. "I, err have. I started…err, reading about smuggling," he lied. "Yes, that's right, and I got so engrossed I couldn't put the book down. Do you know anything about smuggling, Gertie?"

"Lor me no," she laughed. "A bit before my time. Shame really, it would be fun and exciting to have a few hunky rogues about the place these days."

He said nothing, but smiled at her vacuous response.

After collecting the Daily Herald from the post office, Ned sat on Denzil's bench to read it in the sunshine. The pages were full of pictures and details covering the King's funeral. Normally he would have read the articles thoroughly, but on this occasion he found himself unable to concentrate and skipped from cover to cover without absorbing one word. Thoughtfully, he folded the unread newspaper, stood up, put his hand deep inside his pocket and pulled out a fistful of change. It was no good, he needed help and there was only one person he could talk to. Only one person who would understand. Damn it, he would phone his mother!

Knowing there was a telephone kiosk outside the post office, Ned walked back through the village. Everyone he saw, he eyed as a potential suspect regarding Jane's murder, if indeed, murdered she was. Ned still had his doubts. It was, after all, quite bad enough having spoken to a ghost, spirit or whatever you wanted to call her, but one who claimed to have been poisoned, really did stretch the imagination to incredible lengths.

On reaching the telephone kiosk, Ned groaned. There was already someone inside: a woman. When the door opened and she came out, he realised it was Jane's aunt. He cursed beneath his breath, wishing he'd had the nous to eavesdrop on her conversation. She glared at him with cold, unfriendly eyes. He most definitely didn't like her and she promptly became suspect number one.

Ned opened the heavy door of the red telephone kiosk and lifted the cumbersome receiver. He dialled the operator and gave the number to which he wished to be connected. On a distant, crackly line he heard a deep, rich voice answer.

"Hello, Madame Molstanley speaking."

Ned groaned. "Mother, it's me," he snapped, impatiently, following the operator's request for the insertion of coins into the slot.

"Ned," she squealed, reverting to her normal voice, "how are you feeling, sweetheart? Is the sea air doing the trick?"

"Yes and no. That is, it probably would be, but something weird has happened." He then plunged into the story quickly, before his time and money ran out.

"Really, how exciting," said Mother, now back in her Madame Molstanley voice. "I really don't know how best to advise you though, you being a novice to the spiritual world, not to mention a sceptic. I need time to think, Ned, and consult two very good friends of mine. Meanwhile, keep alert."

"Don't worry," said Ned, repeatedly glancing over his shoulder. "I shall be sleeping with one eye open from now on."

"Good. I'll ring the Inn when I have thought things through."

"Excellent. Thank you, Mother. I shall look forward to your call."

"Goodbye, sweetheart, and pleasant dreams."

"Goodbye, Mother."

Ned put down the phone and shook his head. He dreaded to think what his mother's friends might be like.

Walking back through the village he passed the gate of The Police House and momentarily contemplated knocking on the door and reporting his middle of the night experience, but instantly laughed at his stupidity. It was most likely the theft of milk from a doorstep or a missing cat, was as great a crime as happened in a sleepy Cornish village such as Trengillion.

Ned reached the Inn. Frank and Sylvia were in the hallway hanging a picture. They greeted him warmly.

"Perhaps," thought Ned, as he wearily climbed the stairs, "Frank had an affair with Jane, Sylvia found out and she murdered her."

Ned fell onto his bed, head clasped in hands. This was awful! Everyone he encountered was a suspect. Mentally exhausted he fell asleep and did not wake until half past six. Thankful he had not slept longer, he washed quickly, changed his clothes and went down to dinner.

That evening in the snug, Ned chatted to the major again. He both liked and trusted him. The major talked a lot about the War, friends he had lost and the hollow feeling of victory.

"I couldn't go through it all again," he concluded. "Couldn't take the mental torture. I'm too ruddy old now anyway."

Ned asked the major if he knew Willoughby Castor-Hunt.

"Oh yes, he and I always put the world to right when he comes down. Sadly he's a widower too. He lost his wife in childbirth some twenty years ago, and the baby too, poor soul. In spite of being a young man at the time, he's never remarried, so I feel we both have a lot in common. To fill the void in his life though, Willoughby's devoted everything to his work. He's an extremely gifted architect, you see, and has made a great deal of money over the years, especially since the War with the re-building of Britain. But how come you know of him? He's not due for another visit until Whitsun, so you can't have bumped into him."

Ned finished his pint and put the empty glass on the table. "I asked Gertie who lived in the lovely house on the cliff and she told me his name, but that was all."

"I see. Yes, he bought Chy-an-Gwyns just before the War, for a song I might add. It was in a very bad state of repair at the time and he's spent a fortune having it done up. It's beautiful now though, and worth a pretty penny too."

The major insisted on buying more drinks, even though Ned offered first. When he returned with the refilled glasses, Ned craftily turned the conversation to Jane.

"Does she have many friends?" he asked.

The major loosened his tie and nodded. "Yes, she's friends with most of the youngsters in the village. They all grew up here together, so I believe."

"I see, and was she popular?" asked Ned. "When she was here working, I mean?"

The major raised his eyebrows. "Why all the questions? Fancy yourself as an amateur detective, do you?"

Ned laughed. "I'm just curious, that's all. About her disappearance, that is. It just strikes me as a little odd."

The major nodded. "Yes, I agree, and yes, she was very popular here with regulars and guests. She had a smile for everyone."

Ned persisted. "Hmm, I've seen her aunt and I don't think she looks very sociable."

"What, you mean Doris? Good heavens! Doris is alright. A damn fine woman in fact, though she has become a bit of a recluse since Jane's disappearance, I must admit. She was devoted to the girl, you see. She brought her up single handed from quite a young age. Now sadly, she suspects every one of knowing something she doesn't and thinks people are talking behind her back. She would be a bit wary of you, you being a stranger." The major paused, pensively. "I must confess though, it has crossed my mind that they may have fallen out over something or other. Doris and Jane that is. But Doris insists that's not the case."

Ned tilted his head to one side. "May I ask what made you think they may have fallen out?"

"Oh, I don't know, I can't quite put my finger on it but Jane seemed agitated in the days before she went away and I know for a fact she wanted to travel because she told me so herself. She wanted to explore the world, see elephants in their natural habitat, see the pyramids, sail on the Danube, and travel on the Orient Express." The major grinned. "They were just a few of her objectives, and she wanted to see and do all before she settled down and had a family."

Ned raised his eyebrows. "That all sounds very adventurous."

"Yes, we all thought so too but it's good to dream. Sadly though, Doris always poured cold water on her globe-trotting aspirations. Told her not to be daft, and I'm sorry to say, Doris's approach saddened poor Jane."

"I see," muttered Ned, searching for any useful clues amongst the major's inferences. "What a sorry state of affairs."

"Will you be attending church in the morning?" asked the major, unexpectedly changing the subject.

Ned was taken back. He only ever went to church for the School Carol Service at Christmas.

"Err, I don't know," he mumbled, biting his lip, lost for words. "Will you?"

"Of course," the major retorted, pompously, "I escort Sylvia every Sunday. Frank is unable to go as he has to prepare for lunchtime opening, but we always attend, good health permitting."

Ned thought quickly. If lots of people from the village went, it might be the ideal opportunity to observe some of them.

"Then I'll join you, if I may," he grinned, delighted with his spur of the moment plan.

"Splendid," growled the major. "Sung Eucharist is at eleven o'clock. We'll meet you in the hallway at ten forty-five, prompt."

At ten forty-five the following morning, Ned found the major and Sylvia waiting for him. The major was wearing an immaculate suit of dark brown and green tweed. Sylvia was dressed in an elegant, fitted, fawn coat with a matching hat partly covering her neat hair. Ned was glad he had chosen his outfit with care.

"Excellent time keeping," boomed the major, slipping a gold pocket watch into his waistcoat and lifting his hat from the telephone table.

Slipping her hands into soft, kid leather gloves, Sylvia smiled. "The major's a stickler for punctuality, so you've earned yourself a brownie point."

Ned frowned. "A what?"

Sylvia giggled. "Sorry, you've probably never heard that term before, but we had an American staying at the Inn last summer and he used the expression frequently. In fact he awarded me a brownie point every night for his dinner. Don't ask me its origin though, because I've not the faintest idea."

The church bells were ringing gaily as they left the Inn and walked the short distance to the church. As they passed beneath the lichgate, Ned craned his neck to observe the bell tower, denuded of its flag since the funeral of the King. The bells, however, were not visible from the ground.

"How many are there?" Ned asked. "Bells I mean. I can't quite distinguish one tone from another."

"Three," replied the major, "and would you believe, at the moment they're all being rung at once by just one man."

Ned laughed. "But that's not possible, unless he has three hands."

"It is. I've seen it done with my very own eyes. Arthur Bray's our campanologist, and to ring the third bell, he lets down the rope to the floor and puts his foot in a loop on the end. In other words, he rings it with his foot. All very clever stuff."

As they entered the ancient granite building through a heavy, arched door, Ned and the major removed their hats. Inside, a few people were already seated and from behind a faded, red curtain, mournful organ music drifted through the chancel and into the aisle to greet the growing congregation.

"Well, I never, there's Gertie," Ned whispered, much surprised.

"And on her own," said Sylvia. "She usually comes with Nettie, her mother."

Gertie shook her head when asked if her mother was well. "No, she's been up half the night, got the runs, poor thing."

Ned seized the opportunity to join Gertie seated at the back of the church, a much better observation point he considered, than the front.

"I'll keep her company so she's not on her own," he whispered hastily, to his surprised companions.

Impressed by Ned's kindness, Sylvia and the major proceeded to their usual pew near the front of the church, beneath the pulpit.

Gertie was thrilled to have Ned beside her. She considered him very handsome and prayed Betty would be at the service, but knew it unlikely, for she often visited her aunt for piano lessons on Sunday mornings. Ned meanwhile, was equally thrilled. Gertie would be sure to know everyone, hence should any suspicious looking characters appear, she would be able to name them. Both sat looking very smug.

Ned already knew a few faces. Mrs Pascoe from the post office, with her greying hair pulled back tightly in a tiny bun. Although for Church, instead of her usual hairnet, she wore a hat of dark brown felt. With her was Mr Pascoe, a slight fellow, who Ned thought looked hen-pecked. Jim Hughes was in too, with a woman who was, no doubt, his wife. Also present were the Johnsons, and on the other side of the aisle, beside a huge pillar, sat Jane's Auntie Doris.

The door opened and a young couple entered with two young children. Ned elbowed Gertie, gently. "Who are they?"

"That's Police Constable, Fred Stevens, Annie his wife, and their children, Jamie and Sally." Gertie replied. "Why do you want to know, sir?"

Ned smiled. "Curiosity. I just like to know who everyone is."

"I see," said Gertie.

A young man came in, Ned recognised him as Peter, the fisherman friend of Percy Collins. He was followed shortly after by a slim, bearded chap, who removed a cap from his head as he entered the church. Not having seen him before, Ned asked his name.

"That's Sid," Gertie replied, "the school caretaker."

"Hmm," hummed Ned, much interested. "Is he married?"

"Hey, what's your game?" Gertie gabbled, forgetting her manners. "What you wanna know that for?"

Ned managed a pathetic smile and thought it best to ask no more questions.

The service began with a hymn, during which the vicar, Reverend David Ridge, progressed through the church aisles with choir members. At the front, carrying a long, brass cross, was the unlikely figure of Percy Collins, dressed in a long, black cassock and a crisp, white surplice.

Before the hymn ended, a large door at the back of the church creaked open and a clean shaven, middle-aged man, crept in and took a seat at the back of the church on the opposite side of the aisle to Ned and Gertie. Gertie waved to the newcomer and then turned to Ned. "That's Mr Bray," she whispered. "Betty's dad. He's been ringing the bells."

During the sermon, Ned turned over in his mind each of the village's inhabitants he'd encountered since his arrival in Trengillion, but conceded it was not possible to judge a person's character merely by first impressions or looks. Body language, of course, was a different matter, but that was not a viable option with the congregation inside the church, as there was very little to be gleaned from the backs of heads.

During the hymns they stood and Ned was able to observe the congregation with more intent. Noticing Sylvia was not singing, he smiled. The ban issued by Frank, obviously applied to the church as well as the bath and elsewhere. Gertie had a pleasant singing voice, although not as sweet as Jane's. He wondered if she was in any danger as she had replaced Jane at the Inn. He thought it unlikely, but did not want to rule out anything.

At the end of the service they filed out of the church and shook hands with the vicar in the doorway. Ned thought the vicar seemed a nice chap, but then everyone seemed nice. Solving Jane's murder looked far from easy.

That evening, the snug bar was very quiet. Ned sat in the window seat near to a huge, blazing fire, listening to the crackling of logs and the old clock ticking above the flames. The major was talking quietly in the public bar to Jim Hughes, whilst Jim's faithful old dog, Don, slept, contented, on the hearth rug not far from Ned's feet. There was no sign of the Johnsons and only one or two locals were in, conversing with Frank over the curved, wooden bar.

Ned took a swig of whisky and closed his eyes. He felt rested, almost content as he yawned and pushed Jane's plight from his mind.

From the distant hallway he heard the shrill ringing of a telephone bell. After four rings it stopped. Ned took another mouthful of whisky and again closed his eyes.

Sylvia came into the bar. He heard her light footsteps swiftly approaching.

"Ned," she whispered, gently shaking his arm.

He half opened his eyes.

"Ned, we've just had a phone call from your mother." He sat up straight, wide awake, eager to hear the news. "She said, you're not to worry about anything, because she's coming here to see you and has just booked a room at the Inn. God willing, she'll be with you early tomorrow evening. Isn't that nice?"

Ned smiled feebly. His mother! In Cornwall! At the Inn! All feelings of contentment instantly vanished.

Chapter Six

Humming tunefully, Molly Stanley teetered on the thickly padded seat of her dressing table stool and reached for the large, shabby suitcase lying on top of her wardrobe. Once the handle was within her grasp, she lifted it down carefully and blew across the top, sending small clouds of speckled dust into the air. She watched as they floated gracefully to the floor, glistening and twinkling in a golden beam of late afternoon sunlight.

"Fairy dust. Surely that has to be a good omen," she said with a smile of satisfaction.

Resuming the humming, she dropped the cumbersome suitcase onto her gaudy bedspread and put back the stool in its rightful place in front of the dressing table. With a sigh of uncertainty, she then looked through the contents of her wardrobe and thoughtfully considered which clothing to pack for her impromptu trip. Allegedly, Cornwall was milder than the rest of the country, but even so, it was still winter. She pushed to one side her lightweight summer dresses and selectively looked through the remaining items.

Molly was looking forward to seeing Ned again for it was almost two years since they had last met. She had wanted to visit him during his illness but he had insisted he was in good hands, and then before she knew it, she had a phone call to say he was going to Cornwall to convalesce. Molly would have preferred him to stay with her in Clacton. "There's plenty of fresh, sea air here," she had muttered, on hearing the news. But she had to accept the fact Ned was no longer a child and he had to make his own decisions.

From the wardrobe and the drawers of an old chest, Molly gathered several warm, practical garments and packed them neatly into the bottom of the suitcase. She then rummaged through her modest collection of shoes and selected three pairs. Her very best, should she go anywhere special, her favourite and second best, nice and comfortable for travelling in, and her walking shoes, which were actually the ones she wore for gardening, but she considered with a lick of polish they would be more than respectable enough to wear for rambling over the cliff tops or whatever Ned chose to do when they were not ghost hunting.

Once confident all the necessary clothes were packed, Molly left the suitcase and went downstairs to her living room where, from the top of an ottoman, snugly tucked beneath the casement windows, she pushed three matching, floppy, pink cushions onto the floor. She then raised the lid carefully, leaned it back against the wooden sill, and gazed at the contents of the ottoman arranged before her eyes. Her face broke into a huge smile as she excitedly lifted a long, flowing, pale lavender, satin gown, intricately embroidered around the scooped neck, cuffs and hem with bright red poppies. Pulling the gown towards herself, she snuggled her face into the soft fabric. Faint traces of her favourite perfume lingered in the folds. Relishing the scent, she lovingly laid the gown on the discarded pink cushions and delved again into the ottoman to retrieve another item. This time she pulled out a shawl, heavily fringed, crocheted in red wool and flecked with delicate threads of silver. Molly closed the ottoman lid, lay down the shawl beside the gown and neatly put back the pink cushions. With great care, she then unfolded the shawl. Inside was a large, glistening, crystal ball. Molly lovingly raised the glass globe and kissed it affectionately.

"Ned will be surprised to see you," she smiled, although a little apprehensively. For deep down she had to admit she was rather nervous about telling her son of her new found career. Business had dried up a little on the spiritual side and so to supplement her modest income she had taken up fortune telling as a second string to her bow.

Molly's apprehensive smile suddenly broadened into a full, wide, grin of confidence and total conviction. After all, she was happy, independent and able to support herself, therefore any scorn which might come from Ned's lips would be both unjust and unreasonable.

Molly rose to her feet, gathered up the tools of her trade and carried them upstairs to her bedroom. The crystal ball, wrapped inside the shawl, she tucked down amongst the clothing she had already packed. The satin gown she carefully placed on the top. Finally, she added her thick, warm, candlewick dressing gown and sheepskin slippers.

Before she closed the case, she glanced around the room for any objects she may have overlooked. Once satisfied everything needed was inside, she climbed onto the bed and sat on top of the bulging case to push down the lid. When squashed, she was able to fasten the clasps and lock it securely. Pleased with her efforts, she pulled the heavy suitcase from the bed with a thud. She then dragged it downstairs and stood it by the front door.

Molly passed away the evening listening to the wireless and painting her nails. At nine o'clock, having decided to have an early night, she turned off the wireless and prepared a mug of cocoa and her hot water bottle. With everything ready for the journey, except the filling of her travelling bag into which she intended to put some last minute items the following morning, she slipped upstairs to the bathroom, took off her jewellery, tied back her dyed, black hair, removed her make-up and plastered cold cream liberally over her face. Molly had once been a very beautiful woman, and although her looks were beginning to fade, she could still claim a lovely complexion, a fine bone structure, and lips, perfect in shape. It was only the few tell-tale lines, especially around the eyes, which let her down, and for this reason, she wore very little eye make-up as she thought it exaggerated the sagging.

After cleaning her teeth she climbed into bed, wound up the clock and set the alarm for seven. Content that everything was done, she snuggled down between the thick, flannelette sheets, tightly hugging her hot water bottle, and slept.

The following morning, after washing and dressing, Molly filled a small lunch box with ham and mustard sandwiches, made a large flask of coffee and dropped both items inside her travelling bag, along with her hairbrush, comb, hot water bottle and make-up.

For breakfast she poached two eggs and toasted two slices of bread beneath the grill. She was dipping a piece of toast into the runny eggs when the telephone bell rang. Brushing crumbs from her mouth and skirt, she rose and quickly crossed the room to answer it.

"Madame Molstanley," she drawled, in case it was a potential client.

It was, however, her friend Jack, wishing her a pleasant journey and good luck with her mission.

Molly replaced the receiver after his call and smiled. She would miss Jack; his friendship meant a great deal to her. She recalled how very lonely she had been during the first year of her residence in Clacton after she had moved there following the break-up of her marriage. Lacking self-confidence she had stayed indoors. With no friends to visit, the days had dragged and she felt isolated and useless. But Molly and Jack were not romantically linked. He was just a good friend; someone on the same wave length. Jack was a married man anyway, with a crippled, housebound wife. Molly had first met Jack in the library, where feeling herself about to sneeze she had dropped her books whilst trying to reach the handkerchief in her pocket. Jack had come to her rescue and their friendship had blossomed from that day forth. For Jack, she confidently believed, liked her for who she was. Whereas her husband, Ned's Father, had always tried to change her and had scoffed cruelly at her spiritualistic powers.

Molly often visited the home of Jack, and his wife, Gwen. Her eccentricity brightened their lives, and in return, Molly had someone to share her problems with, just as she had done when Ned had phoned to tell her of Jane.

Jack secretly thought Ned must have as vivid an imagination as his mother. Nevertheless, he had advised her to go to Cornwall and offer her services. He knew Molly was keen to see Ned anyway. Therefore, it seemed the perfect solution.

At half past eight, Molly's taxi arrived. She put on her hat, locked her red front door, kissed the horse shoe nailed above the letter box, and said goodbye to the snowdrops blooming alongside the bare stems of her favourite rose, *Peace*. She then walked beneath the wooden gate frame, over which trailed a yellow, winter flowering jasmine.

The taxi driver put Molly's luggage into the boot while she closed the gate securely and climbed into the back seat of the car. She waved goodbye to her little house as the driver started the engine. They then drove off down the road, turned left by the corner shop and headed for the railway station.

Once Molly arrived in London, she crossed the City by taxi to catch her next train from Paddington Station. And as the black cab drove through the bustling streets, she pondered over what her visit to Cornwall might hold. She had never visited the county before and knew very little of it, other than what she had read in books. But if her memory served her correctly, it was a mystical place, where everyone believed in piskies and mermaids, and everyday meals included pasties, saffron buns, clotted cream and heavy cake. Molly patted her stomach. It didn't sound too good for someone always trying to watch her weight.

"And then of course, there's the ghost," she giggled to herself, as the porter carried her luggage along the station platform. Molly thanked him profusely and pushed a florin into his hand after he had found her a seat and put her luggage onto the rack.

Much to Molly's delight, no-one else shared her compartment at the beginning of the journey. This gave her the chance to meditate and prepare mentally for the forthcoming challenge.

As the train pulled out of the station, she leaned back happily in the seat, kicked off her second best shoes, took off her large hat, and gently closed her eyes. She saw Ned's face and smiled lovingly.

"I'll be with you soon, my sweetheart," she whispered. "And then, God willing, all will be well."

Chapter Seven

Ned awoke on Monday morning, sat up and looked at his watch. It was a quarter to eight. He groaned with frustration, aware his mother would be up and ready to start her journey to Cornwall. Lackadaisically, he climbed out of bed, shuffled across the cold lino to the window, knelt on the ottoman and pulled back the curtains. He laughed sardonically. The morning was dull, grey and damp, much like his mood. Rubbing his eyes, he yawned, scratched his head, stepped back from the ottoman and lowered himself down listlessly into the armchair.

"I don't know what you're looking so cheerful about," he mumbled to the portrait of the old fisherman hanging on the wall, as he lit a cigarette. "The state of my health and nerves will rapidly deteriorate once Mother arrives, you wait and see."

Ned leaned back in the chair, overcome with self-pity, as he recalled bitter memories of his childhood and schooldays in particular, where parents were invited along to events such as prize giving and sports days. For those occasions she had worn her usual flamboyant outfits, each one ostentatious in every sense, thus giving his fellow school friends reason to tease and torment him. Although in retrospect, Ned did acknowledge, that the teasing was done in good humour, but at the time he had been hurt, embarrassed and humiliated.

However, far worse than her outfits at school, were happenings at home and in particular her bizarre attempts to make contact with deceased relatives and friends of people they knew. These charades took place frequently in the parlour of their pebble-dashed semi, usually with disastrous, unproductive and sometimes comical results. But most lamentable of all, had to be the heart-rending arguments between *her* and his hard working father. They had blackened his childhood, lost her his respect and scarred him for life.

Ned shuddered at the thought of his mother descending upon the Inn, his safe haven, his temporary domicile, the place to which he'd come seeking peace, quiet and rest. He was apprehensive about the locals' reaction to her flamboyancy but most of all, he was anxious that her high spirited, weird character might repulse Sylvia. With a cry of frustration, he stood, reached for his dressing gown and walked along the corridor to the bathroom.

As he shaved his thoughts became less critical. There was, of course, always the possibility that Molly might be able to shed some light onto the Jane mystery. After all, he had thought so at the time, and that's why he had phoned her in the first place.

"But I didn't expect her to come racing down here," he hissed at his reflection in the mirror.

Angrily, he splashed aftershave over his pale face, packed his toiletries back inside the shaving bag, and returned to his room to dress.

During breakfast, Ned observed the Johnsons were not at their table. In their place sat a portly gentleman with spectacles perched on the end of his broad nose. Propped up against the condiment set on his table rested the local newspaper, which held his attention as he slowly chewed a mouthful of buttered toast.

"Have the Johnsons gone?" Ned asked Gertie, in a hushed voice, as she came in with his pot of tea.

"Yes, sir," she whispered. "Betty told me they left last night after dinner. Mr Johnson prefers to drive at night because the roads are quieter. And before you ask, the new guest is called George Fillingham. I don't know whether or not he's married, but he's here on his own and arrived late last night."

Ned laughed. "Thanks, Gertie." Although, of course, no new arrivals at the Inn would shed any light onto Jane's case. Only the locals were of real interest to Ned.

A little after seven that evening, as Ned lifted his soup spoon from the white, linen tablecloth, a car pulled up at the front of the Inn. Ned groaned as voices, muffled by the ticking over of the car's engine, drifted through the window panes. The car drove off. Ned heard the doorbell clang and from the hallway, Frank's deep voice was audible chatting merrily to jingling bangles. A peal of female laughter echoed along the passage; a jarring laugh which made Ned's flesh creep. He closed his eyes as the jingling and jangling grew louder; the door of the dining room opened. Ned turned; Molly, dressed in shocking pink, stood bordered by the ornate wooden door frame and by her side, Frank grinned, mischievously.

"Ned, sweetheart, darling," she gushed, springing forward to hug her clearly embarrassed son.

Reluctantly he stood, put his arms around her shoulders and sneezed as his face brushed against her tickly feathers and furs. He forced a smile, clearly disappointed to see the contents of her wardrobe had not improved.

"Sit down, Mother," he commanded, gesturing towards the chair opposite. "You're causing a disturbance."

She obeyed as Ned squinted to acclimatise his eyes to the vividness of her figure-hugging suit. Disheartened, he sighed and shook his head. Molly was a talented dressmaker who creatively made her own clothes. Ned just wished her choice of fabric was a little more conservative, especially as, in Ned's opinion, she was approaching the autumn of her years.

When Gertie brought in soup for the major, Ned asked for a bowl for his mother.

"Is this your mother?" Gertie exclaimed, eyes like saucers.

"Yes," Ned scowled, unsure how to interpret the tone of her voice. He caught the major's eye. Beneath raised brows, both men smiled.

"What a quaint place," gushed Molly, casting her eyes, excitedly, around the room. "I've never seen anywhere quite so isolated though. I really thought we were never going to get here."

"Did you have a pleasant journey, Mother?" Ned asked, wishing she would lower the volume of her voice.

She brushed her hand swiftly across a ruck in the tablecloth. "Yes, thank you, although it seems absolutely ages since I left Clacton and for a while I was a bit worried about getting my suitcase down off the luggage rack on the train. I didn't put it up there, you see, because a nice porter at Paddington did it for me. I needn't have worried though, because a really nice young man at Gwinear thingy came to my rescue, so in the end all was well, sweetheart, and I'm here, safe and sound."

"Please don't call me sweetheart, in public," Ned muttered beneath his breath. "It really is rather embarrassing."

She patted his arm lovingly. "Alright then, darling."

She smiled as Gertie put down a bowl of soup. "Thank you, dear. That looks very nice indeed, and I must admit I am feeling rather peckish."

Ned groaned, wondering how long his mother intended to stay.

After dinner Sylvia emerged from the kitchen, her face flushed, her hair hidden beneath a floral headscarf.

"Sorry I wasn't around when you arrived, Mrs Stanley, but I was tied up in the kitchen, speaking metaphorically of course."

The two women shook hands. Ned was relieved that Sylvia seemed not to be at all repulsed by his mother's outfit. He was equally cheered by the amicable conversation as they climbed the stairs.

Molly's room was directly opposite Ned's. Sylvia pointed to her luggage in a corner, brought up by Frank during dinner. She then asked to be excused in order to get washed and changed so that she might help her husband on the bar.

Ned, however, heard none of the dialogue between the two women. He stood speechless with bottom jaw drooping, stunned, as he surveyed his mother's room. In the grate, a coal fire flickered gently, creating a soothing, comforting warmth. Two bowls of pink hyacinths graced the wooden, window sill, filling the room with a pleasing, delicate perfume. A carpet almost covered the entire surface of the floor, with just a foot of heavily varnished, wooden boards showing around the edges, and in the corner, beneath a large oval mirror, stood a white wash basin with hot and cold taps.

"Mother," said Ned, eventually finding his voice, "how is it you have a fire and so forth in your room?"

"Because it's what I asked for," she replied, crossing to the window to draw the curtains and shut out the night. "You know how I suffer with the cold, sweetheart. I couldn't possibly sleep at night without warmth, especially in a strange place. I asked for the best room available, and a fire to be lit. Having said that, I've still brought my hot water bottle with me, just in case."

She gleefully kicked off her shoes and then bounced down on the iron framed, double bed.

Ned glared at the wash basin and then peeped through the curtains. "You're on the front of the Inn too, south facing. You'll get the morning sun in here, if it ever shines, that is. And you'll have a view of the sea. It's not fair."

Molly laughed and patted the bed beside her. "Come, sit down, Ned, and tell me all about this place and your ghost friend. And then, when our dinner has settled a bit, we'll pop down to the bar. I could murder a double gin."

Ned obediently sat down on the green candlewick bedspread and told his mother of the people he had met, and the strange happenings he had witnessed since his arrival in Cornwall.

When mother and son entered the snug bar, the major rose to his feet and offered Molly his hand. "You must be Ned's sister," he said, a twinkle in his eyes. "I can see the likeness."

Molly giggled, Ned cringed.

"Major, this is my mother, Molly Stanley, and Mother, this is Major Smith, who lives here at the Inn."

"Really!" exclaimed Molly, shaking his hand warmly. "How interesting. It must be a bit weird though, living in a pub."

The major gestured for Molly to sit beside him.

"My name is Benjamin, but you're quite welcome to call me Ben."

Molly settled down on the seat in the corner of the snug next to the major whilst Ned went up to the bar to get them each a drink.

"So, what brings you to Cornwall in the depth of winter? Have you come to keep an eye on that good looking son of yours?"

Molly nodded. "I have. He phoned me the other day and sounded rather low. I thought it might cheer him up having his old mother around for a while. He was very ill you know."

"So I've heard, but there is a little more colour in his cheeks now."

Ned returned with the drinks and sat on a stool opposite, his back towards the open double doors. The Inn's latest arrival sat alone in the corner on the other side of the fireplace shuffling through sheets of paper.

"Do we know what brings our new guest to Cornwall?" Ned whispered, when the stranger went outside to the Gents.

The major nodded. "His name is George Fillingham. I was talking to him this afternoon and he's down to look at property in this area because he and his wife want to move here. He was a bank manager in Cambridge 'til he retired last month. They would like to have sea views if possible and if their dream home turns up they would like to be settled by the end of summer."

"If he's looking at houses he ought to have his wife here too," tut-tutted Molly, with disgust. "Women are so much more practical than men when it comes to looking for, and making a home."

The major grinned. "Well actually, Mrs Fillingham will be joining him later this week. She had to look after the grandchildren at the last minute for some reason or other, and as they already had the room booked, George decided to come alone to suss the place out."

"Humph, I don't think I should like to live down here," said Molly, shaking her head. "It's too much the back of beyond."

The major smiled. "That's why I like it. I'm very fond of the place, and some parts of Cornwall, Molly, are quite up with the times."

"Mother lives in Clacton," said Ned. "She likes the busyness there."

"It's a case of what you're used to, I suppose," said Molly, sipping her gin. "I've settled there very well and enjoy my life to a point, 'though I admit I was lonely at first. But I find the people very friendly now, and I have some really good friends and acquaintances."

The door of the Inn opened and from the darkness emerged the soggy, wet figure of Jim Hughes. He took off his raincoat, shook it, and hung it on a coat peg.

Frank gestured towards the dripping coat. "It's raining, I see. No wonder we're so quiet."

"Tipping it down," replied Jim, removing his glasses and wiping them on a grubby handkerchief, pulled from his trouser pocket. "It started just as I was about to leave home, but I think it's only a shower. I wouldn't have come out if I'd not planned to meet Sylvia for a chat about Saturday."

"Ow, what's happening on Saturday?" whispered Molly to Ned, unashamedly listening through the snug's open doors.

Ned shook his head. "No idea."

"It's Flo's birthday," said the major. "Her sixtieth. We're having a bit of a do."

"Flo?" said Ned, puzzled.

"Jim's wife. He's throwing her a surprise party here and wants everybody to come to it. Flo doesn't get out much. It should be a good night."

Molly clasped her hands and giggled. "A surprise party. How exciting!"

Jim, with pint in hand entered the snug to warm and dry himself by the fire. He nodded to Ned and the major and glanced quizzically at Molly.

"Jim, this is Molly, my mother," said Ned, rising to his feet.

Jim bent and kissed Molly's hand. "Pleased to meet you ma'am. It's nice to have a bit of glamour about the old place for a change."

"I heard that, Jim Hughes," laughed Sylvia, emerging through the doorway with a notebook in her hand, "you cheeky so and so."

Jim and Sylvia then went into the empty games room to discuss menus, times, decorations and other last minute arrangements. Simultaneously, George Fillingham collected together his papers, bade everyone goodnight and left for his room.

At half past nine, Jim, having chatted to Pat Dickens for an hour following his meeting with Sylvia, reached for his raincoat and slipped his arms into the still damp sleeves.

"I hope you'll still be here on Saturday," he said to Molly, peeping into the snug before he left, "and that you'll join us for the party."

Molly clasped her hands. "Oh, how wonderful, yes, I'll still be here, and I'd love to attend the party. Thank you so much for asking me."

"You're very welcome, you too of course, Ned. The major's been in on my secret for months."

The major nodded. "Does she still have no idea?"

"None at all. I've told her we're going to the pictures and that I've arranged for Pat Dickens to run us into town. She seems happy with that, so shouldn't smell a rat."

"Well, I hope it all goes to plan," said Ned, "after all your scheming and hard work."

Jim raised his crossed fingers. "Thank you, and I'll see you all on Saturday."

At closing time Ned took Molly to see his room. She was shocked by the lack of comforts.

"It's freezing in here, Ned," she screeched, pulling her jacket tightly across her chest. "How on earth do you ever get to sleep at night?"

Ned grinned. "I usually find the intake of a few pints does the trick."

Tutting, Molly crossed to the window.

"Hark! The rain's stopped," said Ned, as she drew the curtains.

"How on earth can you tell from where you are standing?"

"Because there is a shed, outbuilding, or whatever you might want to call it, out the back, with a rusty, corrugated tin roof, and when the rain falls on it, it's very, very noisy, especially in the middle of the night."

Molly crossed the room towards the door. "Talking of the middle of the night, when shall we go ghost hunting?"

"Whenever you like, but I would imagine you're too tired tonight."

"Oh, good heavens, yes. I'm feeling quite exhausted. I always find travelling tiring."

"Perhaps tomorrow night then."

"Yes, I should like that, but I'm quite sure no-one I've so far met is a murderer. In fact they seem a very nice bunch of people."

"Yes, I know, and I probably imagined the whole thing. It will be nice to have a second opinion anyway."

Molly reached for the doorknob. "Hmm, goodnight sweetheart. Now you get to bed quickly before you catch your death of cold."

"I will: goodnight, Mother."

From beneath his pillow, Ned took his folded pyjamas and tossed them into the chair. As he undid his tie he was convinced the old fisherman's smile was broader than usual.

"Alright, I was wrong. Mother's arrival has actually made me feel a lot better, so you can take that silly grin off your craggy old face."

Across the corridor, Molly undressed and hung her pink suit carefully on a wooden coat hanger in the wardrobe. Wearing her petticoat, she then unpacked the rest of her clothes, leaving in her suitcase, only the flowing gown, shawl and crystal ball. Ned said no-

65

one must know of her spiritualistic talents, as he did not want anyone to guess the real reason for her arrival in Cornwall, but Molly really knew he found it very embarrassing. With a feeling of unease she pushed the case with its controversial contents under the bed, having already decided to leave acquainting Ned with her fortune telling until the moment felt right.

She glanced at the embers of the fire, removed the guard, picked up the poker and attempted to bring it to life. A small flame rose from the ash and clinkers. Molly put one or two more pieces of coal carefully around the flame and then quickly put on her winceyette nightie, dressing gown and slippers. She sat down in the armchair and tucked her legs alongside her bottom to keep warm. Laying back her head, she thought about Ned. She wished he would find himself a nice little wife, someone to look after him and fatten him up a bit. He seemed very skinny, but perhaps the illness could be partly to blame for that. She thought about any possible matches at the Inn, but the only females she had met thus far, were Sylvia and Gertie. Gertie seemed a nice enough girl, but not Ned's type. Sylvia was too old of course and she was married anyway. She liked Sylvia, and Frank. Jim Hughes seemed a nice chap too. As for the major, well, what a gentleman! She was sure she had found a soul mate in him.

Molly rose from the chair and walked over to the mirror above the wash basin. She tied back her hair, removed her make-up and earrings, applied the usual dollop of cold cream to her face, put on the bedside lamp and switched off the main light. Before climbing into bed, she crossed to the window and pulled back the curtains. A full moon was shining; the rain clouds had gone. She switched off her bedside lamp to see more clearly. In front of her lay roof tops bathed in the silvery grey moonlight and beyond, sparkled the flat calm sea. Molly was enthralled. The twinkling water reminded her of glittering jewels on dark satin. She climbed into bed a contented woman, and after snuggling down between the crisp, white sheets, she thought of Jane.

"Well, if you're going to sing tonight, young lady, you'll have to sing very, very loud for me to hear." And with a smile on her face, she fell fast asleep.

Chapter Eight

The following day, Ned escorted Molly around the village to show her the sights. They visited the post office where Molly bought a postcard for her friends, Jack and Gwen. They visited the beach and sat on Denzil's bench, and in the afternoon they took a stroll down the lane by the school, going as far as Gertie's parents' farm, but not calling in for tea and carrot cake as instructed by Gertie. Molly found the village people she encountered very hospitable and gradually conceded perhaps life in the depth of Cornwall was not quite as remote as her first impression perceived. It was a world within a world and Molly rather liked the languid pace of life.

That night, as planned, Ned and his mother crept down to the dining room, hopeful of encountering Jane's ghost. However, nothing happened and the room remained silent throughout their patient vigil. It crossed Molly's mind afterwards, that maybe Ned had dreamt the whole episode: either that, or he may have consumed just one too many pints. She even wondered if glandular fever in any way affected its victim's sense of perception. Nevertheless, she opted to give him the benefit of the doubt, for when all was said and done, it didn't really matter anyway, because she was rather enjoying her impromptu holiday.

"I find everyone here most agreeable," said Molly, the following afternoon as they sat on the bridge at the bottom of the School Lane. "If Jane is dead and was murdered, as you suggest, then I don't think a local person is her killer."

Ned had to agree. "Okay, so let's suppose I did dream or imagine talking to her, and that is a possibility, I must admit. But it wouldn't explain how I heard the singing of a song, which the major ratified as a song Jane used to sing."

Molly laughed heartily. "That sounds like a riddle, but I know what you mean and I absolutely agree."

As they sauntered back up the hill, a car passed by, its driver the skeletal, thin faced man whom Ned had seen driving along the same road a few days before.

"Now, he looks suspicious," said Ned, emphatically.

Molly smiled. "You can't judge a person by his looks, especially when you've had little more than a glimpse. I daresay he's a very nice man, anyway."

Ned could not agree and made a mental note to enquire from Gertie just who he might be.

As luck would have it, when they arrived back the very same car was parked outside the Inn. Inside, Frank was talking to the driver in the hallway. The man did not acknowledge them or even look up as they passed him to reach the staircase, but Ned heard Frank call him Albert.

"Albert," muttered Ned, gleefully to himself. "At last I have a suspect. Albert with the shifty eyes."

With a couple of hours to spare before dinner, Ned opted to join Molly in her room. Standing by the window, deep in thought, he absently watched a large tanker steaming slowly along the horizon.

"How I wish I could see into the future," he muttered, carelessly to himself.

"Really," said Molly, brightly, eyeing the suitcase beneath the bed, as she reached for her slippers, "then perhaps you ought to have your fortune told, sweetheart?"

"Oh, don't be silly, Mother, that's not what I meant. I don't believe in all that stuff and nonsense, as you well know. I'd just like a glimpse as to what the future might hold, that's all."

"It's one and the same thing, surely," scoffed Molly. "And may I remind you, that once you thought it not possible for the living to converse with the dead."

"I still don't think it possible," said Ned, lighting a cigarette and offering one to his mother. "But then I suppose I do. Oh, I don't know what I think anymore, everything is all topsy-turvy at present."

Declining Ned's offer of a cigarette, Molly rose from the chair and nervously pulled out the suitcase from beneath the bed. From it she lifted out the shawl and placed it on the table.

"Sit down," said Molly, carefully unwrapping the crystal ball and tossing the shawl onto her bed.

A deep frown crossed Ned's brow. "What on earth is that thing?" he stammered.

"A crystal ball," said Molly, as though it was an everyday object.

"Well, yes, I can see that, but what I mean is: why do you have one? I mean to say, mediums don't use crystal balls, do they?"

"No, but fortune tellers do," beamed Molly, huffing on it and then polishing the glass lovingly with her handkerchief.

"Oh, no, this can't be true," uttered Ned, aghast. "Since when have you been a fortune teller?"

"Since I found I wasn't making a good enough living by merely being a medium," she responded, triumphantly.

"What! If you needed to supplement your income, why couldn't you have gone out and got a job like a normal person would? You could work in a shop or a factory, or even in a school as a dinner lady. It's robbery to take money from people under false pretences. You're a charlatan, Mother."

"I am not." spluttered Molly, emphatically. "That's a dreadful thing to say about your own mother."

"Really! Tell me, then, what do you know about fortune telling? I mean, have you had tuition, lessons or whatever?"

"Of course not," Molly sneered. "I use my spiritual gifts to guide me along. I'm self-taught and very proud of the fact."

Ned sat down at the table and glared at the hateful ball in disbelief. "Tell me I'm dreaming, Mother, because you know and I know perfectly well that you can't possibly predict my future."

"Oh, but let me try, Ned," she pleaded. "Please let me try. It will be fun and it can't possibly do any harm, can it?"

Reluctantly, Ned agreed, whereupon Molly excitedly pulled her voluminous gown from her suitcase and slipped it over the top of her skirt and blouse.

"Surely you don't need to wear that hideous thing," he sneered. "Oh, this is ludicrous."

"I want to do it properly," she whispered, offended by his ridicule. "Please Ned, try and take this seriously."

Ned sighed. "If Dad could see me now," he muttered beneath his breath.

Molly sat down opposite Ned and took a deep breath. "Now, first you must cross my palm with silver."

"What! Surely you're not going to charge your own flesh and blood for this old nonsense?"

"You can have it back," snapped Molly, impatiently. "It's just what you have to do."

Ned put his hand inside his pocket, pulled out half a crown and grudgingly placed it on Molly's outstretched hand. She clenched her fist, passed her other hand over the crystal ball, fluttered her eyelashes several times, then chanted and muttered undistinguishable words which Ned was pretty sure she was making up as she went along.

"I can see you, Ned," she eventually drawled, eyes fixed firmly onto the crystal ball. "I can see you in the future. You are the headmaster of a boy's school. The boys all like you."

"Oh, really, Mother," snapped Ned, feeling nauseous. "Have you been reading *Goodbye Mr Chips*?" Molly frowned. "After all, you know it's my ambition one day to be headmaster of my own school."

"Quiet, you're interrupting the flow," said Molly, impatiently. She paused and took a very deep breath. "I see you now with a wife and two children, both girls."

"Ah, now that's more like it. What's my wife like? Is she a cracker?"

"She's pretty enough," Molly sighed. "Her hair is dark, her build, slim. She has greeny brown eyes and perfectly straight, white teeth."

"Oh, really, Mother!" hissed Ned, "You'll be telling me her name next."

"Stella Hargreaves," retorted Molly, promptly.

Ned threw back his head and laughed out loud. Molly smiled. It was good to hear him laughing again.

"Anything else?" he asked.

"I see you in a new car; a grey Morris Minor."

Taken aback, Ned ceased laughing. He had a new, dove grey, Morris Minor on order which he was due to collect after Easter, but he had not disclosed this information to his mother and it was unlikely she'd have heard from another source. He felt a little uncomfortable. Molly, however, unaware of the changed expression on his face, continued to stare into her crystal ball. "You are going to move from your flat in London into a house," she said.

"Ah, before or after I'm married?" Ned asked, resuming the flippancy.

Molly ignored him. "And I can see you playing cricket," she said, proudly.

"But you know I play cricket," said Ned. "Can't you see anything about Jane and the happenings here? I mean, that's what I'm really interested in at present."

As he spoke the colour drained from Molly's face. "I can see you crying, Ned. No, no, you're shouting, and you're very angry. Oh dear, you're dreadfully upset. You just kicked the wall right here in this very room, and your eyes are wild and flashing."

Molly rose to her feet, tore off her gown and tossed it onto the open suitcase.

"What! You can't stop now, Mother," he pleaded. "Not when it's just getting interesting. What am I all wound up about?"

"I don't know," she said, grabbing her shawl from the bed and quickly wrapping it around the crystal ball. "I don't want to see anymore. I can't bear to see you upset like that. It scares me."

Ned stood, crossed over to Molly and gave her a hug. "I don't expect it means anything anyway."

"No, probably not," she mumbled, wiping her eyes. But deep down, she was very much disturbed.

By dinner time, Molly had composed herself and was back to normal.

Gertie was waitress and bustled up to their table, carrying two bowls of piping hot leek soup.

"Ah, sir," she said, carefully putting the bowls down on the table. "Tonight is darts' night and we have a home match against the Kings Arms, but Albert Treloar can't make it, so Frank and Sylvia wondered if you would take his place since you're already on the premises. Can you play darts, sir?"

"What! Not very well," he replied, somewhat taken back.

"Oh, darling, don't be bashful," gushed Molly, placing a napkin on her lap, "you were a junior champion a few years back."

"That was for badminton, Mother. It's Dad who is good at darts."

"Oh, well, perhaps you might take after him," she said, shrugging her shoulders. "You must have inherited something from him. Heaven forbid!"

"Albert," queried Ned, ignoring his mother. "What does he look like?"

"What, Albert Treloar? He's a tall, thin chap, middle aged and not much hair."

"That must be him we saw here this afternoon," said Ned, pleased to have more information about a prime suspect. "We passed him on the stairs."

Gertie nodded. "Most likely. Sylvia said he'd been in. They've had to change the day of the Parish Council meeting to today instead of tomorrow and that's why he can't make it."

"What does Albert Treloar do?" Ned asked.

"Oh, you and your questions, sir. He's a farmer. He's not married and lives with his sister, Dorothy, out at Home Farm."

"Thanks, Gertie," said Ned, satisfied. "Tell Sylvia and Frank, I will play darts, but not to expect any miracles."

Gertie laughed. "Oh, we won't expect that, sir. We're bottom of the league anyway. As long as you make up the numbers and hit the board occasionally, that'll do."

Immediately after dinner Ned went to the games room where he found other team members throwing darts to get some much needed practice. Frank was also part of the Ringing Bells team. He joined them when Sylvia finished her chores in the kitchen and relieved him on the bar. The other team members were, Percy Collins, Reg Briers, Pat Dickens and Sid Reynolds.

Reg spotted Ned as he entered the room and hung his coat on the back of the door. "Ned, good to see you again," he said, as the two men met and shook hands. "Sorry I've not been in to continue our chat, but I came down with a cold at the weekend and so haven't been out much."

"I am sorry," said Ned, sympathetically. "Are you feeling better now?"

"Yes thanks, I'm fine, but I've a feeling the wife's coming down with it now."

"Perhaps it'll encourage her to give up the fags," said Percy, casually hitting the bullseye.

"I doubt it," grinned Reg. "Giving up is all talk with Rose. In fact, she asked me to get her a packet of twenty tonight, in spite of a sore throat."

The Kings Arms team arrived as they spoke. They were all strangers to Ned and in from another village. He thought they looked a bit rough and on observing they each bought two pints of beer on arrival, judged his surmise to be correct.

The match went fairly well with the Ringing Bells team lagging behind as predicted, although the score was a little less embarrassing than usual as Percy was on top form. At half time, Gertie brought out refreshments, but Ned was not hungry having recently eaten a very substantial meal. Nevertheless, he enjoyed the break and had an interesting chat with Reg Briers.

To end the match, the last team member to play was Ned, and in order to finalise things he needed a double one to finish his game. During his second attempt, Albert Treloar, having just left the meeting in the village hall, walked in. The rest of the team greeted him warmly, but Ned imagined Albert's eyes burning into his neck and he missed the board again. His opponent, who also needed a double one to finish, took his turn. To Ned's relief, he too failed to achieve his goal. Feeling unnecessarily tense, Ned glanced through the open door into the snug, hoping for a show of moral support from his mother. To his annoyance, she was sitting beside the major, listening to his yarns and obviously enjoying herself. Ned approached the board, the three darts tightly clutched in his sweaty palms. He threw the first; it landed outside the double twenty. He threw the second; it hit the wire, bounced off and landed by his feet. With gritted teeth and half closed eyes, he threw the third. A round of applause broke out. Ned's dart had landed right on target.

Heaving a sigh of relief and feeling in need of a cigarette to sooth his shattered nerves, Ned slid his hand into the pocket of his jacket. His cigarettes were not there. He tried the other pocket. It was empty. After pondering briefly, he reached the conclusion he must have left them on the dining table. He had, after all, departed in haste in order to be on time for the match. He slipped out of the games room, crossing through the two bars and into the passage to the dining room. The light was out and the door was ajar. He went inside, crossed hastily to his table and fumbled around in the semi-darkness searching for the missing cigarette packet. Without warning, the temperature plummeted and immediately he felt conscious of someone or something in the room.

"Hello, Ned," a female voice whispered.

Ned gulped and pinched himself viciously to make sure he was not dreaming. "Jane," he said, eyes darting around in the darkness. "Is it you?"

He heard a faint peel of laughter. "Well, who else might you expect?"

Ned turned towards the window. "Where are you?"

"In front of the fireplace," she whispered. There was a pause and Ned felt a slight draught. "But now I'm by your side."

Ned took a step back. "Stand still," he snapped, aggressively, "you're making me feel giddy."

"Sorry, I'm back by the fireplace now."

"Good, stay there. Now, where were you on Tuesday night? I came down here with my mother looking for you but you weren't here."

"Hmm, let me think. Oh, yes, on Tuesday night I went to visit my Auntie Doris. It was her birthday, you see."

"You what!" gasped Ned, surprised. "Then you're not just confined to this room?"

"Oh, no, I'm free to visit all my favourite haunts, if you'll excuse the pun."

She laughed frivolously.

"Jane, he hissed, glancing over his shoulder to check no-one was in earshot. "Please stop giggling. The other night you told me you'd been poisoned. Is that true?"

"Yes, at least I think so. That's why my spirit cannot rest, you see, and will not do so until the truth about me is known."

"So, who poisoned you, and why, for heaven's sake? There has to be a reason."

"I really don't know, but..."

"Ah, there you are Ned," boomed the voice of Frank. Ned turned to see the silhouette of the large man standing in the doorway. "Come and join us for a drink, there's a well-earned pint waiting for you on the end of the bar."

74

"Thanks. I was, err, just looking for my cigarettes," he mumbled, trying to keep the annoyance from his voice. He followed Frank from the dining room, glancing back over his shoulder as he went, but saw nothing.

After adjusting his eyes to the brightness of the bar, Ned picked up his pint and went to find his mother. He wanted to tell her what had happened but found her still cosily talking to the major.

"Did you win, Ned?" she asked, eagerly, as he approached the table.

"Of course not," he snapped. "That is, I won my game but as a team we lost."

"Never mind, sweetheart, don't let it spoil your evening."

Ned scowled. "Do you have a cigarette, Mother? I seem to have misplaced mine."

"Oh, I have them here, sweetheart." She took them from inside her handbag. "You left them in the dining room." She patted his hand in mock retribution.

Ned made an attempt to smile and hide his frustration. He didn't know with whom he was most annoyed, Molly, Frank, Jane or Albert Treloar.

"I need some fresh air," he muttered, lighting a cigarette. He then went outside to smoke it.

The evening was calm and cold with a full moon clearly lighting the outside of the Inn. Ned sat on an old beer crate, marvelling at the brightness of the stars and pondering the evening's events. He jumped when something brushed around his legs.

"Sod off, cat," he hissed, pushing the creature away. "You'll leave hairs on my trousers."

The front door of the Inn opened. Barley Wine promptly leapt forward and seized the opportunity to get back into the warmth. The door closed and Albert Treloar stood outside pulling on a pair of gloves. Ned watched from the shadows, as he climbed into his car and drove off. The night was very cold. Ned shivered, finished off his cigarette and stubbed it out on the uneven, granite cobbles. As he rose from the beer crate, the door opened again. Someone else was leaving the Inn. Ned kept still as Percy Collins approached his motorbike. Percy was whistling, melodiously. The tune was *Some Enchanted Evening.*

Chapter Nine

During breakfast the following morning, Ned was frustrated by Molly's lack of attention to anything he said. Her mind seemed cluttered with pure trivia and her concentration was focused solely on frequent silly waves across the dining room to the major.

Ned hissed angrily. "Really, Mother, will you please act your age and stop behaving like a giddy sixteen year old. It's most embarrassing."

Molly smiled sweetly. "Sorry, darling. What were you saying?"

"Nothing," Ned mumbled, sulkily. "Nothing that matters, anyway."

Conscious of the angry tone in his voice, Molly watched as he aggressively buttered a thick slice of toast. She smiled, careful to suppress the desire to giggle. He was so like his father, her erstwhile husband, who sulked for days when he was in a mood. She thought it best to ease the situation.

"What shall we do today?" she asked, brightly. "Have you anything planned? The weather looks quite nice so we could go for a little walk."

"Yes, I suppose we could, but for a change I'd like to go somewhere different."

"Oh, definitely, so would I. Perhaps we could take a walk along the cliff tops, if you are feeling strong enough, that is."

"I'm pretty sure I'd be alright. I'm certainly a lot fitter than a week ago. My legs are less jelly-like and I really would like to see a bit more of the coastline."

Molly grinned, delighted by his change of mood. "That's settled then. I wonder which the best way to go is."

Ned frowned. "What do you mean?"

"Which way do we go, east or west?"

"Oh, I see. I've no idea."

Molly's face beamed. "I'll ask the major."

"Major, dear," she called, over the rim of her bone china teacup. "Perhaps you can help us. We're going for a little walkies over the cliff tops today and wonder which way you'd recommend we went, east or west?"

"Hmm," mused the major, "that's a tough one, Moll. East is very picturesque and if you go that way of course you pass the old Penwynton tin mine, which I happen to think is of very great interest. On the other hand, if you go west you pass the Witches Broomstick which is equally fascinating, so really there's not a great deal to choose between the two."

Open mouthed, Molly, placing her empty cup back on its saucer. "The Witches Broomstick! I don't believe it. Whatever is that?"

The major wrinkled his nose. "Well, it's a bit of a tricky one to describe really. It gets its name because of the way rocks have arranged themselves around a patch of sand, you see." He noted the confused look on her face. "If you go that way, Moll, and you look down from the cliffs, you'll see the defined contour of a broomstick. The sand is the brush part and also the handle. The surrounding rocks form the outline of its shape."

Molly frowned; her imagination stretched to its limit.

The major continued, "The only access to it is from the sea, through the handle, if you see what I mean. It's too narrow for a boat though, and for that reason it's inaccessible to all living things except seabirds. Though no doubt crustaceans and fish also find their way through during high water. The locals are very superstitious about it and believe it is the home of evil spirits."

Molly's face broke into a huge grin. "Really!" she squeaked. "How exciting, we shall definitely go that way then. It sounds enthralling."

"It is. Not been there myself for a year or two, but it was a favourite spot of mine when first I came to Cornwall. You'll love it, both of you."

"Come with us today," Molly, eagerly suggested. "We'd really enjoy your company."

"I'd love to," grunted the major, thrilled at being asked, "but I really ought to see the doctor this morning."

"Oh dear, you're not ill are you?" Molly asked, concerned.

"No, it's nothing serious, just an old war wound playing up. It does from time to time. I need something to deaden the pain a bit. The doctor's familiar with my ailments. He's a damn good chap."

With a simpering smile, Molly thanked the major for his advice; she then turned to face Ned again.

"Really, Mother, you shouldn't flirt like that with the major, especially during breakfast, it's most nauseating."

"I'm not flirting," retorted Molly, primly, "I'm merely being sociable. Besides, my sixth sense tells me he desires a bit of female company from time to time and who can blame him."

Ned scowled. The thought of his mother getting close to the major and revealing the dodgy means by which she made a living, filled him with dread.

Before they left, Ned slipped along to the post office for his paper whilst Molly changed into suitable clothing. Much to his surprise Ned found the small shop full and buzzing with the chat of over excited women.

"Oh, I'll not be able to sleep tonight," said one, dramatically wiping her brow with the back of her hand.

"Me neither," exclaimed another, "and I shall have my heaviest rolling pin under the pillow from now on, that's for sure. I don't know what the world's coming to."

"Well, I pity any poor woman living alone, and for a change I shall look upon my old man's snoring as a comfort rather than a curse."

"What's causing all the anxiety?" Ned asked Mrs Pascoe, the postmistress, as he paid for his paper.

"Well, haven't you heard my 'ansome?" she retorted. "It was on the wireless this very morning. That swine, William Wagstaffe's been spotted in Plymouth and we reckon he'll be down here afore we do know it."

Ned threw back his head and laughed. "I very much doubt it. It'll be no more a reliable sighting than any of the others we've been fed these past two years. Unless of course our erstwhile member of parliament has actually become a compulsive globetrotter with an unlimited supply of cash and wants to be caught. No, mark my words ladies, he's tucked away somewhere having changed his appearance so that now even his mother wouldn't recognise him."

Silence tinged with disappointment hung over the post office as Ned, clutching his paper, opened the door to leave. By the time he had closed it, however, the chatter had begun again and even more intense than before.

The morning was mild and pleasant with a gentle breeze blowing up from the south west when Molly and Ned left the Inn; as they strolled down to the beach, the sun made several attempts to put in an appearance, but each time its efforts were thwarted by thick, rolling clouds, intent it seemed on lingering for the duration of their walk.

They left the lane which ran alongside the top of the beach and at the foot of the coastal path began to climb the steep, rugged track leading up to the cliff tops. Half way up, Ned expressed his delight and acknowledged his strength had almost returned to normal, for there was a spring in each step he took and he was able to breathe without stopping frequently to rest.

At the top of the path they stopped and looked along the winding, hilly trail that lay ahead. Close by was the hedged boundary of Chy-an-Gwyns, the large house overlooking the cove. Molly glanced with interest at the name plaque fixed onto a small wooden gate. "Whatever does that mean?" she asked, attempting its pronunciation. "It looks like gobbledygook to me."

Ned smiled. "Well, according to the major, Chy-an-Gwyns is Cornish for house in the wind."

"Really! Fancy that, and quite appropriate too, I suppose. I'm not sure I'd like to live in a windy place though. I mean, it'd be good for drying washing, but a real nuisance if you've just had your hair done."

Before commencing their walk they paused to take in the breath-taking view across endless miles of azure blue sea. Below, just off-shore, a small fishing boat chugged through the calm water followed by a flock of hungry, squawking gulls. Molly pointed to the east, where the chimney of the old mine was clearly visible through a dense multitude of gorse and bracken. They could also see Gertie's parents' farm, and a tractor working in the nearby fields. Ahead of them, to the west, more farm buildings, which Ned estimated to be less than a mile away, lay nestled in the distant hills. He wondered to whom that farm belonged, and made a mental note to enquire once back at the Inn.

They left the curtilage of Chy-an-Gwyns and followed a well-worn, twisted trail through sporadic patches of wild heather, gorse and haphazardly placed rocks. For several hundred yards it ran near to the cliff's edge, and then unexpectedly it reached a large dense area, overgrown with prickly gorse and sprawling brambles, thus causing the path to veer sharply inland through a small triangular meadow. Molly was not amused. In the middle of the field a herd of dairy cows grazed on the short grass near to where the path ran.

"We can't go in there, Ned. If they're bulls they might attack us, and my scarf is red."

"But they're not bulls, are they? They're cows."

"How can you be so sure? You're not a country boy."

"Nor am I an idiot. Look at the udders, Mother, and use your imagination."

Molly giggled, as Ned opened the gate. "Oh yes, silly me. But stay close to me, Ned, won't you? Just in case they turn nasty."

They walked into the meadow and Ned securely closed the gate. "Don't be silly, Mother. They're far more afraid of you, than you are of them."

Molly, tightly clutching her son's sleeve. "I doubt it," she whimpered.

They crossed the field without any mishaps, avoiding both cows and cow pats. On the far side they climbed onto a stile, from the top of which, the tip of Trengillion's church tower was clearly visible in the valley.

Once over the stile, they continued along the path which turned back towards the coast, and in the distance an old weather-worn, crooked signpost, stood near to the cliff's edge pointing out to sea. On nearing it they were able to read the faded lettering, *Witches Broomstick*.

Molly and Ned stepped beyond the signpost towards a rusty railing which ran in both directions for a considerable distance around the edge of the cliff. With curiosity roused, they excitedly peered over the top. Way down below lay a stretch of sand, surrounded by rocks and shaped, just as the major had described, like a witches broomstick.

Ned was enthralled. "I really must bring my camera with me another day and take some snaps to show the children. This is just incredible. Never was a place created by nature more aptly named. Don't you agree?"

Molly shuddered. The side of the cliff was a steep, sheer drop and she was very much afraid of heights. "I don't think the name really conjures up my feelings at present," she gulped, feeling light-headed, turning away, and beckoning Ned to do likewise.

"I'm alright, Mother," Ned laughed, leaning over the fence. "Heights don't bother me one jot, and I might as well have a good look while we're here. You never know, I might even see some of the evil spirits the natives fear."

Molly sat down on a flat rock and removed her right shoe. "You should know better than to mock spirits, Ned. Be they good or bad."

Not wanting to get into a discussion about spirits, Ned looked at his watch and rapidly changed the subject. "We must have walked a fair way. It's almost an hour since we left, you know."

"Well, we've certainly walked a fair way, but I don't think we've come very far. If you take into consideration all the bends, twists and ups and downs, I think you'll find we're still only just outside the village."

Ned nodded. "You could well be right. That farm certainly doesn't look any closer now than it did when we stood outside Chy-an-Gwyns."

Molly removed a tiny stone from her shoe, which had rubbed her foot and made a small hole in her stocking. Leaving her cursing, Ned climbed onto a boulder and contemplated whether to walk on further or go back. Glancing towards the farm, he noticed a pickup truck heading in its direction.

"There must be a road, lane or track leading to that farm," he said, pointing towards the vehicle. "Come on, with any luck we might find our way onto it and then we can walk back by road. At least that way we'll have a change of scenery."

Molly happily obeyed as she had no desire to return the way they had come and meet with the cows again.

They rambled on until eventually they reached a muddy track, deeply rutted through the use of heavy farm vehicles. All indications were that it led inland. They trudged on, and after a short distance found it joined a narrow lane. Ned, who had a good sense of direction, was confident it would lead back to the village.

They passed the farm buildings which had been in their view since they had first set foot on the cliff path. And gouged into the wood of an open five bar gate, beyond which lay a farmyard, saw the name Higher Green Farm.

Beyond the farm, the narrow lane continued to wind sharply downhill. "I think we'll come out in the cove, rather than the village," said Molly, as the road levelled out. "I can still clearly hear the sea."

Ned agreed. "You could well be right. It'll definitely be somewhere like that."

To their right they passed a heavily creosoted five bar gate, with the name Chy-an-Gwyns embossed on a brass plaque. Beyond the gate ran a muddy track leading over the fields to the back of the house whose roof was partly visible through the bare branches of trees, stunted and bent from frequent exposure to south westerly gales.

"That windy place must be worth a pretty penny," said Molly, as they approached a sharp bend.

Before Ned could answer, a small dog emerged around the corner and ran in circles around their feet, yapping as it bounced up and down on its short, stubby legs. Both stopped quite still and stared at the creature in amazement. Neither before had ever seen such a peculiar looking animal.

"Whatever sort of dog is that?" asked Molly, who knew absolutely nothing about canine breeds.

"God only knows," said Ned, as they attempted to break free and walk past the barking animal. "Looks like a crossbreed of some sort."

They heard a sudden female voice cry out, "Shut up, Freak, and come here you gormless mutt."

The dog ceased barking instantly, as around the corner emerged his mistress. She had red hair, was heavily made up and wore a short skirt with a thick baggy jumper, but no coat. Ned gasped and stared in amazement. It was the woman he had encountered on the train.

All three remained silent as they passed each other by.

"Do you know that Jezebel?" hissed Molly, accusingly, once they were out of earshot. "The look on her face told me she knew you."

Ned chuckled. "Well, I'll be damned. She was on the train, but I never dreamt she'd turn up here of all places." Still laughing, he glanced back along the lane. "I wonder who on earth she is. And what about that dog! Did ever you see such a bizarre pair?"

Molly nodded. "What did she call it?"

Ned laughed. "Freak. She may look a bit odd, but I would imagine she has a good sense of humour."

"Humph! I don't know about that. She looked a right trollop to me, and that clothing is more suited to the seedy, street corners of a city, than to a lovely location such as this."

Ned kept quiet. A person's sense of dress was not something he wished to discuss with his mother.

As they walked around the next bend, both heaved a sigh of relief. They were back in the village on the lane at the foot of the cliff path where they had first set off. Pleased with their walk, and the discovery of a new route, they strolled happily back to the Inn. And as they walked through the door, the sun finally succeeded in breaking through the thick, white cloud.

Chapter Ten

During breakfast on Friday morning, Molly sat quietly with a very glum face. "It's no good, Ned," she said at last. "I've been through the entire contents of my wardrobe here and I don't have anything to wear for the party tomorrow night. I'm in the depths of despair."

Ned gasped and counted to ten quickly beneath his breath. "But surely something amongst that vast array of colour would be suitable," he finally spluttered, recollecting the glimpse he'd had of Molly's clothes when she had recently put away a pair of shoes.

"But they're not party clothes," scoffed Molly, annoyed by his lack of understanding. "Everything I brought with me is for day wear. I didn't expect to be invited to a party, you know, and I don't want to let the side down by not dressing in an appropriate manner."

Ned realised there was no point in arguing. "So, what would you like to do about it?"

"I thought we might pop into town," Molly suggested, hopefully. "I'm sure they must have a nice little dress shop there, although of course I do prefer to make my own clothes. But on this occasion I realise that's quite impossible."

Ned groaned. He doubted any local shops would sell clothing in the flamboyant styles and colours Molly favoured, but then concluded, that might possibly be a good thing.

Gertie entered the dining room to clear away their dirty dishes. Ned asked her about any buses that might be going into town.

She responded with her usual enthusiasm. "Oh yes, we have two on Fridays, sir. One at ten-thirty and the other at two-fifteen. It takes three quarters of an hour to get there, so if you go in at ten-thirty you can catch the one-fifty back. That's what I do when I go into Helston."

Molly clapped her hands gleefully. "Wonderful! Thank you, Gertie dear. What do you say, Ned. Shall we go?"

Ned was not at all enthusiastic about shopping with his mother, or anyone else for that matter. It was a task he loathed, be it for food, clothing or whatever, but he could not dampen this sudden bout of happiness and so reluctantly agreed.

Gertie added. "The bus stop here is by the post office, and you'll be dropped off in Helston near the Blue Anchor. They brew their own beer there, it's called Spingo, and I'm told by the lads it's very good."

Ned grinned. "Thank you, Gertie. I might need a tipple of something stronger than beer though after shopping with mother."

"Pleasure, sir," she grinned, with an unexpected wink. "Hope you have a nice day."

They found Helston to be larger than expected, for when both had first arrived in Cornwall by train, only a few houses in residential areas were visible from their taxis.

Molly stepped from the bus enthusiastically, determined to enjoy one of her favourite pastimes. They left the bus and walked along the street, glancing in shop windows and entering the first store to show any sign of promise. Alas, much to Molly's dismay, it sold no party clothes or evening wear.

"Just frumpy old clothes in drab colours for frumpy old women," Molly said, shuddered, as they emerged from the shop. "And so much in brown too. How could anyone possibly wear brown, by choice?"

"This is a rural area, Mother. A post war rural area at that. What's more, farmer's wives, fisherman's wives and rustic folk would look absolutely ridiculous traipsing about the countryside, wearing shocking pink."

"I suppose so," sighed Molly, somewhat downhearted.

They continued up the street towards the Guildhall.

"There are an incredible amount of pubs in this town, aren't there?" said Molly, totting up those she had seen on her fingers. "Goodness only knows how they all make a living."

At the top of the hill, by the Midland Bank and Boots the Chemist, they turned a corner and walked into Meneage Street. Outside Joy Williams, they stopped and looked at the china and glassware display in the window.

"Let's just pop in here and buy Flo a nice vase for her birthday. That one in the corner has rather taken my fancy."

With vase wrapped and securely tucked beneath Ned's arm they went into a second ladies outfitters, full of hope, but once again they were profoundly disappointed, as it also sold nothing to whet Molly's appetite. The matronly shop assistant, however, was very helpful, and suggested they tried Abbots, further up the street. "Cross over the road and carry on past Rowe's, Gilbert's, and the TSB Bank, you can't miss it. It has lovely stained glass running around the tops of the windows."

They thanked her profusely and left the shop with a small degree of optimism.

Abbots was only a small shop, but much to Molly's delight, judging by the window display, albeit sparse, it did appear at least to specialise in evening wear. The shop bell rang merrily as they opened the door. Inside a pretty, slim girl, smiled to greet them.

Ned sat down on a wicker chair by the counter to rest and wait patiently for Molly to be shown several dresses, but unfortunately, very few gowns were brightly coloured, and much to Molly's disgust, the only styles in her size were black.

"I'm going to a party, dear," said Molly, frustrated. "Not a funeral."

The shop assistant smiled sweetly. "I know many ladies who actually prefer to wear black for parties. It's a very flattering, sophisticated and slimming colour."

"Are you suggesting I'm fat?" spluttered Molly.

"Oh no, madam, no, not at all. I was just trying to explain why some of our evening wear is in black. If I might say so, you have a lovely figure, madam."

After swallowing the gratuitous flattery, Molly reluctantly agreed to try on some of the gowns, and eventually emerged from the dressing room wearing the one she disliked the least.

"Good heavens!" Ned spluttered, amazed by the transformation. "You look stunning, Mother, absolutely stunning."

The shop assistant nodded in agreement. "It's a perfect fit and could have been made for you, madam."

"A real head turner," added Ned.

"Do you think so?" Molly smirked, patting her stomach.

"Absolutely! It'll take the major's breathe away."

With raised eyebrows, Molly turned to the assistant. "I'll have it then, dear."

She returned without hesitation to the changing room, after stating categorically she had no desire, whatsoever, to try on any of the other gowns on offer. And ten minutes later they left the shop with Molly happily carrying her latest purchase wrapped in brown paper and tied up neatly with string.

"Do you think that girl was Stella Hargreaves?" Ned asked, smiling with gratitude at the shop assistant through the glass door, as they proceeded to walk along the pavement.

"No. Her hair is the wrong shade and she has slightly crooked teeth," said Molly, emphatically.

"Did you get what you wanted in town, ma'am?" asked a bright eyed Gertie, as they sat down to dinner that evening.

"Yes thank you, dear. I bought a nice new dress and I have to say, I'm quite delighted with it."

Gertie smiled, dreamily. "I've got a new frock too. Mum made it. I'm really excited about the party tomorrow. It should be really good. Everybody's going to be here for it, and Sylvia's making tons of food."

Ned was looking forward to the party also, but for a different reason to everyone else. He was hoping to eavesdrop on conversations and do a bit of amateur detective work on Jane's behalf. He expected his mother to do likewise, but her thoughts at that moment seemed to be occupied solely with fluttering her heavily mascaraed eyelashes at the major. "So like a woman!" Ned mumbled, his voice tinged with a note of despair.

"How's your war wound, dear?" called Molly to the major, across the dining room.

"Much better today, thanks, Moll," he beamed. "Doctor did the trick."

"Splendid," said Molly, rubbing her hands together. "We can't have you missing all the fun tomorrow night."

Gertie arrived with their desserts.

"Who's that with George Fillingham?" Ned whispered, suddenly noticing he was not alone.

"Bertha, his wife," she replied in a hushed voice. "Mrs Fillingham arrived at lunch time and she seems really nice."

The bar was very quiet, compared with a usual Friday night. Most people stayed at home to save their energy and money for the following evening.

Molly retired to bed at half past nine in order to get plenty of beauty sleep.

Ned was in bed before Frank rang last orders. And when Sylvia wiped down the tables after closing time, only the major remained seated in the bar.

Chapter Eleven

The following morning, Ned peeped around the door of the public bar looking for his mother to inform her he was off to the post office to collect his newspaper and buy a sixtieth birthday card for Flo as they had forgotten to get one the previous day in Helston. He was greeted by four women, all wearing headscarves to conceal bulging curlers. Preparations for the surprise party were well underway and the bar was a hive of activity. Rummaging through a box of once brightly coloured, but now faded, crepe paper streamers, knelt Sylvia. Molly, red in the face, sat slumped on a stool, attempting to blow up balloons along with another woman unknown to Ned. On introduction, he discovered she was Farmer, Pat Dickens' wife, May. Gertie stood at the bar pouring tea into cups from a large brown teapot. She winked mischievously at Ned as he leaned lazily on the dark, wooden door frame.

"You gonna give us a hand, sir?" she asked, hopefully.

"Err, when I return perhaps," he muttered, hoping his unwillingness wasn't too obvious. "If you've not already finished that is."

He pulled up the collar of his jacket and walked down the passage, leaving the ladies to do their good work. With a shiver, he then stepped outside into the brisk east wind.

Several people greeted Ned as he strolled along the road. Thanks to Molly, he had become quite a well-known figure in the village and most people were keen to express their liking for that fresh faced lad from up London.

Inside the post office, Ned shuffled through the birthday cards and bought the only one he could find specifically for a sixtieth birthday.

"As you can imagine we've had quite a run on them," smiled Mrs Pascoe, as he paid for card and newspaper. "Been selling like hot cakes they have, and I ordered extra as well when Jim first mentioned Flo's do."

Ned grinned. "Then it's just as well I've come in early this morning otherwise I might have been unlucky."

As Ned approached the Inn, he paused. None too eager to return indoors and listen to the babble of over excited women enthusiastically making things pretty, he decided to stroll down to the beach and relax on Denzil's bench for a while and read his paper in peace. He found, however, it was too chilly to sit for long. The bench, in its exposed position, offered no protection from the biting east wind. Reluctantly, Ned closed the paper after reading only the front cover. Cursing the fact he was not wearing his overcoat, he rose, walked across the shingle and threw a pebble into the approaching waves. He heard it plop in the distance, and watched as the grey, salt water, splashed and tumbled just inches from his brown leather brogues.

Ned shivered, partly from the cold and partly from his fear of drowning. He thought of Jane and wondered where her body was buried. For he believed without doubt that she was dead and the villain responsible for her untimely end was walking free.

In front of him stretched countless miles of the English Channel. Could Percy have murdered her and dumped her body out at sea? It was possible. He owned a boat and must have had ample opportunity to do so. Furthermore, with a heavy weight tied to her waist, she would surely never get washed ashore.

Ned shuddered. The idea of Jane decaying on the sea bed both repulsed and appalled him. For even though they had never met in life and he knew nothing of her looks, other than her alleged beauty, in a strange way he felt emotionally involved and he wanted to help her find eternal rest.

Back inside the Inn, Ned found the ladies still decorating the bar. Teetering on a chair, Gertie was attempting to pin a streamer into a beam. Seeing Ned from the corner of her eye she lost concentration and dropped the pin. Obligingly, he stooped to retrieve it.

"See a pin and pick it up and all the day you'll have good luck," Gertie chanted, as he dropped the pin into her outstretched hand.

"What do you think?" asked Molly, showing off a balloon onto which she had neatly painted, Happy Birthday Flo.

Ned surveyed a heap of colourful balloons gently quivering on a table in the breeze from an open window. "Lovely, but surely you're not going to paint all that lot, you'll be here all day."

"Good heavens, no. I'm just doing four. Two for each bar. Look I've done those already." She pointed to two white balloons hanging from the beam above the fireplace in the snug.

Alongside the bar, May Dickens and Sylvia each held the end of a red streamer, which they twirled until its twist was symmetrical, they then handed it to Gertie to pin onto a beam. Again she dropped the pin.

"Would you do this for me please, sir?" she asked Ned. "You're so much taller than me and I seem to be all fingers and thumbs this morning."

Ned took off his jacket, threw it onto a table and climbed onto the chair. Gertie watched, open mouthed, as he stretched to reach the beam and his shirt pulled away from his trousers.

Frank entered the bar with a tray of coffee mugs. Glad of a break, May Dickens sat beside Molly and chatted about the ups and downs of being a farmer's wife. "It's a hard life, it really is. Up early each and every day to milk the cows, but I wouldn't swap it for all the money in the world, and nor would Pat."

"Where is your farm?" Ned asked, joining in the end of conversation.

"Up on the cliffs. Higher Green Farm, it's called."

"Really! That's the one we passed the other day," said Molly, warming to her new found friend. "It's quite near to the Witches Broomstick, isn't it?"

May laughed. "That's right. In fact some of the locals even call it Broomstick Farm."

Because Sylvia needed the dining room re-arranged in order to lay out the birthday buffet, the Inn's residents agreed to have dinner at the earlier time of five o'clock. The party guests were due to arrive from seven o'clock onwards, and Jim was expected with Flo around half past seven. According to the latest information, Flo still suspected nothing and was genuinely expecting her birthday treat was to be a rare visit to the pictures, although she had mused to her friend, Nettie Penrose, during an afternoon visit, how she thought it a little odd Jim wanted her to wear her best frock to the cinema.

"God only knows why," she'd said to Nettie. "No-one will see me in the dark and I probably won't even take my coat off."

"Perhaps he just wants you to feel special," Nettie had replied. She'd then prattled on nervously about the mending and ironing she had to do, indicating that's how she'd be spending *her* Saturday night.

At twenty five minutes past seven, Pat Dickens arrived at the Hughes' cottage wearing his old, everyday coat over the top of his best suit. He kissed the birthday girl on the cheek, patted Don's head, and gave the thumbs up sign to Jim, whilst Flo opened the birthday card he'd just given to her. Don wagged his tail eagerly, anticipating a trip out, as his master reached for his coat. Flo put the card from Pat and May on the mantelpiece and then stroked his silky head. "I'm afraid you'll have to stay here, old fellow. We can't take you to the pictures. It's not allowed."

"Ooh, he can come with us for the ride," said Pat, knowing Jim never went to the Inn without his faithful friend. "And I'll keep him with me 'til I pick you up later. He'll be no trouble."

"Good idea," said Jim, helping Flo on with her coat.

As they approached the car, Pat fumbled in the deep pockets of his overcoat as though looking for something. "You don't mind if I just pop into the Inn quickly before we go into town, do you? I think I must have left my specs in there last night and I really ought to have 'em on for driving."

"Of course not," Jim hastily replied, knowing this was part of the plan. "The film doesn't start 'til half past eight, so there's plenty of time."

Pat left the car parked outside the Inn and returned minutes later clutching the glasses case which had been waiting for his collection on the bar. Instead of climbing into the driving seat, however, he put his head through the car window.

"Flo, just pop in quickly and see Sylvia will you, she wants to wish you a happy birthday and give you a card, but can't leave the bar as Frank's down the cellar changing a barrel."

"We've plenty of time, love," said Jim, noticing her hesitation.

Pat opened the car door, Flo stepped out and obligingly walked towards the Inn, followed closely behind by the two men and faithful Don.

Inside, behind drawn curtains, both bars were in darkness and only the flickering glow of the fire in the snug produced any light.

"What on earth's going on?" asked Flo. "Where's Sylvia? Is there a power cut?"

Near the coat pegs, someone giggled. Flo turned hastily as Sylvia switched on the lights and people emerged from various hiding places singing *Happy birthday*. Flo, completely overwhelmed, burst into tears.

"Jim Hughes, is this your doing?" she sobbed.

Jim kissed her flushed cheek and handed her his handkerchief,

"Nothing but the best for my Flo," he whispered. "You deserve it, love. Happy birthday."

Ned was delighted with the turnout. Everyone he knew, or knew of, was at the party, and many more besides. Molly likewise, was infinitely happy. Wearing her new gown and looking extremely glamorous, she raised many eyebrows amongst the male party goers, unbeknown to their wives and sweethearts. Not that Molly was a threat to any woman. She had eyes only for the major, and he likewise, had eyes only for her.

"Moll!" he'd spluttered, when first she'd emerged in the new black dress. "You look gorgeous, absolutely gorgeous." And after that the compliments kept on rolling in.

"Perhaps wearing black isn't such a bad thing, after all," she grinned to her bemused son. "But I draw the line at brown, Ned. I'll never wear brown."

Although Molly would have preferred to spend the entire evening in the company of the major, she knew Ned wanted her to mingle amongst the guests and find out anything she possibly could about Jane's past. Therefore, when she saw Doris sitting alone in the dimly lit snug, sipping a glass of sweet sherry and staring absently into the fireplace, she went to her side.

"You look deep in thought, Doris," she whispered, softly. "Are you alright?"

Doris turned, her eyes brimming with tears. "It's Jane," she sighed. "I was thinking of Jane. Whenever I come here I expect to see her smiling face. She loved this place, you see. Loved the people. I just wish I knew what'd happened to her. Where she is."

"Have the police tried to find her?" Molly asked, sitting by her side.

Doris nodded. "Yes, of course. She's been on a missing persons list for months, but it's never achieved anything. They think she's gone off travelling or something daft like that. And I suppose if there's no evidence to point otherwise, they've no reason to regard her being missing as out of the ordinary. But I know she'd never go off without saying. She was keen to travel, admittedly, but even though she knew I disapproved, she would still have told me, and she certainly wouldn't have gone away without telling her friends."

"It does seem odd, I must admit," said Molly. "I wonder, did she have any enemies. Anyone who might want to harm her?"

"The police asked me that. But no, not that I'm aware of, anyway. I never heard her say a bad word about anyone. By all accounts, she was a very popular girl."

Molly impulsively put her arm around Doris's thin shoulders. "Someday there will be news," she whispered. "Someone, somewhere must know the whereabouts of your niece."

"It'll be bad news when it comes," Doris sobbed. "It sounds negative to say it, but I just know she's dead. I feel it in my bones."

Molly recoiled. She felt very uneasy. What could she say? If Ned really had spoken to Jane's ghost, then Doris was right. Jane was dead and it would be cruel to give her false hope.

Flo Hughes sauntered in from the public bar to thank Doris for the amethyst brooch she had received as a birthday present, and pointed out it was already securely pinned to the bodice her best frock.

Not wanting to spoil Flo's evening, Doris quickly brushed away her tears and smiled. "You were looking forward to seeing that film, weren't you, Flo?"

Flo laughed. "Yes, but we're still going to see it, only next week now. A party is so much more fun."

Molly subtly slipped away, leaving the two old friends to chat. She found Ned and told him what Doris had said.

Behind the busy bar, Sylvia and Frank were helped by both Gertie and Betty. Molly eyed them with interest.

"Gertie looks very pretty tonight," she commented. "Betty's far too skinny though. She needs to put on a few pounds."

"Mother, don't be so critical. It's possibly genetics that make her slim and not malnutrition."

The major appeared from nowhere, beaming. "Ah, there you are, Molly. Been looking for you everywhere." He handed her a large gin.

Ned thought it best to leave and mingle with the other guests. He started with the games room, where Harry the Hit-man stood by the darts board talking to Albert Treloar. Harry's shirt sleeves were tightly rolled up revealing even more grotesque tattoos. Ned subtly moved a little closer in an attempt to hear the topic of their conversation. Harry spoke in an East London accent, convincing Ned even more, that he was a gangster of some sort. The subject of discussion between the two men, however, was anything but sinister. They were chatting about a renovation programme for the village hall.

Ned moved on. In the snug someone firmly grabbed him by the arm.

"Ned, you've not met my wife yet have you?" He turned to see Jim and Flo Hughes. Ned kissed Flo on the cheek and wished her a happy birthday.

"Thank you, and thank you for the lovely vase too," smiled Flo, her cheeks flushed. "It's very pretty, and my favourite colour as well."

"You're very welcome, but I can't take any credit as Mother chose it. It was her idea too as she believes a woman can't have too many vases."

Flo laughed. "Absolutely. And I do love my flowers."

"You used to work here at one time, didn't you?" Ned said, remembering being told so by Frank.

"That's right. I did the cooking and looked after the bed and breakfast side of things. I was mighty glad to give it up though and let Sylvia take over as it was becoming a bit of a strain."

"Ah, but you still make the pasties and quite delicious they are too."

Flo was delighted with the compliment. "Yes, I still make the pasties, and that's quite enough for me now."

Ned realised she would have worked with Jane, but thought better of bringing Jane into the conversation on such an occasion.

"Sorry I'm late," panted a voice from behind. They turned to see Reg Briers approaching, a box of chocolates tucked beneath his arm. He kissed Flo's hand in a chivalrous manner, and wished her a happy birthday.

"Thank you," Flo smiled, as he gave her the chocolates. "My favourites. Is Rose not with you?"

"No," said Reg, clearing his throat, "I'm afraid she's in bed with a cold."

Ned frowned, puzzled, convinced Flo's look was verging on one of happy relief.

As the evening wore on and the drinks flowed more freely, so the chatter of raised voices increased in volume and conviviality. Pat Dickens, intoxicated by both atmosphere and strong cider, climbed onto a chair and announced he felt like dancing, much to the embarrassment of his wife, May. Sylvia obligingly cooperated and suggested they move back the tables while she fetched her old gramophone record player. The tables, therefore, were hurriedly pushed aside by all available males, leaving a substantial floor space in the public bar. Annie Stevens, wife of Police Constable, Fred, shuffled through Sylvia's record collection and chose a selection suitable for dancing to. She then carefully put the first record on the turntable and turned the volume to maximum.

"May I have the pleasure of this dance, Moll?" asked the major, clumsily attempting to bow to his aspired partner.

"Of course," she giggled, springing to her feet, even though both were painfully pinched by her best shoes.

"I bet that dress was a tricky little number to squeeze into," the major grunted, putting his arms firmly around her waist and pulling her close.

"Hmm, and I might need a hand getting out of it, Benji," Molly giggled, slipping her arms tightly around his neck.

"Mother!" exploded Ned.

Molly laughed helplessly. She had not seen her son standing nearby. As the major whisked her away she gently shook her head. How like his father, Ned looked, when he adopted that superior, pompous attitude.

The music, chatter, laughter and dancing continued. Gertie was given a short break and sought out Ned for a dance. Glad to have the company of someone nearer his own age, he took her arm and escorted her onto the makeshift dance floor. She pulled him close, as Annie, following a request from Flo, put on a slow Waltz. Ned cringed. He had no more knowledge of Waltz steps than he had of knitting techniques. But Gertie didn't care, nor was she bothered when he frequently trod on her toes. She was dancing with Ned and that was all that mattered. She just hoped Betty was watching.

Albert Treloar was dancing also. Or rather stumbling around in an attempt to dance with Gertie's mother, Nettie Penrose, who he held awkwardly in his long, thin arms. The strong Somerset cider he was drinking, however, caused his feet temporary loss of control, and on turning, he lost his balance and tumbled headlong across the floor with Nettie landing ungracefully on top of him. On raising their heads, they found the slow Waltz record laying broken in two beside their entwined feet, alongside the upturned gramophone player. The fall had knocked both musical implements from the table, thus causing a premature end to the dancing.

Fred Stevens attempted to get the music going again, but within minutes pronounced the gramophone dead, leaving a red faced Albert to plead with Sylvia for forgiveness and a promise to get it repaired as soon as possible.

At eleven o'clock several people left, including Albert Treloar who was driven home by his non-drinking sister, Dorothy.

Ned looked at the clock. It was past closing time and quite obvious Frank had little regard for the licensing laws when there was money to be made and people were having a good time. And as the village police constable, Fred Stevens, was one of the many still in the bar, drinking, what did it matter?

Faces, however, had turned somewhat glum. The happy chatter having subsided with the rhythm of the music. More entertainment was needed and the major swiftly decided he had the perfect solution.

"Ladies and Gentlemen," he slurred, a little incoherently, after rising to his feet. "My good friend Molly here, is a medium. Might I suggest she attempts to contact someone out there for us?" Teetering, he pointed towards the window.

Ned looked aghast. His jaw dropped. He could not believe his ears. His mother must have revealed to the major details of her dodgy occupation. A few cries of astonishment went through the still substantial crowd. It was Jim Hughes who clapped and agreed it was an excellent idea.

Molly, somewhat surprised by the major's proposal and far from feeling sober, nevertheless, jumped at the opportunity of being the centre of attention, and readily agreed to the challenge.

"I shall need total silence if I am to make contact with the spirit world, and also another large gin to aid my concentration," she burbled, taking a seat at the table by the window in the public bar. She then turned to Ned. "Darling, be a treasure and fetch down my long gown, please. It's in the suitcase under my bed."

Ned groaned. He was extremely cross and very much afraid. What if his mother, even in her drunken state, should contact Jane in the presence of everyone? Or worse still, what if Jane's murderer was at the party and he turned nasty? Ned felt sick as he went to Molly's room, but consoled himself, that at least Doris had already left, and Fred Stevens was still around, even if a little inebriated, should there be any trouble.

Ned scowled and hissed at Molly as he handed the satin robe to her, but she was oblivious to his concerns and grinned nonsensically as two women helped slip the robe over her black dress. Another table was pushed up to the one at which Molly sat. Everyone then shuffled around to sit or stand as near to Molly as they could get. Frank turned out some of the lights to create an atmosphere. Betty screamed making everyone jump. The sudden change of ambience jangled her nerves. When everyone was settled, Molly closed her eyes, hiccupped and asked the spirits to guide her towards any lost soul wishing to communicate.

"Try and contact Denzil," Percy suggested, flippantly. "We all knew him."

"I shall contact...hic, whosoever is out there wishing to com, com, talk to...hic, whosoever is here," slurred Molly.

Ned closed his eyes, looked heavenwards and prayed.

Molly outstretched her hands over the table and closed her eyes tightly.

"Is there anyone out there?" she drawled in a low, husky, voice.

Nothing happened.

"Is there anyone out there? Hic," Molly asked again.

The only sound was the ticking of the clock, the faint crackling of flickering flames from the fire in the deserted snug, and the irregular sound of collective breathing.

Someone coughed nervously. Ned's stomach rumbled. Outside a sudden gust of wind whistled around the window by which the party-goers were assembled. No-one dared move. All eyes were riveted on Molly's flushed, blank face. An unexpected loud crack, reminiscent of thunder, pierced the atmosphere followed by a blinding flash. The heavy window curtains billowed out across the wooden sill and flapped angrily against the back of Molly's head, but she did not move. On the ceiling above, two paper streamers rustled vigorously, and the plates in the snug bar rattled as though shaken by an earthquake. Four brightly coloured balloons slipped from a beam and floated gracefully downwards. As they reached the floor, one of the lights Frank had left on behind the bar, flashed, sparked and popped intermittently.

Molly's face turned from flushed pink to mottled grey.

"Someone wishes, hic, to speak." She took a deep breath. "To whom do you wish to speak, spirit?" asked Molly, her voice almost inaudible, and very, very deep.

Carefully, and precisely, she began to mouth the name. "Wi, Wi, Will, William," she muttered. "You wish to speak to, hic, to William Wagstaffe."

Chapter Twelve

Frank leapt away from the panic stricken group and fumbled in the semi-darkness for the light switch praying restored illuminations might quash the hysterical outburst, he then endeavoured to revive Sylvia, away in a dead faint alongside the bar. The thought of William Wagstaffe in their midst was too much for the women folk to bear. Some sobbed, others sat trembling with ashen faces. The younger ones screamed uncontrollably. Flo Hughes, like Sylvia, fainted, and Molly, her face now devoid of colour, stared vacantly into space as though in a trance. Even the bewildered men cast eyes of suspicion over their shoulders towards their fellow men unsure how to interpret the chilling request of Molly's conjured up spirit.

Once Sylvia was revived and sitting up fully conscious, Frank, in desperation, rang the bell in order to take control of, and calm the pandemonium.

"For God's sake," he boomed. "Pull yourselves together. Wagstaffe's only been on the run for a couple of years and you've all known each other for far longer than that. I don't know where the ruddy man is, but he's certainly not in here tonight, is he now?"

Gradually everyone calmed down. The women dried their eyes, some even laughed. Molly sat pale faced and speechless.

"Good God, that gave me a scare," Nettie Penrose, sighed, blowing her nose. "Frank's quite right of course, but even if Wagstaffe's not at the Inn, it doesn't mean he's not in the village, does it?"

"Absolutely, and I shall make a point of looking under my bed from now on," said Flo, nervously sipping from the glass of brandy given to her by Frank. "Even if Jim does think I'm daft."

When near normality returned and most people had gone home, Frank filled up the glasses of those remaining.

"On the house," he chuckled. "I think it's time to wind down a bit."

He locked the front door and switched off the outside light. The remaining few then moved into the snug. Gertie and Betty were freed from their bar duties and Betty promptly made a bee line for Percy at whom she had been making eyes all night. Seeing this, Gertie flounced off and sat down unceremoniously beside Ned.

"You're mum's brilliant," she said, taking a large swig from her half pint glass of sweet cider. "She really scared me back then, but it was a joke, wasn't it?"

Ned thought it might be best to agree. "Most likely," he said. "Mother has a habit of becoming the life and soul of the party."

In a trice, Gertie had spread the word, and soon the consensus of opinion was Molly had conjured up the imaginary spirit for a joke. There was much relief, and although Ned was thankful the possibility of William Wagstaffe actually seeking refuge in Trengillion was no longer the main topic of conversation, he was still very keen to question his mother, now recovered, regarding the truth behind her extraordinary performance. The opportunity to do so, however, did not arise, for the major was constantly at her side, or, as on Ned's last observation, kneeling on the floor, tickling her feet in an attempt to cure her hiccups.

Jim Hughes, delighted with the success of the evening and considerably merry, bought a round of drinks for everyone. Reg Briers, perched on a stool, began to sing. Gradually others joined in, and the major insisted on buying a further round to moisten their dry throats.

Ned's head felt muzzy as the smoke filled room began to spin in a hazy blur. On the table beside his legs, he pushed aside an ashtray overflowing with cigarette butts, to make room for his brim-full glass of whisky. Gertie, close by his side, linked her arm tightly through his and rested her warm head on his shoulder. His nose twitched as the scent of her strong perfume mingled with the tobacco smoke in her hair, roused his sense of smell. She was dreamily singing. Singing about boatmen rowing.

Ned attempted to sing, but when he opened his mouth no sound emerged from his dry lips. He felt dizzy as the room continued to spin. And on the beams above, the colourful plates inspired by the melodious harmonies, appeared to dance and jiggle to the rhythm of the music.

The following morning, Ned awoke convinced he was going to die.

He attempted to open his eyes and lift his head from the pillow, but his head ached beyond belief. He ran his dry tongue across his dry lips and tried to swallow, but his mouth was devoid of moisture. Through a hazy blur he sensed a presence in the room.

"Jane," he murmured. "Jane, is that you?"

Gertie's voice greeted his ears and a pillow hit him hard in the face.

"Jane!" she screeched. "Who's Jane? Is she your girlfriend?"

Ned groaned as he forced open his eyes. To his amazement, Gertie stood at the foot of the bed doing up the buttons of her new frock.

"Who's Jane?" she shouted, again.

"Um, I, I don't know," Ned mumbled, feebly. "I must have been dreaming."

Gertie leaned across the bed. "You don't have a girlfriend, do you, Ned?" she asked, attempting to soften her voice.

"No, no, no I don't. God, I feel like crap."

"That's alright then," beamed Gertie, sitting down on the bed to put on her stockings and shoes.

On rising she turned and gave him a big kiss. "I must go. See you at breakfast."

She glanced in the mirror on the wardrobe door, roughly ran her fingers through her hair, and then giggling, skipped from the room.

Ned rolled over and looked at his watch. It was half past seven.

"Breakfast!" he groaned. "How could anyone possibly eat breakfast?"

He instantly went back to sleep and slept for a further two hours.

On waking, he crept along the corridor to the bathroom where he drank two large glasses of water before taking a bath. Still feeling very fragile, he then dressed and went downstairs to see if anyone else was around.

In the bars, Frank and Sylvia were cleaning up the mess from the previous night. He offered to help, but found he could not bend to pick up anything without a severe pain thumping inside his forehead and an appalling feeling of nausea rising from his chest to his throat.

Sylvia laughed, but not unkindly. She had limited her intake of alcohol to three glasses of gin and orange. Feeling fine, she left for the kitchen to make Ned a bacon sandwich and a cup of strong coffee.

The food and drink helped to settle his churning stomach, but had little effect on his throbbing head.

"You going to church this morning?" Frank laughed, putting a match to the kindling wood stacked carefully in the fireplace.

"Ugh, it's Sunday," Ned moaned. He turned to Sylvia. "Are you going?" he asked.

"I don't know, it all depends how Benji is feeling."

Ned cringed. He found events of the previous night a massive blur, but amidst the haze he did recall hearing his mother call the major, Benji.

"I really must have a word with her," he mumbled. "Silly woman, making a ridiculous exhibition of herself like that."

"Hey, you leave her be," said Frank. "Let her have her bit of fun. She's a born entertainer that lady. Best night we've had in here for years. Isn't that right, Sylvia?"

Sylvia nodded. "I thoroughly enjoyed it, despite the scare."

Ned kept silent, as he recalled his mother asking for William Wagstaffe. Had she done it as a joke? The opportunity to find out had so far not arisen.

At a quarter to eleven, the major descended the staircase and entered the bar with a radiant Molly on his arm.

"Are you ready for church?" he asked Sylvia, who was clearly amused.

"Of course," she smiled. "Just give me a minute."

She left to fetch her coat and hat. Ned likewise, went to his room and slipped on his overcoat. If everyone else was pretending they felt fine, then damn it, he would do the same.

The church was much quieter than the previous week. No Percy singing in the choir. No Police Constable Fred Stevens and his wife, Annie. No Jim and Flo Hughes, and much to Ned's surprise, no Gertie. He felt relieved, yet at the same time disappointed. He didn't want a relationship, especially a short fling. He was in Cornwall merely to rest. His life was centred elsewhere and he saw no place in it for Gertie.

Just before the service began, Sid Reynolds arrived and sat in a pew on the opposite side of the aisle to the party from the Inn. Ned tried to recall whether or not Sid had been at the birthday party, but was unable to decide either way.

The vicar's sermon was about sin. Ned felt as though it was solely directed at him, but eventually convinced himself it could apply to just about everyone at the party. "Even the old dears were knocking back the sherries," he chuckled to himself.

During the afternoon Ned slept for another hour. On waking he felt a lot better. As he sat in the fireside chair putting on his shoes, he noticed one of Gertie's hairclips on the floor. He picked it up and slipped it in his pocket. From the corner of his eye he was aware of the old fisherman smiling from his frame on the wall.

"I expect you've witnessed many such evenings as last night in your day," he grinned, as he tied up his shoe laces. He stood to reach for his jacket, and whilst doing so was convinced the old fisherman actually winked.

Ned left his room and crossed the corridor to his mother's room. He knocked gently on the door in case she was sleeping.

"Come in," he heard her call.

Ned found her sitting by the fire toasting her feet with an open book on her lap. She greeted him warmly.

"Come in and sit down, sweetheart," she said, pushing her feet inside her slippers, "and tell me all the details of things that happened last night, which regrettably neither I nor the major can remember."

Ned sat down on the rug in front of the fire beside his mother's chair.

"I was hoping you'd be able to do the same for me. There are lots of things I can't remember, like going to bed for instance."

"Oh, but surely you must remember William Wagstaffe," she sighed, eyes looking heavenwards.

Ned laughed. "How could I forget? Now I hope you're going to put my mind at rest and tell me, like everyone believes, it was a tantalising hoax."

Molly slowly shook her head. "Oh, but it wasn't a hoax, Ned. I truly wish it was. I feel so guilty for causing such mayhem but I really did hear a voice. I can't remember whether it was male or female, but I do recall it was distant and angry. If only I'd been sober. I could kick myself for drinking so much. With a clear head it would probably have made more sense."

Ned groaned. "Oh, God, I can't believe this is happening. It's too ridiculous for words, and I don't suppose you've a clue as to what the voice was saying either."

Molly shook her head. "Not really. All I actually remember is muffled crackling. You know, like when there's interference on the wireless. It wasn't until I asked to whom he, she, or it, wished to speak, that I was able to make out the name. It then kept repeating William Wagstaffe, over and over again."

"But what on earth can this signify? Surely Wagstaffe can't really be in Trengillion? I mean, why would he be here? It is, after all, to use your own words, the back of beyond."

Molly shrugged her shoulders. "But then, why not? He has to be somewhere, and the back of beyond is a good place to hide."

"Yes, and I know it's always been my belief that he is heavily disguised and in hiding. But I really can't accept that he's down here."

"Hmm, maybe not, but deep down I can't help but wonder if there might be a connection between him and Jane?"

"No, surely not. Why should there be?"

Molly sighed. "I don't know. The major and I were talking about him last night. He went to school with him, you see. Wagstaffe that is. The major was quite chatty because he was under the influence of alcohol. But this morning when I mentioned it he didn't want to talk about it. I think it disturbs him to have known someone capable of murder. Especially with the victim being a poor, defenceless woman."

"You like the major, don't you, Mother?" said Ned.

She smiled. "Yes, I do. He makes me feel, well, you know, very special."

Ned reached up and touched her hand, lovingly. "Just don't get hurt, Mum," he whispered. "Be ruled by your head and not your heart."

Molly's eyes prickled as she felt them fill with moisture. It had been a very, very long time since he had called her Mum.

Chapter Thirteen

By Sunday evening, even though everyone had recovered physically from Saturday night's excessive merry-making, the party's extraordinary happenings were still the main topic of conversation amongst the regulars of the Inn, and Molly's spiritual encounter with someone on the *other side* asking to speak to the infamous William Wagstaffe, whether believed to be genuine or otherwise, was known by all of Trengillion's inhabitants far and wide. Frank was delighted with the gossip. It brought villagers to the Inn who had never set foot through the door, all eager to set eyes on the up-country spiritualist who had caused more excitement in the community than they had ever known before. Even Ned was amused, and, if the truth be known, a little proud.

During breakfast on Monday morning, the Inn's residents were entertained by a very high spirited Bertha Fillingham, eagerly questioning Gertie about Trengillion and the surrounding neighbourhood. For the previous day, she and George, had found their ideal retirement home - Sea Thrift Cottage - perched on the cliff tops near to Higher Green Farm. Gertie extolled the virtues of the area with her usual enthusiasm, causing Bertha to raise her over excited voice in both pitch and volume. She babbled at high speed, non-stop, unable to do her breakfast justice, stating she just couldn't wait to go into town with George to put in a very realistic offer with the estate agents handling their dream property.

Molly sighed thoughtfully as she stirred two lumps of sugar into her tea. Part of her envied the Fillinghams the prospect of a new life in Cornwall, but at the same time she felt it must surely be difficult to let go of the past, especially if, as in the case of George and Bertha, one had lived in the same house for more than thirty years.

Molly lay down the teaspoon in the saucer and thought of Clacton and her friends Jack and Gwen. She tutted. How remiss of her, they had not crossed her mind for days, not since she had sent them a postcard on her first morning at the Inn, even though she had promised to keep them well informed of the happenings in Cornwall. She smiled to herself, thinking how difficult it would be to say much on a postcard, as one never knew who might read it.

"I'll go with you to the post office this morning, Ned, if you don't mind. I really must get another postcard for Jack and Gwen and let them know, I'm at least alive and well."

"Of course I don't mind. In fact I've nothing planned for this morning, so we could go for a walk afterwards if you like."

Molly sighed. "I'm afraid I can't today, Ned. The major and I are going to visit Doris at eleven for coffee. We think she needs more company. She seemed so low on Saturday night, poor soul, and it must be dreadful for her not knowing what has happened to her beloved Jane."

A beautiful morning greeted them as they left the Inn. The sky was powder blue, almost cloudless, and on a grassy bank beyond the lichgate of the church, clumps of pale yellow primroses lay snuggled together in the dappled shade of a leafless sycamore.

"I do believe there's a hint of spring in the air," said Molly, enthusiastically. "It almost feels warm enough to be outdoors without a coat."

"Mmm, I agree, and for that reason I think I'll ask Sylvia if we can go out on the horses today. She keeps offering to take me for a trot and I reckon today would be simply perfect."

Molly raised her eyebrows. "I didn't know you could ride a horse."

Ned laughed. "I can't. Well that is to say, I can, but not very well. There is much room for improvement, to say the least."

"Really. I'm intrigued. So where and when did you learn?"

"Last summer George and I went to stay with his parents for a weekend cos it was his sister's twenty first birthday and she was having a big party. The family live on a farm, you see, and have several horses, so George and I went out riding along with his sister whilst we were there. I enjoyed it, even though it was difficult to stay in the saddle at first. It was a rather thrilling experience."

"Who's George? I don't think I've heard mention of him before."

"Oh, you must have. He's a teaching friend of mine. My best friend in fact. I've known him for nearly five years now." Ned laughed. "He insisted I went to the party because he thought he might be able to marry me off to his little sister. But when we got there, we found she already had a steady boyfriend."

"Really, what's her name?"

Ned grinned. "Not Stella Hargreaves. And before you ask any more searching questions, she's now engaged to that boyfriend."

As they reached the post office, a Ford Prefect drove past loudly honking its horn. It was the Fillinghams on their way into town. Ned and Molly waved vigorously and then entered the busy shop.

Back at the Inn, Ned left his mother at the foot of the stairs and went in search of Sylvia. She was in the kitchen and to his surprise, stood at the table tying together a brace of pheasants by their necks with binder twine.

Ned entered the room and looked down at the colourful plumage with interest. "Pheasant for dinner tonight, I assume."

Sylvia wiped her blood stained hands on the floral pinafore covering her clothing. "Actually, no. Jim brought these in only this morning, so they're not ready yet. Game needs to be hung for at least two days, you see, and so these beauties are going out to the wash-house until Thursday."

"Hung! Do you mean that literally?"

Sylvia smiled. "Yes."

"Would you consider me as a simpleton if I asked why?"

"No, of course not. Hanging merely improves the flavour and helps tenderise the meat. To be fair, I wouldn't expect a city dweller to know that. There is much to be learned from country living, Ned. I gained some knowledge from my Land Army days, and the rest from Jim Hughes. What Jim doesn't know about game and shooting isn't worth knowing. However, I assume you're not here for a lecture on game."

"No, as interesting as it is. I'm actually here to see if the offer still stands to take out the horses for a trot. It's a gorgeous day."

"Oh dear, I'd love to say yes, really I would, but not today. We've new guests arriving at lunchtime and I've not prepared their rooms yet."

Gertie, busy in the sink washing the dirty breakfast dishes, heard what was said and peered over her shoulder.

"I'll go with you, Ned," she said, eagerly. "I've got to go and check them anyway. That's if it's alright with you, Sylvia."

"Of course, Gert, that's fine by me. The poor creatures could both do with a good run. What with the party and everything, they've not been ridden since Friday."

Ned rubbed his hands, gleefully. "Brilliant. I'll just pop up to my room and get changed. Where and when shall I meet you, Gertie?"

"I'll be another twenty minutes or so yet. So you might as well walk over to the stables and I'll see you there."

Ned was given directions to the stables, he then ran upstairs and changed into his oldest pair of trousers, a thick woollen sweater and his brown brogues, which he noted were in desperate need of a polish.

Leaving the Inn he walked along the side path and into a small rear courtyard, paved with large, irregular shaped slabs of granite. The yard was enclosed by several single storey outbuildings. Inquisitively, Ned peered inside the first, a low, windowless, structure, which he guessed may once have been a pigsty. A modest heap of coal lay to one side. Logs occupied the rest of the space. Ned stepped back outside and straightened up his back.

In a shady corner behind an old well, the door of another building was slightly ajar. Ned pushed it open and stepped inside onto the spotlessly clean cherry red tiled floor. It was the wash-house. In a corner, its bowl covered by a heavy wooden lid, stood a large, brick-built copper. Ned assumed it was no longer in use, for on the opposite wall, beside a deep Belfast sink, stood a modern electric copper. Ned lifted its lid and peeped inside, the residue of water lay in the bottom. He replaced the lid and turned around. Beside the door, beneath the curtained window, the surface of a scrubbed wooden table was littered with a wicker laundry basket, bags of blue rinse, washing powder, blocks of green Fairy soap and a wash dolly. Tucked beneath, was a large galvanised tub containing dirty washing and a selection of empty tin baths. From the handle of a mangle, which turned the rubber rollers, hung two pairs of wooden wash tongs. And dangling from a beam on the ceiling, hung the unfortunate brace of pheasants.

Ned went back outside and crossed to a well in the middle of the courtyard. He wondered if it contained any water. He peered into the darkness but could see nothing. Intrigued as to its depth, he picked up a small stone and dropped it inside. Within seconds he heard a distant splash.

Above his head, tightly wound around a large spindle, was a thick rope. From it dangled a cast iron hook. Ned turned the spindle's handle. It creaked, and moved grudgingly. He was tempted to attach an upturned bucket lying on the granite slabs and lower it into the water, but decided against it. He must not keep Gertie waiting.

Leaving the yard, he wandered into a grass meadow. It ran behind the churchyard and away into the valley. Through gaps in the tall hedgerows, Ned was able occasionally to glimpse the roof tops of buildings which ran alongside the village's main road. From the bottom of the field he started to climb up the gentle slope towards the stables. Approaching the paddock he saw the two horses, Winston and Brown Ale, heads to one side, eagerly peering out of the stable door. Ned climbed over the five bar gate and dropped down onto the clipped grass. Brown Ale neighed. Ned stroked the nose of each horse in turn and gave them sugar lumps which he'd taken from a bowl in the dining room.

Gertie arrived ten minutes later, having first changed into slacks and a hand knitted sweater which she kept at the Inn for riding. Ned watched as she opened the stable doors and released the horses into the paddock for a brief trot around while she sorted out the riding gear. Feeling useless, Ned leaned on the gate, lit a cigarette and looked out across the valley to admire the view.

"I'll take Brown Ale, if you don't mind," shouted Gertie, before calling the horses back to her side. "I've never ridden Winston before and I think he might be a bit too big for me."

"I don't mind at all," said Ned, carelessly. "One horse is much the same as another to me."

Gertie frowned, unsure whether his blasé statement indicated he was a very skilled horseman or a complete novice. She hoped it was the latter.

"Have you ridden much before?" She asked.

"I'm afraid not," he grinned, throwing his cigarette butt over the wall.

Gertie smiled broadly. It would give her a chance to show off her riding skills if Ned was a bumbling amateur.

Once mounted, they went down the slope of the adjoining meadow into the valley and then followed a short, hoof marked track into the village, where they crossed the main road and turned down the lane between the school and The School House. Neither spoke. Eventually they reached land farmed by Gertie's parents.

"I'm sorry about the other night," Ned blurted suddenly, as they left the lane and rode along the edge of a freshly ploughed field.

"Sorry! For what?"

"Well, I don't know really, cos if the truth be known I can't remember anything that happened after the singing started. It's all a complete blur and I certainly don't remember going to bed."

Gertie threw back her head and laughed. "That's just about the story of my life. I'm an easily forgettable blur."

Ned winced. "No, no, please don't say that. It's not what I meant to imply at all. It's just, I can't remember. Really I can't. I mean, you and me. Sorry, I feel such a cad. Such a fool."

Gertie smiled. "That's because there's nothing to remember. You fell asleep the minute your head hit the pillow."

"Oh God. What must you think of me? I'm so sorry."

"Stop apologising. It actually makes me giggle when I look back on it."

"I'm no match for Casanova, am I?"

Gertie shook her head.

"Right, let's change the subject. How about you telling me about yourself. At present I know nothing, other than you work at the Inn."

They trotted gently along the edge of a field where decapitated cauliflower stalks protruded through the dark earth, each denuded following the harvest of its yield.

Gertie ducked to avoid an overhanging hawthorn branch. "There's nothing much to tell really. So I'll keep it brief. I don't want to bore you and send you to sleep again."

She cleared her throat and took a deep breath.

"Right. I'm twenty years old and the only daughter of Cyril and Nettie Penrose, who you already know, and I live at Long Acre Farm, where we are now. I went to the village school and my best friend is Betty Bray. We've known each other since we started school and we've never fallen out. Not over anything serious anyway." She sighed. "Ever since I was little I'd wanted to be an

111

actress, but it's not the sort of thing ordinary girls do, is it? I mean, there are no drama schools or anything like that nearby, so the only experience I've ever had is the annual show we put on in the village hall each autumn. It's always great fun, and you'd be surprised how many normally straight laced people like acting the fool. Anyway, when I left school I didn't know what to do. The bus service into town's not that great, although Mum did offer to drive me in. But really, I didn't want to work in a shop or a factory, and I hate paperwork so definitely didn't want to work in an office. That left no other choice so I opted to work on Dad's farm."

Ned looked surprised. "What driving tractors, herding cows and suchlike?"

"Yes. Dad taught me to drive a tractor, and you can take that smirk off your face, I was as good as any man, just as the girls were in the Land Army during the War."

Ned smiled. "I don't doubt it for a minute. So what happened next?"

Gertie sighed deeply. "Jane disappeared. I heard Frank and Sylvia needed help at the Inn. It was summertime, you see, and so they were quite busy. I decided to think about it but it didn't take me long to make up my mind. If the truth be known it was a bit frustrating anyway, getting dirty all the time, often working alone, and I must admit I did get rather tired. Dad didn't have any trouble finding someone to replace me, there's always boys leaving school looking for work."

"What about Betty?" Ned asked. "She doesn't seem to do many hours at the Inn."

"She does one day a week so that I can have a day off, and helps out too when there's something on like Mrs Hughes' birthday. She has a job in town, you see, working in a small factory. Her mum works there too."

"I see. So what do you do when you have time off? I mean, country life must be a bit of a drag cos there's not a great deal to do, is there? Surely you'd like to go to big shops, visit museums and see live shows at the theatre. Not to mention the opportunity to go to parties and so forth."

"No, I don't crave those things." retorted Gertie, promptly, as she dismounted to open a gate into the next field. "It's a case of what you're used to I suppose. I love it here and I'd hate to be a towny like you. Anyway, we still have the occasional party. You witnessed that for yourself the other night, even if you can't remember much about it."

Ned glanced sideways as she haughtily settled herself back in the saddle on the brown mare. "Touché," he said.

She promptly turned towards him. Her face was flushed. "Race you across the field."

Ned surveying the level field of green pasture ahead. "Right, you're on."

Gertie won the race with ease and laughed as Ned reached the hedge a poor second. He thought how pretty she looked. Her eyes shone brightly and glowed with satisfaction and pride. She clearly relished his defeat.

To hide his breathlessness, he looked away from her face and glanced across the fields to the beautiful Cornish coastline. White, frothy waves repetitively splashed onto the rugged rocks and dozens of gulls followed behind a small fishing boat heading towards the cove. He felt a pang of empathy with Gertie's way of thinking and wondered if he could ever be anything but a towny.

Back in the paddock, Gertie unsaddled the horses and led them into the stables. Ned left her to do the chores, for it was obvious she was more than capable of the job in hand and any contributions from him might be more of a hindrance than a help. He wandered off, sat on a wall and lit another cigarette. He felt warmed by the ride and the gentle heat radiated from the watery winter sunshine. Ned poked the dead match between the stones and rolled up the sleeves of his thick sweater. He thought of Jane. If his memory served him right, she too had been fond of horses.

Arriving back at the Inn, Ned and Gertie found an unfamiliar van parked outside on the cobbles. Attached to its tow bar was a trailer carrying a small motor boat. Ned looked at it quizzically.

"Wow! I see the new guests have arrived already," Gertie giggled, a note of excitement in her voice.

"Guests," repeated Ned. "Why have guests brought a boat with them in the depths of winter?"

Gertie ran her hand along the side of the boat. "Because they're treasure hunters. They've come to look for some wreck or other apparently lying at the bottom of the sea off this coast. I don't know how long they are here for, but it could be a while if they have difficulty finding it. Isn't it exciting?"

"Well, I should think they must already have found treasure. This boat must have cost an absolute fortune."

"Really? I don't know about that. But Sylvia did say something about one of their dads being loaded."

"How fascinating!" Ned exclaimed. "This really will be something to tell the children back at school, especially if they find the wreck while I'm still here."

Gertie fetched her bike from the shed and rode home without going into the Inn. Ned went to his room, changed, and then crossed the passageway to see if his mother was yet back. He tapped gently on her door.

"Come in," she called.

Ned found her sitting on a chair by the window in a stream of sunlight, writing the postcard.

"Hello, sweetheart," she said, looking up. "You've got colour in your face at last. That's good. I take it Sylvia took you out on the horses."

"No, she didn't actually. She was too busy, so I went with Gertie."

Molly raised her eyebrows. "Do I smell a hint of romance?" she asked, hopefully.

"No," Ned retorted, firmly. "We're just good friends, that's all."

Molly lowered her head and continued writing the postcard to hide her smile.

"How was Doris?" Ned asked, sitting on the bed.

"Quite cheerful today. She said how much she loves the springtime, although of course, we could still have lots more bad weather yet."

"Did she mention Jane?"

Molly shook her head. "No, and I didn't want to raise the subject either. I don't think there's much more she could tell us, anyway."

Ned stood, crossed to his mother's side by the window and glanced down towards the Inn's entrance. The van, trailer and boat were no longer there. He assumed the new arrivals had taken the boat down to the beach.

At dinner that evening, a radiant Bertha Fillingham sat with her amused husband, George. Their offer on Sea Thrift Cottage had been accepted and already she was planning its redecoration and where to put each item of furniture they possessed. Her bubbling delight spread to the other guests, thus causing the atmosphere to buzz with optimism and enthusiasm.

In due course the two new arrivals entered and sat at the table where once the honeymoon couple had dined. They were both in their mid-twenties, of similar height, equal good looks and striking, corn coloured, blond hair.

Molly turned to Ned and nodded her head in their direction. "They should cause quite a stir amongst the local females."

The same thought had crossed Ned's mind and he felt a pang of jealousy as Gertie, eyes sparkling, placed bowls of soup on the table in the alcove.

Later, in the bar, Frank introduced the two young men to the locals. Des Granger and Larry Blewett, both from Dorset. They shook hands amicably with those present and all agreed, in whispers, they seemed a very nice couple of lads.

The major in particular was very interested in their visit, for he was keen to learn how they intended to search for the wreck which lay on the seabed.

"We'll be snorkelling," said Larry, when questioned. "For the time being, that is. At the moment we're just keen to locate it. But next year we hope to dive and search in earnest. Don't we, Des?"

"Dive?" queried the major. "But surely diving equipment is only available to military and police divers."

Des nodded. "Yeah, you're right. My dad's a Navy frogman and it's through him we've got interested in looking for wrecks and so forth. But next year, like in America, Aqua-Lungs should be commercially available over here too. My cousin lives over there, you see, and he sent me a copy of this fantastic new magazine called *Skin Diver*. We're really keen on the idea. It's going to be a fascinating hobby when we get all the latest gear, cos there are loads of sunken vessels yet to be discovered on the seabed and some, no doubt, went down with valuables on board."

The major nodded with enthusiasm. "And you will of course declare any treasures you might find to the necessary authorities."

Larry grinned. "Yeah. Everything will be all legal and above board. Couldn't be anything else really cos my old man's a barrister and I don't think he'd appreciate seeing his only son in the dock."

"Then I wish you both well and I shall watch your progress with great interest," said the major.

Later, as Ned stood in the public bar, observing who was talking to whom, Percy Collins came in with his friend Peter. In turn they each asked Frank for a pint. Ned watched as the new arrivals spoke to the fishermen. He thought Percy seemed distant and had a worried look on his face, or was it just his imagination? No, Percy looked troubled. He kept glancing towards the window and biting his nails in an agitated manner. Was he afraid of what lay out there? Was he afraid of what the treasure hunters might find hidden beneath the waves? If so, Ned believed he knew exactly what that something was.

Chapter Fourteen

On Tuesday morning, Des and Larry left the Inn after breakfast for their first exploratory trip out to sea. Gertie excitedly informed Ned and Molly of this when they entered the dining room at half past eight. They also learned that the young men had arranged to have an early breakfast in order to catch the tide.

Molly shuddered. "Ugh, it's far too cold to go in the water this time of year. They must be mad."

"I know," Gertie agreed. "And I said so to Des."

Molly picked up the teapot. "According to the major, they have dry suits or some such paraphernalia, but it wouldn't suit me. Going in the sea that is."

Gertie giggled. "I thought you meant wearing a dry suit wouldn't suit you."

"God forbid," said Molly, warmed her hands on the heat generated from her full teacup. "The mind boggles."

In the afternoon, Ned left Molly reading and wandered down to the cove hopeful of seeing Larry and Des. Their boat was not on the beach when he arrived, so he assumed they were not yet back. The only people around were Percy and Peter, sitting on a plank of wood supported by old oil drums, outside the net loft, where they mended crab pots ready for the summer. Both men nodded to Ned as he walked by. He greeted them in return. Percy looked happy. Ned was surprised. If there was any truth in his theory regarding Jane, then Percy ought to be feeling very uneasy with Larry and Des out at sea, and not laughing and joking with his best friend.

Nonplussed, Ned crossed the beach in order to sit on Denzil's bench and while away the time. The beach was deserted. The two cottages which overlooked it stood empty and forlorn. But that was to be expected, for during a conversation with the major, he had learned that the people who owned them only came down in the summer and occasionally at Christmas.

A few gulls squawked overhead as Ned lowered himself onto the bench. He watched as they circled beneath the white clouds and then flew up over the village in search of food. When they disappeared from view, he turned and looked at the sea, where small waves splashing continually along the same stretch of sand. Mesmerised, he tried to establish whether the tide was ebbing or flooding. He finally concluded it was high water and the tide was on the turn.

The church clock struck three. As the echo of its chimes faded away, Ned became aware of the distant humming of an outboard motor. He raised his head, leaned forward and looked out to sea. As he had hoped, Des and Larry's small boat was emerging around the cliffs. Ned watched as the boat reached the water's edge. Percy and Peter, having ceased work, waited to help the two newcomers in. Then together, with the aid of the mighty winch, the boat was pulled ashore to join the small row of fishing boats resting beyond the high water mark.

Ned, conscious of the young men chatting in the distance, cursed his inability to hear the nature of their conversation. For a while he watched from afar trying to decipher hand gestures and body language. Eventually, his inquisitiveness became too much to bear. He rose from the bench in a casual manner and walked across the beach with both ears strained, desperate to eavesdrop on their discussion. Once in earshot he was able to hear their dialogue, clearly. To Ned's dismay their chat was boat talk, which meant little or nothing to him.

They all waved to him as he sauntered past. He waved back and then continued to stroll away from the beach. However, seconds before he was out of earshot he heard Larry ask, "Did you ever find your dad's car keys?"

Percy laughed. "Yeah, thank God. They were in my ruddy sea boots all the time. I knew they couldn't be far away. The old man would have killed me if I'd gone home and said I'd lost them. That car's his pride and joy."

Ned's jaw dropped heavily with disappointment as he stepped onto the road and headed for the Inn. So that was why Percy had seemed anguished the previous night. He had just lost some damn, silly car keys!

On Wednesday the wind was too strong for anyone to venture out to sea, and so Larry and Des, determined to make use of their free time, spent the day in their rooms, where they passed the hours studying sea charts and ancient maps. Molly, likewise, went to her room after breakfast and stayed there. She hated the wind, thus had no desire to leave the Inn.

"Besides," she told Ned. "The book I'm reading is very absorbing, and so this weather gives me the ideal opportunity to finish it."

Ned, restless, did not want to be confined indoors. He put on his coat, scarf and gloves and went out with every intention of taking a walk. He did not wear his hat, however, as he knew from experience it would be futile in such a wind.

He decided to walk the cliff path to the east of the cove and maybe even get along as far as the old mine. But when he reached the top of the cliff, he found it was as much as he could do to stand in the strong, south-westerly gusts. Nevertheless, he persevered and staggered on in the direction of the mine, clearly visible on the distant horizon. However, he was unable to walk any further than a row of six Coastguard cottages, for the wind behind forced him to travel at a pace not of his choosing, thus causing him to realise, walking back into the wind would be an almost impossible task. With a sigh of defeat, he lowered his head to protect his face from the elements and retraced his steps, with great difficulty, back along the cliff path and down into the cove.

At the bottom he stopped and sat down on a boulder sheltered from the wind by the back wall of the winch house. From there he watched the waves as they thundered and crashed noisily onto the continuously moving shingle, convinced the wind had strengthened considerably during the short time he had been away from the Inn.

By early evening, the wind had reached south westerly gale force nine. And in the public bar of the Ringing Bells Inn, as Pat Dickens poured pale ale from a bottle into his pewter tankard, he informed those present, the Shipping Forecast predicted storm force ten.

"So I've heard," said Frank, putting Pat's empty bottle into a crate beneath the bar. "I should think we're in for a pretty quiet night, trade wise that is."

Jim Hughes nodded. "I covered up my geraniums in the greenhouse this afternoon with orange boxes I'd scrounged off Maude Pascoe. I didn't want 'em to get damaged, cos likely as not a few panes of glass'll get broke. The greenhouse is rather exposed, you see, and catches the south westerly winds real bad. Daft place to have it, I suppose, but we put it there cos it's a nice sunny spot."

"You sound like a keen gardener," commented Molly. "I've always thought it would be quite nice to have a greenhouse, but my garden back home is rather small."

"You could always have a lean-to," suggested Jim.

"Mmm, well, not really. I rent my home, you see, so it might not go down too well with the landlord, knocking nails into his walls and so forth."

Before Jim could respond, the door of the Inn flew open, and Percy ran in breathlessly with Peter close behind. They asked for volunteers to help with the boats. There was the possibility of the sea reaching the road in the early hours of the morning at high tide, and they wanted to move all the boats off the beach to the safety of a grass verge opposite.

Without hesitation, Pat Dickens and Jim Hughes placed their drinks on the bar and left with Percy and Peter. Ned, Frank, the major, George Fillingham, and Gertie's father, Cyril, followed. Larry and Des, on arriving from their upstairs rooms shortly after, promptly left too when Sylvia conveyed the news. Only the ladies remained at the Inn to fret and worry.

Sylvia stood, a lone figure behind the bar, her face pale as she watched the clock tick slowly by. She had witnessed winter storms before and shuddered, remembering the night when Denzil Penhaligon had gone missing in December during her first year at the Inn. He should not have gone out. The forecast had been bad. He told his family he would not be long - just a couple of hours - while he caught a few mackerel for supper. No one knows quite what happened, but he did not return. His boat was found the next day, battered and broken against the rocks in the shadow of the old Penwynton mine. His body was washed up several days later. It had been a grim and bleak Christmas for everyone that year.

Bertha noticed her worried look. "They will be alright won't they?" she nervously asked.

"Yes, yes of course," said Sylvia kindly, forcing a smile, as she poured a glass of stout. She then left the bar with her drink and joined Bertha and Molly by the fire. "They'll be alright as long as they have their feet firmly on the ground."

The three women sat cosily in the snug bar with Jim's Labrador, Don, each thinking about the men in their lives helping the fishermen in unfavourable circumstances: Bertha, and her beloved George, each looking forward to their retirement in Cornwall, Sylvia, and her much loved Frank, and Molly, not only with her son, but someone who, in a very short time, had come to mean a great deal to her.

The wind screeched relentlessly across the earthenware pot of the Inn's tall, brick chimney. It squeezed through every gap surrounding the rattling sash windows and whistled down the dark, wide chimney void, causing flames around the burning logs to flicker wildly in the excessive draught. And as the clock on the chimney breast above the crackling logs, struck the half hour, the first drops of rain began to fall and bounce heavily against the thick glass panes.

The minutes ticked by. The raindrops rapidly increased in number until their resounding pitter-patter finally outdid the howling of the wind.

Bertha listened, deep in thought. "George only has on his lightweight jacket," she muttered. "And his heart is not strong."

Molly patted her hand, reassuringly. "There are enough of them out there," she said. "Your George won't be needed to do any heavy work, although I daresay the poor soul will be getting pretty wet."

As the clock over the fireplace neared nine, they heard the sound of approaching voices. Sylvia sprang to her feet as the voices grew louder and rushed to the door to welcome the men folk in. All were drenched to the skin, except Percy, Peter, and some other fishermen who were wearing oilskins.

Wet coats and jackets were rapidly hung over the backs of chairs, across vacant stools and empty tables. No-one grumbled about the weather, instead an air of excitement hung over the Inn as they happily chatted, thankful to be safely back in the warm and dry.

"It's nearly storm force ten already," said Frank to Sylvia, as he reached for a dozen tumblers, into which he emptied a bottle of whisky.

Sylvia placed the glasses of whisky onto a tray ready to hand out to the shivering men. "It sounds like it. I don't envy anyone on a ship tonight."

The major settled in his usual place in the corner of the snug beside Molly. Ned, teeth chattering, joined them. Molly hugged and kissed them both. They tasted of salt. "We were so worried. It seemed you were gone forever."

"Good God, Moll, you shouldn't have been worried." The major gestured his appreciation to Sylvia as she handed him a glass. "They're brave men that make a living from the sea and what we did tonight was absolutely nothing in comparison. Nothing at all."

Ned, rubbing his hands together to revive his circulation, nodded in agreement.

The men, warmed by the whisky, chatted freely and excitedly. George Fillingham in particular, having spent his entire working life sitting in the bank, revelled in the thrill of having done something useful, in spite of his weak heart.

"A refill for everyone, please, Landlord," he boomed, rising to his feet. "The drinks are on me." He and Bertha were due to return home the following day and he wanted to show his appreciation to the people he hoped soon to be his friends and neighbours.

Cyril Penrose downed his second whisky and then bade everyone goodnight. He was keen to get back to Long Acre Farm to make sure his wife, daughter and animals were safe.

"Are the horses alright?" Ned asked Sylvia, as Cyril and a few of the fishermen left the bar.

"They should be fine, Ned. Gertie and I settled them before it got dark. They'll be well protected. The stables are quite sheltered when the wind is in the southwest."

Jim Hughes asked Frank if he might use the telephone. Flo was in town for the night staying with her sister and brother in law, and he wanted to make sure all was well with them and reassure her he was safe also.

"Of course," said Frank. "Go ahead, you know where it is."

Jim returned from the hallway minutes later. "Phone's dead. Hardly surprising, I suppose."

Pat Dickens cursed and said he had better get along home too or May would be fretting. He put on his wet coat and opened the door.

The wind rushed in, sending rain and debris across the bar floor. It took all Jim's strength to close it after Pat's exit.

Apart from the Inn's residents, the only other people remaining after Pat's departure, were Jim Hughes, Peter and Percy. And so Sylvia, in an attempt to muffle the sound of the rain lashing against the glass panes and the screaming wind whistling through every gap in the old windows, drew the thick curtains. Meanwhile, Frank, chilled by his damp trousers, threw a couple more logs onto the already blazing fire. Don, curled up and asleep on the hearth rug, woke, moved back a few feet to avoid overheating, and then promptly closed his sleepy, brown eyes again

The major, enjoying the drama brought about by the stormy weather, went to the bar and bought a round of drinks. As he handed the last glass to Percy, the lights began to flicker intermittently and after sixty seconds of teasing, they all finally went out.

"Damn," grumbled Frank. "We'll be lucky if we get the ruddy power back before tomorrow afternoon now." In disgust, he picked up his pint and joined everyone else in the snug, whilst Sylvia lit candles she had brought from the kitchen that morning after hearing the forecast.

"Old Josh would be fretting by now if he were still with us," laughed the major. "He hated power cuts, didn't he?"

"Josh?" queried Ned. "Who's Josh?"

"A dear old chap, who used to live in Well Cottage," Sylvia answered, as she sat on the hearth rug beside Don. "He did odd jobs here when fishing got too much for him, he was well into his seventies by then, but still insisted on working in order to pay his rent. Bless him."

"Fine fellow," the major agreed, "I'd many an interesting chat with him over the years. He could certainly spin a yarn or two."

"So what became of him?" asked Molly, "I take it he's no longer around."

Frank sighed. "He died. Got pneumonia real bad and didn't recover. He should've gone into hospital, of course, but he refused. He wanted to stay here at the Inn. Sylvia nursed him constantly without a word of complaint."

"Didn't he have any family of his own then?" Ned asked.

123

Percy laughed. "I couldn't imagine old Josh married with kids, he was a confirmed bachelor and didn't have any time at all for women. Daft bugger!"

"Not until Sylvia came along," grinned Frank, nudging his wife affectionately. "He was smitten with you, wasn't he love?"

"I reminded him of his mother," smiled Sylvia, modestly. "She died when he was eleven. I think that's why he didn't want to get attached to any woman. The pain of losing someone close was too great."

"How long ago is it since he died?" Ned asked, thinking of Jane.

Frank wrinkled his nose. "Must be nearly a year now, 'twas before the summer anyhow."

There was a sudden crash outside. Everyone jumped.

Bertha squealed and tightly clutching her husband's arm. "What on earth was that?"

"Sounds like the ruddy Ringing Bells board," grumbled Frank. "It often blows down when we have a sou'westerly. It's a damn nuisance."

"You'd better go and get it, Frank," said Sylvia. "Or it'll only be fit for firewood by morning."

Percy jumping up and slipping on his oilskins. "I'll go, seeing as I have suitable clothing and so forth. There's no point in you getting wet through again, Frank."

Frank nodded gratefully and rose to close the door as Percy stepped out into the wind and rain. Ten minutes passed by before the young fisherman returned holding the mischievous board. He said it had been impossible to distinguish anything in the pitch-dark, and it was not until he tripped over the board that he eventually found it lying, intact, outside the Gents.

As the clock approached ten, with only candlelight and the fire's glow to illuminate the bar, Bertha suggested Molly try and contact someone from the *other side* again. Sylvia, horrified, quickly quashed the idea. "No, I'd be scared to death, Bertha. Especially with no electricity to light up the nooks and crannies on my way to bed. It gives me the creeps just thinking about it."

Ned likewise, thought it a very bad proposal, but for different reasons to Sylvia.

"Ooh, I don't know," grinned Percy. "Whoever Molly got hold of the other night might still be around and could probably tell us where that rat, Wagstaffe is. Half the village are convinced he's around here, you know, and they'd all love to make the News by finding him."

Feeling uncomfortable, Ned tried to think of a way to change the subject. Molly came to the rescue. "You went to school with William Wagstaffe, didn't you, Ben?" She smiled sweetly. "Tell us what he was like?"

Bertha Fillingham gasped. "Really, how fascinating! Did he seem a potential murderer when you knew him, Major?"

The major knocked ash from his cigar into the ashtray on the table and glared at Molly, clearly agitated. "It was a very long time ago."

"Oh, but do please tell us what he was like," Bertha begged, excitedly.

The major groaned. "Well, alright, if I must. It's going back a fair bit, mind. It'd be well over thirty years in fact since we first met." He paused, hoping someone might interrupt and go off on a tangent, but the small gathering were captivated and ready to hang in his every word. With no choice, he continued. "I first met him when we both started at the same school. We'd have been eleven, I suppose. He was a skinny chap, small for his age and always seemed rather nervous. We weren't close friends, but we were in the same year. If I remember correctly his best friend was Freddie Jackson. Freddie went on to be Head Boy. Anyway, as the years ticked by, William grew into a fine looking lad. Excellent cricket player too. And he always had a flock of girls following him around on such occasions as permitted us to mix with the outside world. He had dark, wavy hair, seductive eyes, and I used to envy him his good looks. In fact most of us boys did. It was, I recall, his ambition to be a politician, and eventually Prime Minister, and for that reason he worked extremely hard and got damn good exam results. That's really all there is to tell. I've not seen him since we left school and were it not for his success in achieving his ambition and the abominable goings on a couple of years back, I doubt I would ever have heard of him again." The major sighed and gently shook his head, "The lad certainly didn't seem potentially violent, but then evidence seems to indicate a crime of passion, for which anyone of us might well be capable, I suppose."

"Oh, no, never. Not me," spluttered Bertha, emphatically. "I could never take anyone's life, no matter how much I might despise them."

Molly agreed. "Me neither, although I often used to think I could murder my husband. He was such an unreasonable monster."

"Mother!" snapped Ned. "Be fair, the fault was not entirely his, and there are two sides to every story."

Percy intervened, took a ten shilling note from his pocket and put it on the table. "My round, I think."

In spite of the blazing fire, Molly felt chilly and asked Sylvia if she might take one of the candles to her room to fetch a cardigan.

"We can do better than that," smiled Sylvia, producing a torch from beneath the bar.

"Battery's flat," grunted Frank. "That's why I didn't offer it to Percy when he went out to look for the board."

Ned stood up. "It doesn't matter, I'll go." He picked up a candle, firmly stuck to a saucer with melted wax. "We don't want you setting fire to the place, Mother."

"Thank you, sweetheart. You'll find my nice thick, purple cardy on the back of the armchair."

As Ned left the bar, a deafening clap of thunder, boomed loudly from across the sea. Ned paused, until its rumble faded away. He then proceeded up the dark staircase, guided only by the light of the flickering candle which cast eerie shadows on the surrounding walls.

The room struck cold as Ned opened Molly's door. Ned looked at the grate, the fire was burning low. Knowing his mother's passion for constant warmth, he carefully put down the candle on the table, closed the door and removed the fire guard. From the brass coal scuttle he took three, large pieces of coal and laid them, with precision, on top of the greying embers. Pleased to have done a good deed, he replaced the fire guard, lifted the cardigan from the back of the chair, draped it across his arm and picked up the candle.

Walking towards the door, he felt a cold, biting, breeze sweep around his ankles. His trouser legs began to flap. Puzzled, he turned. Observing no visible reason for the breeze, he resumed his passage towards the door. On reaching for the latch, a rustle from behind caused him quickly to turn again. Dumbfounded, he watched as the embroidered cloth hanging from the table, flapped and fluttered as though in a strong tunnel of wind. Simultaneously, the candle in his hand, flickered, hissed and softly fizzled out in a magical puff of violet smoke.

Confused, afraid and unable to see, Ned fumbled in his pockets for a box of matches. He cursed bitterly, realising they were downstairs on a table in the snug alongside his cigarettes. With heart pounding, he attempted to reach out for the wall and feel his way towards the door. But as he stumbled into a chair, he sensed he was not alone in the room.

"Is that you, Ned?" whispered a now familiar voice.

"Jane," he blurted, deeply relieved that the presence was at least familiar to him. "I might have known it'd be you. What on earth are you doing in here and why did you put my candle out? I can't see a ruddy thing now."

She giggled. "Sorry, but this has always been my favourite room, and if you must know, I've come to watch the storm."

As she spoke, the room was illuminated by a bright flash of lightening, which glowed across the sea like a spectacular silver firework. Ned squinted and then gasped in amazement, for by the window, momentarily, stood the figure of a young woman. He could not see her face for her back was towards him, but she was dressed in red.

Rapidly, the room reverted to total darkness. Ned, in a state of shock, jumped nervously as a loud clap of thunder echoed through the Inn, shaking the walls as it crackled and rumbled violently overhead. Holding the back of the chair for support, he stood mesmerised, until the boom slowly faded to a distant murmur and the only audible sound remaining was of the wind whistling eerily down Molly's chimney. And as the rain lashed heavily against the window panes, Ned, in a daze, remained frozen to the spot until the flame on his candle slowly reignited, revealing to him there was no-one in the room but himself.

Chapter Fifteen

By morning, the wind had abated to a light south westerly breeze. Ned awoke at half past seven, sat up in bed, yawned and rubbed his eyes. Having suffered a poor night's sleep, he felt sluggish and tired, for the howling wind, continually battering the shed's corrugated tin roof, along with the image of Jane's unexpected apparition, had repeatedly disrupted his dreams and kept him awake for many hours.

Before going down for breakfast, Ned called into his mother's room to report his brief sighting of Jane, for he had been unable to say anything the previous night, due to the presence of others. Molly was astounded to hear Ned's story.

"If only she would put in an appearance while I'm in here," she sighed, dropping powder compact and lipstick into her handbag. "I would so dearly like to ask that young lady a few questions."

"So would I," mused Ned. "But she never stays around long enough for me to engage her in a proper conversation."

Molly laughed. "Oh, well, there's always another day, I suppose, but if this is her favourite room, I shall sleep with one eye open from now on."

With the absence of electric lights to take away the darkness of the bleak, grey morning, the dining room appeared very dim and gloomy for breakfast. This alarmed Molly, for it struck her the loss of power might result in the kitchen being unable to produce a pot of tea.

"Don't worry," Gertie laughed, amused by the downcast expression on Molly's face. "We cook by solid fuel as well as electricity, so breakfast will be as normal."

Molly sighed, much relieved, as she took her seat at the table, "Thank God for that. I don't function properly until I've had at least two cups of tea."

"Did the storm keep you awake, last night, Moll?" called the major from his corner.

"Good heavens no," she grinned. "I'd had far too many gins for that. How about you?"

"Slept like a log. Once my head hit the pillow I didn't know a thing 'til this morning."

"Has there been much structural damage done do you know?" Ned asked Gertie, as she brought in the welcome pot of tea.

"I would imagine so. We lost part of our big barn roof and there were loads of slates and branches along the main street when I biked in to work this morning."

"I trust your father got home alright?" commented Molly, removing the cosy from the teapot.

"Yeah, eventually, but he said the brook at the bottom of the hill had risen quite a lot because a big tree had fallen across it and the water was beginning to trickle across the road when he went over the bridge. It couldn't have been too bad though, cos it was alright when I came in this morning."

Heads turned as Larry and Des entered the room and sat at their table.

"You'll not go out to sea today, I expect, will you lads?" laughed George Fillingham.

Larry grinned. "No fear. We've already been down to the cove to suss things out and as you'd expect there's a huge ground swell out there."

"And for that reason the boats will all stay put on dry land 'til it calms." said Des, placing a napkin on his lap. "Meanwhile, have you heard about the lane leading to Higher Green Farm? Apparently, part of it has subsided."

Ned raised his eyebrows. "What, badly?"

"Well, no, not really, you can still get along it because Pat Dickens got by this morning on his tractor. He was telling us about it when we went to check the boats an hour or so ago. He said he's never known it happen before and he's lived here all his life."

"Dear, dear, sounds like Harry and his men will be kept busy for a while," grunted the major. "If there's a lot of damage done, that is. Still, it's an ill wind and all that."

"Harry?" queried Molly. "Do I know him?"

"Of course you do, he's often in for a pint. Nice bloke. Works damned hard. I like him a lot."

When Ned went to fetch his daily paper, he found Trengillion a hive of activity. On the cobbled area in front of the Inn, Frank was precariously balanced on top of a tall wooden ladder, his arms outstretched, re-hanging the Ringing Bell's board on its wrought iron bracket. Along the main street, villagers were out and about, eagerly exchanging stories of the storm as they gathered broken slates, swept up twigs and debris from trees and shrubs, and gathered litter, scattered from upturned bins. On several damaged rooftops, temporary sheeting was already in place, as protection from the elements until such time as insurance claims could be assessed. Outside the school, Sid Reynolds was sweeping up fragments of glass from a shattered window which, left partly open, had broken free in the wind.

Inside the post office, Bertha Fillingham was saying goodbye to Mrs Pascoe, the post mistress. "We dearly hope to be back and settled in by summer," she said, with sincere enthusiasm, dropping a bag of peppermints into her handbag. "I can't wait, I'm so excited. I love it here."

"Leaving already?" said Ned, lifting a copy of the Daily Herald from the shelf.

Berths sighed. "Regrettably, yes. I've left George loading up the car, so I imagine we'll be off as soon as I get back."

"Well, you take care, Mrs Fillingham," said Ned, earnestly, shaking her hand. "I won't be here, of course, when you come back, but I hope you'll both be very, very happy in your new home."

"Oh, thank you, Ned," she said, warmly. "And you take care of that wonderful mother of yours. She and her doings have made this visit very memorable, one way and another. She's a treasure, an absolute treasure."

Bertha Fillingham left the post office, avoiding the huge puddle by the door and walked off down the road, humming happily with a spring in each step, each movement endorsing the enthusiasm she'd so passionately expressed.

Ned paid for his paper, walked back through the village and then down to the beach, for he wanted to see for himself how much damage had been done by the storm. He found several men sweeping away seaweed, debris and shingle, deposited over the narrow road, during high water, in the early hours.

The cottages overlooking the cove, Ned observed, appeared to have escaped unscathed. He assumed this was due to protection from the high cliffs. However, on taking a second look he noticed one had lost some thatch and the gate of the other hung on only one hinge.

Ned crossed the shingle towards the choppy sea. Stretching out for miles between land and horizon, huge waves churned, broke, rumbled and foamed before reaching land and crashing noisily onto the already battered shore. Ned stepped back to avoid salt spray rising like early morning mist from the great waves. He was not at all surprised boats were staying on dry land. The ocean looked most unwelcoming, extremely dangerous and capable of inducing horrendous bouts of sea-sickness.

Hearing a loud engine, Ned turned to see a lorry emerge and stop outside the cottages. From the driver's seat jumped Harry the Hitman, who ambled over to the men clearing the road. Ned glanced at the lorry. In the back, lay a ladder, planks of wood, a heap of hard-core and bags of sand. It suddenly occurred to him that Harry the Hitman was Harry the builder, of whom the major had spoken so amicably during breakfast.

Ned watched the men talking. Harry's strong East London accent boomed above the others. In spite of the major's favourable words, Ned wondered how long he had been in the village and whether or not he had known Jane.

"Questions, questions, questions," he mumbled, "and seldom do I get any damn answers."

He left the beach and walked back to the Inn, still clutching his unread daily paper.

The following day, the sea was considerably calmer and so Larry and Des, both tired of being kept on land, went to sea, as did Percy and Peter, in search of mackerel. Many of the other boats were laid up for the winter and each year stayed ashore until Easter when the crabbing season began. Percy and Peter were also crabbers, but they occasionally went out in the winter to catch a few fish to keep body and soul together. And if the fish were in abundance, then they would salt down the surplus to use as bait for their crab pots in the summer.

Molly had an appointment in Helston at eleven o'clock to have her hair set, and as the major had a dental appointment at a similar time, he'd offered to take her into town in his old car. Ned, uncertain how best to spend his day, contemplated the options and eventually decided on a walk along the back lane to Higher Green Farm so that he would be able to see for himself just how much damage had been done to the road by the storm. He then proposed to follow the track from the farm out onto the cliffs and walk back along the coastal path.

It was a beautiful morning, with clear blue skies, very little wind and brilliant sunshine, the heat from which caused Ned to remove his jacket and throw it across his shoulder before he even reached the damaged road.

Overhead, a plane flew high in the sky, leaving behind a defined white streak across the vivid blue. Ned stopped and watched as the line of vapour spread like ink on blotting paper, before it finally dispersed altogether.

On reaching the damaged part of the road, Ned found Pat Dickens and Jim Hughes shovelling vast quantities of rubble from a tractor and trailer into a large crevice which ran for several feet along one side of the road surface. The lane, Ned discovered, belonged to Pat, so its repair and upkeep was his responsibility.

Ned chatted briefly to the two men and then continued walking upwards towards Higher Green Farm. At the top he stopped, turned and looked back downhill to the village nestled in the valley. It was very picturesque. Thatched cottages, granite houses, the church and the Inn, bordered the winding main road which ran downhill and ended abruptly as it reached the beach and the vast ocean. Ned glanced back over the village to the paddock where Winston and Brown Ale friskily galloped across the short grass. He squinted. Someone was with the horses but it was impossible to ascertain whether it was Gertie or Sylvia. He wished he possessed binoculars and made a mental note to purchase a pair on his return to London.

Ned turned back and continued walking up the lane, past Higher Green Farm and onto the track leading to the cliff path. When he reached the Witches Broomstick he stopped, laid his jacket onto the old railing and fumbled about in the pockets for his cigarette packet. Only one remained. He removed it, slipped it between his lips and lit it. As a puff of smoke rose above his face, he crumpled up the empty packet and tossed it over the cliff's edge. Ned watched as it landed far below on the sand and instantly felt a pang of guilt. Creating litter was an act for which he frequently scolded his young pupils.

Leaning on the old railings, he looked out to sea. Miles and miles of uninterrupted blue lay between shore and horizon, nothing else was visible to the naked eye. Ned glanced down at the rocks and boulders below. Had the recent storm moved any of them? He thought it looked much the same and had unquestionably encountered many such storms before.

When he finished his cigarette, he left the railings and the cliff edge, climbed over the stile and crossed the field where the herd of cows grazed. One or two of them raised their heads as he passed by, but most were oblivious of his presence.

On leaving the field, Ned stepped back on the coastal path, which in spite of the winter months, still showed visible patches of wear and tear caused by ramblers and strollers during the holiday season and beyond. All around, Ned surveyed bright yellow gorse in flower and he concluded its beauty could surely not be surpassed, even on a glorious summer's day.

On approaching the end of the cliff path, Ned looked at his watch; it was still early in the day. He deliberated whether or not he should walk down to the beach, where perhaps he might see the two boats come in. However, as he turned the corner at the end of the path which ran around the boundary wall of Chy-an-Gwyns, he saw from the cliff tops, both boats were already on the beach. Disappointed, he turned to continue his walk, but intuitively he sensed something was amiss. He turned back. Larry stood on the beach and judging by his hand waving gestures, appeared either angry or distressed. He was addressing Percy and Peter. Des stood by his side. Ned wished he was nearer, for it was not possible to hear, or even guess what was being said.

On impulse he began to run down the steep, rugged path, slipping and sliding, sending small stones rolling. He reached the bottom and stepped onto the lane, glad to have a solid surface beneath his feet. By the cottages near to the beach, he met Larry, running, dripping wet and with nothing on his feet. On seeing Larry's white face, Ned felt his heartbeat quicken.

"What's wrong?" he panted, as goose pimples rose on his rapidly chilling body. But Ned already knew the answer. It was obvious. They had found Jane.

Chapter Sixteen

Standing alone with heart pounding wildly, Larry's words reverberated through Ned's racing mind. "We've found a body," he'd croaked, whilst heading towards the village and the telephone kiosk. "We've found a body."

Shocked and dumbfounded, Ned steadied himself and sat down on the garden wall of one of the cottages. When he finally felt composed, he walked, still dazed, down to the beach, where Des, his hands trembling, endeavoured to roll a cigarette, whilst relaying the details to Percy and Peter. The two astounded fishermen, slowly absorbed the devastating news, each overwhelmed with astonishment and disbelief.

As he approached the three men, Ned glared angrily and accusingly at Percy. Was he a guilty man? If Jane's body had been found at sea then he would have had ample opportunity to dispose of her. However, Percy's body language did not indicate guilt. He looked genuinely shocked and not at all uneasy. Desperate for more information, Ned crossed the shingle to join in the conversation.

"I've just seen Larry. What happened?" he asked, eagerly, avoiding eye contact with Percy. "He told me you'd found a body. Where in the sea was it?"

"It wasn't," said Des, licking the cigarette paper and tapping the finished result on the back of his hand. "It wasn't in the sea, anyway. It was it in the Witches Broomstick. Well, it still is."

"The Witches Broomstick!" gasped Ned. It was now his turn to feel the colour drain from his face. "But I don't understand. How on earth did you find it in there?"

"I didn't find it. It was Larry's doing and he was by himself. I think it's shaken him up a bit. Well, I know it has, and I must admit I feel a bit shell shocked myself."

Ned was confused. "So what exactly happened? I mean, why was Larry in the Witches Broomstick? How did he get in there? I was led to believe the place was more or less inaccessible."

Des lit his cigarette and discarded the match over his shoulder. "It is, and the whole thing's a bit of a fluke really. You see, we went out to sea as usual this morning, but to be honest, I think we'd both had one pint too many last night so we were feeling pretty lazy. Anyway, as we passed the Witches Broomstick, Larry said how he'd love to go in there sometime and have a good poke round. I told him to go then, it was such a gorgeous morning and the sun was really quite warm, and I was more than happy to stay in the boat and do a spot of sunbathing while he'd gone."

"You mean, he swam in there?" muttered Ned, who was unable to swim.

"Yes, you can get to it through the gap quite easily, although anyone who wasn't a competent swimmer might struggle cos the water's quite choppy around the rocks. Anyway, I watched him swim until he was out of sight and then I lay down in the boat. It seemed like I'd only just got myself comfortable, when I heard him come splashing back, shouting at the top of his voice. He scared me cos I wondered what on earth was wrong. It's daft, but I thought he might've been attacked by a shark, even though I know there aren't any of the killer types around here. Anyway, he managed to climb aboard with a helping hand from me and he said he'd found a cave, gone inside, and there, slumped up against the wall, was a body."

"How horrible!" said Peter, sympathetically.

"Was it male or female?" asked Ned, feeling slightly light headed.

Des laughed. "What! I've no idea. From what Larry said I'd guess it's little more than a skeleton. And without a bit of flesh and so forth, I shouldn't think he'd have a clue. I know I wouldn't."

"So do you think it had been washed up there?" Ned persisted.

Des, shrugging his shoulders. "Dunno. Remember, I've not even seen it and poor old Larry was too shocked to go into much detail."

Larry returned shortly after, the colour back in his face.

"You alright, mate?" Des asked. "You look a bit better."

Larry nodded. "Yes, thanks, I'm fine now. It was just a bit of a shock, that's all."

Ned questioned Larry, but he was unable to be any more specific than Des.

"My instincts were to get back here as quickly as possible and ring the police. Stupid really, cos that poor sod's been dead for ages, so another hour or so wouldn't have made any difference. I could kick myself. If I'd stayed longer I could have had a good nose around and weighed up the situation."

"So what did the Old Bill have to say?" asked Percy.

"They're on their way out here now and they want us to stay put and wait for them. The village bobby should be here first though cos he lives nearby apparently and they said they'd ring him straight away."

The only subject on anyone's lips at the Inn that evening was the body. During the afternoon, watched by a steadily increasing number of spectators, the beach had been overrun with police officers, both plain clothed and uniformed. Larry and Des, whose names rapidly became well-known, helped as much as they were able, and took police officers and frogmen out to the Witches Broomstick in their boat, where after a thorough search around the rocks and shore line, they all eventually returned, along with the body.

No one of course knew the identity of the decayed corpse. Everyone assumed it was a stranger. A holiday maker perhaps, who had fallen from the cliffs during the summer, or some foreigner, possibly a sailor, who had had the misfortune to have fallen from a boat or ship and been washed ashore.

The Inn was far busier than a usual Friday night, as everyone made it their destination in order to ascertain they were up to date with the latest gossip and facts. Hence by nine o'clock, both bars were full and every seat taken.

Frank, Sylvia and Gertie worked non-stop serving drinks to the thirsty locals. For the more they talked the more they drank, hence the atmosphere was tinged with both excitement and jollification. Frank rubbed his hands gleefully, as the ten shilling notes piled up in the cash register, half wishing a body could be washed up in Trengillion every Friday.

Just before closing time the door of the Inn slowly opened. Above the noise no-one noticed Doris, wearing her slippers and no coat, creep in. She stood a lonely figure alone in the doorway eyeing the boisterous crowd. Her eyes red from crying. Her face pale and blotchy.

It was May Dickens who spotted her first. Alarmed by her appearance, she left her seat, crossed to her friend's side and grasped the cold hands in her own.

"Doris, whatever's wrong, love?" she asked. "You look dreadful."

Doris gazed blankly into May's face. Her eyes again filled with tears.

"Jane," she whispered, through quivering lips.

"Jane," repeated May, puzzled. "I don't understand, Doris. What do you mean?"

"Fred Stevens has just been in with a nice police lady. The body they found today. They said, they said, it was, it was, a young woman."

The colour drained from May's face. "No, oh God, no," she whispered. "Surely you don't mean…"

"He wanted to know the name of Jane's dentist. They're going to check her dental records."

The laughter in the bar died away, until the only voices audible were faint whispers of those too far distant to comprehend the nature of the dialogue brought about by the arrival of Doris Jones.

"They think it might be Jane, then?" said Pat Dickens, rubbing his forehead. "Christ! It never even crossed my mind that…" His voice trailed away.

Dumbfounded by the news, the gathering was too shocked to speak and the silence was not broken until Molly gently tapped May on the elbow and spoke. "Perhaps it might be better if we took her up to my room," she whispered.

May nodded. The two women then led Doris away from the stunned crowd in the bar, followed by the major.

Once the news sunk in, everyone began to talk at once, for it had not occurred to even one of them, that the body might be that of Jane. Certainly, they all knew she was missing, but they chose to believe popular rumours that she had gone away, even though they knew Doris refuted this and had reported her disappearance to the police. The new developments also caused confusion. For if it was Jane, and there were many who had their doubts, then a new question arose.

How on earth had she found her way to the Witches Broomstick? She could not have fallen from a boat and got washed up ashore, as she seldom, if ever went in boats, for she suffered badly with sea sickness. It was unlikely, also, she had got into trouble whilst swimming, for she seldom swam in the sea as the water was too cold, and it was a long way for even the best of swimmers to go as far as the Broomstick.

"She must have fallen from the cliffs and got washed into the cave," said Albert Treloar, adamantly. "It's the only way."

"Don't be daft. She couldn't have fallen, not with that railing there," scoffed Harry. "Not unless she'd been sitting on top of it."

"She could have fallen off somewhere else," snapped Albert. "The railings don't run all the way along the cliffs."

"Perhaps, if it is Jane, she was picking wild flowers," suggested Gertie, tearfully. "She often took wild flowers home to Doris and some really pretty ones grow on the side of the cliffs."

"Surely not," tutted Jim Hughes. "She was a clever girl. She'd never have taken such a risk."

Ned stunned into silence, sat in the corner of the bar as the inane chatter buzzed around him. Staring into his half empty glass of beer, he felt sick. Sick, light headed and sorrowful. Unable to bear the babble of voices any longer, he rose from his seat, hands over ears, and passed through the crowd, into the hallway and headed towards the stairs.

Outside the dining room he paused. The door was ajar and so he crept inside. It felt peaceful. The noise from the bar was muffled by the thick walls. Ned closed the door, crossed to the table in the window, sat down and leaned his aching head, back onto the cold wall. Two facts troubled him. Firstly of course, he did not believe as did everyone else, that Jane's death was an accident. Jane said she had been poisoned and Ned had every reason to believe her. The second troubling fact, was that the discovery of Jane, categorically ratified his ability to dabble with the unknown. He knew that he'd not dreamed up his encounters with Jane, although he had doubted it at first, but her remains were rock-solid evidence she really was dead and that knowledge brought the reality home. This also meant, his mother, who for many years he had considered to be a charlatan, really did possess talents to converse with the dead. Ned did not know whether to laugh or cry.

Shortly after, he heard familiar voices in the hallway. He went to the door. Outside, Molly, May and Doris stood with the major, who was buttoning up his overcoat. May had offered to stay with Doris overnight, but she would not hear of it.

"I'll be alright," she said, with dignity. "It has helped so much being able to talk to sympathetic ears. You've all been very kind." She took the major's arm as they headed for the door. He had insisted, at least, she let him escort her home.

After their departure, Ned, Molly and May returned to the bar. Everyone had gone except Pat, who was waiting for his wife. Gertie and Sylvia were occupied washing dirty glasses which stretched the entire length of the bar, and Frank was wiping down the empty tables. Gertie with her hands in the sink was not her usual bouncy self. Understandably she was very subdued. Sylvia likewise, dried the clean glasses and put them back on the shelves in silence.

Frank finished wiping the last table and dropped the damp cloth onto the bar.

"Rum business all this," he muttered, as he started to empty the brimming ashtrays. "To think all this time our poor Jane's been out there in the Witches Broomstick and we knew nothing about it."

"If it is Jane," snivelled Sylvia.

"It's bound to be, if you think about it," said Frank, sitting to ease his aching back. "It would explain why no-one's seen neither hide nor hair of her these past six months. We should all have listened to Doris a bit more, poor soul."

"It can't be Jane," sobbed Sylvia, as a glass slipped from her trembling hands and smashed on the tiled floor. "It can't be." She threw the tea towel onto a crate of empty bottles and fled from the bar.

"Shall I go after her?" Gertie asked.

Frank shook his head. "No, best leave her alone. It's been a bit of a shock. She was very fond of Jane. We all were."

He bent down and picked up the broken pieces of glass, while Molly took Sylvia's place drying up. And as Pat and May were about to leave, the major returned.

"Is she alright, do you think?" asked May, tying her headscarf beneath her chin.

"She's as well as can be expected. She half hopes it is Jane, so that she can bury the poor girl and have peace of mind, but then she feels guilty for feeling that way."

Frank drove Gertie home when they finished work. He would not let her cycle as he felt she was understandably unstable and he didn't want to lose any more of his staff to unfortunate accidents.

The following morning as Ned walked to the post office he saw a police car parked outside Ivy Cottage and he knew inside poor Doris would be receiving news that the body had been identified as Jane. He bought his paper and as often before walked down to the beach to read it, although its contents were of little interest to Ned in his current state of mind. He stared, his face expressionless, at the sea, flat like a millpond, its waves little more than mere ripples.

A car engine disturbed the peace. Ned turned and watched as a police car stopped and parked outside the thatched cottages. Two police officers stepped out and crossed to Percy and Peter, making withy crab pots outside their loft. One officer made notes in a little book, while the other questioned the two fishermen.

After the police had finished their interview they returned to their black car and drove off. Ned, desperate to know of any developments, eagerly called to the fishermen. "Any news, yet?"

Percy rose and sauntered across the beach towards the bench. "They didn't say, they just asked us loads of questions, mostly about the Witches Broomstick, seeing as we understand the sea and all that."

"Oh," Ned muttered, disappointed. He was anxious for the police to discover Jane had been poisoned and realise her death was not an accident. He was anxious for a murder investigation to get underway.

Later that morning, Ned returned to the Inn. The bar was open so he went inside and much to the surprise of Frank ordered a large whisky. Jim Hughes was at the bar also, having just delivered the pasties. He was talking to Albert Treloar who had called into the Inn for much the same reason as Ned.

"Have either of you heard if there's any more news about the body?" Ned asked, after paying for his drink.

"It was Jane they found," said Jim, sadly. "That I do know. The police broke the news to Doris this morning. They're now trying to establish the cause of death. Poor kid."

"I heard a bit of gossip this morning," said Albert. "And malicious gossip at that. It's being hinted that she may have taken her own life and chucked herself off the cliff because she were expecting a little 'un. But I think that's nonsense and Dorothy was livid when I told her what I'd heard."

"I should think so," said Jim. "That's a wicked thing for anyone to have said. I just hope Doris doesn't hear such rubbish; she's upset enough as it is."

On Monday morning, Ned ran down the road beneath a threatening black cloud. Tucked under his arm was a copy of the Daily Herald. He reached the Inn and crossed the threshold just as the first hail stones fell. Quickly he pushed shut the door to keep out the bitterly cold, north east wind. Relieved to have avoided a drenching, he ran up the stairs to his room, threw the paper on the bed and removed his coat and hat. As he breathed into his cupped hands, to restore life to his tingling fingers, he crossed to the window and watched as the huge, hail stones bounced off the old tin roof and battered against the glass panes of his window, before falling to the ever increasingly white ground below.

Ned shivered. It was too cold to stay in his room. He picked up the newspaper and crossed the landing to see if his mother was in. He found her sitting by the fire, happily knitting.

She smiled. "I thought you might appear when I saw the hail stones."

He stepped towards the grate and held out his hands to warm on the flames. "It's freezing out," he grumbled. "I thought it's supposed to be milder down here."

"And so it is," said Molly. "They have snow up North and it's spreading down to the Midlands."

"Ugh," groaned Ned. "It had better not get this far."

"Anything interesting in the news?" asked Molly, eyeing the newspaper which he had dropped onto the floor.

"I've not looked yet," he replied, relishing the warmth of the fire. "I haven't really had a chance."

He picked it up, took a fleeting look over the front cover and then sat, cross legged, on the floor with the paper spread out on the rug. To the rapid clicking of Molly's knitting needles, he then glanced casually through the open pages with little interest as to its contents, until one solitary article suddenly caught his eye. *Body found in Cornish Cove,* he read.

Ned felt the pace of his heart beat increase, as it thumped loudly in his chest and ears. For some reason he had not expected a local story to make the national press. But it was not the article that sent his heart racing, it was what lay beneath it. A picture of Jane. Just her head and shoulders. She was smiling broadly, her face framed by thick, wavy hair resting gently on the shoulders of a floral dress.

Ned picked up the paper and showed it to Molly. Neither of them had ever seen a picture of Jane before.

"Gertie's right," Molly whispered, "she was very beautiful. What a dreadful loss. Poor, poor Doris."

She passed the paper back to Ned and again he gazed at the picture. It brought a lump to his throat. He felt choked and emotional, for it was uncanny to look into the eyes of someone to whom he had spoken and yet never known.

A little later Ned returned to his room and carefully tore Jane's picture from paper and placed it in his wallet. With her face now firmly engraved in his mind, he felt more conviction than ever that he had to help her seek justice.

He turned to the portrait of the old fisherman.

"Bear witness to this, old fella," he said, fist clenched. "I vow I shall not leave Cornwall until Jane's killer has been found. Even if it means not being able to return to London and consequently losing my job."

Chapter Seventeen

Over the following days, details of the police enquiry began to emerge and circulate with great rapidity around Trengillion and the surrounding area, but just how much was fact and how much was fiction, no-one knew for sure. Everyone blindly believed that which they chose to believe and dispassionately disregarded the rest. The general consensus of opinion was, however, that Jane's body had definitely not been washed up in the Witches Broomstick, for it appeared she had been found well beyond the high water mark, hence a tragic swimming accident was not an option. Besides, the local paper reported she was not wearing a bathing costume, but was clothed in the remains of her favourite red dress. Results from a post mortem also revealed she had no broken bones, so a fall from the cliff or the maliciously suggested suicide was also out of the question, and neither did she bear any signs of violent injury to her head or any other part of her anatomy. Furthermore, rumour speculated the police did not suspect foul play. Although they were very mystified as to why a perfectly fit and healthy young woman should venture into a cave, sit down and die, as the only explanation seemed to be she had climbed down the cliff side successfully, but through inexperience had been unable to climb back up again, and subsequently had starved to death. The locals thought this a ridiculous conclusion. They knew no-one had ever climbed down the cliff face at the Witches Broomstick before, and the first would certainly not be a woman wearing a thin cotton dress who religiously kept her finger nails well-manicured. No, there had to be some other explanation, but try as they might, no-one could think of anything plausible. Consequently, the subject was done to death by every tongue in the village and beyond.

"Could there be a tunnel leading into the cave somewhere?" suggested Jim Hughes, one night at the Inn. "There's always been rumours of one used by smugglers in years gone by."

"The police divers checked the day after they removed the body," said Larry, always in on any debate concerning his astonishing find. "We were with them at the time."

"There were a few tunnels," Des added. "Well, caves anyway. They were all small though and every one had a dead end."

The major snorted. "Smugglers wouldn't use a tunnel with such an inaccessible entrance in any case. If you can only get to it by swimming then that would make it very difficult for boatloads of contraband. Ridiculous idea."

"I suppose so," said Jim, trying to visualise smugglers swimming through the handle of the Broomstick with barrels of brandy on their backs.

"Damn baccy would get wet anyway," chuckled the major, taking a cigar from the tin in his pocket. "And that, gentlemen, would never do."

Ned listened to the conversations tirelessly. If Jane had been poisoned, as she claimed, he thought it unlikely that any traces of poison would remain in a body so badly decomposed. She was a mere skeleton according to Larry, who had been present when the police had recovered her body. Ned felt sick and angry at the thought of lovely Jane being abandoned and left to rot in a grotty cave. He was also sickened by the speculative tittle-tattle which seemed to achieve absolutely nothing. To him there seemed also only one explanation as to how she came to be in the cave. Someone must have poisoned her, put her into a boat, travelled to the Witches Broomstick and then swam with her lifeless body into the cave and left her there believing she would never be found. So once again this led Ned back to his number one suspect, Percy. Yet somehow Percy did not look or behave like a guilty man. He genuinely seemed deeply sorry that Jane had been found dead, and Molly told him he took flowers to Doris after the discovery and sat talking to her for a whole afternoon. No, Ned did not really believe it was Percy. Besides, he had to admit he really liked him.

Standing beside the window in his room, Ned pondered over other boat owners in the area. Undoubtedly there were many with whom he was not acquainted. After all, Jane had gone missing in

August so there would have been a lot of activity on the sea then and a considerable number of holiday makers around too.

He thought of William Wagstaffe. Was he part of the equation? No, it was absurd to suggest just because he had murdered his mistress he would ever murder again. Besides, no-one had ever mentioned Jane having a liaison with a stranger and he would be considerably older than her anyway.

Ned tossed things over in his mind until his head ached. He contemplated going to the police and telling them all he knew, but conceded the idea was preposterous. They would never believe him. He would be labelled a crank or a crackpot. Worse still, they might think he was telling wild stories in order to cover his own guilt.

"This could take forever to solve," mused Ned, as he watched Barley Wine leap onto the old tin roof and curl into a massive ball, intending to do nothing other than sleep in the warm sun. It then occurred to Ned he had booked his room only until the end of the following week. He promptly turned and walked away from the window. It was imperative he find either Frank or Sylvia to enquire if it was possible to stay a little longer. His bank balance could take the extra expense, as he had recently inherited a small sum of money from a great aunt.

Downstairs, Ned found Frank in the bar, bottling up and humming *The White Rose*.

"Hello Ned," he said, pushing aside an empty crate with his foot. "Everything alright, you look puzzled?"

"Do I? Well yes, I'm fine, thanks, but I was just wondering if it would be possible to have my room for say, an extra couple of weeks?"

Frank grinned. "You starting to prefer the old country life then? It's much better here than your old cities."

"No, or rather yes. I'd just like to stay a little longer, that's all. I'm not ready to go home yet."

Frank chuckled. "Best go and find the wife then, she takes care of the guest side of things, although I'm pretty sure it'll be alright."

"Okay," said Ned, eagerly. "I'll do that right away. Have you any idea where I might find her?"

"Out with the horses, I expect. She goes down to see them at least once a day. I sometimes wish I had four legs."

Ned left the Inn, walked through the back courtyard and across the field towards the stables. As he opened the paddock gate, Winston and Brown Ale eagerly trotted across the field to greet him. He closed the gate quickly and stroked their noses in turn, apologising profusely for having entered their domain with no lumps of sugar in his pockets. The two horses followed closely behind as he walked towards the stables. When he entered the building, they cantered off.

Ned looked around. To his surprise there was no-one there. He had assumed Sylvia would be busy inside mucking out or doing whatever horsey people do, but the stables were quite empty. He walked back out into the sunshine and glanced across the surrounding countryside. Apart from the horses, now running around the paddock, the only sign of life was a flock of sheep idly grazing in a nearby meadow. Ned decided to wait. Perhaps he had arrived at the stables ahead of Sylvia, or maybe she had already been and gone. Frank, did after all, only say he expected she would be with the horses.

Ned climbed up onto the old stone wall which separated the paddock and the field which led back to the Inn, and with both arms outstretched to maintain his balance, he teetered along the top, careful to avoid tripping on brambles or treading on loose stones. Near to the gate he found a flat, grassy spot, which looked suitable for sitting on. Cautiously, he lowered himself down, facing the village, his back to the paddock, and rested his heels on the tips of a large, conveniently placed protruding stone.

To pass the time, Ned lit a cigarette and glanced across the field towards the Inn, where only its roof was visible above the hedges and through the trees.

Next to the Inn stood the church, and close by, lower down in the valley, the chimneys of the Vicarage were just visible nestled amongst the leafless trees. Ned thought the village a beautiful spot and tried to imagine himself living in a rural location such as Trengillion. He concluded, however, that as a bachelor, he would probably die from utter boredom, but as a married man, it would then be a totally different scenario and such a location would undoubtedly be the ideal environment in which to bring up children.

Ned thought about a wife and his mother's prediction of Stella Hargreaves. He laughed out loud. He had already conceded defeat regarding his erstwhile scepticism over Molly's claims regarding spiritualism, but her ability to tell fortunes, well, that was absurd. She even admitted herself, that she was a self-trained novice. He would never, ever believe it possible for anyone to predict the future.

He thought of Jane. Lovely, beautiful Jane, and wished he had been in Cornwall the previous August so that perhaps somehow he might have prevented her death.

"Ned," said a puzzled, slightly hostile voice from behind. "What are you doing here?"

He jumped with surprise and quickly turned. Sylvia was standing behind him in the paddock, frowning as she attempted to comb her hair with her fingers.

"Sylvia," he spluttered, foolishly. "Where did you spring from?"

She scowled. "Well, the stables of course. Have you been sitting there long?"

"What? No, no, I've err, been out walking and only just sat down here for a rest." For some reason he didn't want to tell her the truth and admit he'd actually looked inside the stables and seen she was not there.

She looked relieved and forced a smile. "Had you arrived earlier you could have helped me. I've been polishing saddles."

He tried to suppress the automatic desire to frown. He knew she was lying and wondered where she had really been.

"Anyway, I'm glad I've bumped into you," he said, hiding his confusion and rising to his feet on top of the wall. "I wonder, would it be possible for me to have my room for say, an extra couple of weeks? I asked Frank earlier but he said bed and breakfast was your department."

"Well, yes," she said, surprised. "We're not expecting any more visitors until Easter now and even then, not all the rooms are taken."

"Good. So I can stay?"

She shrugged her shoulders. "Of course. You've almost become part of the family. Will your mother want to stay longer too?"

"That's a good point, I don't know. I've not actually mentioned it to her yet, but I'm pretty sure she'll be in no hurry to go home."

Ned walked along the top of the wall in preparation to drop onto a flat patch of grass below, but as he was about to jump, he noticed the figure of a man hurrying across an adjacent field. Ned scowled and looked down at Sylvia who was petting the horses. Had this man and Sylvia been somewhere together? If they had it would explain Sylvia's aggressive attitude and untidy hair. Ned stared hard at the man again before he disappeared from view. He could not be sure, but he thought he recognised him. From behind he looked very much like the school caretaker, Sid Reynolds.

Chapter Eighteen

Walking back to the Inn together, Ned glanced sideways in an attempt to catch a glimpse of Sylvia's hands, but to his annoyance she had both tucked deep inside the pockets of her jacket. He wanted to see if her hands showed any signs of polish, but then reflected it didn't matter if they did, as she may well have polished the saddles earlier. What did matter was that she was not in the stables when she had said she was. She was lying and Ned meant to find out why. If she was having an affair with Sid Reynolds, well, that was her business, but he felt cheated, annoyed and though he would never admit it, extremely jealous.

They said very little during the short walk, and when they reached the Inn, Sylvia slipped off to her own quarters and Ned went up to his room, slammed shut the door and threw himself down angrily into the chair.

"Women!" he complained bitterly to the empty grate. "Why do they have to be so damned complicated."

Profoundly agitated, he stood, crossed to the window, opened it and peered outside. The only sign of life was Sylvia's damn, lazy cat, still curled up on the old tin roof. He closed the window aggressively and sat down restlessly on his bed. From the corner of his eye, the portrait of the old fisherman came into view. Ned stood up again, looked at the painting with interest and wondered whether it was the portrait of a local person or just a picture of no-one in particular. He made a mental note to ask Frank when next they met.

He returned to the bed and lay down to rest, but found anxiety only intensified as he tried to relax. Feeling in need of a sympathetic ear, he decided to find his mother. He slid off the bed, left the room and crossed the landing. He knocked on the door, went in and found his mother wearing her third best shoes and doing up the buttons of her coat.

"Oh, are you going out?" he mumbled, annoyed by her lack of consideration.

"Yes, sweetheart, the major and I are going for a little stroll. It's such a nice day. Why, is anything wrong?"

"Well, yes, sort of," said Ned. "There's something I want to tell you."

"Then go ahead, the major and I didn't set a time, we just left it that I'd call for him when I'm ready."

Relieved to have someone to hear his dilemma, he told of, without stopping for breath, the events of that morning.

"Sid Reynolds and Sylvia! No, I don't believe it!" chuckled Molly. "Although actually, I do recall seeing them deep in conversation only last night. And Sid looked really happy."

"Humph," said Ned, even more dejected. "There's definitely something fishy going on then."

"It certainly looks that way. We'll have to keep an eye on them if Sid pops in tonight," said Molly, quite excited. "Meanwhile, I'll try and question the major subtly. You know, ask if the Newtons' marriage is unsteady and so forth. But don't worry, I won't implement you in any way."

"Thanks," said Ned, cheered by his mother's willingness to help. "I'll leave you to it then. Enjoy your walk."

During dinner that evening Molly seemed very subdued. Concerned, Ned asked the reason for her lack of good cheer.

"It's the major," she replied, avoiding eye contact with her son. "I really don't know what's got into him. He was fine when I saw him this morning, but this afternoon he seemed a bit odd, and when I questioned him about the Newtons, you know, asked about their marriage and the likelihood of there being a rift, it seemed to anger him. He was annoyed that I should even suggest such a thing. In retrospect, I think perhaps I wasn't quite subtle enough."

"Oh dear," sighed Ned, sympathetically.

"I think I've upset him. In fact I know I have. He wasn't his usual bright self when we first left the Inn, so I ought to have been more tactful. Talking about the Newtons' marriage just pushed him over the edge, so to speak. He hardly spoke for the rest of the walk. He's very fond of Frank and Sylvia, you know. They're like family to him. I didn't say you had reason to suspect Sylvia of infidelity, of course. I think if I had, he would have walked off and left me alone in the middle of nowhere."

Seeing that Molly was feeling uncomfortable, Ned changed the subject and told her he had booked his room for an extra two weeks. He had forgotten to mention earlier that was the reason for seeking out Sylvia in the first place.

Molly's mood brightened a little. "Oh, that's a good idea, sweetheart. If you don't mind, I think I'll do likewise."

"Of course I don't mind. You're as intrigued as I am to know what on earth's going on here. There has to be some dodgy character somewhere with skeletons in his cupboard who we've not yet encountered."

Molly giggled, excitedly. "Talking of dodgy characters has just reminded me. Guess who I saw today?"

Ned grinned, pleased to see his mother cheerful once more. "I've no idea. Who was it?"

"That dreadful trollop with the red hair and awful scruffy little, yappy dog."

"Really!" said Ned, with interest. "Where was this?"

Molly giggled. "Outside her house. And you'll never guess who she is. I still can't believe it myself. The major told me when I asked. This was before we'd fallen out, of course."

Nonplussed, Ned shook his head. "So, who is she?"

"Rose Briers, the headmaster's wife," said Molly, triumphantly. "Would you ever believe it?"

"What!" She can't be. She looks nothing like a headmaster's wife. Not that there's a particular way such a person should look, but you know what I mean."

Molly lowered her voice. "Well, she is. She was coming out of The School House gate and dressed just as tarty as the other day when we saw her. She completely ignored me, of course, but uttered simpering greetings to the major."

"The plot thickens," said Ned, still shocked, as he finished his dinner and placed his cutlery neatly in the centre of his empty plate.

Molly sighed deeply. "Not that discovering the identity of the headmaster's wife helps us in any way. I don't know, Ned. What are we going to do next? About Jane, that is. How on earth can we speed things up a bit? We seem to be getting nowhere fast."

Ned agreed. "I don't know. I've actually seriously been thinking of going to the police."

Molly was shocked. "You can't, Ned. They'd think you're mad. I've had plenty of experience regarding that sort of thing, believe you me."

"I know, but I thought perhaps, if I went to see, P.C. Stevens it might be a bit more, well, you know, low key. He's always seemed a pretty likable chap to me."

"Oh, I don't know," said Molly, trying to pierce the remaining peas on her plate with the prongs of her fork. "I think he might have to report anything he's told, even in confidence, especially if it's of a serious nature, like this is. I don't see talking to him would be a good idea at all."

"How about his wife then. What's she like? I've never actually spoken to her before."

"Annie, she's a treasure, and would probably be very interested in our story, seeing as she is related to Doris, that is."

Ned was surprised. "I didn't know that. In what way is she related?"

"They're cousins. I only found out yesterday and forgot to tell you. Annie's father and Doris's mother were brother and sister. Annie's father married quite late in life, hence the twenty year age difference."

Gertie came in to clear their plates and bring in the puddings. They stopped their conversation and Molly commented on Gertie's new hair-do.

"Oh, do you like it?" she grinned. "I had it done in Helston this afternoon. It was getting a bit long and I was fed up with it."

Molly smiled. "It's very nice, dear. It suits you."

Gertie returned to the kitchen, plates in hand, head held high. A compliment from Ned's stylish mum was a compliment indeed.

"She's a nice kid," said Molly, lifting her spoon and fork.

Ned groaned. "She's not a kid, Mother. She's only five years younger than me."

"She's a kid until she gets the key of the door," said Molly.

Ned didn't retaliate verbally, but attacked his jam sponge and custard with unnecessary vigour.

Later, whilst Ned was in conversation with Pat Dickens in the public bar, Sid Reynolds entered the Inn. Pat was telling a very long winded rigmarole about a problem he'd had with one of his tractors, hence Ned was unable to get away. He caught Molly's eye. She nodded in response and crossed the floor towards Sid at the bar. Nearby she paused, stroked Don, and made a casual comment to Jim Hughes about the weather. She was close enough now to eavesdrop on Sid's remarks to a radiant looking Sylvia, standing behind the bar.

"I feel like a new man," she heard him whisper, loudly, as Sylvia handed him his drink. "You've made me so very, very happy."

Sylvia winked. Sid blew her a subtle kiss. Molly froze with a mouthful of gin, some of which trickled slowly down her chin, leaving a streak in her face powder. She had heard enough!

Pat Dickens turned, saw Jim Hughes, and proceeded to tell him about the troublesome tractor. Molly, still dazed, grabbed Ned's arm, dragged him into a corner and told him what she had heard.

"I can't believe that I've just witnessed such blatant flirting," hissed Molly, indignantly. "And Frank stood not more than five feet away. It's outrageous."

Ned felt his anger rise. "Well, it's nothing to do with us. But I wouldn't want to be in his shoes," he said, nodding towards the new found philanderer. "Not when Frank finds out."

"If he finds out," said Molly. "Anyway, it answers your question as to why Sylvia wasn't in the stable. She was obviously gallivanting off somewhere with lover boy. Come on, Ned, let's sit down, my feet are killing me and I feel all of a dither."

They went into the snug and sat in the window seat near to the fire.

"You're not going to join the major tonight, then." said Ned, noticing the major, sitting alone in his corner, reading a book.

"Certainly not!" hissed Molly. "He's behaving like a stuffy old fool, and as you know I cannot tolerate fools. I had enough experience of that with your father."

Normally, Ned would have sprung to his father's defence. He thought, however, on this occasion, to do so would be inappropriate. He could see through his mother's infuriation that she was really quite upset and on the verge of being tearful.

153

The door of the Inn opened, and much to Ned's delight, P.C. Stevens and his wife walked in.

"Evening, Fred. Evening, Annie," boomed Frank.

Fred helped his wife off with her coat and hung it on the hooks by the door. "It's Annie's birthday, so I thought I'd bring her out for a well-earned break."

"Lovely," smiled Sylvia. "Happy birthday, dear. Is Doris looking after the children?"

Annie nodded. "Yes, she volunteered to baby-sit, so we've taken her up on the offer. I think she was glad to have something to focus on other than, well, you know."

"Of course," said Sylvia. "Say no more."

Watching from inside the snug, Ned turned and whispered to Molly. "If the opportunity arises, one of us must speak to Annie and tell her our secret."

"What! Are you sure, Ned? I mean, once we've told someone there's no going back and we simply don't know how she'll react!"

"We have to," said Ned. "Time is running out and we're getting nowhere fast. We desperately need someone to help us. Besides, Annie would have been here last August. She knows the area and I should think she knows more about this case than anyone else in the village, barring her husband of course."

"And the person guilty of Jane's murder," Molly added.

As luck would have it, the men began to play dominoes in the public bar. Ned joined them, and Annie carried her drink onto the snug where she sat beside Molly near to the fire. No-one else was around, even the major had joined in the game.

Molly, flustered at first, talked about any subject which entered her head, before finally turning the conversation to Jane.

"I suppose there's no more news?" she said, after they had covered the subject lightly.

"No," sighed Annie, somewhat subdued. "I think to be honest, the police are as mystified as the rest of us. It's likely the inquest will return a verdict of accidental death."

Molly bit her lip. She had to say something. Ned was right.

"Annie," she whispered, nervously. "There's something I ought to tell you. We, that is, Ned and I, can't go to the police because they'd simply think us mad. But, umm, we're sure we know something

154

which is vital to the outcome of Jane's case. Oh, dear, this is a dreadful question to ask, but have you ever considered the possibility of her death being, err, murder?"

The colour drained from Annie's face. "Murder," she repeated, slowly. "Whatever do you mean? There's no evidence whatsoever to indicate murder. Besides, Jane was the dearest, sweetest girl I've ever known. No-one would murder her. No-one."

Molly tightly grasped Annie's shaking hands and explained all that had happened since Ned had first arrived in Trengillion. Annie listened to every word in stunned silence, and then sat thoughtfully, allowing all she had heard to sink in. After several minutes she turned to Molly.

"Ned's a school teacher, isn't he?"

"Well, yes," said Molly, surprised by the question. "Why do you ask?"

"Oh dear, this is going to sound really, really silly. But last summer," her voice dropped to little more than a whisper. "Last summer a fair came to Cornwall. Jane and I both went to it and we took the children. You know how children love fairs?"

Molly nodded.

"Anyway, outside an over-ornate caravan, conveniently placed next to a tea tent, an old gypsy woman was reading tealeaves. Jane and I thought it would be a bit of a laugh to have our fortunes told, so we each bought a cup of tea and joined the queue. It cost three shillings, but we thought it would be money well spent."

Molly turned pale and goose pimples rose on her arms. "Oh God, what did she say?"

"Well, everything she said to me could apply to just about anyone and everyone, but with Jane it was different. Jane said that to begin with, the fortune teller told her pretty much the same as she had told me, but when she looked into her cup a second time she went all peculiar and started twitching. She then told her, that one day a school teacher would come to her aid and set her free."

"Good God," spluttered Molly, shocked, "that's really creepy to hear, even for a believer like me."

Annie smiled. "Of course, it made no sense at all to us then. We laughed in fact as we tried to imagine a teacher wearing his black gown and mortar-board riding into the village on a white horse and rescuing her from captivity, following abduction by an evil villain. We neither of us dreamt it could possibly mean after she was…"

Annie, unable to finish the sentence, took a handkerchief from her sleeve and wiped her moist eyes. She didn't want anyone to see the tears.

"Molly, something tells me that you're right in what you say, and for the sake of Jane and of course poor, poor Doris, I'll do anything you want to get to the bottom of this."

Molly squeezed Annie's hand. "Thank you so much, and thank you for not laughing at me. You don't know how much this means for us to have another brain with fresh ideas to help work things out."

Annie, although still stunned, asked herself the same questions Ned and Molly had asked over and over again. Who would want to kill Jane and what could possibly be their motive?

"As far as I know," mused Annie, returning her handkerchief to the pocket of her cardigan, "she didn't have an enemy in the world."

"So it seems. But what about Percy? What sort of relationship did he and Jane have?"

Annie smiled. "Percy wouldn't hurt a fly, and I don't think the two of them were anything more than just good friends, really. I mean, certainly they used to be in the company of each other a lot, and I think he was rather sweet on her for a time. But he's a nice, kind and considerate lad, and usually they were with the rest of their group, anyway. You know who I mean, Peter, Percy, Jane, Gertie and Meg, they were all very good friends. And still are, of course, those that are left."

Molly picked up her gin and tonic and took a sip. "Meg! Who's she? I don't think I've come across that name before."

"Haven't you? But then again I suppose you wouldn't have. She's the vicar's daughter, and a real beauty."

"Ah, so might I have seen her in church?"

"No, I very much doubt it. She doesn't go out a great deal socially these days. You see, her mother was severely disabled following an accident last summer, so she spends a lot of time looking after her, especially on Sundays when the vicar is out for much of the day. They're a very close family."

Molly nodded. "I see. And do the vicar and his poor wife have any other children?"

Annie shook her head. "No, Meg is an only child."

"Hmm, so is Ned."

Annie glanced at the men playing dominoes in the public bar. "I wonder why Jane has never told Ned who poisoned her. I mean, surely she must know."

Molly shook her head. "He seems to think she doesn't, which I must admit, does seem a bit odd."

"Yes, very weird. And has he spoken to her since her body was discovered?"

"Regrettably, not, although he has tried to reach her on several occasions. It's most frustrating. She seems very elusive."

"That's a shame. We shall have to think up a plan. As you say, we can't go to the police and I certainly can't tell Fred. He thought I was bonkers just having my fortune told, and said it was a load of tosh. Let me sleep on it and see what I can come up with, and then I'll be in touch."

She uttered these words just in time. The game of dominoes was over and the men were mingling once more.

Chapter Nineteen

Sunday morning was wet and dull. So dull, Ned needed the bedroom light on to dress by, and the bathroom light on to shave. When he went downstairs for breakfast, a solitary one hundred watt bulb glowed beneath the fringed lampshade in the centre of the dining room ceiling and the large bay windows were misted with patchy condensation. Ned hated dark mornings and grumbled continuously as he ate his fried bread, bacon and eggs.

"Did you get out of bed the wrong side this morning, dear?" Molly asked, as she poured herself a second cup of tea.

Ned frowned. He could not tell his mother he had slept badly because he was unable to banish from his mind images of Sylvia with Sid Reynolds. He therefore, continued instead to complain bitterly about the weather.

"We're in March now," he moaned. "It should be getting more spring like, yet it's nothing but one miserable, cloudy, dull day after another."

"Don't be ridiculous!" Molly retorted. "We've had some beautiful weather during our stay here, and even if it is now March, we're still in winter."

Ned remained in a bad mood as he changed for church. He would not have gone, but he wanted to see if that awful blighter Sid would have the audacity to put in an appearance, and if he did, how Sylvia would react.

He walked with Molly to the church without speaking, kicking up stones as his mother talked continuously. She was beginning to get on his nerves. He wished he was a little boy again and then he could stamp in one of the numerous puddles and splash her legs to relieve his anger.

On entering the church, they found very few people were assembled, and so with a vast array of seats to choose from they took a pew towards the back in order to view the congregation as it arrived.

Sylvia and the major were the first to put in an appearance, and as usual both were dressed immaculately. Sylvia smiled. The major merely nodded and spoke out of politeness. Ned heard his mother sigh deeply.

Fred and Annie Stevens appeared next with their two children, Jamie and Sally. Close behind, followed Pat and May Dickens.

Gertie breezed in soon after with her mother and best friend Betty. Close on their heels were Percy and Peter. Ned was surprised to see Percy did not go into the vestry to join the choir, but instead sat with his close friend and colleague.

A group of elderly ladies, several couples, and a few families all unbeknown to Ned, rapidly filled the remaining pews on the right hand side of the aisle. And finally, looking very smart, his hair and beard trimmed, and wearing a new suit, appeared Sid Reynolds. Ned glanced at him with a loathing he had never before realised he was capable of, and angrily suppressed a strong, uncharacteristic, desire to hurl the hymn book towards the back of Sid's neatly combed hair.

After the service, during which Ned nodded off to sleep several times, only to be woken abruptly, by sharp stabs in the ribs from Molly's elbow, Sylvia and the major were the first to leave. Sylvia was needed back to the Inn to help Frank with the lunchtime opening. She did not speak to Sid as she left. Sid was in conversation with Gertie, Betty, Percy and Peter.

Molly noticed Fred Stevens was chatting to the organist, and so she slipped away to have a word with his wife, Annie. Ned meanwhile, was collared by Pat Dickens, who wanted to update him on the troublesome tractor saga.

Molly seemed quite satisfied regarding the outcome of her brief conversation with Annie, and so invited Ned along to her room once they stepped back inside the Inn. Ned, still sulking, and in an even more disagreeable frame of mind after being talked at by Pat Dickens, reluctantly agreed.

"Annie's had a brilliant idea," said Molly, like an excited schoolgirl, as she carefully hung her damp coat on the back of a chair and stood her umbrella to drain on newspaper beside the fireplace. "And I sense we might be in for a break-through."

"Really," said Ned, carelessly leaning against the window sill and exhibiting very little interest.

Molly sat down, removed her best shoes and put on her slippers. "Yes! Tuesday, I am told, will be the monthly Beetle Drive, and it will be here at the Inn. Lots of people attend apparently, as it's to raise money for modernising the village hall kitchen."

Ned lit a cigarette to emphasise his disinterest. "How exciting! Why don't they hold it in the village hall, then? And what is a Beetle Drive, anyway?"

Molly sighed deeply to stifle her impatience. "They have it here because it's better attended than it would be in the village hall. And a Beetle Drive is a game where people sit around tables and take it in turn to throw a dice. Each number represents a part of a beetle's body. It's a case of seeing who can complete a beetle first. The winner of each table then moves on to the next table and the overall winner is the first person to complete the circuit."

Ned frowned. "I see. I think."

"I've never actually played it," said Molly. "But Annie says it's good fun."

Ned yawned. "Okay, I'll accept that. So what's Annie's bright idea?"

"Well, she thinks if we could start a rumour claiming that Jane was murdered, it would give us a chance to watch the reactions of people. See if anyone behaves in a suspicious manner, looks alarmed, breaks out in a sweat, you know the sort of thing to look for."

Ned snorted with unkind derision and carelessly flicked ash into the bowl of faded hyacinths. "And how does Annie propose we start these rumours?"

"Well, that's easy. She wants us to do that. For example, on Tuesday night, I could say to you, in a loud stage whisper, of course, that I'd overheard a couple of women in the village talking, and one of them had said, she'd heard rumours that Jane Hunt had been murdered."

Ned forced a weak smile. "Could be interesting. But wouldn't it look a bit suspicious coming from you? After all, nearly everyone here knows you're a medium, so your involvement might well not have the necessary impact."

"Then you can do the talking. It makes no difference to me. In fact, it might be better if it came from you."

Ned was not convinced, but accepted anything was worth a try. They certainly had to do something soon, as the inquest into Jane's death was due to open before long.

"Annie says we must try and stand near to Albert Treloar, as he's one of the biggest gossips in the village."

Ned frowned. "But what if he's the guilty man? He'll not pass on any tittle-tattle, will he?"

"More will hear than him, we'll make sure of that. Besides, if he is guilty, he'll still react in some way or other and probably even leave the premises."

"In which case I'll follow him," said Ned, his enthusiasm mounting.

"Well, I can't see as anything would be achieved by you doing so, but that's up to you."

"So, will Annie be at the Beetle Drive?"

Molly nodded. "Yes, which is perfect. As luck would have it she's Secretary to the Village Hall Committee, so Fred will be at home, out of the way, looking after the two children."

Ned felt a little more cheered and even conceded a minute pang of excitement as he contemplated possible results for Tuesday night.

"Shall we go down for a drink?" he suddenly asked. "To celebrate!"

"Rather premature, don't you think? But why not! A drink's a good idea and there's always such a nice atmosphere in the bar on Sunday lunchtime."

Since it was still raining, Ned went to his room in the afternoon. Beer consumed during daytime always made him feel sleepy. He did not undress, but lay on top of the bed and stared up at the ceiling, where he tried to make pictures from the cracks in the plaster. He was not one hundred per cent certain that Tuesday night would be very fruitful and secretly thought there must be other ways to make headlong progress.

He yawned. "Oh, Jane, Jane, if only you would be more helpful! We're trying our best, really we are, but, oh, I don't know."

He awoke, shivering, several hours later and quickly put on his thickest pullover and warmest jacket. Rubbing sleep from his eyes he peered through the window. The rain had stopped and the sky looked brighter. Not that it mattered as darkness was imminent.

Ned turned and caught the eye of the old fisherman.

"Damn it, I still haven't found out who you are."

He took the painting from the wall, blew dust from the top of the frame and turned it around. On the back someone had written, Claude Gilbert, 1883. Repeating the name to memorise it, he returned the picture to its hook and made a mental note to enquire just who the old fisherman may have been.

When Ned went down to dinner, he found Frank in the hallway, replacing the receiver following a telephone call.

"Ah, the very man. Perhaps you can tell me, Frank, who Claude Gilbert was?"

Frank laughed. "Claude. Why he was Josh Gilbert's great uncle. You know who Josh was, don't you? We told you about him the night of the storm. The old boy who did odd jobs here for a while. Claude, his uncle, was a fisherman, but a bit of a rogue as well, so I believe. Why on earth do you want to know?"

"Because there's a portrait of him in my room," said Ned.

"Oh, yes, of course. I'd forgotten about that. It was painted by one of Claude's fancy up-country friends who owned some property down here. It got handed down to Josh when the old boy died. Josh had a lot of time for his great uncle, you know, especially when he was a youngster, that's why he kept it in his room."

"His room?" queried Ned.

Frank chuckled. "Yes, that's right. When Josh came to stay here and Sylvia nursed him, your room was his room, if you see what I mean. In fact he died in there, on your very bed."

Ned's jaw dropped. Frank noticed and grinned mischievously.

"Now don't you worry, Ned, old Josh won't hurt you. He was a nice old chap. Besides, I don't believe in ghosts and suchlike."

Ned smiled weakly and made a feeble effort to laugh, consciously aware that ghosts and suchlike were very much part of the Inn.

On Monday morning the Inn was shrouded with thick fog. As Ned walked through the village to collect his paper it was difficult to make out the outlines of the buildings on either side of the road, and what little traffic there was drove by very slowly. Ned passed the church and looked up at the tower, the turrets were veiled with a thick, swirling mist. He passed The Police House, where he imagined Annie Stevens bustling around whilst trying to recollect any strange behaviour or events during the past seven months. When he reached the post office, he was greeted by Mrs Pascoe who apologised for the non-arrival of the papers.

"It's the weather," she fretted. "Bert Simms was in earlier and he was saying it's as thick as a bag in town and further up the line, so the papers won't be here until maybe as late as lunchtime."

"Never mind," sighed Ned. "If you'll reserve me a copy of the Daily Herald, I'll call in for it this afternoon."

Mrs Pascoe assured him she would. He bought two packets of cigarettes and left.

Outside the post office he paused, with no paper to read, he felt rather lost. It was not the sort of day on which to take a walk or sit on Denzil's bench. From the other side of the road he heard the voices children at play, he crossed the road and glanced over the wall into the playground, hopeful of seeing Reg. Some of the girls were skipping, others played hopscotch, whilst the boys chased around, playing what looked very much like Cowboys and Indians.

Through the mist, near to the school's entrance, Ned spotted an attractive young woman, stooped down as she looked at the knee of a little girl crying bitterly. Ned wondered who the young woman was. He had not seen her before and made a mental note to ask Gertie.

Back at the Inn, Ned went to his room and picked up one of the books he had borrowed about smuggling. He lay on the bed and looked down the index for the name Trengillion. To his surprise it was there. He turned to the appropriate page and found a brief article which mentioned a notorious smuggler called, Billy Gilbert. Opposite was a rough sketch of Billy. Ned studied the picture, albeit only a few lines, and felt sure he could see a resemblance between fisherman, Claude, hanging on wall in his room, and the face of Billy, looking up at him from the page.

Ned laughed. "I wish you could talk, you old rogue," he said, turning to Claude. "I'm sure you and this chap here must have been related."

There was a tap on the door. Molly poked her head into the room.

"Ah, there you are, Ned. I was just wondering if you would like to come with me into town. I've checked with Sylvia, the bus goes at 11.30am today, it being market day. We could have a bit of lunch whilst there."

"But what about the fog. Surely the bus won't be running on time. It's as thick as a bag?"

"The fog's cleared," said Molly.

Ned dropped the book and looked towards the window. He was amazed to see the sun shining brightly.

"Would we be shopping for anything in particular?" he asked, turning to face his mother.

"Only wool. May Dickens has given me a lovely knitting pattern for a pullover and I thought I'd knit one for you."

"In that case I'd definitely better escort you. I can't risk you being tempted to choose pink."

That evening, after dinner, Molly, eager to cast on the pullover, returned to her room, vowing to join Ned for a drink later. And as the major was not in his usual place either, Ned was the only customer when he went into the bar.

"A pint of your usual?" asked Frank, as Ned sat down on a stool.

"Yes please, and one for yourself."

The sound of children's voices passing by outside reminded Ned he had forgotten to ask Gertie about the pretty young woman in the school playground. Instead he asked Frank.

"Well now, I imagine that would be young Meg. She teaches at the school and she's certainly as pretty as a picture."

"What, the vicar's daughter?"

"That's right, but it's no good you taking a shine to her because she's spoken for."

"Really," grinned Ned, sipping his pint. "So who's the lucky chap?"

"Sid Reynolds. He asked her to marry him last Saturday."

"Frank!" snapped Sylvia, as she walked behind the bar for a glass of lemonade. "You're not supposed to tell anyone. It's a secret."

"Well, Ned won't spill the beans, will you, lad?"

Ned, mouth gaping in a state of utter confusion, slowly shook his head.

"They want to keep it secret until the weekend," said Sylvia to Ned. "Then make an official announcement at Meg's twenty first birthday party."

"Sorry, Sylvia," mumbled Frank. "It just sort of slipped out."

"Don't worry, I won't breathe a word," Ned promised. "But did you say, Sid asked Meg to marry him on Saturday?"

Sylvia, answering for her husband. "Yes, and you probably even saw him when you were standing on the paddock wall. I did, just after I'd spoken to you. He would have been on his way back from the Vicarage then. I knew where he had been of course, because he'd asked for my advice the night before."

"Advice," muttered Ned, very confused. "Advice about what?"

Sylvia laughed. "Sid is fifteen years older than Meg. He was worried people might think it too big an age difference. We had a long chat about it the other evening. I told him to go for it. He's absolutely crazy about her."

Suddenly everything made sense. Sylvia had not been romping in the fields with Sid. Sid had been at the Vicarage asking Meg to marry him. And Sid's gratitude to Sylvia was for her advice. Ned tried hard to conceal his delight. He did not hate Sid Reynolds! Sylvia was not an adulteress! He was no longer jealous!

"Would you like a drink, Sylvia?" he asked, on impulse, grinning like the Cheshire cat.

Sylvia nodded. "Thank you very much. I'll have a bottle of stout if I may, but not until I've freshened up and changed into something a little more becoming."

Ned handed Frank half a crown to pay for the drink and then put the change in his pocket.

By the time Molly came down, the bar was a little busier and she was happy, having completed several rows of the new, dark green pullover.

"What are you looking so smug about?" she asked, as Ned bought her a gin.

He laughed. "Come into the snug and I'll tell you."

They sat down near to the blazing fire and Ned told Molly about his conversation with Frank and Sylvia.

"So you see," he concluded. "Sylvia and Sid are innocent of all the accusations we made against them, and you won't say a word about the engagement, will you?"

"Of course not," said Molly. "But I don't quite understand."

"Don't understand what?" snapped Ned, impatiently. "It's quite elementary. Sid was at the Vic..."

"Yes, yes, I can see all that," interrupted Molly. "But what mystifies me is, if Sylvia wasn't out with Sid on Saturday, when she claimed to have been in the stables. Then where on earth was she?"

The smile disappeared from Ned's face as the feeling of euphoria vanished. Damn it. He hadn't thought of that!

Chapter Twenty

On Tuesday morning during breakfast, Molly was still mystified as to the whereabouts of Sylvia on Saturday afternoon. Ned on the other hand, was uninterested. She had not been with Sid, so as far as he was concerned, the matter was of no interest.

"Let's not dwell on it, Mother. Our priority now should be finding out who poisoned Jane. I'm actually looking forward to this evening, I must admit."

"You're right I suppose, and I'm sure there's an innocent explanation. I'm just peeved that the whole silly episode caused me the loss the major's friendship. He hardly speaks to me now, and when he does, it's merely out of politeness."

"Perhaps you could apologise," suggested Ned, happily buttering his thick slice of toast.

"Apologise! For what?" Molly snapped. "He's the one in the wrong."

Ned thought it best to change the subject. "How's my pullover coming along?"

"Very well. I've nearly finished the front, but I don't like working with dreary, dark colours, they strain my eyes so."

Ned looked intently at his mother and smiled. Her daffodil yellow blouse certainly brought a splash of colour to the otherwise drab dining room, although he could not see the necessity for quite so many frills. He put his hand on hers. "Don't worry about the major, Mum. I'm sure he'll come to his senses soon."

As Annie predicted, the Inn was busy that evening, with people arriving to secure good seats as soon as Frank opened the doors. Many of them were unknown to Ned and Molly, but it was evident by the chat and laughter that the fund raising enthusiasts were all well known to each other.

"Most of our locals are keen to see new fittings in the village hall kitchen," said Annie, after Molly commented on the many strange faces. "At present there are no cupboards or work surfaces, and there is no hot water either. And as it's used by lots of different groups and organisations, the hall's refurbishment has great appeal. That's why I was confident there'd be the usual good turn out."

Ned was impressed by the growing numbers. Even the vicar put in an appearance, much to the delight of two elderly ladies who discussed with him the church flower rota as he stood by the door with a pint of beer clasped firmly in his hands.

At half past seven, Ned and Molly seized the opportunity to circulate and mingle. The Beetle Drive was not due to begin until eight o' clock, and as the seats around the tables rapidly filled up, Molly excitedly whispered, "I've a really strong feeling that tonight is going to be quite productive."

"I hope so," said Ned, absently, enchanted by Sylvia's elegant dress. "Otherwise it'll be back to the drawing board."

Just before eight o'clock, as Annie and Nettie Penrose were distributing the Beetle Drive cards, the door of the Inn swung open. The chatter instantly subsided and was replaced by lingering tut-tuts and groans. Reg Briers had arrived, and with him was his controversial wife, Rose.

"Evening, Reg. Evening, Rose," Frank smirked, a twinkle in both eyes.

Ned sensed that Frank was amused to see Rose had decided to put in an appearance.

"Hello, Frank, sweetie," she drawled, approaching the bar where she leaned across and stroked his beard.

"Hussey," whispered Molly, beneath her breath.

Intrigued by the silence, Ned glanced around the gathering. All the women had stopped their vivacious chatter and sat with expressions of disapproval on their glum faces. The pleasant atmosphere had disappearing and Ned could feel the tension rising. The men, however, took on a completely different stance to the women. They preened themselves, stretched their necks, straightened their ties and tidied their varying coloured heads of hair.

Reg handed Rose a glass of whisky and dry ginger. From it she took three large gulps and then placed the glass on the table while she removed her coat. Beneath it she wore a tight, blue skirt with a slit up the side which barely covered the tops of her stockings. The skirt itself just about covered her knees and the red, figure hugging,

V neck jumper she wore, clung like a limpet to her curves, revealing a cleavage which set a few pulses racing and mouths dribbling.

Rose and Reg sat down at the same table as Harry the Hitman, and his wife, Joyce.

Ned grinned. He thought the Briers looked an unlikely pair. Reg was five foot nine, the same height as Rose who was wearing high wedge heeled shoes. Reg's hair was thick and fast turning grey. No-one knew Rose's true colour for she had continually dyed it an artificial shade of auburn for as long as the village folk could remember. Reg was smartly dressed in a conventional striped suit, white shirt and silk tie, while Rose, many would say, had the worst possible taste in clothing imaginable.

The Beetle Drive finally started just after eight. Ned, who had never been to one before, thought the notion sounded rather ludicrous. He found, however, that playing was addictive and soon threw each dice enthusiastically, willing it to show the number he needed.

There was a lot of laughter once the initial shock of Rose Briers' attendance had been overcome, and at the end of each round, everyone talked excitedly about the near misses they had encountered whilst trying to complete their beetles. Ned even won a couple of rounds, which he admitted to his mother, made the first half of the evening quite enjoyable.

At nine o'clock they had a break, during which May Dickens and Flo Hughes sold raffle tickets, most people refilled their glasses and Ned and Molly prepared to put their scheme into action. Before doing so, however, Molly looked around hoping to see Annie, for she wanted to give a signal indicating they were ready to go ahead with the plan, but Annie was nowhere to be seen. Albert Treloar was standing near to the main entrance of the bar talking to Gertie's parents and so Ned and Molly, despite Annie's absence, casually edged their way in his direction and chatted about nothing in particular as they went.

"Have you sent a postcard to any of your work colleagues yet?" asked Molly, still looking for Annie.

"Yes, of course," Ned replied, knowing that was a cue to turn the conversation gradually around to Jane.

Meanwhile, unbeknown to them, Rose Briers, who had now consumed several glasses of whisky and dry ginger, excused herself from the men trying to peer down the top of her jumper, picked up her handbag and left for the Ladies outside.

Rose shivered as she carefully walked in her wedge heeled shoes across the uneven cobbles and into the unheated empty building where she hurriedly entered the one solitary cubicle and locked the door. After she had pulled the chain and adjusted her clothing, the rapid hissing of water pouring back into the cistern gradually faded away. When it stopped she became aware of running water elsewhere within the building. She opened the cubicle door. To her astonishment the small room was filled with steam. Water gushed freely from the hot tap, splashing the surrounding tiles before it swirled and disappeared down the plughole. Yet there was no-one else present. Rose picked up her handbag and stepped out into the steamy room. Puzzled, she crossed to the sink to wash her hands and turned off the tap. It was not until she raised her head to reach for the towel that she looked into the mirror above her head.

The piercing scream which emanated from the quivering mouth of Rose Briers, rang through the ears of everyone inside the Inn. Several men and a few brave women rapidly put down their glasses and ran out to see what was wrong. They found Rose, still screaming hysterically, as she pointed to the mirror. Jaws dropped in disbelief at what they saw. Written in the steam were the words, *Who killed Jane Hunt?*

Harry went to comfort Rose. Still trembling she let him embrace her and did not resist when he forced her head to rest on his chest. Once calmed, she then told the inquisitive crowd what had happened.

"Tosh!" spluttered, a frowsy, middle-aged spinster. "I bet you wrote it yourself."

Rose lifted her head from Harry's chest. "Of course I didn't" she snapped, vehemently. "Why should I?"

"Wouldn't surprise me if you had," retorted a jealous wife. "It's obvious you've done it to draw attention to yourself, cos that's what you're like."

"What! That's absurd."

Pat Dickens stepped forward and looked at the mirror closely. "Well, someone clearly did. But what I want to know is what it means, and whether there's any truth in it. Surely that's far more important than who wrote it."

Everyone talked at once. Ned, who was amongst the witnesses, turned to Molly. "Annie, do you think?" he whispered.

Molly nodded. "It must have been, no-one else knows."

"I'm going back inside," Rose shouted, her cheeks pink with anger. "It's bloody freezing out here and I need a drink."

Pushing aside onlookers, she stormed out of the building and returned to the Inn. Meanwhile, the steam slowly dispersed. The chilling message on the mirror began to fade, and with nothing left to see, everyone else left also.

Back inside, tongues wagged, as those who had remained in the bar were informed by those who had gone out to investigate, just what all the commotion was about. Looks of shock and fear crossed their faces.

"Thank goodness Doris has a headache and isn't here tonight," said Flo Hughes, shaking her head in disgust. "I'd have hated her to have witnessed this little outburst."

"But do you think there is any truth in the message on the mirror?" whispered May, sipping her sweet sherry. "I mean, it's a pretty serious accusation isn't it?"

"No," Flo tutted. "I don't believe it for one minute. Some heartless soul did it for a lark and I wouldn't be surprised if it's not that awful Briers creature either. She's capable of just about anything."

Frank, wearied by the mayhem, rang the bell in an attempt to regain order. "Come on, ladies and gents. Let's get on with the Beetle Drive. After that you can chatter 'til the cows come home."

Most people calmed down, although there were some who could not resist muttering beneath their breath and Ned thought the vicar looked most uncomfortable. Soon, however, everyone was concentrating once again on throwing the dice and getting the numbers needed to complete their beetles. At the end of the twelve games, Maude Pascoe from the post office was declared the winner and won two pounds, and the vicar, who came last, was awarded the booby prize: a tin of toffees.

As soon as the excitement of the game was over, the tongues began to wag again, until almost everyone was of the same opinion. Rose Briers had maliciously written the message.

Ned caught Annie's eye. She looked cross. This convinced him she was responsible for the stunt but was not happy about it being labelled a ploy by Rose. The frowsy, middle-aged spinster who had shouted at Rose in the Ladies, was again wagging her finger accusingly.

Rose's face was as red as her lipstick. She stood up.

"Now look here you silly, stupid, people. How many more times do I have to tell you, I did not write that message on the mirror? Why should I? Even I think it's in very bad taste, unless of course there is some truth in it. In which case I suggest you stop harassing me, think before you open your mouths and start using that grey matter, albeit in very small quantities with some of you, between your ears."

"She's right, you know," said Harry, suddenly. "I think someone knows something about Jane's death and they're trying to warn us."

"So, which one of us wrote the message?" asked Albert, dispassionately. "That's what I'd damn well like to know."

Pat Dickens spoke next, "Like I said when we were out there, it doesn't matter who wrote it, what matters is whether or not it's true."

"It doesn't have to be any of us here tonight, anyway," said Frank. "The toilets are always unlocked so anyone from anywhere could have slipped in and written on the mirror."

Annie was smiling.

"But, but…" stammered, May Dickens, turning grey. "If the message isn't a hoax and Jane really was murdered, then someone from the village must be a murderer."

Nettie Penrose turned to Annie. "Is there any truth in this? Do the police suspect that poor Jane's death wasn't an accident? And if so, why haven't we been told?"

A hushed bar waited for her reply. Annie, caught off guard, felt her hands turn clammy with fear. She had not expected to be questioned and she knew she must not let the side down.

"I, I, don't know," she muttered, hoping the embarrassment she felt didn't show. "Fred doesn't confide in me over police matters."

Gertie wept. "This is awful. To think there might be a murderer amongst us. Poor Jane. Who could possibly have done such a thing?"

Percy put his arms around her shoulders and stroked her head gently, as loud chatter broke out and angry voices searched for names of people against whom they bore a grudge. The major, shocked on hearing the names of decent people abused and tossed around as likely suspects, stood up and banged his fist firmly on the bar. Everything went silent, for the major was a greatly respected figure in the village.

"For heaven's sake, pull yourselves together. I find this smearing of civilised characters both distasteful and distressing. Being at loggerheads will achieve absolutely nothing. If you're not careful this bickering will divide our close knit community for many, many years to come. You must *not* make unjust accusations against those not here to defend themselves. If Jane was murdered, and I hope to God the poor girl wasn't, then someone must have had a pretty good motive. Please, I beg you. Think before you speak so vindictively."

Impulsively, Molly reached up and put her hand on the major's shoulder. "Well said," she whispered, "well said."

Beaming, he turned to his erstwhile companion. "Moll, your glass is almost empty. Pop a double gin in here please, Sylvia."

He passed the glass over the bar. "How about you, Ned. Another pint?"

"What! Well, thanks, yes," Ned muttered, surprised, by the rapid change of circumstances.

"I'm sorry," said Molly, as the major slipped the refilled glass into her hand.

"Sorry," he grunted, passing a ten shilling note across the bar to Sylvia. "Sorry for what?"

"Annoying you the other day. It's a very bad habit I have. Being tactless, that is."

The major laughed, took her arm and led her to his corner in the snug. "Don't be daft, Moll. It wasn't your fault, it was mine. After we'd arranged to take a walk, I looked in the paper and saw my ruddy shares had taken a mighty tumble. Put me in a bit of a mood, I can tell you, and you bore the brunt of it. They're up again today though, I'm very pleased to say."

Molly moved closer to his side and kissed him on the cheek. Right at that moment she didn't really care who had killed Jane.

Normality returned after the major had spoken. Glasses were filled and the chatter was more amicable. The anger and aggression subsided to be replaced by a sense of excitement.

Ned, delighted to see his mother happy again, wandered around the bar to look for Annie. He wanted to congratulate her on the change of plan. He found her hurriedly folding raffle tickets with May and Flo. Unable to say anything in the presence of the other two ladies, she just raised her eyebrows and smiled. Ned beamed and commented on the success of the Beetle Drive as a fund raising event.

From the hallway the shrill bell of the telephone rang. Sylvia slipped out to answer it. She returned promptly and rushed to Annie's side.

"That was Fred on the phone. He said not to panic, but young Jamie has fallen down the stairs. He's complaining his arm hurts. Fred says, sorry, but could you come home straight away, as Jamie wants his mum."

Without hesitation, Annie sprang from her seat, grabbed her coat, bade everyone farewell and was gone.

"Damn!" muttered Ned, beneath his breath, realising he would have to wait until the following day, or even longer, to talk things over with Annie.

Most people left after the raffle was drawn, especially as the first ticket pulled out of the hat, belonged to Reg, who let Rose, choose first prize from the fine selection of generous donations.

Only Sylvia, Frank, the major, Molly, Ned, Larry and Des remained in the bar after the last of the villagers had gone home, and Larry and Des returned to their rooms as soon as their glasses were empty.

"Would you like a hand with the tidying up?" a joyous Molly asked Sylvia.

"Yes, please," she replied, eyeing the bar and tables cluttered with empty glasses and brim-full ashtrays.

"You wash and I'll dry," said Molly, grabbing a tea towel as she walked behind the bar.

Frank sat down, lit a cigarette and offered one each to Ned and the major, who promptly sat on either side of their landlord.

"No time for a break," Sylvia tutted, swilling a sherry schooner around in the sink. "All the tables need wiping."

"I can't do 'em," grunted Frank, wrinkling his nose, "because they're cluttered up with dirty glasses."

He winked at Ned and the major, and then lifted both his feet onto one of the low stools.

"Men!" hissed Sylvia. "They never do anything to keep you happy."

But Sylvia was wrong. The three men laughing and blowing smoke into the already smoky atmosphere would all go to considerable lengths, to keep Sylvia Newton happy.

Chapter Twenty-One

Molly was the only one seated in the dining room when Ned went down for breakfast the following morning. She greeted him with sparkling eyes and a broad smile, indisputable evidence regarding the true extent of her regained happiness.

"What an evening," she said, as he took his place at the table opposite, "I don't think I've ever witnessed quite such a hullabaloo before in my life."

Ned nodded as he picked up his serviette. "Yes, it was a bit chaotic, wasn't it? But it's very frustrating that neither of us got the chance to speak to Annie. I'd love to know what she thought of it all."

"Well, I shall find out soon as I'm going to pop round and see her later.

Ned poured himself a cup of tea. "Good, because I'm bit baffled as to why she didn't tell us of the change of plan."

Molly picked up the teaspoon in the sugar bowl and sprinkled a generous portion over her porridge. "It was most likely a spur of the moment decision. You know, she was probably in the Ladies washing her hands, saw the steam, did it on impulse, ran out before anyone saw her and didn't get the chance to tell us before chaos broke out."

"Hmm, I expect so. You'll find out later anyway."

"Yes, I shall. I do hope her little boy is alright."

Larry and Des walked into the dining room, followed shortly after by the major, who bade mother and son a sincere good morning.

Molly winked and Ned acknowledged his greeting warmly, after which the topic of conversation was changed to knitting for fear of being overheard.

After breakfast, Ned followed his mother up to her room. She wanted to tell him all she had found out about Rose Briers during a tête-à-tête with the major the previous evening.

"It's nothing earth shattering," said Molly, as Ned closed the door. "The major's not one to gossip, but even he can't hide the fact he disapproves of the woman's irresponsible behaviour."

"I thought she seemed rather popular with the men," smiled Ned, kicking off his shoes and lying down on his mother's bed.

"Not men like the major!" retorted Molly, primly. "Only the weak would succumb to the advances of that trollop."

"I see, so what can you tell me about 'that trollop'?" said Ned, with a smirk, clearly amused by his mother's small minded attitude.

"Well, she's not from these parts for a start. Poor Reg met her one summer whilst on holiday in Blackpool. Apparently, she worked in the hotel where he was staying and for some reason he took a shine to her. God only knows why: the man obviously has impaired vision. Anyway, from what the major says, their marriage came about because several people in the village had let it be known that they thought it would be more fitting for the headmaster of their school to have a wife. It appears for some reason they didn't approve of the fact he was a bachelor. Anyway, to cut a long story short, he asked Rose to marry him!"

"What, while he was still on holiday in Blackpool?"

"Precisely," scoffed Molly, taking a seat. "Not only that, but they went out, there and then, got a special licence, and so he came back a married man with a wife in tow."

"Good old Reg! I bet the locals were shocked when they first saw her."

"Well, not really, because according to the major, she was just about normal then. She still had dyed red hair and wore too much make-up, but at least her clothing was a lot less revealing and she was apparently quite timid, although I find that hard to believe."

"Timid! Hmm, perhaps then it's the whisky and dry ginger that makes her so loquacious."

"Whisky and dry ginger, fiddlesticks! She's vociferous by nature."

"Well, whatever her natural disposition is I thought she and Reg seemed perfectly happy together last night and surely that's all that really matters. Personally, I can't see what all the fuss is about. There are two sides to every story and it can't be much of a life for poor Rose living in such a hostile environment."

Molly was flabbergasted. "Ned, have you taken leave of your senses?"

"No, it's just I like to see some good in everyone and I think maybe she has been judged too harshly."

"Humph, as far as I can see the hostility is of her own making. There's nothing to stop her from behaving in a respectable and acceptable manner. She should feel honoured to be the wife of a headmaster. And as for that dog! Well, what more can I say?"

She shook her head angrily, picked up her knitting, removed the ball of wool from the ends of the needles and proceeded to knit with vigour.

Tired of the mud-slinging, Ned purposely changed the subject. "What time are you going to see Annie?"

"Soon," said Molly, still tight lipped. "I want to finish the front of this pullover before I go and I've only a couple more rows to do now."

"In that case, if you don't mind, I'll go out and get some fresh air. I might even be able to find someone to go horse riding with me."

"Good idea. You run along then and I'll see you later when I've learned what Annie has to say."

Ned left the Inn and crossed the field to the paddock, hopeful of finding Sylvia with her four legged friends. He was not disappointed. As he approached the stables she was clearly visible inside, mucking out. He leaned on the old wooden door frame and watched as she tossed clean straw over the floor from the end of a pitchfork, completely oblivious of his presence, until the dust from the straw tickled his nose and caused him to sneeze.

"Ned," she squeaked, jumping back in alarm. "Good God, you startled me."

He pulled a handkerchief from his trouser pocket and wiped his nose. "Sorry. The sneeze came out of the blue."

With a shake of her head she continued to toss the straw. "Are you just passing by or have you become attached to the horses?"

"Well, actually, a bit of both. I was wondering since the weather's fine, if there was any chance of taking Winston out for a run. Actually, I exaggerate; it would be more of a walk, or at most a gentle trot."

Sylvia's face broke into a broad smile and she laughed. "I see. Gertie told me you weren't the most accomplished of horsemen. But yes, of course you can take out Winston. You'd better not go alone though. I intended to take one of them out myself anyway, so just give me a few minutes to finish this and then we'll take them out together."

When the stables were neat and tidy with everything back in place, Sylvia saddled up the two horses and Ned opened the paddock gate. They then crossed the field into the valley, went along the hoof marked track and out onto the main road which ran through the village. By the school they turned down the lane leading towards Long Acre farm.

"Have you been up to the old mine yet?" Sylvia asked, raising her hand to greet an elderly cyclist wheeling his bicycle as he neared the top of the hill.

"No, actually I haven't. I had every intention of going there on the afternoon of the terrific storm, but the wind had other ideas so I got no further than the Coastguard Cottages. The major speaks well of it."

"Quite rightly too. We'll go there today if you've no objections. It's always been a favourite spot of mine and somewhere I frequently visited when first I came to Cornwall."

They took a bridle path through green meadows and alongside freshly ploughed fields, lined with lifeless hedgerows and leafless trees. From the bough of a young elm tree, flocks of squawking starlings sat on every available branch.

"They have plenty to say for themselves," said Ned, amused by their noisy chatter.

"If you think that now, you should hear them before they go to roost. Hundreds of them flock together in the trees and make their presence very audible. I love them! They seem to have such human like characteristics."

Ned observed catkins swinging in the breeze from a hazel shrub close by the path. "I do believe there are real signs of spring at last," he commented, reaching out to touch the catkins. "Thank goodness. I've just about had enough of winter."

Sylvia smiled. "There are lambs in the fields of Long Acre Farm, so Gertie was telling me yesterday. I love the spring, but winter has

179

its charms too. In fact I really like all seasons and I'd hate to live anywhere where it was much the same all year round."

"Lambs," mused Ned. "Do you know, I don't think I've ever seen a real spring lamb? Not in the flesh. Isn't that dreadful?"

Sylvia nodded. "Yes, but that's the price you pay for city life. The countryside has so much more to offer. I love it."

As the fields gently sloped southwards, the sparkling blue sea became increasingly visible, stretching faraway beneath the sun's bright rays towards the distinct, clear line of the distant horizon.

"Look at that, Ned: isn't it beautiful? Like glitter sprinkled from above. And we have it right here on our doorstep, in our very own back garden, whenever we feel the need to see it."

At the final gate before the cliff path, they dismounted, tied the horses' reins to the large granite gate post and then walked along a short rugged track leading to the remains of the old mine.

Ned was very impressed. He craned his neck to see the top of the tall, round chimney standing alongside the ruins of the engine house. "It's really, really big, close up. Huge, in fact. I'm surprised as they always look pretty small from a distance."

Sylvia laughed. "And they were much bigger still in their heyday before they became sad relics." She lovingly slapped a large granite quoin. "Cast your mind back, Ned, and try to imagine what it must have been like up here then."

Ned turned and surveyed the magnificent coastline. "Hmm, rather nice. Idyllic, quiet and peaceful," he said, thoughtlessly.

"Quiet!" snapped Sylvia, her eyes wild with animosity. "Are you crazy? The sound of thudding stamps boomed out for miles around. It was anything but quiet and peaceful."

"Oh," said Ned, rather foolishly. The presence of Sylvia seemed to have addled his mind and slowed down his ability to think straight.

"And have you any idea what it must have been like underground during the last century?" she continued. Ned shook his head. "The shafts of this mine go right out beneath the sea. Conditions were very, very cramped, stiflingly hot, stuffy and airless. In fact, temperatures sometimes rose as high as one hundred and forty degrees Fahrenheit and often there was not enough air to keep even a miserable candle alight. In fact, many miners frequently put out their candles and worked in the dark purely to conserve air. And as if that wasn't enough, they worked in fear of rock falls and explosions! Many of the men developed tuberculosis, bronchitis, rheumatism and God only knows what else. By the time they reached the age of forty, they were clapped out wrecks. It was a terrible, terrible life!"

"Sorry," said Ned, surprised and cowed by her anger, "I should have known better. The beauty up here clearly belies the horrors down below."

Sylvia sat down on the tussocks of grass, leaned back against the old granite wall, removed her headscarf and shook her hair free. Ned sat down beside her but did not dare get too close.

She half smiled, her anger having partly subsided. "I'm sorry," she said, reaching out to pat his arm. "I shouldn't have snapped at you like that. It was very unkind of me, but it makes me so angry when I hear people, like yourself, make such silly comments. It was old Josh who told me about the horrors of mining. He lost several of his friends in dreadful accidents. I can see why you were misled, though, because in spite of this mine's gruesome past and history, it is very beautiful up here and this is my most favourite spot in the whole wide world. That's why, paradoxically, in spite of all I've said, when I am gone, I should like my ashes to be scattered up here."

Ned scowled. "Oh, for God's sake, no. Don't speak of death, especially on such a lovely day. There has been enough of it lately with the on-going Jane mystery."

Sylvia rose as the colour drained from her face. She walked towards the cliff's edge and looked down below where the waves repeatedly crashed onto the rocks. "Poor, silly Jane," she muttered, her eyes tinged with tears.

"Silly?" mumbled Ned, rising to stand by her side. "Why silly?"

Sylvia turned to face him. "Because she died, Ned. And because I'm sure whatever it was that caused her death, it could well have been prevented. Just as Denzil would still be alive and with us today had he not chosen to go to sea when there was a bad forecast. So many bad things in life, it seems, could be avoided with just a little more forethought."

Ned nodded, thoughtfully. "So true."

"Jane was a very dear friend as well as a very good and much liked worker."

"So I've heard. May I ask what your theory is regarding the mirror episode? That's if you have one."

Sylvia laughed. "The mirror! I think it must have been a prank, albeit a very tasteless prank. Someone has a warped sense of humour and takes great pleasure in seeing others running around like headless chickens. What do you make of it all?"

Ned shrugged his shoulders. "I don't know. Remember I'm a stranger here and therefore I don't think it's fair for an outsider such as myself, to comment. What's more, I never knew Jane."

"No, of course not." She looked at her watch. "I ought to be getting back."

"Must you?" Ned asked, disappointed by the abrupt end to the excursion.

"Yes. I've a hundred and one things to do, although I really would much rather stay here a little longer."

Reluctantly, Ned walked with her to where the horses grazed on clumps of grass. They then rode back to the village together. On their return Gertie was waiting outside the stables.

She smiled brightly. "Ah, there you are. Frank sent me down to tell you there have been a couple of enquiries this morning about room bookings for Easter. He's taken the telephone numbers and wants you to call them back as soon as possible."

"Right," said Sylvia, dismounting. "In that case, Gertie, if you'll help Ned with the horses, I'll go straight back now."

She handed the reins of Brown Ale to Gertie and Ned watched as she crossed the field back to the Inn.

"Which way did you go?" Gertie asked, leading both horses towards the stables.

"What?" mumbled Ned, realising she had spoken.

Gertie repeated her question.

"Sorry. We went down the lane by the school, over the fields and then up to the old mine. It's really nice there."

Gertie laughed. "Well, yes, of course. I know that. I am after all very well acquainted with our local beauty spots and the old mine's not far from our farm."

She unsaddled the two horses as they drank thirstily from the trough.

Ned walked towards, and then leaned on, the five bar gate. In the distance he saw a solitary figure crossing the field in the valley and heading towards the Vicarage.

"There goes Sid. No doubt on his way to visit the beautiful Meg."

Gertie crossed to Ned's side. "Hmm, that's right. Meg always goes home during the school dinner break. But how do you know about Meg and Sid?"

Ned grinned. "Frank let it slip out the other night and he got a right scolding from Sylvia for doing so. I know they are engaged too. But don't worry, I've not told anyone. No-one other than Mother that is."

Gertie giggled. "Trust Frank! But they're not officially engaged yet. Not until Friday, when it will be announced at Meg's twenty first birthday party. Mind you, I think quite a few people have guessed already."

"Will the party be at the Inn?" Ned asked, hopefully.

"No, it's at the Vicarage. It's only going to be a quiet affair, just family and close friends."

"I see. I hear Meg spends a great deal of time looking after her invalid mother. I suppose that's why I've hardly seen anything of her."

"Yes, it's all very sad really. Pearl, that's Meg's mum, was a beautiful lady before the accident. She was the life and soul of the church. Everyone liked her and she'd do anything for anyone. And now she has an ugly scar across her face, she's confined to a wheelchair and doesn't go out much at all."

Ned was intrigued. "So what happened? What sort of accident was it?"

"She was knocked off her bike while cycling home from a W.I. meeting one evening last summer. Poor thing. She injured her back badly and spent a month in hospital."

"How awful," said Ned, wondering what W.I. stood for. "So who, or what, knocked her off?"

Gertie's look was one of disdain. "A car. A car driven by Albert Treloar. It's rumoured he was drunk at the time."

"Good God!" said Ned, shocked. "For some reason I've never liked that man."

Gertie laughed. "He wasn't very popular last summer with anyone here either, I can tell you that. Gradually though, most people have forgiven him, including the vicar and his wife, so who are we to bear a grudge? And he was very, very sorry. In fact he lay off the booze for a whole month while she was in hospital."

"I take it, he'll not be on the party guest list, then."

Gertie laughed. "No, I shouldn't think so."

"Are you going?"

"Oh, yes! Betty, Meg and I were at school together. The lads will be going too. Percy and Peter that is."

Ned sighed. "So Jane would also have gone, had she still been alive?"

Gertie nodded. "Yes, of course. Poor Jane was a bit older than Betty, Meg and me, but she was still one of our set and she'd definitely be there. I feel ever so bad over what happened to Jane. I mean, I really did think she might be, well, you know, pregnant. She wasn't quite herself, you see, in the days before she disappeared. She seemed distant and sorta vague. It might have been my imagination, of course, but she definitely wasn't her usual bubbly self, and for that reason I assumed she was worried about something. A baby seemed the obvious conclusion."

Ned found Molly in her room when he arrived back at the Inn. She was busy casting on for the back of the pullover. She lay the knitting down promptly on her lap as he closed the door.

"How was Annie's little boy?" Ned asked.

"Fine, fine. His arm's not broken, thank goodness. Just sprained. But you'll never guess what?"

"Sorry," said Ned, confused. "I'm not sure what you mean."

"The mirror!" said Molly, excitedly. "When I saw Annie she gave me a big hug and said what a brilliant idea it was to write that message on the mirror. Well, I thought she was boasting at first, but then realised she was paying us a compliment. She was dumbfounded when I said we hadn't done it, because neither had she. Do you realise what this means, Ned? If it wasn't Annie and it wasn't us, then someone else around here must have reason to believe Jane was murdered."

Chapter Twenty-Two

The mirror's eerie accusation which had occurred during the Beetle Drive, consequently provided the villagers with ample ammunition with which to communicate frequently with each other about its sinister implications. And Ned, Molly and Annie, all eager for any helpful clues or useful information, mingled with people, whenever and wherever they could to eavesdrop on any conversation from which they might learn the nature of the latest suppositions.

Annie listened intently outside the school playground each day, and looked forward to forthcoming meetings of the Mother's Union and the Women's Institute. Ned kept his ears to the ground each morning when he collected his paper from the post office and Molly chatted to all the women with whom she had become acquainted since her arrival in Cornwall.

All sorts of theories were debated and discarded as to why someone felt it necessary to take the life of an amicable and harmless person such as Jane. But for all the chatter and gossip, none of the locals could come up with a believable suspect, or even an over imaginative motive.

"What does Fred make of all this?" Molly asked, as she sat drinking coffee with Annie in The Police House on Thursday morning.

Annie sighed deeply and shook her head. "He has no idea who's responsible for the writing on the mirror but is reluctant to put a stop to the tittle-tattle in case there's any truth in any of it. It's all very odd, I must admit, and it's making me feel very edgy."

Molly agreed. "Same here, I feel most uneasy. Someone other than us obviously suspects foul play and I'd really like to know just what they've found out. In fact right now, I'm as keen to find out who wrote on the mirror as I am as to know who killed Jane. It obviously wasn't the murderer, unless of course, he's tuppence short of a shilling."

"But if someone knows something, why haven't they been to the police?" asked Annie. "Unless of course we've another medium in the village and Jane's been chatting with them too." Annie laughed. "Like you, they wouldn't dare report it, would they? Because they'd be labelled quite crazy."

Molly chortled, but had to admit, even the possibility of that couldn't be ruled out.

On Thursday evening, the Inn was surprisingly busy and so Ned and Molly, knowing that Annie would not be in, took it upon themselves to eavesdrop amongst the locals, a task Molly thoroughly enjoyed.

"It's quite amazing the twaddle some people talk when they've had a drink or two," she whispered to Ned, having just listened to a conversation between Larry, Des and Harry the Hitman. "Larry reckons one day there'll be a tunnel going out underneath the English Channel linking this country with Europe. Did you ever hear anything so daft?"

"Well, I don't see that it's an impossibility," said Ned, thinking of the mine shafts running beneath the sea bed. "And it has been talked about for years. But to be honest, I can't see any virtue in such a venture. I mean, surely the fact Britain is an island was to our advantage during the War."

"Quite right," agreed Molly. "And let's hope it always stays that way."

After a while the noise in the bar was too loud to hear without straining and making eavesdropping look obvious, and so Molly happily joined the major in the corner of the snug.

Ned went to refill his glass and found Reg Briers leaning against the bar. He felt uncomfortable as he recollected events from Tuesday night and Reg immediately picked up the vibrations. He smiled. "Please don't feel embarrassed just because you've met my dear wife, Ned. She's really quite harmless and her bark is far worse than her bite."

Ned, not knowing what to say, gave a false laugh and grinned foolishly.

"A pint for the lad please, Frank," called Reg. "And I'll have a refill too."

"Thanks," said Ned, finally finding his tongue.

"Rose isn't a happy woman," continued Reg. "That's why she's so argumentative. Although on Tuesday I think she had good cause. She may have her faults, bless her, but telling lies isn't one of them and she'd never make a statement like the one on the mirror unless she had very good reason to do so."

"But why doesn't she get on with anyone?" Ned asked, sipping his beer. "Why all the bad feeling, and how on earth did it start in the first place?"

Reg sighed. "Well, I suppose that's partly my fault. She thought being a headmaster's wife would be exciting and if I'm honest I probably painted too bright a picture for her about life down here. She'd never been to Cornwall before we met. She didn't really even know where it was. We met in Blackpool, you see: that's where she was born and bred, so she was used to bright lights and the rest of it, a sharp contrast to dear Trengillion. Poor Rose, she'd not been here more than a fortnight when she overheard a couple of women making spiteful comments about her hair. She turned on all women after that and it's just gone from bad to worse."

"Oh dear, I saw on Tuesday night there was no love lost between Rose and the local females. But she doesn't seem to have a problem with the men."

Reg laughed. "No, no, she doesn't. She flirts with them just to annoy their wives and sweethearts. I've tried to get her to stop, but she says it's the only bit of fun she gets from life."

Reg left just after nine thirty. He was not one to over indulge in the consumption of alcohol, especially on weekdays. The most important things in his life were the school, the education of his young pupils and, Ned surmised, his bizarre wife.

Not wanting to remain in the bar after his brief conversation with Reg, for its content had left him feeling somewhat down-hearted, Ned feigned a headache, calmly made his exit and walked along the passage to the hallway.

At the foot of the stairs he was met by a hissing, yowling Barley Wine, who flew past him with black fur standing on end and his tail resembling the bristles on a chimney sweep's brush.

"Mind out, you dozy ragbag," Ned muttered, smiling sadistically at Barley Wine's obvious discomfort as he fled down the passage.

He turned back towards the stairs.

"I hate cats," whispered a low, familiar voice, breaking up the consequent silence.

Ned grabbed the old oak newel post and cast his eyes rapidly around the hallway. "Jane, is that you?"

"Yes, 'tis none other than me."

Ned squinted and peered into the dark shadows. "Where exactly are you?"

"I'm sitting on the staircase under the picture of Saint Michael's Mount and I'm waiting for you."

Ned climbed part way up the stairs. "Where on earth have you been all this time?" he hissed, in hushed annoyance, after first checking there was no-one around. "I've so many questions I need you to answer."

She giggled. "I've been here, there and everywhere."

"Really! Well, while you have been, here, there and everywhere, a new development has occurred. So stay put wherever you might be now and don't you dare move."

She giggled. "By development, do you mean the message on the mirror?"

"What! How do you know about that?" he asked, frustrated because she was not visible and he felt daft talking to someone whose presence was not evident.

"I know all about it, because I did it. Aren't you pleased with me, Neddy?"

"You!" Ned choked, deeply shocked, and forgetting to keep the volume of his voice low. "But I don't understand."

"Oh dear, why not? After all it's very simple, really."

"Humph, then you'd better explain."

"Okay. Well, the other afternoon, Sunday I think it was, as you lay on your bed looking up at the ceiling, you said, 'Jane, Jane, if only you would be more helpful.' So I did as you asked and helped."

"I don't believe what I'm hearing," said Ned, unsure whether to laugh or cry. "In my wildest dreams I would never have guessed it was you! And what were you doing in my room anyway?"

"Well, it was me and I was in your room because I popped in to see how you were, nothing more. Anyway, that's not the reason I've been sitting here waiting for you tonight. I'm here now because I have something very, very important to tell you."

Ned groaned, dreading what news she might have to impart. "Go on then. I'm all ears. Please enlighten me."

Ned felt her voice softly whisper close to his ear. "I want to you know that destiny will now run its course, and to warn you, Ned, that whatever happens, you must never, never, never, lose heart."

"What!" Ned spluttered, angrily thrusting forth his arm in an attempt to touch her. But it was too late. The inevitable had happened. She was gone.

"Women!" groaned Ned, as he blundered up the rest of staircase. "They even talk twaddle when they're dead!"

Ned slept badly that night. Jane, Sylvia and Rose invaded his dreams causing him to wake frequently, perturbed and distressed. At half past six he arose, took a bath, shaved and waited patiently in his room for breakfast time.

Molly was late coming down. She and the major had had a late night. Had he been in a better frame of mind, Ned would have told his mother about his meeting with Jane the previous evening. As it was he couldn't be bothered. Gertie, waiting on the tables, was very happy, extra bubbly and irritatingly giggly. Her voice jarred Ned's nerves.

"Women!" he grumbled, "God! They really are annoying me this morning."

Ned strolled through the village for his daily newspaper. Women were gossiping inside the post office and gossiping outside the school. He walked down to the beach, where two women had the audacity to be sitting on Denzil's bench! Ned felt he had to get away. He returned to the Inn, threw his unread newspaper in the chair and changed his clothes.

Claude, the old fisherman grinned down from his frame. Ned felt sure he was laughing in a mocking manner. He seized the frame and turned the portrait round to face the wall. "You can stay like that until I get back," he scolded, as though talking to a badly behaved pupil. He then left the room and banged the door shut behind him.

He left the Inn and strutted across the field to the paddock where he sat down on the old stone wall. The sun shone brightly and the birds sang tunefully.

"Thank God! No women!" he chuntered to a blackbird, unaware it was a female, busy gathering twigs to build her nest.

He took from its packet a cigarette and lit it. For five whole minutes, Ned relaxed and felt almost content until he saw, coming across the field, a figure in the distance. "Sylvia!" he groaned.

Confident she had not seen him, he jumped down onto the grass inside the paddock and crept alongside the wall towards a thick hawthorn bush. Behind the bush he hid. Through a small gap in the glossy, green foliage of thick ivy entwined around the bare hawthorn branches, he watched Sylvia as she opened and closed the five bar gate. She then went into the stables and let Winston and Brown Ale out into the paddock. Ned kept very still. He didn't want to attract the attention of the horses and give away his hiding place, for how could he possibly explain his actions, if Sylvia were to find him hiding behind a hedge? Ned frowned. Why was he hiding behind a hedge?

"This is crazy," he muttered, rising. "I'm behaving like I'm half sharp. Women are driving me nuts."

He clambered out from behind the bushes, brushed down his clothing and marched proudly, upright towards the stable door. Once there, he looked inside, but there was no sign of Sylvia. He searched around, just as he had done the time before. She was nowhere to be seen.

From above, Ned heard a muffled cough, followed by a creak and rattle near the rafters. Quickly, he glanced towards the top of a wooden ladder propped against the back wall of the stable. To his amazement he saw a beam of torch light flash against the roof of the building. Someone was coming up from some sort of concealed place. Ned did not wait to see who, or what, but fled from the stable and returned to the safety of his hiding place behind the hawthorn bush.

Five minutes later he saw Sylvia emerge from the stable. She did not even look at the horses but headed straight for the gate. She left the paddock and walked back across the field towards the Inn. Beneath her arm she carried a red biscuit tin. Puzzled, Ned watched until she was out of sight.

Chapter Twenty-Three

Completely bewildered by that he had just witnessed, Ned crept back inside the stables. The old wooden ladder had moved and was lying on the floor alongside the wall directly opposite the horse's stalls. With a pang of excitement, he scurried to the door and peered outside to make sure no-one was about. The coast was clear. He crossed to the ladder, picked it up and leaned it against the back wall in exactly the same position as he'd seen it a short time before. With caution, he then climbed up the rungs until he was able to see the top of the wall. Amazed by its depth - between three and four feet - he glanced in both directions. At equidistant intervals rested the ends of five large, wooden roof trusses.

He climbed up another rung. Between two trusses, part hidden amongst rubble, dry earth and cobwebs, he spotted a rusty metal sheet. Ned lifted it, peeped beneath, and saw four wooden boards. He felt a pang of excitement. Were the boards covering the entrance of a secret tunnel or passage? Charged with enthusiasm, he pushed aside the metal sheet and carefully propped it behind the nearest roof truss. With heart thumping loudly, he then attempted to lift one of the boards, but to his dismay, it would not budge. He tried another, it too would not move. Puzzled, he ran his hands over the boards. Towards the back he felt a heavy metal bolt. He climbed up another rung, stretched across and slid back the bolt. To his delight, he discovered the boards were firmly joined together to create a small trap door.

Light-headed by the thrill of his discovery, Ned eagerly lifted the trap door. Beneath was a rectangular hole, edged with decaying wood which he estimated to be about twenty inches by thirty in size.

He peered inside, but with no light, could see nothing. Without hesitation, he scuttled back down the ladder to get the torch he recalled seeing hanging from the wall beside the saddles. Before returning to his discovery, however, he crept out to the back of the stables to view the building from outside. Along the edge of the paddock was a steep bank into which the stables were built. Hence from outside, no back wall was visible and the top of the bank was level with the guttering on the roof.

Fascinated, Ned hurried back inside, climbed the ladder and shone the torch into the hole. A few dirty, granite steps appeared in the beam of light. Intrigued, Ned clambered on top of the wall, tucked the torch beneath his chin and gradually lowered himself inside. When his feet reached the solidity of granite, he slowly climbed down the steep, narrow steps, steadying himself with both hands on the wall, until his feet touched firm ground below.

Once he felt stable, he let go of the wall, grabbed the torch and quickly flashed it around his surroundings. As anticipated, he found he was in a tunnel or passage, but its dimensions barely provided sufficient headroom for the average size person to stand upright, and the walls were no more than four feet apart. Ned shivered, the tunnel was cold, airless, claustrophobic and musty.

After brief consideration and against his better instincts, Ned decided to explore in order to establish whether the passage actually led anywhere or if it was nothing more than a secret hidey hole. Hence, it was with a feeling of unease, he tore himself away from the comforting glimpse of light and the outside world, and left behind the open trap door.

Treading carefully on the uneven floor of loose earth and rubble, he warily made his way along the dark passage. Almost immediately it began to slope steeply downhill.

The damp walls and roof were held back by old timbers, many of them rotten and decaying in parts. Ned had no idea where the passage might lead, but he sensed he was deep inside the bank which ran along the back of the stables.

Eventually, the tunnel narrowed. The height dropped to less than four feet. Ned bent himself double, determined to persevere and with difficulty stumbled on until he found his way blocked by a pile of stone and earth. He cursed, assuming the obstruction was the result of a roof fall.

Relieved, yet also disappointed that he could go no further, he reluctantly began to make his way back, quietly confident that he had found the passage used by smugglers in a bygone age, and no doubt the very passage which for many years, school children and grown-ups alike had unsuccessfully sought.

As he stumbled over damp, rocky earth, eager to breathe in fresh air, Ned decided, he must, on his return to the Inn, read Frank's books meticulously, before contemplating another visit to his new found discovery, to see if any made reference to the tunnel.

Ned's pace quickened as the five granite steps appeared in the beam of torch light, for he was eager to get back outside. And then suddenly it struck him that no natural light was showing from the trap door above. Alarmed, he ran towards the steps and climbed them with haste, only to discover the trap door was closed. Presuming it had dropped shut accidentally, he pushed against it. It did not move. He tried again and again using all his strength, but it would not budge. Ned froze, realising someone must have closed the door and bolted it.

Deeply annoyed, he sat down on the cold bottom step, held his head between his hands and cursed. He was a prisoner, there was no other way out. Agitatedly, he stood up, frantic questions racing through his mind. How was he ever to set himself free? Who on earth had trapped him in? And furthermore, was it deliberate? As far as he was aware, the only person who knew of the passage was Sylvia. And why would she ever want to visit it anyway? The place was quite empty. Ned then remembered the red biscuit tin which she had carried beneath her arm. Had she taken it from the passage or was it something which had lain in the stables? Ned didn't know, and at that particular moment, didn't really care.

He climbed the steps and tried the trap door again. It still would not move. In frustration, he thumped it hard, swore bitterly and desperately cried out for help. His call generated no response. Finally, accepting defeat, he knew he had no choice other than to make his way back along the tunnel.

Feeling sick and disheartened, he stumbled through his gloomy surroundings, over the rubble and loose earth, until eventually he reached the uncomfortable, cramped spot where the roof had fallen in. He groaned. It looked as though the only possible way of escape was to dig through the rubble, and even then it was likely the tunnel might lead to a dead end.

Ned began to pull away at the heap of stones and earth. In doing so a little more fell from above. Afraid and disheartened, he switched off the torch to conserve the battery and rested to restore his strength.

Five minutes passed by, but to Ned it seemed like five hours. He willed himself to try again on a different part of the roof fall. He must not give up. Carefully, he pulled away the stones and dropped them into a heap by his feet. More earth and rubble fell, revealing a large, oblong stone. Inspired, Ned calculated if he could make a hole big enough to climb through beneath the large stone, then it might act as a lintel and hold back the rubble above.

Fired up with hope and enthusiasm, he pulled out stones and handfuls of earth, until he'd made a large opening. Holding his breath he pushed his hand through the gap. To his delight there appeared to be nothing on the other side, thus indicating the roof fall was relatively small.

Much cheered, he continued to work until he was confident there was sufficient room to squeeze through. Ned peered into the hole to see what lay beyond but could see nothing as it was quite dark. With the torch he looked again. The other side appeared much like that along which he had already walked. With relief and a little optimism, he removed his jacket and pushed it through the gap. He heard it drop on the other side. Clutching the torch and holding his breath, he carefully, so as not to disturb the fragile sides, slid himself through the opening.

To his relief, he reached the other side with considerable ease but he was still unable to stand upright as the tunnel's height was little more than three feet. As he picked up his jacket, he heard a rumble overhead. In panic he stumbled away from the roof fall and fell flat on his back.

Ned laughed, much amused, as he realised the source of the noise. The tunnel obviously ran beneath Pat Dickens' lane at the foot of the cliff path and the roof fall was, no doubt, a result of the road collapsing during the storm.

Ned picked himself up and brushed down his trousers. If he was correct in his surmise regarding Pat's road, then he was not far away from the sea. This meant there was no question as to why the tunnel existed. It was most definitely the handiwork of smugglers. But why would Sylvia know about it? She was not of Cornish birth and had reputedly only been in the area for a few years!

"Someone else must be in on this secret," whispered Ned. "But who?"

He put his jacket back on and continued to stumble along the passage. At one point the roof was so low he had to crawl through on his stomach. But then to his joy it suddenly became wider, a glimmer of light shone in the distance, his ears were met by the sound of tumbling waves and he was able to breathe in the fresh smell of seaweed and salt water. Further on, the stones beneath his feet gradually turned to dry sand and the tunnel opened out into a cave. Ned shuddered as it dawned upon him where he was. In the Witches Broomstick and the very cave where poor Jane's remains had been found.

Relieved, yet saddened, he walked out into the welcome sight of daylight. The sun was still shining and he was grateful for the little warmth it provided. He brushed the earth from his clothes, took in a deep breath and washed his hands in a shallow rock pool.

Above him towered the sheer side of the high cliff. Its perpendicularity clearly showing there was no way he could possibly climb his way out. Ned ambled down to the water's edge. Swimming was not an option either. He shouted for help, hoping someone might hear on the cliff path above. No-one acknowledged his cry. He sat down on a rock and looked at his watch. It was twenty minutes past three.

Ned's stomach rumbled. He was hungry and wished he had eaten more breakfast instead of sulking over women. Women! What he'd give to see one of them now. Though perhaps not Sylvia. He did not think he wanted to see her.

He remained sitting on the rock until his backside felt numb, and then walked around on the wet sand to stretch his legs. The tide was coming in and the sun was slowly creeping behind the high cliffs above.

Ned realised the chance of him being found before nightfall was nil. It would not be until he failed to appear for dinner that the alarm would be raised. His mother would begin to worry. Gertie too perhaps, although her head would more likely be filled with hopes and anticipations for the party at the Vicarage. Molly would tell the major he had been in a foul mood during breakfast and the major would undoubtedly conclude Ned had gone off in a huff and would return eventually when in a better frame of mind.

If only he had told his mother where he was going. If only he had told someone. As it was, no-one would know where to look, except the person who had deliberately trapped him in the tunnel.

As the light finally faded and night fell, Ned crept back inside the cave. He had gathered together a few bits of dry seaweed and lumps of driftwood. He carefully piled them in a little heap and attempted to start a fire. The seaweed lit, smouldered briefly for a few seconds, and then went out.

In despair, Ned lit his last cigarette, sat down on the dry sand and leaned back against the wall of the cave.

What if no-one ever found him?

He thought of Jane, and suddenly realised why she had been found in the Witches Broomstick. She too must have come along the tunnel. If he was right and the roof fall had occurred as a result of the storm, then nothing would have obstructed her pathway.

But why would she have been in the tunnel?

A shiver ran down Ned's spine. Perhaps, she had been poisoned as she claimed, and her body dumped in the tunnel behind the stable, where the villain who had administrated the poison, hoped it would never be found. If so, maybe she had not been dead, but just unconscious, and on coming round had found the strength to crawl along the passage.

Ned felt sure he was right. It made sense. But how could anyone have carried her up the ladder and dropped her into the entrance of the tunnel. Even someone as petite as Jane was reputed to be, would have been difficult to manoeuvre as a dead weight.

"It must have been someone very strong," thought Ned, as he racked his brains to think who it might be. He guessed most of the farmers and fishermen were pretty muscular. Harry the Hitman too.

Ned pulled his jacket tightly round his chilled body, thankful he had on Molly's warm pullover. He tried to sing and cheer himself. It worked for a while but his throat soon became hoarse.

He craved a drink of water, or better still a pint of beer.

Ned shone the torch on his watch. It was ten minutes past ten. The party at the Vicarage would be in full swing and his mother would be frantic with worry at the Inn.

His eyes began to feel heavy. If he could sleep it would pass away some of the time. Ned yawned as he tried to recall Jane's last words.

What was it she had said?

He remembered. It was, 'Never, never, never lose heart'.

He had been cross with her at the time, but as he sat, a lonely, unhappy figure, he realised it made sense. 'Never, never, never lose heart'.

"I won't," he muttered. And gradually he fell asleep, unbeknown to him, on the very spot where Jane had breathed her last breath.

Chapter Twenty-Four

On Friday morning, Molly, unaware of her son's impending misfortune, went to Ivy Cottage for a coffee and homemade scones. Doris had invited her round when they had bumped into each other outside the village hall earlier in the week. Molly, who entertained Doris with her stories, observations and gossip, was always a welcome guest at Ivy Cottage, and as the two women had discovered they had a lot in common, the chat was not entirely one sided.

On this particular occasion the time slipped by unnoticed, and Doris insisted that Molly also stay for lunch, hence it was mid-afternoon before she returned to the Inn. Having not seen Ned since breakfast, she tapped gently on the door of his room. There was no reply. Instinctively, she peeped inside. Ned was not there, but his folded newspaper lay in the chair and the portrait of the old fisherman hung with his face to the wall.

Molly smiled. It was evident Ned had left his room in much the same mood as she had found him during breakfast.

She closed the door and happily returned to the warmth of her own room. And as she had nothing planned, she made up the fire and began to read a book which Doris had loaned her.

Later, when Molly went down to dinner, she expected Ned to be already seated in the dining room. She was surprised, therefore, when she saw his empty chair. The other guests arrived, but Ned was not amongst them.

The major noticed her unusual lack of vivacity.

"Anything wrong, Moll?" he asked, concerned. "You look a bit glum."

She frowned. "It's Ned. I expected him to be here. I've not seen him since breakfast."

"Hmm. Probably gone for a long walk and lost all track of time. You know what these youngsters are like."

Molly forcing a smile. "Yes, maybe."

Gertie bustled in with the soup. Her eyes sparkled. Thoughts of the party were clearly all that occupied her mind. She stopped when she found Molly alone.

"Oh, where's Ned?" she asked, bluntly, clutching two bowls of steaming winter vegetable.

Molly shook her head. "I don't know. Have you by any chance seen him at all today?"

Gertie shrugged her shoulders. "Not since breakfast and he were in a right mood then, weren't he?"

Molly did not answer. Gertie put down just one bowl of soup and gave the other to the major.

After dinner, on the insistence of the major, Molly went into the bar. He deemed a double gin would make the situation more tolerable. Reluctantly, she sat down in the corner of the snug, where he handed her a full glass.

The evening dragged on. Molly frequently rose to look at the clock above the fireplace. Everyone who came in she questioned about possible sightings of Ned. Larry and Des had seen him, but only briefly, on the beach before they had gone out to sea.

Various suggestions were made as to his possible whereabouts, such as a trip into town or a visit to the pictures. Molly was not convinced by any of the conjured up theories. All were totally out of Ned's character.

Just before eight, Sylvia breezed into the bar wearing a beautiful, pale blue dress. The major's eyes lit up as he waited at the bar for the pint Frank was pouring.

"Is Cinderella going to the ball?" he asked, smitten.

She laughed. "Only for a little while. I'll be at the Vicarage for no more than an hour as it wouldn't be fair to leave Frank to do all the work alone."

"You can stay as long as you like, love," Frank grinned. "I'm quite alright, as long as you're back in time to wash the glasses. I hate washing glasses."

Molly rose and looked from the snug doorway to see the cause of the frivolity. Sylvia's outfit made her gasp.

"Oh, I do like your frock," she said, approvingly. "What a beautiful colour. Is it new?"

Sylvia beamed with pride. "Thank you. Yes, I bought it today."

"What, in Cornwall? In Helston?"

"Yes, I got it in Abbott's. New stock in. It only arrived yesterday."

Molly smiled feebly. "I don't suppose you saw Ned in town by any chance, did you?"

"Ned! Why no," muttered Sylvia, baffled. "Should I have?"

Molly sighed. "No, I suppose not. It's just that he appears to have gone missing. No-one's seen him since this morning."

Sylvia frowned. "Really! How odd. But I expect he'll turn up. Don't worry."

But Molly did worry. She sipped her gin with little enthusiasm as the long evening dragged on. She felt uneasy. What if Ned had found out something about Jane's murder and landed himself in trouble? She wished there was someone in whom she could confide. The major was out of the question and she knew that Annie would be at Meg's party with Fred.

At closing time Molly left the bar in despair.

"If he's not back by morning I'm going to the police," she told the major, as they slowly climbed the stairs.

The major rested his hands on her shoulders. "And if that's necessary I'll escort you. Meanwhile, try and get some sleep, Moll."

Feeling miserable, she shuffled along the landing to her room. Once inside she closed the door and wearily sat in her chair beside the dying embers of the fire. In her mind she turned things over yet again. She knew something was wrong. Call it a mother's instinct, women's intuition or whatever you wanted, Ned was in trouble. Yet she could not go to the police before morning. Ned was a grown man, anyway. She was not responsible for his actions or his whereabouts. He was free to come and go as he pleased and that is how the police would see it.

She undressed slowly, neatly folded her clothes, laid them on the back of the chair and then slipped into her warm flannelette nightie.

With little enthusiasm, she tied back her hair, went through her rigorous beauty routine and then climbed into bed.

Molly thought sleep would be impossible, but she drifted off with ease. Her brain was tired. Her mind was cluttered. Sleep was a way of escaping the mental torment she was experiencing.

The following morning, she awoke at six o clock and remembered instantly that all was not well. She slid out of bed, put on her dressing gown and slippers and walked briskly down the passage to the bathroom. On her way back she stopped outside Ned's room and gently tapped on the door. There was no reply. She turned the handle quietly, crept inside and switched on the light. The room was just as she had seen it the previous day. Ned's bed had not been slept in and yesterday's Daily Herald lay unread in the drab, fireside chair.

Molly closed the door, returned to her room to dress and put on some make-up. To pass the time she raked through the ashes in her grate, screwed up a few sheets of an old newspaper and laid them on top of the clinkers. She then placed sticks of kindling wood, which she found tucked behind the coal scuttle, on top of the paper, and finally put on a few pieces of coal. From her handbag she took a box of matches and lit the newspaper in several places. Once the fire was burning nicely, she sat down beside it and read to while away the time.

At twenty minutes past eight, she went downstairs for breakfast. No-one else was in the dining room, so again she sat down alone.

Gertie brought in a pot of tea. Her eyes looked tired. The party had obviously been a success. She glanced at the empty chair.

"Still no Ned? she mumbled, attempting to stifle a yawn.

Molly shook her head and turned to face the wall to conceal her tears.

Gertie sighed sympathetically and returned to the kitchen.

Molly put a little milk into her teacup, removed the cosy from the brown earthenware pot and poured steaming hot tea onto the milk. She then picked up the teaspoon, stirred two lumps of sugar into the strong, brown liquid and watched as it swirled around in the blue and white striped cup.

She picked up the cup to warm her hands. She then closed her aching eyes, the swirling tea clearly imprinted on her eyelids. In her mind, the colour of the hot, brown liquid slowly transmogrified to the bluey green hue of the sea. Tumbling waves framed by a thick, murky haze drifted before her eyes. She was looking down from the cliff tops onto rolling seas, jagged rocks and rippled sand. Sand, on which stood the solitary figure of a young man. Molly gasped and opened her eyes. The cup dropped from her hands and tea spilled into the saucer. She had seen Ned. Clearly, she had seen Ned, looking lost and forlorn, standing on the water's edge.

Inspired by her foresight, she sprang to her feet and knocked over the chair on which she had been sitting. Feelings of hope and optimism pulsated through her body. She laughed with confidence. She knew where Ned was. Without hesitation, she fled from the dining room, down the passage into the hall, through the door and down the road towards the cove.

No-one was on the beach, but Percy and Peter were on the roadside tinkering with the engine of Peter's old van. Breathlessly, she ran towards them. "Please, please, help me," she cried.

Peter, alarmed by her wild appearance and strange behaviour, caught her as she stumbled on the uneven road. "What is it? Whatever's wrong?"

"It's Ned," she stammered, as the brisk south westerly wind ruffled her black hair. "He's trapped inside the Witches Broomstick!"

"Trapped in the Witches Broomstick," repeated Percy. "What the devil is he doing there? I don't understand."

"He went missing yesterday," gabbled Molly. "He's not been back all night but I know that's where he is. Please take me there in your boat. He must be rescued."

The two fishermen, bewildered and unable to comprehend all that Molly was trying to tell them, looked at each other and nodded. Peter then closed the bonnet of the van, and without asking further questions, both took the boat down to the water's edge, where they helped Molly on board before pushing the vessel into the frothy waves.

It was cold at sea. Molly pulled her cardigan tightly across her chest and folded her arms to keep warm as the little boat chugged and tossed on the lumpy waves around the cliffs and into the south westerly wind. The Witches Broomstick soon came into view and Percy skilfully steered the boat towards the entrance, avoiding rocks just visible beneath the shimmering water. When the vessel stopped, Peter, in the boat's bow, shouted through the narrow gap between the rocks which surrounded and formed the broomstick's handle.

"Ahoy, is anybody there?"

Above the sound of water gently lapping around the boat's wooden hull, they heard a faint, but distinct reply. Molly abruptly stood up. The boat rocked. Without waiting another minute, she clawed the slippers from her feet, flung them into the bottom of the boat and jumped overboard.

"Come back," yelled Percy, horrified. "Come back. Let me go."

But Molly, a superb swimmer, was away from the boat and through the gap between the rocks, before Percy had time even to untie his shoe laces.

The sight which greeted Ned as his mother emerged from the sea was one he vowed to remember for the rest of his life. Her wet, lank hair. Her tears. Mascara running down her pink cheeks and her favourite purple cardigan, heavy with salt water, hanging unevenly around her knees.

Screaming his name, she clambered over the shingle, onto the sand and into his open arms.

Percy emerged from the sea shortly after. "Good grief," he spluttered, seeing mother and son dancing on the wet sand. "You were right. What the devil are you doing out here, Ned?"

The three of them shivered in the early spring sunshine, all talking at once, asking each other questions through chattering teeth.

Peter, unable to see the gathering on the sand, called to them from the boat. Percy shouted back to say all was well.

"I think we'd better go," he said, "before we all freeze to death."

Ned looked alarmed. "But I can't swim."

Molly took his arm. "No problem. It's not far to the boat, so I'll take you. I did a life-saving course a while back."

"What! Where?" Ned asked, surprised.

"Clacton of course. I'm used to the sea, you know."

As the boat headed back to the cove, Ned told Molly, Percy and Peter what had happened. They listened in disbelief, although Ned deliberately omitted to mention Sylvia. He claimed he had found the tunnel by chance and his inability to get back out was an accident. He wanted to save Sylvia's involvement for the ears of Molly and Annie only.

Back ashore, Molly and Ned thanked the two fishermen profusely and assured them they were both alright before they returned indoors to get out of their wet clothing. Percy did likewise.

Thankfully no-one was around inside the Inn and so Molly and Ned were able to creep in unseen. Ned insisted his mother take a bath first and get herself into dry clothing whilst he went into his room and changed into his dressing gown. Not until both were warm, dry and sitting on the rug by the fire, did Ned tell his mother what had really happened. She listened in amazement. When she heard of Sylvia's involvement she was shocked.

"It's all too close for comfort," she said. "I would never have suspected Sylvia of being tied up in this."

"Me neither. But she may yet be innocent of any wrong doing."

"She knew about the tunnel leading to the Witches Broomstick," said Molly, "so was withholding evidence when the police were investigating Jane's death. She must have known all along how Jane had got to the Witches Broomstick."

"I agree, but I'm sure all is not what it seems," said Ned, eager to defend Sylvia, in spite of his doubts about her.

Molly rose to her feet. "I'm going to see Annie. Hopefully Fred will be out and I'll be able to see what she thinks we should do next."

"Good idea, and while you've gone I'll take forty winks. A cave is not the most comfortable place in which to spend a night."

"Feel free to lay on my bed. It's warmer in here than in your room. I'll be back as quick as I can."

She took her coat hurriedly from the wardrobe, left the room, slipped down the stairs, out of the Inn and round the corner into the village. On reaching The Police House she heaved a sigh of relief. Fred's car was not there, only his bicycle leaned on the garden side of the privet hedge, indicating he was not home.

She knocked eagerly on the front door. Annie answered and the two women went into the dining room.

"It's quiet here," said Molly, sitting down at the table.

Annie smiled. "Yes, it is. Fred has taken the children to stay with his parents for the weekend, to give us a break."

"That's nice. Where do they live?"

"Newquay."

"Very nice, and how's Jamie's arm?"

"Fine; I think the fuss was really over the initial shock. He seldom mentions it now. But what is it you want to tell me? I know there's something, it's written all over your face and your hair's wet."

Molly poured out the story she had heard from Ned about the previous day's events. Annie listened, stunned.

"So do you think Sylvia went back to the stables and shut Ned in?" Annie asked.

Molly sighed. "I don't know, I really don't know. I can't believe that she would and Ned did say he saw her walk back across the field. What's more, I know for a fact she went into town yesterday because she bought a new frock."

Annie nodded. "Yes, I know, she was wearing it last night."

"And she hasn't in any way been behaving oddly. Besides, why would she do such a thing?"

Annie sighed. "No reason at all as far as I can see. I reckon someone else must know about the tunnel, and that someone must be the person who poisoned Jane and hid her body down there."

"I'm inclined to agree. But whoever can it be?"

"What on earth are you two talking about?" asked a puzzled voice.

They quickly turned their heads. Fred was standing in the doorway and he'd heard nearly every word of their conversation.

Chapter Twenty-Five

As Molly was eager to get back to the Inn and talk further with Ned, she left Annie to explain to Fred everything that had happened regarding the mysterious circumstances relating to Jane's death. On her return, she found Ned still in her room, lying half asleep on top of the bed.

He raised himself onto one arm as she hurriedly entered the room and closed the door. "Back already. That was quick."

Molly hastily took off her coat. "Yes," she puffed. "Unfortunately, or fortunately as the case might be, Fred turned up and heard most of our conversation. I don't think it will be long now before he arrives here asking questions, because Annie will have no other choice than to tell him the truth."

Ned sat up, rubbed his eyes and swung his legs over the side of the bed. "Thank God for that. I feel it's time greater brains than ours were involved in this whole ghastly business. It needs someone with a bit of authority, a lot of know-how and hopefully some answers."

Molly sat down in the armchair and warmed her hands by the fire. "I couldn't agree with you more. But how are you feeling? You still look a bit peaky to me."

"I'm alright. A lot better anyway than I would be if I'd never been found. I must admit, I am rather hungry though. I've not eaten since breakfast yesterday morning and I used up a lot of energy last night just trying to keep warm."

Molly looked at her watch. "Hmm, and I didn't have breakfast today. I didn't even drink my tea. You wait here and I'll just pop downstairs and see if there's anyone in the kitchen."

She returned ten minutes later with two mugs of tea, four slices of hot buttered toast and a pot of ginger marmalade on a tray.

"I found Gertie and she made up this tray for us. Sylvia wasn't there, thank goodness. Apparently, she went out straight after breakfast to await a delivery of straw for the stables or something like that. It might have been awkward if she'd been there and started asking questions."

Ned eagerly took a slice of toast from the tray and spread it thickly with marmalade. "Did Gertie comment on the fact I've turned up alive and well? That's if she'd missed me, of course"

"Oh, she missed you alright, but I just made light of your return. She seems a bit vague this morning, anyway. I think she's suffering the after effects of a night out."

Ned raised his eyebrows. "Surely she didn't drink too much at the Vicarage."

Molly shrugged her shoulders. "I don't know about that. The vicar obviously likes a drink because I noted he had at least three pints of beer at the Beetle Drive."

A sudden sharp knock on the door made them both jump.

"Come in," said Molly, expecting it to be the major wondering why he had not seen her at breakfast. It was, however, Frank who peeped around the door, a quizzical look on his face.

"Molly. Fred Stevens is downstairs and he'd like a word with you and Ned, if that's alright."

"Yes, that's fine. Would you send him up please, Frank?"

"Course," he said. "I hope everything's alright."

Molly smiled nervously. She couldn't possibly even hint to Frank why the village police constable wanted to see her and Ned.

Fred listened to mother and son's account with great interest. It tied in exactly with that told to him by his wife, although he made it clear from the start that he was very sceptical about Ned's claim to have conversed with Jane's ghost.

"Do you feel strong enough to come with me to the stables?" he asked, intrigued by the notion of a tunnel. "I'd like to see this hidey hole for myself, before I report it."

"I'm fine," said Ned. "Now I've had forty winks and a bite to eat, I'm as right as rain."

Molly rose from the armchair and reached for her coat. "If you don't mind, Fred, I'd like to go too. I'm as curious as you to see the tunnel, despite the fact I have a horse phobia due to a fall from a pony when I was a nipper which resulted in a broken arm."

Ned was astounded. "I've never heard you tell that before."

"That's because recollection of it fills me with embarrassment. The pony was very small, you see, and it didn't even break out in a trot. I felt such an idiot at the time and if I'm honest, I still do." She shuddered. "I can still hear my friends laughing."

They found Brown Ale alone in the paddock, drinking from an old tin bath. Ned stroked him affectionately and then looked inside the stables where fresh bales of straw were piled inside the door. The ladder, he observed, was back in its rightful place. He hung the torch, which he'd had in his possession since the previous morning, back on the nail beside Brown Ale's saddle. Winston's saddle was missing. He assumed Sylvia had taken him out after the straw had been delivered.

He lifted the ladder, propped it up against the wall and climbed to the top. The sheet of metal was back over the trap door. He pushed it to one side and felt for the bolt. It was firmly in place, leaving him with no doubt, that someone had deliberately made him a prisoner. Ned slid back the bolt and lifted up the trap door. He peered into the dark, musty hole, shuddered, climbed down the ladder and reached for the torch.

"You'd better take this," he said, handing it to Fred. "It's as black as pitch down there."

Fred took the torch and climbed the ladder. At the top he switched it on and flashed it over the dirty granite steps.

He frowned. "Hmm, I don't think I'll be going in there. It looks grim to say the least and I'm none too fond of small, tight spaces. I think it best if I leave its examination to the experts."

He closed the trap door and pulled the metal sheet back over the top. Once he was safely on the ground, Ned removed the ladder and placed it back where it belonged, alongside the wall.

Ned scratched his head. "I wonder why the ladder's here. I mean to say, there's no use for it, is there? Other than to get up to the tunnel, that is. So who brought it here?"

Fred nodded. "Good point. I think it's time I asked around a bit and tried to find out just how many people know about this tunnel, and of course why there's a ladder here. It seems to me that at present the only people in the know are you, Ned, and Sylvia."

"I wonder if Frank knows," mused Molly, watching a spider scuttle across the floor towards a scattering of straw.

Fred nodded. "So do I and I mean to find out."

As he spoke, they heard the thud of horse's hooves approaching. Assuming the rider to be Sylvia, Fred insisted they remain in the building out of sight. It was Sylvia. Her clear voice rang out uttering words of praise to Winston as she dismounted. Having minimised the chances of her giving him the slip, Fred confidently marched outside, followed by Ned and Molly.

Sylvia was taking the saddle from Winston's steaming back as he drank thirstily. She jumped when she saw the small party emerge from the stables.

"Fred, Molly, Ned, why on earth are you all here?"

Fred pulled a notebook and pencil from his pocket. "I think you know the answer to that, Sylvia."

Frowning, Sylvia walked into the stables, hung up Winston's saddle and then returned back outside. "No, no, I've not the foggiest idea. Perhaps you'll kindly enlighten me?"

"The tunnel," said Fred, opening up his notebook. "What can you tell me about the tunnel?"

Sylvia scowled. "Tunnel? I'm sure I don't know what you're talking about."

"Come on, Sylvia, let's not play games. Ned saw you come out of it yesterday, so you might as well tell me the truth."

Sylvia's eyes flashed and she glared angrily at Ned. "Have you been following me?"

Fred didn't give him a chance to reply. "Just answer me, Sylvia. If you've nothing to hide you can tell me about it. Honesty's always the best policy. Come on, tell me what you know."

Sylvia looked back at the stables. Her bottom lip quivered. "But I promised," she whispered. "I promised I'd never tell anyone!"

Fred's eyebrows rose sharply. "Promised. Promised who?"

"Must I say?"

"Yes, of course."

Sylvia sat down on an up-turned bucket and sighed deeply. "I don't suppose you have a cigarette, do you, Ned?"

He shook his head, conscious that her hands were trembling. Molly fumbled in her handbag, pulled out a packet of Embassy and offered one to Sylvia. She half smiled as Molly lit it for her. "Thanks."

Sylvia looked at Fred as smoke wafted from her mouth. "You remember Josh Gilbert, don't you?"

Fred nodded. "Of course I do. Nice old chap, a fisherman, who lived in the village all his life. He did odd jobs for you at the Inn after he'd retired."

Sylvia smiled. "That's right, and it was Josh who told me about the tunnel."

"Josh! But how come he knew about it. I mean to say, folks in the village have been looking for it for donkey's years. Why did he never tell anyone else?"

Sylvia eyes watered. "Because he was ashamed."

"Ashamed! Why? I'm confused. Perhaps you'd like to explain."

"Okay. It was last year when Josh was on his deathbed that I heard about the tunnel. Poor old Josh was delirious at times and kept muttering about his Great Uncle Claude. Having no idea who he was talking about, I asked who Claude was and so he told me.

Claude, I learned, was, as his title implies, Josh's great uncle. And he was already an old man when Josh was born. But nevertheless, they became very close. Josh used to visit his great uncle often as a boy and listen to tales of the sea. He lapped up all the old yarns and in his eyes Claude was a hero. But then one day, when Josh was about sixteen, he learned from another fisherman, that Claude was actually the son of Billy Gilbert, the notorious smuggler. Furthermore, Claude had followed in his father's footsteps, so to speak, on the wrong side of the law. At first Josh didn't believe it. He insisted it was a pack of malicious lies. And so he went to see his uncle to tell what he had heard. To his utter dismay, Great Uncle Claude confessed it was all true.

It was after Josh had learned the truth that Claude told him about the tunnel. Josh was horrified, but at the same time he *still* idolised his great uncle in spite of his dishonest ways. You see, up until he'd learned the truth he'd always believed Great Uncle Claude to be a retired, honest, hard-working fisherman. It had never occurred to him that he might do anything as corrupt as smuggling. Poor Josh. He was very religious, and it saddened him greatly to know he was related to the disreputable Billy Gilbert, of whom he'd heard plenty and had little regard. He confessed to me as he lay dying in order to clear his conscience. 'To prepare me for meeting the Lord,' he said.

And he begged me never to tell a soul about Claude's bad ways, or the tunnel, cos he didn't want his name blackened and people to think ill of him when he was gone." Sylvia burst into a flood of tears. "I feel so bad now," she sobbed. "You shouldn't have made me tell, Fred. I've broken a promise. I feel utterly untrustworthy."

Fred watched as she brushed aside the tears with her fingers. "I'm sorry, Sylvia, really I am, but I had to know."

"I've never breathed a word to anyone about the tunnel and Josh's unscrupulous ancestors," she whispered. "I've not even told Frank."

Fred leaned forward and patted Sylvia's shoulder affectionately. "You've done the right thing telling us and as far as I'm concerned I see no reason at all for anyone else to learn of Josh's secret."

"Thank you."

Fred held Sylvia's arm as she rose unsteadily from the up-turned bucket. "Just one more question. Have you ever been along the tunnel?"

She paused before speaking. "Yes, I must confess I have. Not often, just three times, or maybe four. The first was soon after Josh's death. I went out of curiosity, thinking it would be exciting. Although to be perfectly honest, I didn't really expect to find it and I was fascinated when I did. It's so cunningly hidden. I went inside to have a poke around but didn't go along very far. It's pretty miserable down there. Very claustrophobic with nothing to see but earth, wood and stone. To be honest, I couldn't wait to get back out again and into the fresh air."

Ned nodded in agreement.

"And the last time?" asked Fred.

Sylvia sighed. "Yesterday, when Ned must have seen me. You see, I was mucking out and thinking about Jane and her being at the Witches Broomstick. I, like everyone else was puzzled as to how she got there. Then I suddenly remembered the passage. Josh told me where it came out, so I thought I'd see if it would have been possible for Jane to have gone that way."

"And you found it blocked," said Ned.

"Yes, and I was very relieved as I didn't want to go any further." She shuddered. "Ugh, it was horrible. Cold, inhospitable and cheerless. When I realised Jane couldn't possibly have gone that way, I came back as quickly as I could."

"Had you found the tunnel not blocked, would you have told me?"

"Oh, Fred, of course I would. For although I'd have felt disloyal to Josh, I'd have accepted that helping Jane was a justifiable enough reason to betray him."

"Good. And so what did you do next?"

"Do next? What do you mean?"

"I mean after you came out of the tunnel yesterday."

"Oh, I see. Well, nothing really. I had other things on my mind."

Molly laughed. "Like buying a new frock."

For the first time since the questioning had begun, Sylvia smiled. "Well, yes, exactly. One has to get one's priorities right."

Fred sighed. "Do you think there's any chance that Jane might have known about the tunnel?"

Sylvia shrugged her shoulders. "If she did she never mentioned it to me and we rode the horses many times together from here."

Fred nodded. "Yes, I know she was a good horsewoman. Rack your brains, Sylvia, and see if you can think of anyone else who might know about the tunnel."

Sylvia shook her head. "I can't think of anyone, but then it's more than possible other people do know. I mean to say, Billy and Claude Gilbert weren't the only ones to smuggle around here and use this tunnel. They had numerous colleagues and henchmen, so I suppose it's feasible the descendants of any of them may have learned, just as Josh did."

Fred nodded and then closed his notebook. "Thanks Sylvia. I'm really sorry if I've upset you. But you do understand that I'm just doing my job."

"Of course. But why all this interest in the old tunnel all of a sudden? Is it because you thought it might lead to the Witches Broomstick?"

Ned spoke before Fred had time to open his mouth. "Partly. But, it's also because I went down there to have a look after I saw you come out and someone deliberately trapped me inside."

Sylvia gasped. "What! Oh my God, no. So that's why you weren't at dinner last night. How on earth did you get out?"

"I dug my way through the roof fall and walked to the Witches Broomstick. I was eventually rescued this morning by Peter, Percy and Mother."

"What! So you were there all night?"

"Yes."

Sylvia looked shocked. "How horrid! But surely you don't think it was me who shut you in?"

Ned shook his head.

"Did you find everything in its normal place this morning?" Molly suddenly asked.

Sylvia frowned. "In its normal place! Like what? I don't quite understand the question."

"Like the ladder," said Molly.

"The ladder! Well yes, I suppose so. I've not touched it this morning. I assume it's in its normal place."

"Ah, that reminds me," said Fred. "I do have one more question, Sylvia. Why is there a ladder in the stables, I can't see a use for it?"

Sylvia smiled. "Actually, it belongs to Harry Richardson and he left it here ages ago. You see, before Frank bought me Winston, he had the stables checked over by Harry to make sure it was in a reasonable state of repair. After all it hadn't been used for donkey's years. He found the roof leaked in a couple of places and so he cured it by giving the slates a cement wash, and for that of course he needed a ladder. I suppose he's long forgotten about it, even though Frank reminded him frequently after the roof was first done."

They all walked back to the Inn together, each deep in their own thoughts. Ned wanted to ask Sylvia about the red biscuit tin she had carried the previous day. Had she brought it up from the tunnel or had it been in the stables all along? He decided to say nothing, as it was probably of no consequence. And he would feel very foolish if it turned out to be a sandwich tin.

News of the tunnel spread like wildfire around the village, and once again, Jane's case was the main topic of conversation. Its discovery also caused everyone to revise their original beliefs as to how Jane came to meet her death. No longer were holiday makers or gypsies suspected of being involved: it had to be someone local, someone familiar with the history of the area. The cause of death was also a contentious issue. If Jane had been murdered, as the mirror claimed, and her body tossed into the tunnel, then how was it possible her remains were found half a mile away, at the other end, in the Witches Broomstick? It was common knowledge that her badly decomposed body bore no signs of violence. It was therefore supposed, she had not been dead when the trap door had closed so cruelly behind her. This then raised the question as to what kind of murderer would leave his task incomplete and by what method was her life supposedly taken? Suggestions of strangulation and suffocation seemed the most popular solutions, as in either case it was possible that death might look evident through loss of consciousness, and it was assumed her killer would be unlikely to hang around to make sure his mission was complete, for fear of being discovered. So the verdict was quite simple. Someone had strangled or suffocated Jane, hidden her body in the tunnel, where she had eventually regained consciousness. She then found herself trapped and walked until she got to the Witches Broomstick, and there she had died of starvation.

There were others though, who preferred still to believe it was an accident. Their verdict being she had gone into the tunnel after hearing about it from a source unknown, the door had slammed shut behind her and she had found herself trapped, much like that nice lad from up London. Except poor Jane didn't have a mother who was a medium, fortune teller or whatever Molly was, who knew where people were by simply looking into a cup of tea.

Molly's status rose dramatically in Trengillion following Ned's rescue, although lots of the locals, as a precaution, were careful what they thought when she spoke to them, just in case mind reading was another of her talents which had yet to come to fruition.

On Monday evening Gertie waited on the tables, a huge grin spreading from ear to ear.

"And what are you looking so happy about, young lady, may I ask?" smiled Molly."

"Can't tell you," she giggled. "It's a secret!"

Ned looked heavenward. Women and their secrets! He thought it unlikely she would be able to keep quiet for more than five minutes before blurting out that which she was quite obviously longing to reveal.

"Have you won a competition?" asked Molly.

"No."

"It's clearly something very nice. Are you learning to drive, perhaps?"

"Well, that wouldn't be too difficult as I can already drive tractors. But no, that's not it. Try again."

"You've got an exciting new job," said Ned, feeling he ought to make a contribution to the silly game.

Gertie held out her left hand to show a modest diamond ring. "I'm engaged to be married, but not officially until Wednesday. That's why I wouldn't tell."

Much to Gertie's delight, Molly was very surprised. "Really! So who's the lucky young man?"

Wringing her hands, Gertie blushed and giggled. "Percy! He asked me to marry him on Friday night at Meg's birthday party. I'm so happy, I could cry."

Molly raised her eyebrows, sharply. "I didn't even know you and he were going steady."

"That's cos we've not been. But we've known each other for years. All our lives in fact. I've always had a crush on him, and he on me, but he was sweet on poor Jane too. Anyway, on Friday night at the party he popped the question. He said he'd lost Jane for ever and couldn't bear the thought of losing me too. Isn't that romantic? We went to buy the ring this afternoon. I'm so happy!"

"Congratulations," said Ned, much dazed. "Percy's a decent chap. You'll make a nice couple."

She giggled. "Thank you. You know, Ned, when first you arrived here I thought perhaps you might be the one for me, but I soon realised I couldn't possibly even think of marrying a towny. I'd die if I didn't have grass beneath my feet and the sea on my doorstep!"

"That's very poetic, dear," said Molly, surprised.

Ned forced a smile, recalling, how not long ago, she been all over him. He watched her skip back happily to the kitchen and then plunged his spoon into the leek and potato soup.

"Women are so fickle!" he muttered beneath his breath.

On Wednesday evening Gertie and Percy had a small engagement party at the Inn. Most of the regulars were there along with their wives and sweethearts, all glad of an excuse to get together, let down their hair and catch up with the latest gossip. Sylvia put on a buffet as a present to the happy couple, Betty baked and decorated a cake, and others showered them with practical gifts such as towels, bed linen and kitchenware.

To Ned's delight, Sid Reynolds arrived with the beautiful Meg. He watched as the youngsters mingled and laughed together, much as he did with his chums back in Hammersmith. He felt a sudden pang of homesickness. Seeing him alone, Percy left the others and approached his table. "Won't you come and join us? You look a bit lost tonight."

Thrilled at being asked, Ned smiled. "I'd love too. Thank you."

Percy reached out and took Ned's near empty glass. "Here, let me get you a pint. I don't feel you're a rival anymore now there's a ring on Gert's finger."

Ned laughed. "I never was, Percy. Really, I never was."

Later, on his way back from the Gents, Ned was apprehended by Pat Dickens. "I hear you've seen the underneath of my lane. Can't believe the old tunnel's been there all this time. I couldn't even begin to imagine how many times I must've driven over it."

"Yes, and you or someone else, actually drove over it just after I'd scrambled my way through the roof fall. It gave me a bit of a scare until I realised what it was."

Pat tutted. "Dear, dear, it must have been a nasty experience, stuck down there overnight. It wouldn't have suited me. I like my bed too much."

"It wasn't very pleasant, and of course it was made worse, my not knowing whether or not I'd ever get out."

Pat sighed. "Poor old Jane! If only we'd known she was there too, trapped and stranded. She must've been ever so scared, poor kid. I'm really baffled as to how she managed to get down there in the first place, though. But she always was the adventurous type. You know, wanting to go gallivanting off round the world and stuff like that."

Ned tilted his head to one side. "You don't believe the rumours suggesting she was murdered then?"

"Good heavens, no!" said Pat, emphatically. "I've thought about it a great deal, and May and me have discussed it a lot too. Jane were a lovely girl, you see, and I can assure you there's no-one around here as would have done anything to harm her."

Ned said nothing. It was common knowledge Molly had been able to predict his whereabouts in the Witches Broomstick, but Fred had insisted Ned having conversed with Jane should be kept quiet. He had not even reported it to his bosses for fear of ridicule. If there were any truth in the claim Jane had been poisoned then he wanted it kept hushed. Hence the words *poison* and *ghost* were never uttered.

"What I want to know," said a slightly inebriated Albert Treloar, "is, if the tunnel was used by smugglers, then how the devil did they get their goods through the narrow handle of the Witches Broomstick?"

The major agreed. "That's what I'd also like to know. We're all in agreement that even the smallest of boats couldn't squeeze through that tiny gap without doing serious damage to the hull."

"I had quite a bit of time to think about that," said Ned, who had momentarily abandoned the youngsters in the public bar to scrounge a cigarette from his mother who was happily chatting to the old timers in the snug. "And the only solution I could come up with was, that maybe they had a long narrow raft onto which they unloaded the boat's contents and then swam with it through the gap to the shore."

"Feasible," the major agreed. "Quite feasible. It certainly had to be something like that. But however they did it, it must have been a right palaver."

"They must have been a brave bunch," said Nettie Penrose, admiringly. "You wouldn't catch me out there in the dark with all the evil spirits and suchlike."

Reg Briers laughed. "I expect it was the smugglers who started the rumours of evil spirits in the first place, Nettie. What a perfect ploy to discourage potential onlookers from witnessing illicit doings."

At half past nine, the door of the Inn suddenly flew open, and a very excited Rose Briers, who had thus far not attended the party, breezed in breathlessly with Freak yapping relentlessly round at her ankles.

"Guess what?" she gasped, looking at the rapidly turning heads and raised eyebrows, as she leaned on the bar for support. "There's just been a newsflash on the wireless. Some old bloke's dog has unearthed the remains of a body buried in a spinney up country. The police are not giving out any details, but there's much speculation that it will be the remains of William Wagstaffe's housekeeper, Grace Bonnington."

Chapter Twenty-Six

The police, who had descended on Trengillion in great numbers following Fred's report of new developments in the village, left after a few days convinced that Ned's imprisonment in the tunnel had been nothing more than an unfortunate accident. For although they were very interested, at first, to discover a way for Jane to have progressed to the Witches Broomstick, they soon concluded that she, like Ned, had ventured into the tunnel and due to unforeseen circumstances had quite simply been unable to get out again. They were of the opinion, that in both cases the heavy trap door had fallen accidentally and the bolt had jerked into place due to the vibration caused, as happened in four out of ten cases when they reconstructed the situation. Either that, or Jane and Ned had been unable to open the door, simply because they had pushed on the side of the hinges, rather than the bolt. The verdict on Jane's death would therefore, inevitably, be accidental.

Ned was devastated. He thought his discovery of the tunnel would provide the evidence needed to open a murder case. Instead he had given the police grounds on which to close it. Fred was not happy either, but had to go along with the views of his superiors.

Annie, Ned and Molly, met on Denzil's bench to express their outrage.

"So, it looks as though finding Jane's killer is down to us," said Molly, clearly annoyed. "Which takes us right back to square one."

"I just can't believe the police are dropping the case," snapped Ned, vociferously. "It's absurd. Their second-rate investigations are a downright travesty of justice."

Annie, partly in defence of her husband, was a little less outraged. "I suppose there's always the possibility that they're right and it may in both cases have been an accident."

Ned leapt up from the bench. "No, no, no! Someone deliberately trapped me in that tunnel and the same goes for Jane too. If she had been trapped down there through her own misfortune, whilst fit and healthy, someone would have heard her calling for help. It was

August remember! Holiday makers would have walked the cliff path. She would never have just sat down and died! I believe she reached the end of the tunnel exhausted and died from poison administered to her by someone whose neck I should dearly like to get my hands around just now. Jane was murdered. I know it, because she told me so and if you're honest with yourself, Annie, you know it too."

"But there's no evidence to suggest murder," Annie retorted. "The police couldn't get any fingerprints from the trap door or the sheet of rusty metal. Police need evidence, a motive and a suspect. This case has none of those things. There's nothing even to prove that Jane reached the Witches Broomstick by way of the tunnel. It's all circumstantial."

"I know the police think I'm a complete and utter wimp who is incapable of opening a trap door, but how do they explain the sheet of metal being back in place, eh?"

"They think as the trap door fell shut it must have caused the metal sheet to topple back over the door. Remember, they didn't have the opportunity to examine it closely because you and Fred had moved things and poked around before Fred reported it to the police, so the evidence they found was flawed."

"Yes, alright then, but what about the ladder. How is that supposed to have got back in its usual place? Did the vibration cause that to move too?"

"Don't be silly, Ned. Sylvia says she doesn't remember putting the ladder back in place when she went to the stables on the Saturday morning, but at the same time she can't swear to that fact, and certainly not in a court of law, as she easily may have done it without realising or thinking."

Molly sighed. "So what do we do next?"

"We wait," said Annie. "If you're right about all this, Ned, then something will happen soon."

"Wait! But for how long? We're due to go home soon. I can't sit around here forever, even though I've vowed not to leave until this whole damn business is cleared up. In reality, I know I have to return home and go back to my job."

Ned hurled a handful of pebbles into the sea to emphasise his anger. The subsequent splashes succeeded by relieving a little of the tension.

"Perhaps Annie's right," said Molly. "And something will happen soon. I mean to say, if it becomes common knowledge the case is to be closed, should a verdict of accidental death be reached, then whoever is responsible may well be off their guard and make a silly move."

In the afternoon, Molly went into town to have her hair done. Her roots needed touching up as a white stripe was beginning to appear amidst the black, causing her, she complained, to look like a badger.

Ned spent the afternoon in the warmth of his mother's room, having remembered he was supposed to be attending a birthday party at the weekend in London. Knowing he would not be home by then, he wrote a fairly detailed letter to his school teaching friend, George Clarke, telling him of events at the Inn, but deliberately not mentioning his dubious new found talents. He finished off the letter vowing to be home shortly before the Easter holiday, after which he added a post script, expressing his eagerness to hear all the gossip from George and his much missed circle of friends.

He was posting the letter when the bus arrived back from town. Molly rushed down the bus steps and kissed Ned on the cheek, causing him to cough on the inhalation of the nauseating perfume which always seemed to emanate from the heads of ladies who had recently been in the hands of the hairdresser.

Later, in the snug, May Dickens complemented Molly on her hair. "I'm always saying I must get mine done. As you can see I'm getting very grey now and it makes me look and feel so old."

Molly laughed. "I dread to think how grey I'd be if I left it to grow out. I haven't allowed my natural colour to be seen for years, other than when my roots show, that is."

"Same here," grinned Sylvia, enjoying the female chit-chat.

"No," said Molly. "You don't dye your lovely hair, surely?"

Sylvia smiled. "I do, as regular as clockwork. This is my natural colour, but like you, if I'm not careful the grey will show through."

"But you're not old enough to be going grey!" exclaimed Molly.

"Thank you, but I'll be thirty eight next birthday. That's enough about age though. It's something which seems to increase with alarming regularity once one passes the age of twenty one, and it's by no means my favourite subject."

Pat Dickens, meanwhile, talked to Ned and asked more questions about the tunnel. In response Ned suggested Pat ask Frank if he might be allowed go inside for a poke around. It was after all, on land belonging to the Inn, one end of it anyway. Pat, thrilled by the suggestion, went to enquire from Frank if such a visit would be permissible.

The next morning Ned awoke in a melancholy mood, wanting to be alone with time and space to think. After breakfast he slipped away from the Inn and headed towards the cliff path on the westerly side of the cove.

The morning was chilly, nipped by a brisk north westerly wind gusting through the village and out to sea. Ned was wrapped up well, wearing his overcoat and scarf tied snugly around his neck. Overhead, a few grey clouds threatened rain. Ned eyed them with uncertainty but felt confident the weather would stay fine for the duration of his walk.

He scrambled along the rough path towards the cliff tops, passing clusters of bright yellow celandines nestling cosily beneath bushes and hedgerows. Near to the front gate of Chy-an-Gwyns, he stopped, walked to the cliff's edge and looked to the sea below crashing relentlessly onto the cliff face and swirling around huge rocks part hidden beneath the rolling waves. No boats were visible, not even a ship on the distant horizon. He returned to the coastal path and ambled along the winding track, across Pat Dickens' field of cows and over the stile until eventually he reached the Witches Broomstick. Holding tightly to the railing, he looked over the side and shuddered. It was the first time he had seen the location of his nerve-racking confinement since his dramatic rescue.

He watched dreamily as the Broomstick's patch of golden sand disappeared beneath the tumbling waves, evoking memories and vivid pictures of the night spent in the cave. Again the same question sprang to his mind. Why had someone trapped him in the tunnel? He was confident no-one knew he, Annie and Molly had reason, other than the mirror's declaration, to suspect Jane's death of being murder, hence there was no cause for anyone to think he, or they, might be on their trail. Whoever trapped him, therefore, must have done so simply because he had found the tunnel. And so who might that be? The only person he knew of was Sylvia.

He pondered briefly whether it was plausible to suspect Sylvia of killing Jane. Certainly, she would have known her well and had every opportunity to lace her drink. But what could possibly be her motive? Had Frank flirted with Jane perhaps? Ned thought this unlikely. Frank had eyes only for Sylvia and he was not the womanising type. No, try as he might, Ned could think of no reason to suspect Sylvia. Also there was the fact that the murderer had somehow carried Jane into the tunnel. He tried to imagine Sylvia climbing the ladder with Jane across her shoulders. He laughed. It was absurd!

So who else might it have been? Pat Dickens, Jim Hughes, Cyril Penrose, Reg Briers, Sid Reynolds, Percy Collins, Peter Williams, Harry the Hitman, Frank Newton, the vicar! No, it couldn't be any of them, he liked them all. Even Albert Treloar was alright once you got to know him. But what about the major? He had forgotten him. Ned chuckled. What would his mother say if she knew he had even contemplated such a thing? No, it could not be the major anyway, because he would not have known about the tunnel.

There was no doubt the tunnel was at the heart of this mystery, and the fact had to be faced that the guilty party would hardly be likely to confess to knowledge of its existence, anyway.

Ned sighed deeply as Annie's words then came back to him regarding lack of evidence to prove Jane had accessed the Witches Broomstick by way of the tunnel. He groaned, weighed down with frustration and ready even to concede perhaps, his imagination had been over active and his imprisonment nothing more than an unfortunate accident.

As Ned watched a piece of driftwood inside the Witches Broomstick repeatedly sink beneath the waves and re-submerge as the water retreated, he sensed something snuffling around his legs. He stepped back and looked towards the ground as a familiar female voice shouted, "Freak, come here, you sodding dog."

Ned turned abruptly and Freak barked as Rose Briers came into view.

Beside the huge bolder, she came to a standstill and attempted to push strands of hair, driven by the wind, away from her face. "Well, well, well, if it isn't Reg's teacher friend from up the line."

Ned cringed. He was in no mood to banter with Rose Briers.

"Where's Mummy?" she asked, glancing around.

Ignoring her, Ned turned around and resumed his observation of the sea.

Not one to be slighted, Rose stepped forward and leaned on the railing beside him.

"Why do you dress in that hideous manner?" he sneered, seeing her short skirt through the gap of her flapping, unbuttoned coat. "It's what I'd expect to see in the seedy back streets of London."

She laughed. "Frequent visitor there are you?"

Ned ignored her again.

"I dress like this because I'm bored, bored, bored!" she snapped. "There, is that a satisfactory answer?"

Ned scowled, angered by her attitude and her unwelcome presence. "Don't be ridiculous! How can you be bored? The wife of a headmaster should occupy her time usefully and actually find it fulfilling. Life's what you make it, but it seems to me you're just hell bent on making your own life a misery and that of everyone else too!"

"Don't preach, you sound like Reg on a bad day. Anyway, how can you expect me to fit in here when everyone hates me?"

"They don't hate you," said Ned, irritated by her negativity. "It's all in your mind. Anyway, out of curiosity, what's the natural colour of your hair?"

"It's brown, a horrible mousy, brown, a bit like yours, only a lot lighter."

Ned winced. "There's nothing wrong with that, so why do you dye it?"

Rose shrugged her shoulders. "Because it makes me different to them, I suppose. But more likely because they hate it."

"And I suppose the same reason goes for the excessive make-up and hideous clothing?"

Rose half smiled. "If you must know, the powder's to cover my horrible freckles and I like my bright lipsticks and eye make-up. As for my clothes, I did dress sensibly once upon a time when I worked in a Blackpool as hotel receptionist, because I really liked my job and the people I worked with. That's why I'm resentful, if the truth be known, because I gave it up. I thought marrying a headmaster would be bettering myself, you see. I think it could have worked too, had it been anywhere other than this one-eyed dump."

"So, what went wrong?"

A pained expression crossed Rose's face. "I'd not been here long when I overheard a couple of old bats talking about me outside the school one day. They didn't know I was there, of course. One of them said my hair and make-up brought shame to the village and I looked like a harlot."

Ned smiled. "And so you decided to shock them further by dressing to fit the label you'd been given!"

She grinned. "Well, yes. It gave me a big kick to upset the evil, gossiping old women."

Ned recalled Reg saying flirting with the married men to upset their wives was the only pleasure she had in life. He felt a sudden pang of sympathy. "It's never too late to change back, you know."

"Oh, but it is. Besides, if I changed they'd think they had beaten me and I couldn't possibly endure that."

Ned thought it wise to change the subject.

"Have you heard any more news about the body in the spinney? I've seen no mention of it in any of the newspapers."

She shook her head. "No, it's most annoying. But I suppose no more will be said until a positive identification has been established, if it ever is. After all there can't be much of poor old Grace left."

"No, I suppose not. Do you think he'll ever be found?"

"What, William Wagstaffe? I hope so, but then again, I hope not. He's become rather a hero of mine, that's why I don't want him caught. But at the same time I'd like to see what he looks like now and find out where he's been. I was really excited when I thought he was in Cornwall the other week."

"Why do women like men who live on the wrong side of the law?" Ned asked. "I just don't understand it."

Rose shrugged her shoulders. "Escapism, pure escapism. And dreams of a more exciting life."

A seagull gracefully landed on the rocks behind them. It squawked, flapped its wings rapidly and flew off when Freak leapt forwards, barking madly.

"Shut up, you dozy mutt," snapped Rose, as she buttoned up her coat to keep out the ever freshening wind. She turned to Ned. "I'd better be getting back now. Reg will be home soon for his lunch."

Ned was surprised. "You prepare Reg's lunch then?"

"Of course, I'm not completely heartless and I bear no grudge against poor old Reg."

"I'll walk back with you, then. That's if you've no objections to a companion with horrible mousy brown hair."

They arrived at the Inn just as the first few drops of rain started to fall.

Rose thanked Ned for his company as they separated, and she headed for The School House.

On impulse he called after her. "Rose, not everyone hates you. I think you have a certain charm!"

She turned and waved. "That's because you're a daft up-country bugger," she laughed.

Chapter Twenty-Seven

The following morning, after spending an enjoyable hour sitting on Denzil's bench reading his newspaper in warm sunshine, Ned returned to the Inn. As he closed the heavy side door, Frank crossed the hallway with a steaming cup on a saucer in his hands. Simultaneously the telephone bell rang.

"Sod it!" cursed Frank, turning to approach the offensive object. "Would you just pop this coffee out to Sylvia please, Ned, so it don't get cold. She's out in the vegetable garden somewhere."

Ned nodded, lay down his newspaper on a chair and took the coffee from Frank as he picked up the telephone receiver. Ned then left the Inn, walked through the courtyard, past the well, and out towards the garden, treading carefully as he went so as not to spill coffee in the saucer.

The vegetable plot lay behind a high granite wall, with access only through a wrought iron gate. Ned could not see Sylvia as he latched the gate but observed the door of a large wooden shed was open and assumed she would be inside, but she was not.

He glanced around the garden for signs of life. Behind a tall holly hedge, thick, grey smoke pothered heavenwards, buffeted by a gentle westerly breeze. He left the path and walked around the hedge where he found Sylvia, happily throwing garden debris and prunings onto a small, crackling bonfire. He handed her the coffee and said it was from Frank.

"I like the smell of a bonfire," he said, approvingly. "It reminds me of when I was young and I used to visit my grandparents. Granddad always seemed to be burning garden rubbish in those days."

Sylvia took a sip of her coffee. "I don't suppose you get a chance to do any gardening in London, do you?"

"Good heavens, no. I live in a flat and don't even possess a window box. I know absolutely nothing about horticulture."

Sylvia smiled, thoughtfully. "Everyone should have a garden, it's a very therapeutic, productive and worthwhile hobby."

"Therapeutic?" repeated Ned, puzzled.

Sylvia pushed a branch back onto the fire which had toppled from the top. "Yes. If I'm feeling low, depressed, bad tempered or even just tired, I come out here, get my hands in the soil, smell the flowers, admire the vegetables and relax in the peace and quiet. It's very soothing and I love it."

"Flowers?" Ned queried, conscious there was not a flower in sight.

She smiled, aware of his questioning tone. "I shall be sowing seeds soon. I grow lots of annuals in the summer, mainly for cutting. It's so nice to have fresh flowers around the Inn, especially ones with a pleasant scent. Sweet peas are my favourites. I grow several varieties."

Ned cast his eyes over the plot. "Do things grow well here, close to the sea, I mean? I'm thinking the air must be tinged with salt when the wind blows from the south."

"Most things grow fine, after all I'm able to put on plenty of horse manure."

Ned laughed. "That's something else I remember - Granddad nipping out with a bucket and shovel every time the horses went by. He said it was good for the roses."

"It's good for lots of things," said Sylvia.

Ned ducked as a sudden gust of wind blew smoke in his direction. "It's probably a silly question, but how do you get the manure from the stables to the vegetable garden? It's a long way to carry in buckets."

Sylvia giggled. "In the wheelbarrow, of course." She pointed to the wooden barrow leaning against a wall.

Ned groaned. "How daft of me, you must think me a right idiot."

"Well, you did say you knew nothing about horticulture, and to be fair, I don't suppose you see many wheelbarrows in London."

Ned glanced across the valley to where the stables were visible in the distance. "Another thing I keep meaning to ask is, does the field between here and the paddock belong to the Inn?"

Sylvia nodded. "Yes, but Frank insists the villagers treat it as their own. It's not really used very much, which is a shame, although children do play in there occasionally, and once a year the school and church use it to hold their combined garden fete. This summer we're going to start fundraising so that we can buy some swings and possibly even a slide."

Ned felt a sudden pang of dismay, as he visualised the village in summer: children on swings, sunbathers on the beach and paddling in the sea, families picnicking down the lanes, the Inn's clientele enjoying a pint outside on a warm sunny evening and ramblers walking the cliff paths with no need of a coat. He felt saddened that he would not be around to join in the activities. In fact, once he had returned to London, the chances were he would probably never see Trengillion and its inhabitants again.

The church clock struck midday.

"Good heavens," Sylvia gasped, peeling off her gardening gloves. "Is that the time already? I have to go, Ned. I'm supposed to be taking over the bar from Frank. He has a funeral to attend at half past twelve."

"Oh, anyone I know, or knew?"

Sylvia shook her head. "No, the deceased is an old chap whose name I can't remember. He lived in the village at Rose Cottage and used to come to the Inn long before I arrived down here. In fact I don't think I've ever seen him because he's been housebound for quite some time."

She handed Ned the garden fork. "Don't put anything else on the fire, but keep an eye on it for a few more minutes, please. I'll pop out and check it again this afternoon. Meanwhile, if you'd shut up the shed in case it rains, I'd be most grateful."

She dashed off, untying her headscarf with one hand and carrying the empty cup and saucer in the other. Ned watched until she disappeared behind the hedge, he then poked the fire with the fork. He leapt back in alarm as flames flared up, rapidly devouring dried holly leaves and twigs, which hissed and crackled in the intense heat. When the flames dyed down to a gentle smoulder, he stuck the fork forcibly into the earth and walked around the holly hedge to view the remains of the winter vegetables.

Near to the gate, long, crooked, knobbly stems with Brussels sprouts clinging like limpets to their sides, towered over Savoy cabbages whose outer leaves had been nibbled by unwelcome slugs and snails. A dozen or so cauliflowers, each the size of a football, occupied a large patch and alongside the path ran a row of big, healthy leeks.

Ned walked towards the shed. By it, part of the garden was dug over, ready and waiting, he assumed for seeds. He bent down and touched the earth. It felt cold and damp.

The area in front of the shed was sheltered. Ned leaned against the wooden construction and gazed across the rooftops between the Inn and the sea, where the cliff tops were just visible through the gaps. It was very peaceful: the only sound, the distant echo of falling waves and the sporadic cry of rooks in the churchyard's tall trees.

From the lifeless branch of the old apple tree, two blue tits pecked at a dangling lump of fat, watched through the half closed eyes of Barley Wine curled up in the sun on top of a nearby wall. Ned tried to imagine himself in his own vegetable garden, sitting on a bench, pipe in hand, surveying the fruits of his labour. He was surprised by the enormity of its appeal.

Before closing the shed, curious as to its contents, Ned slipped inside for a quick peek. Behind the door he found a sack of potatoes and wondered if they had been grown by Sylvia or whether she bought them from one of the farmers. He decided the latter was most likely for the vegetable garden was not over large.

From hooks on the ceiling, dangled bunches of large, flat onions. On the floor their dried, golden, skins, danced in a draught from the open door. Above a workbench, three shelves were piled high with rows of neatly arranged flower pots, stacked methodically in varying sizes. Against the wall, leaned a selection of forks, spades, rakes, hoes and other objects which Ned could neither name nor imagine the use of.

From the small back window, the paddock, the stables and the old stone wall on which he occasionally sat, were visible across the valley. The rooftops of the Vicarage were also apparent and from two of the four tall chimneys, grey smoke rose upwards towards the clear blue sky.

A squawking seagull landed heavily on the shed roof. Ned, unaware of the loud thud's source, turned quickly in panic and hit his head on a large coil of rope hanging from a beam. Dazed, he stumbled, lost his balance and fell to the floor, knocking from a shelf, a trug containing hand forks and trowels, and a seed tray stacked with secateurs, short canes and neatly wound pieces of string.

"Bugger!" muttered Ned, angrily, picking up the scattered objects and bundled them, higgledy-piggledy, back into the trug and seed tray. Once done, he stood quickly, eager to return the items to their rightful places. But his task was momentarily delayed. For tucked away neatly at the back of a deep shelf, was a red biscuit tin.

Ned froze. He recognised the tin as that which Sylvia had carried when emerging from the stables on the day he had ventured into the tunnel. His heart thumped noisily and his head began to spin. Quickly, he looked outside to make sure the coast was clear. No-one was about. With shaking hands he slid the tin from the shelf and stood it on the bench. Anxious to see its contents, he carefully removed the lid. His eyebrows rose in surprise. For inside the tin lay many packets of seeds, some commercial, others saved, dried and sealed in brown envelopes with names and dates carefully written on the fronts in Sylvia's neat handwriting.

Ned laughed as he briskly shuffled through the tin. After establishing it contained nothing other than seeds, he replaced the lid in triumph and returned it to the back of the shelf. He felt extremely happy. Jubilant even! The tin after all, was the only remaining question mark hanging over Sylvia's head, and it contained nothing sinister. Sylvia was innocent of all theories suggesting she might in any way be linked to Jane's death.

Ned felt ten feet tall as he closed the shed door and strode behind the holly hedge to establish the bonfire was safe. Once done, he left the garden in search of his mother to relay the excellent news.

"Seeds!" spluttered Molly, astonished. "What, nothing but seeds?"

"Yes, I went through the whole lot."

She sighed. "So, we've been all round the houses, so to speak, and we're no nearer now, knowing if, and by whom, Jane was murdered, than the day I arrived here. How very extraordinary."

"That's right. We've not the slightest shred of evidence against anyone. We've found no-one with a motive, no-one behaving in a suspicious manner and what's more, we now have no untied ends."

Molly laughed. "I never did see myself as an amateur detective. Just as well really."

Ned had found Molly in her room, repairing the hem of a skirt which had started to come undone after she had caught it on the corner of a chair. Molly always carried a needle and cotton reels of various shades in her handbag. She claimed a button or hem might come adrift at any time.

As she continued with her needlework, Ned rose, crossed to the window and looked out towards the sea.

"Will you be leaving here when I go home?" he asked, thoughtfully.

Molly sighed. "I expect so. I can't afford to stay here much longer. I still have to pay my rent in Clacton, you know, whether I'm there or not."

"So that will be the end of you and the major then?"

"Please, Ned, please. I don't want to think about it," she said, without looking up.

Ned watched his mother as she folded the repaired skirt and returned the needle and cotton to her handbag. She had changed so much during the past few weeks. Been so happy. He wondered just how content she really was living alone in Clacton, and he sharply rebuked himself for not visiting her often, vowing in future he would make a much greater effort to keep in touch.

On Friday, Ned and Molly discovered during breakfast, through Gertie, that it was Sylvia's thirty-eighth birthday, in spite of Sylvia wishing the event be kept quiet. Most of the locals, however, were already in the know, so the Inn was busy that evening with well-wishers. And on the bar, Gertie and Betty both worked with Frank, giving Sylvia a chance to mingle with her friends and acquaintances.

Larry and Des also had cause to celebrate. At long last they believed they had found the exact location of the ship wreck they had been seeking. They each bought a round of drinks for everyone at the Inn, in lieu of their anticipated, impending wealth, which they hoped would come to fruition when they returned with their eagerly anticipated Aqua-Lungs the following year.

Throughout the evening, Sylvia never had an empty glass in her hand, for devotees, eager to show appreciation for their landlady, continually showered her with drinks. Hence by closing time she was considerably inebriated.

Unable to stand without swaying, Sylvia finally flopped down on a seat near to the door. Frank noticed this and asked Gertie to pop along to the kitchen and make a cup of very strong, black coffee. Annie, concerned for Sylvia's welfare, sat by her side and chatted in an attempt to keep her awake long enough to drink the coffee when it arrived.

Sylvia, her face flushed and her speech slurred, burbled and giggled in response to her companion's light hearted banter.

"That's a beautiful necklace," commented Annie, reaching to touch the sparkling blue stone dangling around Sylvia's throat. "I love the way it catches the light."

"It is pretty, isn't it? It's my birthstone, an aquamarine. Gem of the sea."

"Very appropriate."

"It's very precious too, cos Jane bought it for my birthday last year."

"Jane," whispered Annie. "Poor, dear, Jane!"

Sylvia's eyes rolled. She attempted to sit up straight and unsuccessfully tried to grab Annie's arm. "Don't believe the silly mirror, Annie. It was talking a load of rubbish. Jane wasn't poisoned, you know. Definitely not. She wasn't poisoned, it was definitely an accident." And with that brief statement, she fell helplessly to the floor and passed out.

The major and Frank rushed forward and picked Sylvia up, just as Gertie arrived with the coffee.

"Follow us with that, please, Gert," said Frank. "We're gonna take her to the bedroom to bring her round."

Ned watched the small party leave the bar. He then put down his pint on a table, in order to pay a visit to the Gents outside.

By the door, sitting alone in silence, he noticed Annie, a blank, anguished expression on her pale, white face. He took a seat by her side. "Annie, whatever's wrong? You look as though you've seen a ghost."

As she turned and looked into his face, he saw there were tears in her eyes. "Did you not hear what Sylvia said?" she whispered.

Ned shook his head. "Not really. Surely most of her burbling was pretty incomprehensible."

"Not all, I could understand most of what she said, especially when Jane's name cropped up."

"Jane. She mentioned Jane."

Annie nodded.

"What did she say?"

A tear trickled down Annie's pale face. "Sylvia said, 'Don't believe the silly mirror, Annie. It was talking a load of rubbish. She wasn't poisoned, you know. Definitely not. No, she wasn't poisoned, it was definitely an accident.' Ned, don't you see what this means? We've none of us ever breathed a word to anyone, but Fred, about Jane being poisoned. So how does Sylvia know?"

Chapter Twenty-Eight

Frank awoke the following morning and crept quietly out of bed so as not to disturb his sleeping wife, although it was obvious by her gentle snoring she was unlikely to be woken by anything less than an earthquake. Usually they rose at the same time, but he decided that on this occasion it would be best to let her sleep for as long as possible, otherwise she would be feeling very much under the weather all day long, and certainly would not be able to face cooking a meal for the residents in the evening.

After dressing, he leaned over the bed, kissed her flushed cheek and tiptoed quietly from the room.

In the kitchen he found Gertie busily preparing things for breakfast. She smiled when she saw Frank alone. "No Sylvia this morning?"

"I think it best if we manage without her for a while," he grinned, as Gertie poured him a cup of strong tea. "I very much doubt she'd be a great deal of use, anyway."

Together they cooked the breakfast and Gertie waited on the tables as usual.

"How's our lovely landlady feeling this morning?" laughed the major, as Gertie placed a teapot on his table. "Not too good, I should imagine!"

"We'll have to wait and see. She hasn't got up yet, but when she does I expect she'll have a thumping headache. Poor thing."

It seemed Sylvia was not the only one to incur the curse of a hangover. Larry also looked extremely fragile as he and Des took up their seats in the dining room. "I can't think whatever made me start drinking beastly spirits," he moaned, running his hands slowly down his clammy grey face. "I must be bonkers!"

Ned went to fetch his paper as usual after breakfast, eager to pass away the time until he heard from Annie whether or not Fred thought Sylvia's comment the previous night was incriminating enough to be passed on to his superiors.

It was a beautiful morning with a real touch of spring in the air. Ned passed the baker, tunefully whistling as he delivered freshly baked bread from the back of his van to each house. Outside the church, Sid Reynolds, his feet firmly placed on a wooden step ladder, lavishly painted creosote onto the ancient lichgate, while Meg, standing close by, trimmed back straggly grass overhanging the stone wall which bordered the churchyard. Several people were out mowing their lawns, filling the air with the pleasant, sweet scent of freshly cut grass.

Once the paper was purchased, Ned walked down to the cove, where Harry the Hitman was white-washing Cove Cottage, and Percy and Peter were painting their fishing boat.

"The village is a hive of activity this morning," commented Ned. "I feel I'm the only person being lazy."

"It's always the same in the lead up to Easter," mused Peter, dipping his brush into a tin of dark blue paint. "Easter marks the beginning of a new season, fishing, tourism and so forth."

Ned sighed deeply. "Yes, I suppose so and I'll be back home by then."

After reading his paper and watching the approaching tide gradually wash away a silly face he had drawn on a small patch of sand, he left the cove and returned to the Inn. As he set foot on the cobbles, a police car turned the corner and pulled up alongside him. Three people stepped out. Fred in uniform, a policewoman, and a tall, distinguished looking man in plain clothes. Ned nodded to Fred, and then tore upstairs to his mother's room. "The police are here," he panted excitedly, rushing to the window.

Molly was sitting by the fire knitting a grey pullover for the major. "Good heavens! So they've taken Sylvia's mention of poison seriously then. I hope she's up."

Ned walked away from the window. "I'm going downstairs. I simply have to find out what's going on."

"Don't be silly, Ned. The police are hardly going to invite you in to hear their questioning."

"Well, of course not. But that doesn't matter as I intend to eavesdrop."

"Ned, you mustn't," said Molly, aghast. But he was gone.

"Impetuous, just like his father was as a young man," muttered Molly. Although she had to admit, she too was curious to know the outcome of the police visit.

Downstairs, Frank showed the police into the public bar. Sylvia, having finally risen, was cleaning out the fireplace in the snug. As she turned to see to whom Frank was talking, she pushed away a stray strand of hair from her face, leaving behind a black, smutty mark on her forehead.

Frank, his brow creased with confusion, told her the police wanted to ask a few questions. She groaned. He noted her white face, but was unsure whether to attribute its paleness to the police presence or the effects of a hangover.

Sylvia rose to her feet, brushed ash from her skirt, left the snug and slipped behind the bar to wash her blackened hands in the sink.

"Please, sit down, Sylvia," commanded Fred, as she re-emerged, drying her hands on a tea towel. She obliged, choosing to sit in the window seat, where the sun was shining onto the brightly polished table. The police officers sat likewise. Frank, however, chose to remain standing.

"Mrs Newton, please allow me to introduce myself. I am Detective Inspector Williams. With me is W.P.C. Wright, and I believe you are already familiar with P.C. Stevens?" Sylvia nodded. "Good. Now I'd like to ask you a few questions regarding the death of your former employee, Jane Hunt."

Sylvia stiffened, gulped, cleared her throat and attempted to smile. "Please, go ahead, although I can't see how I can be of any more help."

"Hmm, you are aware, of course, that rumour has it that Miss Hunt was murdered?"

Sylvia shrugged her shoulders. "Well, yes of course, it all started here on the night of the Beetle Drive and that silly message on the mirror."

"So I'm led to believe. And may I ask if you personally have any thoughts or theories about how she may have met her death?"

Sylvia scowled. "I don't believe she was murdered, if that's what you mean. I'm inclined to go along with your theory that it was nothing more than a tragic accident."

The detective inspector's eyebrows rose. "Really! So, you have never expressed an opinion, as to, if it was murder, how someone might have taken Miss Hunt's life?"

"No, not that I recall," she snapped. "I really can't see what you're getting at. I've already told you that as far as I'm concerned it was an accident."

"I see, so you have never suggested her death might have been brought about by poison?"

Fred noticed Sylvia wince. "No, no, I have not." She enunciated each word with precise clarity.

"Hmm, is that so? Then let me refresh your memory, Mrs Newton. Last night, you said, and I quote, 'Don't believe the silly mirror. It was talking a load of rubbish. She wasn't poisoned, you know. Definitely not. No, she wasn't poisoned, it was definitely an accident.'"

"Did I?" scoffed Sylvia. "I don't remember. In fact, I remember very little of last night. It was my birthday yesterday, you see, and regrettably I had too much to drink."

"So I understand."

"Anyway, if I did say, whatever you say I said, so what? Am I not allowed to speculate like everyone else?"

"Of course, Mrs Newton. But something has been brought to my attention which I was unaware of until this morning. That being, we have reason now to believe that Miss Hunt may after all have been murdered and a poisonous substance used to bring about her death, and you seem to be the only person to have mentioned the word poison."

There was a long pause, during which Sylvia, through a muzzy haze, tried desperately to recollect the previous evening's events.

"Who said I talked of poison?" she eventually muttered.

"A very, very reliable witness," answered the inspector promptly.

Sylvia's face darkened. She felt sick and tired. Her head ached unbearably and her stomach churned.

"You knew about the tunnel," the inspector continued. "You go to the stables every day. You had ample opportunity to poison Jane. You..."

"...But, but, why would I kill Jane?" interrupted Sylvia. "This is crazy. She was my friend. It's ridiculous to think it was me."

"At present only you know the reason why, Mrs Newton," the inspector whispered gently, noticing a look in her eyes which he had seen many times before in his long career. "You did kill her, didn't you?"

Sylvia kicked the table leg and rose defiantly to her feet. Outraged by the accusations, she declared herself innocent and turned to face her accusers. In a mirror, hanging on the wall, she caught a glimpse of the black smudge on her face. Frowning, she licked her finger and vigorously attempted to rub the stubborn mark from her throbbing forehead. When lowering her arm, she caught sight of the blue aquamarine stone still hanging around her neck from the previous evening. It sparkled in the sunlight, just as on the morning of her birthday the previous year when she had first lifted it from inside the neatly wrapped box. She smiled, recalling Jane's delight when she had hugged her, overcome with genuine appreciation. Sylvia stared into the mirror deep in thought, both hands clasped firmly over the necklace. Her vision blurred and tears welled up in her eyes.

"Sylvia," whispered Frank, shocked by the sudden change in her mood. "Sylvia, what's the matter? Please, tell them this is all rubbish."

"I'm sorry," she whispered, turning and looking into Frank's eyes. "I'm so very, very sorry."

Ned standing in the passage outside the door, which stood slightly ajar, felt his knees give way. His back slid down the wall until he was crouched beside the old wooden door frame.

"Mrs Newton, did you kill Jane Hunt?" asked the inspector, now standing and with a note of impatience in his voice.

She flopped back down on the window seat. "Yes," she croaked. "Yes, yes, yes. I killed Jane. But I didn't want to."

Frank stumbled forward and knocked over a stool as he grabbed the arms of his sobbing wife. With force, he pulled her to her feet.

"No," he shouted, shaking her violently. "No, you didn't! You couldn't have! Why would you? I don't understand!"

Fred sprang forward to separate Sylvia and Frank. W.P.C Wright gripped Sylvia's arm tightly and helped her back into her seat.

Sylvia raised her head. "I can't live this lie anymore," she sobbed. "Always thinking someone might find out. Never being completely sure whether or not anyone had seen me."

Frank's face turned an ugly shade of red as his wife's words sank in. "But why?" he bellowed, leaning forward and banging his fist heavily on the table. "Why ever would you want to kill a lovely girl like Jane?"

"I can't tell you, Frank. Please don't ask me."

The inspector who had been standing since Sylvia had confessed, returned to his seat. "If you can't tell us *why* you took Miss Hunt's life, Mrs Newton, perhaps you'd care to tell us exactly *how* you took her life."

Sylvia looked horrified. "You want me to relive that day."

"Yes, I do. Please take your time."

The policewoman fetched Sylvia a glass of water from behind the bar. Frank grudgingly gave her his handkerchief to wipe her running eyes and nose. Fred Stevens returned to his seat and stared into space, too stunned even to speak.

"Alright, I'll tell you what happened that day, but nothing more. I shall not tell you why and so please, don't ask me again." She dried her eyes. "We often went riding together. Jane was a fine horse woman, far better than me; she was a natural and really should've gone in for show jumping on a large scale. On the day she died, we went out on the horses as on many occasions before. It was a beautiful day. Hot and sunny, and Jane was wearing her favourite red dress. Red suited her. But then all colours suited her. Anyway, I'd prepared a picnic for us to eat when we returned to the stables. I often did this during the summer, so Jane thought nothing of it. But what she didn't know was that on this occasion, I'd poisoned the coffee. She had a cold at the time, so it must have tasted almost normal to her, because she didn't say anything. After we'd eaten I left her sitting on the grass and went to attend the horses. By then she was complaining she didn't feel well. I took my time, and when I returned she was lying face down. I assumed she was dead."

Sylvia paused. Frank, his face as white as a sheet and shocked by her words, lowered himself clumsily onto a stool.

"Go on, please," said the inspector.

"I had a long piece of rope in the stables. I dragged Jane inside and tied one end of it around her waist. The other end I carried up the ladder and dropped it over the rafter nearest the tunnel's entrance. I tied the loose, dangling end of the rope to Winston's saddle, and then led him towards the stable door. The rope hoisted Jane up to the roof. Once she was level with the tunnel's entrance, I ordered Winston to stand still. I then ran back up the ladder, pushed Jane over the open trap door and commanded Winston to walk backwards, so that he lowered Jane inside. Once the horse's job was done, I removed his saddle and sent him back outside to join Brown Ale. I then untied the rope from Jane's waist, closed the trap door and bolted it firmly in place."

The bar fell into total silence. Even Ned, from far out in the passage, could hear the ticking of the clock above the fireplace in the snug.

Frank tried to speak, but so deep was the shock, his vocal chords had ceased temporarily to function.

"She couldn't have been dead," whispered Sylvia, staring into space, tears streaming down her cheeks. "She must have regained consciousness long enough to crawl through the tunnel to the Witches Broomstick. I was devastated when Larry and Des found her and knew before long someone would find out about the tunnel. But to my relief, when I went down there, I found a roof fall and so for a while I felt safe."

"Did you go to the tunnel often?" asked the inspector.

"I did prior to Jane's death. It used to give me a thrill going to the Witches Broomstick by means of a way which no-one else knew of. But after Jane was down there," she shuddered. "I kept out."

Fred, finding his voice, rose to his feet and stared across the table into Sylvia's eyes. "How could you? How could you take the life of someone in such a cold, calculated and heartless way? You of all people. We looked up to you. Respected you. But..."

Detective Inspector Williams reached out and touched Fred's arm. "...That's enough, Constable Stevens," he ordered, firmly.

Fred took a deep breath to quell his anger and then sat back down.

"How on earth did you manage these past months to act normal and show no signs of emotion with all this on your conscience?" Frank mumbled, at last finding himself able to speak. "I don't understand. You didn't even get in a flap when Jane's body was found."

Sylvia glanced into his cold, dark eyes, where instead of the loving look she was so used to, she saw utter loathing. "I was very scared at first. But eventually I convinced myself after six months there would be little or no trace of poison. Besides, there was nothing to suggest it had been anything but a tragic accident."

They all jumped as the door burst open and Ned staggered in, his face purple with rage.

Sylvia cowered in her seat.

"It was you who trapped me in the tunnel," he shouted. "You did so knowing full well there had been a roof fall and that I'd never get out."

Sylvia clenched her fists tightly. "I had to, Ned. You found my tunnel. I knew if you started talking, fingers would point towards me. I had no choice."

He lurched towards her. "You bitch. You heartless, murdering bitch! How did you know I was there?"

"I saw your shadow as you dashed out of the stable door," she sobbed. "I didn't know it was you though, Ned. I just knew someone was about. When I went outside I could sense piercing eyes watching me from the bushes. So I walked home across the field as normal as possible."

"Then you crept back, found I'd gone inside the tunnel and locked me in."

"Yes," she screamed, rising to her feet and knocking over her glass of water. "Yes, I did. But I didn't know it was you, Ned. I didn't know it was you. It wasn't until Molly said you were missing, that I realised."

"Guilty of murder and guilty of attempted murder," he yelled. "May you rot in hell."

He turned and stormed towards the door. Sylvia tried to go after him but the policewoman held her back.

"I'm sorry," she shouted. "I'm very, very sorry. It was never my intention to harm you, Ned." She flopped back down on the window seat. "I never wanted to harm anyone."

He did not look back, but left the bar and climbed the stairs to the sound of her sobbing uncontrollably. At the end of the landing he entered Molly's room and slammed shut the door. Molly, still knitting, raised her head in alarm. The clicking needles stopped abruptly when she saw his ashen face.

"Ned," she whispered. "Oh, no! I heard shouting. Please don't tell me it was Sylvia all along."

Ned nodded, crossed to the window and violently kicked the wall.

"Damn it," he groaned. "She killed Jane and tried to kill me. I hate her! I hate her!" He paced the room, cursing, swearing, thumping and kicking everything in his path.

Molly rose, dropped the knitting in her chair and attempted to reach him. He resisted and tried to walk away. She caught his hand and pulled him down gently to sit beside her on the bed.

"Let it out, Ned," she whispered gently. "It's no use bottling it up."

The tears welled up in his eyes and ran down his flushed cheeks. He cried until his throat was hoarse.

Half an hour later, they heard the Inn door close. Ned and Molly crossed to the window and looked down below. The three police officers were there and with them was Sylvia, handcuffs clasped firmly around her wrists. The inspector climbed into the front passenger seat, after Sylvia and the police woman had taken their seats in the back. Beneath the gently swaying, Ringing Bells Inn board, Fred was talking to Frank. He patted his shoulder affectionately. He then climbed into the driver's seat and closed shut the car door. The engine started and slowly the car pulled away. Sylvia looked out of the small back window. She saw Ned up above and blew him a kiss. He watched the car round the corner until it was out of sight. And at that moment, Ned knew he would never see Sylvia Newton again.

Chapter Twenty-Nine

The Inn remained closed during that Saturday lunchtime. After the police had departed, Frank locked the door, switched off the lights and went to the back living room where he sat alone amongst the books and clutter.

Word soon spread of Sylvia's arrest and several people eager to know more, went to the Inn on pretence of needing a pint to help quench their insatiable thirsts, when in reality, their only thirst was for information regarding the truth behind the gossip.

Molly, after Sylvia's departure, went to the major's room to tell him of the morning's events. Deeply shocked, the major in turn went to find Frank, whereupon the two men sat together, comforting each other over the tragic loss of a woman both had loved.

"It must have been something real awful she wanted kept secret to have killed poor Jane, like that," wept Frank, his anger long having subsided. "But for the life of me, I can't even begin to imagine what it might have been."

The major likewise was nonplussed.

They sat together for several hours talking quietly, reminiscing and drinking tea, until their commiserations were disturbed by a gentle tapping on the door.

"Come in," croaked Frank.

Molly entered with a plate of corned beef sandwiches. "I've just been to the kitchen and made these," she said, forcing a half smile. "I know you'll not be feeling hungry, but you must eat something and keep up your strength."

Frank thanked her. "You're a good woman, Molly," he said, taking the plate from her hands. "Sylvia would be touched by your thoughtfulness as she was a firm believer in eating well and not skipping meals."

"What are you going to do about the Inn?" asked the major. "I mean, we can't sit down here forever when there's a business to be run."

"Sod the business," mumbled Frank. "Sod everything!" He then rebuked himself. "I'm sorry, Ben. Please forgive me. You're quite right of course. My locals are also my friends and I can't just shut them out and not let them know what's going on."

"Would you allow the major and I to run the bar tonight?" Molly asked. "I've done a little bar work before, albeit a long time ago, and the major's very familiar with the place."

"Would you? Would you do that for me?" he asked, taking a sandwich to please Molly. "I'd be very much obliged if you would. I'll be around of course, should there be any problems."

"We'd be only too pleased," the major assured him. "You've only to ask, Frank, and we'll help you out any way we can."

And so that evening when the inquisitive locals went to quench their by now unbearable thirsts, they found a different, but not unknown, couple of faces behind the bar. Gertie meanwhile, having heard the news on the grapevine, came into work early to establish the truth behind the rumours and to cook the residents' evening meal. After which, she appointed herself to the job of looking after the kitchen, with Betty's help.

Trade was brisk throughout the evening as word spread that the Inn was open as usual. Everyone it seemed, fancied an evening out. Women who were usually more than happy to stay at home whilst the men went to the Inn to discuss, fishing, football and the price of potatoes, suddenly felt in need of a small sherry or a glass of lemon and lime and the opportunity to have a chat with their female contemporaries.

Inevitably, there was only one topic of conversation, although still no-one had any knowledge of just how Jane had met her death. Only those involved knew the details and they chose not to disclose them for the time being. The major did say, however, when asked, that at present no motive was known, as Sylvia refused to co-operate with the police on that point. This gave the gossiping tongues something new to chew over and set their imaginations into working overtime. By the end of the evening, most concluded that the only plausible motive was infidelity. Sylvia had obviously been an adulteress and Jane had found out. This would explain her silence. She was keeping quiet because she didn't want to incriminate the person with whom she had been unfaithful. This caused the women to eye their husbands with suspicion, as they tried to recollect any periods of strange behaviour during the months prior to Jane's disappearance.

On Sunday morning Ned awoke and looked from his window. A thin layer of white frost sparkled on the old tin roof. He shivered, put on his dressing gown and slipped along the landing to the bathroom. Once washed, shaved and dressed he went downstairs to see if he could help in any way. He found Gertie and Betty busy in the kitchen preparing breakfast and his mother with the major in the bar cleaning and polishing ready for Sunday lunchtime opening.

"How's Frank?" asked Ned.

"I'm alright, lad," he answered, emerging from the cellar. "I'm keeping myself busy, as I find it helps deaden the pain."

Frank had put in a brief appearance late the previous night, where he found, much to his relief, people did not flock around him asking awkward questions. Instead they kept their distance, much as people do following bereavement, when embarrassment causes them to be at a loss for appropriate words. This suited Frank fine, meaning he could come and go as he pleased. He had no desire to work behind the bar, however, at least not for the time being, hence he was extremely grateful to Molly and the major for stepping in, especially as he planned not be around during Sunday lunchtime opening as he intended to visit Sylvia, once he'd eaten breakfast and the cellar work was done.

Since his mother and the major would not be attending church, and Gertie was in a flap at the prospect of cooking her first roast dinner that evening, Ned likewise was delighted to give it a miss. And since his services were not required at the Inn, he decided to get away and walk down to the beach.

The bright sunshine had long since chased off the early morning frost, leaving behind a clear, sunny day with blue skies and a chilling wind blowing from the east.

Ned left the Inn clutching his Sunday newspaper for there was no Daily Herald on the Sabbath. He strolled down to the cove with every intention of sitting on Denzil's bench, but on arrival, found it occupied by young children, excitedly watching a small dog running around in circles chasing its tail. When the dog finally came to a standstill, Ned realised it was Freak and so he cast his eyes eagerly over the somewhat deserted beach looking for Rose. At first it appeared she was nowhere to be seen, but then from behind he heard a piercing, tuneless whistle. Freak's ears pricked up immediately and he tore across the beach like a streak of lightening. Ned turned. Rose was sitting in the distance on rocks near to the stream, sheltering from the wind with her fur coat wrapped tightly around her slender body. Ned crossed towards her not knowing what frame of mind she might be in. He heaved a sigh of relief when he saw her smile.

"How are things at the Inn?" she asked, as he sat down beside her.

"Pretty grim. Everyone's keeping themselves occupied almost as though nothing's happened, but you can tell Sylvia is on the mind of each and every one of them, especially Frank."

"Poor Frank. It's funny you know, but do you remember what I said about William Wagstaffe and him being a sort of hero of mine."

Ned smiled. "Yes, I remember."

"Well, now we've had a real murder here in the village and I really did believe it was an accident; murder doesn't seem at all exciting or romantic anymore. In fact, the thought of Sylvia killing poor Jane by whatever means is horrible, just horrible!"

"So there does beat a heart beneath that brassy exterior. I refer to your mention of poor Jane."

"Oh, I never had anything against Jane, or Sylvia for that matter. I certainly didn't hate them like I do the gossiping old crones. In fact if the truth be known I envied Sylvia her lifestyle. I mean, it must be quite satisfying working at the Inn, a bit like hotel work, I suppose."

"Hate is a very strong word," said Ned, embarrassed to recall telling his mother he hated Sylvia.

"Maybe," smiled Rose, jumping down from the rock. "Anyway, I really must go now. Reg will be home soon from church and it's time to prepare and cook the vegetables."

They walked back to the village together and separated at the Inn.

Ned, not wishing to return indoors to his room or go to the bar for a pint, decided to stay outside in the welcome sunshine. And instead he went to Sylvia's vegetable garden.

Everything there was much as he had seen it the time before. The bonfire had burned away completely, leaving behind a residue of ash which pothered and swirled in each gust of wind that blew.

Ned walked to the shed and took out an old chair, which he recalled having seen on his previous visit. He placed it in the sun against the side of the shed and sat down.

Looking across at the desolate garden, Ned thought of Sylvia locked up in a prison cell and was surprised to find he felt only pity for her. Gone was the anger and hatred, and in their place unexplained questions dominated his thoughts.

"What a mess," he sighed to four sparrows, busily pecking around on a patch of earth amongst the weeds. "What a horrible mess!"

Ned put his hand inside the pocket of his jacket and pulled out his cigarette packet. He lit one and threw the match carelessly onto the patch of freshly dug earth. The church clock struck midday. Time for the major and his mother to open up the bar.

Ned picked up the newspaper which he had previously laid down on the path. He opened it and glanced through the pages. Nothing of much interest caught his eye. It all seemed rather dull in comparison with events in the village. The only article he read in full was about the body found up-country in the spinney, and even that was disappointing, as it was not Grace Bonnington at all, but an unidentified male.

Ned closed the paper, lit another cigarette and leaned his head back on the shed wall, where, much to his surprise, tired through having had a poor night's sleep, he dosed off in the warmth of the sun.

When he awoke, the sun had disappeared behind a grey cloud. Ned shivered, rose quickly and folded the chair, eager to get back indoors. He then returned the chair to the shed. From the back window, he looked across the valley to the empty paddock and wondered if anyone had thought about the needs of the horses. He made a mental note to ask Gertie.

As he turned to leave the shed, Ned remembered the red biscuit tin containing the seeds. He didn't know why, but something compelled him to take another look. He removed the items on the front of the shelf, pulled the tin from its hiding place, laid it on the bench and removed the lid.

The seeds were still there. He lifted out some of the packets and shook them. They all had something inside. He shuffled through the entire contents, and then tipped them out onto the bench.

At the bottom was a manila envelope marked sweet peas, in Sylvia's neat handwriting. Ned thought it seemed bulky for just seeds. He opened it up and inside, along with a dozen or so dark, round seeds, found a small bundle of photographs tied with a pale blue ribbon. Ned was astonished. It seemed a strange place to keep old pictures. Carefully he untied the ribbon. The first picture was of a young man in R.A.F. uniform. He was handsome and Ned considered could not have been much older than himself when the picture was taken. The next was of a couple on horseback, the same young man and surely the young woman with him was Sylvia, her hair a lighter shade. Other pictures were of children, a farmhouse, and young women posing together on bales of hay, wearing Women's Land Army uniforms.

Ned felt a pang of guilt, aware he should not be prying into Sylvia's past and private life: her life, he assumed, before she had moved to Cornwall.

He shuffled through the pictures quickly as they meant nothing to him, until one, the very last one, caught his eye. It was a picture of a man. A fine looking, prosperous man. Ned frowned. He felt sure he recognised the face. Yes, of course. He had seen it many times before in the newspapers. It was William Wagstaffe!

Chapter Thirty

Locked up, all alone in a prison cell, Sylvia Newton sat and reflected on her bleak circumstances. Circumstances caused by one crazy moment of reckless, impetuous behaviour.

Two hours had passed since Frank's departure, yet still her throat ached from crying and pleading for his forgiveness.

Outside the day was growing old. Sylvia crossed to the window and gazed out to the beautiful, winter sunset glowing over the chimneypots and rooftops of that peaceful Sunday afternoon town. The same sunset, she reflected, would also be lighting the skies over Trengillion, framing the silhouette of the dark, leafless trees around the Inn and the church tower, and then finally, as the daylight faded, the sun would sink in a blaze of colour behind the bank and the stables in the paddock.

Sylvia sighed, knowing she would never see another summer. Never dig over the stale earth of winter and put in new life with seedlings in springtime. Never smell the beautiful perfume of her favourite sweet peas, or gather apples in the autumn. Never sit in her favourite spot by the old tin mine, or paddle in the sea. Never ride her beloved horses across the buttercup filled meadows. Never scramble over the cliff tops or walk along the pretty winding lanes.

She left the window and sat down on the plain, hard bed and stared around at the cold, bare walls. She wondered just how many people had occupied the cell before her, wishing they too could turn back the clock and change events which had led to their imprisonment. Yet deep down, Sylvia knew she could never regret leaving London and fleeing to the West Country. Her twenty three months in Cornwall had been some of the happiest in her life. And she really did love good, kind-hearted Frank: just as she had loved the two other men in her life, before him. She had loved all three and lost all three. For she knew without doubt, that life with Frank was over now forever.

Sylvia rose and touched the bars across the window which kept her a prisoner. But already she knew how pain and suffering afflicted those who craved freedom. For her conscience had for two long years yearned to function free of guilt, persecution, torment and remorse. But it was not until she had seen the sparkling aquamarine in the mirror during the police questioning, that she had finally realised she was no longer able to endure the pressure of living a deceitful lie. Living, with a false identity.

She sat back down, and reminisced fondly over the days when, whilst working in London, she had met her first husband, Richard Bonnington, a young, handsome R.A.F pilot. Following a whirlwind romance, they had married in October 1939, shortly after the outbreak of War. Richard had been so proud when the opportunity had risen for him to fight for his country.

Sylvia lowered her head and stared at the grubby, bare floor, remembering the heartache that had followed the ecstasy. For in less than two years after her wedding day, she found herself a widow. Richard's plane had survived the bullets of hostile guns long enough to limp, wounded, out of enemy territory. But sadly, before reaching the friendly shores of home, he had plunged into the cold waters of the English Channel and his body was never recovered.

With Richard gone, she had eagerly seized the opportunity to escape city life and its painful memories by joining the Women's Land Army. This enabled her to spend the remainder of the War, deep in the heart of the Northamptonshire countryside, not far from the orphanage where she had grown up.

Sylvia smiled, those years were happy years. She made some good friends, enjoyed working with the magnificent Shire horses and acquired some useful horticultural skills. She learned to love working with the earth and communing with nature. She found peace of mind in the country and this slowly enabled her to overcome the bitterness she had first encountered following Richard's untimely death.

However, when the War was over and she was released from the Women's Land Army in January 1946, she craved city life again. She wanted to feel the pavement beneath her feet and shed overalls for fashionable clothes, shoes and stockings. She returned to London and, as luck would have it, succeeded in securing the position of housekeeper to a successful politician and his family. But luck, Sylvia found, had a nasty habit of running out.

It was never her intention to fall in love with William Wagstaffe. It just happened. And for three wonderful years during their clandestine affair, she had been joyously happy, confident William also shared her enthusiasm for their passionate relationship.

Sylvia trembled as she recalled the dreadful day when her world had fallen apart. It was the morning of January the first 1950. William, his wife and children were staying with friends on their country estate, just outside London to see in the New Year. She was all alone in the house when he'd returned unexpectedly to collect his briefcase, which he'd inadvertently left behind. Delighted to see him, she'd greeted him warmly when he breezed into her room. She received no such greeting in return, however: his face was sombre, his attitude cold. Without warning, or feeling, he told her bluntly their affair was over and she must leave his house. He confessed he had wind of an impending promotion and could not afford the revelation of a seedy affair thwarting his chances and destroying his career.

Dazed, she had listened in disbelief. Could this really be the man she loved so dearly, standing there before her, insisting she, with no choice, must pack her bags, leave and find another position elsewhere?

Sitting on the bed in her cell, Sylvia gulped, as a cold shiver engulfed her entire body. If only back then she'd had time to think, had some inclination beforehand of his waning love for her, instead of realising, too late, on that dreadful January morning, she occupied no place in his heart or his life, was surplus to requirements and a threat to his glittering career.

Regrettably she had acted with haste. She had panicked, a slighted woman. From the plate off which she had eaten the night before, she grabbed a steak knife and, screaming of her hurt, her anger, her grief, had plunged it deep into his chest. Her screams faded as he staggered backwards and stumbled into a chair. His limp hands grasped for the knife. With eyes grief-stricken and lips trembling, he had attempted to speak. Then he fell, and all movement stopped. She stepped forward as he lay lifeless on the floor, but knew, even before she sought his pulse, that he was dead.

With the knife still embedded in his chest, she hastily wrapped him in a sheet from her bed, dragged him down the stairs, across the hallway and out onto the gravel driveway. Thankful the grounds were surrounded by a camouflage of trees and evergreen shrubs, she managed, through pure adrenalin, to manoeuvre his body from where it lay on the gravel, into the boot of his car. After closing the door quietly, so as not to attract the attention of any passers-by, she hastily returned to the house and from beneath her bed pulled a red biscuit tin containing money she had saved, old photographs and her identity papers. From her wardrobe, she took a change of clothes, pulled gloves from a drawer and then with haste, ran down the stairs and out of the house to the potting shed.

Wearing the gloves, she seized a garden spade and threw it on the back seat of the car. Thankful William had left the keys in the ignition, she started the engine and cautiously drove along back roads to a nearby spinney. From there, sobbing, she unceremoniously buried his body in a shallow grave, still wrapped with the sheet from her bed and with the steak knife embedded in its chest.

The spade, its duty done, she thrust deep into a holly bush until it was no longer visible. She then changed into clean clothes, dropped the bloodstained garments into a large paper bag, wiped all traces of her finger prints from the boot handle, and drove William's car to a disused factory car park, abandoning it there.

With nowhere to go, no home and no belongings, she walked briskly to Paddington Station, hiding her face beneath the brim of her hat. At the station she bought a one way ticket to Devon and caught the first available train. On reaching her destination, she booked herself into a small hotel, and from there, walked the following day to an isolated spot, where she burned her blood stained clothes, her identity card, birth certificate and marriage certificate. She watched sadly as the flames engulfed her true identity. Grace Bonnington was no more.

As luck would have it, she and William Wagstaffe had shared the same blood group, hence police went in search of him, assuming she had been the victim of a brutal murder.

For several weeks she lay low as the story made front page news. Meanwhile, she dyed her hair from light to dark brown, changed the style and made a point of always wearing a hat partly to cover her face. Instead of Grace Bonnington, she now used the name, Sylvia Spencer.

Sylvia had been a friend, she as Grace, had made during the War in her Land Army days. They had shared a room in the Northamptonshire farmhouse and kept their identity papers and birth certificates together in Grace's red biscuit tin.

On June 30th 1944, as the War dragged on, the real Sylvia Spencer had gone to London to meet her boyfriend, home on leave. She left her friends at the farm in the early hours of that cold, dank day, after which, she was never seen again. It was assumed she must have been killed by the doodlebug, which caused mass destruction when it exploded in the street outside the Air Ministry at Adastral House, where she and her boyfriend had arranged to meet. Her remains were never found and identified, and as, in the excitement and rush to catch her train she had forgotten to take with her, her identity papers, they had remained ever since in Grace's red biscuit tin.

Grace, with optimism, had kept Sylvia's papers over the years, always hopeful that one day, her friend would turn up alive and well. But this was never the case.

When Grace, now Sylvia, thought the coast was clear, she moved from Devon on to Cornwall. She wanted to be as far away from London as possible. She chose the Ringing Bells Inn for her stay simply because the name appealed to her and in no time at all she had fallen in love with Frank.

Sylvia sighed. Things would have been perfect then were it not for Jane.

She sat down on the floor beside the bed and rested her arm on the rough, grey blanket. Poor Jane! If only she had not gone to visit her aunt and uncle in Kent, as it was there she saw a picture of Grace Bonnington on a sheet of newspaper lining the bottom of a drawer. Jane, a sharp girl, had noticed the resemblance between Grace and Sylvia, and on returning to the Inn had asked awkward questions. Sylvia, not wanting Jane to voice her opinions to others, told her the truth and begged her never to breathe a word to anyone. Jane had promised solemnly, but Sylvia was afraid. She could not take the risk that Jane might one day betray her.

"God forgive me," whispered Sylvia, not for the first time during the long months that had followed Jane's death.

254

Sylvia looked at her bleak future. She knew already that the body found in the spinney, which at first everyone assumed to be her, would in time be identified as William Wagstaffe. Her picture would then appear in all the papers and it would not take long for the locals to realise that Grace Bonnington and Sylvia Newton were one and the same person.

Sylvia could not bear the thought of being taken back to London to face trial for William's murder. She could not face the press, the questions and the pain it would cause poor, innocent Frank. And what would be the end result when she was found guilty of not one, but two murders? Death! Death by hanging!

"I shall be hung by the neck until I am dead," she whispered. "For the Judge will see me as nothing other than a ruthless killer. A woman without compassion. A woman whose acts of violence know no bounds."

Sylvia rose and crossed to the table where a kind policewoman had allowed her several sheets of paper and a pencil. On them she wrote a letter to Frank confessing everything she had been unable to tell him earlier. It was easier when written, as she would not have to witness the horrified look on his face when he finally learned the bitter truth.

When she had finished, Sylvia folded up the sheets of paper, left them on the table and climbed back onto the bed. From the sleeve of her cardigan she took the handkerchief which Frank had given to her during the police questioning back at the Inn. She spread it out in front of her and removed a small packet of razor blades which she had taken from the bathroom cabinet on her last visit there before they had taken her away. She slipped one of the blades from the packet and dropped the rest onto the floor.

She knew it would be painful. But so too was suffering a long, lingering death, due to the cruel administration of poison after crawling through a gruesome tunnel desperately in search of help. At least William's death had been quick. The knife must have pierced his stone, cold heart.

Sylvia lay back on the bed, rested her head on the thin pillow and forcefully cut deep into both her wrists. The blood splattered onto her crisp, clean blouse, and the blade fell onto her skirt.

Staring towards the window, she watched the moon and smiled. That same moon would be beaming down on Trengillion, the Inn and the sea. She thought of her beloved horses, of her friends, of Frank, of William, and of Richard. She felt no hate. No bitterness and no self-pity. She felt no pain. And as the tears trickled from Sylvia's eyes, so the blood trickled from her slender wrists and her white lips whispered faintly the same words over and over again, "God, please forgive me and judge me not too harshly." Until finally, the moon disappeared. Her vision blurred. Consciousness was lost and she was freed from the torments of her troubled, guilty mind, forever.

Chapter Thirty-One

The following morning, as Ned walked along the road returning from the post office, he was conscious of a pair of eyes gazing at him from the front cover of his folded newspaper. Eyes which seemed familiar, yet try as he might, he could not recollect where he had seen them before.

He walked on a little further, his mind filled with curiosity, until the suspense became unbearable. In the middle of the road he stopped, unfolded the paper and looked at the face in full. He gasped loudly. In bold print, the name beneath the picture, said Grace Bonnington.

With heart racing, Ned read that the mysterious body found buried in the spinney up-country had been identified as William Wagstaffe. Wagstaffe, it revealed, had been murdered, and Grace Bonnington was wanted for questioning in connection with his death.

In disbelief, Ned clumsily folded the paper, his mind plagued by images of the pictures he had found in Sylvia's red biscuit tin, and in particular the one of William Wagstaffe. He felt dizzy and sick. He took in a deep breath. He knew where Grace Bonnington was and he guessed, before long, everyone in Trengillion would know also. The dyed hair and change of style was not enough to disguise the true identity of Sylvia Newton.

In a daze, Ned unsteadily walked down the road lost in thought. He passed the postman, whistling, as he propped up his red bicycle against the wall of Well Cottage, and waved absentmindedly to Sid Reynolds as he passed by in his car. Outside the church Ned stopped. Suddenly, everything fell into place and at long last, after weeks of confusion and deliberation, he finally believed he knew why poor Jane had died.

In a state of shock, he rounded the corner to the Inn. A police car stood outside. He went into the hallway, wiped his feet and turned down the passage looking for signs of life.

At first there appeared to be no-one around, but then he heard gentle sobbing emanating from the dining room. Inside, he found

Gertie and Betty, both snivelling at the table in the window. His mother, with red eyes, sat nearby. The major, and Annie Stevens were with her.

Molly began to rise as her son neared the table. Ned threw down the paper. "You obviously know about this, then?" he blurted. "To think all this time we've been living in the presence of a cold blooded, double murderer. Whatever made her do such things? The woman's unhinged. I wonder how many other skeletons there are in her closet. I can't believe..."

"...Ned, Ned, please, that's enough," said Molly, tears welling up in her eyes again. "I will not have you speaking ill of the dead, whatever the circumstances might be."

"But I'm not, am I? I'm talking about Syl...." He stopped as his mother's words sank in.

"I don't understand," he muttered, glancing around at the saddened faces. "What's going on?"

"Sylvia's dead," whispered Molly, wiping her eyes.

"Dead!" The word stuck in Ned's throat like a piece of raw apple.

"She took her own life," croaked the major. "Silly girl slashed her wrists. They found her this morning."

Ned flopped into the nearest chair. "Good God. Does Frank know?"

"Yes, of course," whispered Annie. "Fred and Detective Inspector Williams are with him now. I came round to tell you all before you heard the news from another source."

"Excuse me," choked Ned, feeling his eyes begin to water.

He hastily left the room and stumbled up the stairs in a daze. For the first time during his stay in Cornwall, he yearned for the solitude of his cold, bleak room.

Later, when Ned felt more composed, he left his room and the Inn and slipped round the back to Sylvia's vegetable garden. Inside the shed he took from its hiding place, her red biscuit tin and tossed the seed packets aside. He removed from the bottom, the bundle of photographs through which he had looked the previous day, but shown to no-one else, and then put them into the pocket of his jacket.

Back inside his room, he spread out the photographs on his eiderdown and then read more thoroughly the article on the front page of the Daily Herald. It told of Grace being the widow of R.A.F pilot, Richard Bonnington, and in a cold, calculated manner, how she had worked as housekeeper for the Wagstaffe family in Chelsea. She was wanted for questioning regarding the death of William Wagstaffe. The article did not, however, disclose the method by which he had died.

Ned cast his eyes sadly over the pictures which told of happier times, he then gathered them up with reverence, and bound them back together with the piece of blue ribbon. He decided first to show them to his mother and the major, and then when things had quietened down, he'd give them to Frank.

Ned sighed, as he tried to imagine just how low Frank must be feeling. He had suffered so much in the past few days. First he'd had to endure finding his wife the murderer of Jane, and now it seemed, the murderer of William Wagstaffe also. She had lied about her true identity and finally taken her own life.

"Poor Frank," muttered Ned, with deep, deep feeling. "Poor, poor Frank!"

Frank Newton sat restlessly staring into the grate, where a pile of ash and clinkers from the previous day's fire, looked as cheerful as the life which he saw cast before him. The police had gone and he was left alone to comprehend that which he had been told.

He picked up the letter Sylvia had written before she had died. In it she had explained to him about her liaison with William Wagstaffe and the tragic consequences which followed. He read the words slowly and thoroughly for the second time from beginning to end.

Frank found it difficult to imagine Sylvia really being Grace Bonnington. She would always be Sylvia to him. She had even signed the letter, Sylvia.

He stood up and shuffled his way through to the kitchen. He would make a pot of tea, that's what Sylvia would do if she was faced with a similar predicament. It seemed to be a woman's remedy for just about everything.

Frank poured the boiling water from the kettle into the old brown teapot, gave it a stir and put on the lid and the tea cosy. He then placed it on a tray along with his own cup and saucer, a bottle of milk, some sugar lumps and the tea strainer.

Sylvia would have put the milk in a jug, but Frank thought dirtying jugs an unnecessary extravagance.

Carrying the tray carefully, he slipped back along the passage, into the living room and closed the door. He could hear voices coming from another part of the Inn, but he didn't want to speak to anyone for a while.

He sipped his tea whilst looking at the front page of the newspaper. Next to Sylvia, a small picture of William Wagstaffe was inserted. Frank stared at him, his eyes full of loathing. How dare this jumped up, pompous, egocentric, politician treat his Sylvia so! Frank had no time for politicians, whatever their persuasion. He did not blame Sylvia for killing William Wagstaffe. He just wished she hadn't.

"Wouldn't it have been nice if she'd done as that miserable sod wanted and left his house?" he mumbled. "She could then have caught the train from Paddington without blood on her hands, and come to Ringing Bells, married me and everything would have been perfect. But she should never have killed Jane. Jane was a smashing girl and the poor kid hadn't done anything wrong. Not like that swine, Wagstaffe. Poor Jane, you shouldn't have killed, Jane, Sylvia. That was a wicked, wicked thing to do."

Frank tossed the newspaper onto the dusty table, stood up and poked the ash in the fireplace. He contemplated lighting it, but could not be bothered. He could not be bothered to do anything. But what about the Inn? It would be opening time soon. He had better find the major and Molly to see if they were alright to open up again. But then, what about the next day and the day after that? Could he ever be the happy landlord again? Perhaps he should go away for a while. Take a break, collect his thoughts together and plan his future. "A future without, Sylvia," choked Frank, as tears welled in his eyes. It was a harrowing thought. If the major and Molly couldn't help him out, then he'd have to plod on regardless, just as he had done before Sylvia had arrived. And he could always ask Flo Hughes to sort out the bed and breakfast side of things for a while, as she had done before in days gone by. Then there was Gertie and Betty. They were a couple of good girls. They would help.

Frank folded up Sylvia's letter and placed it behind a framed picture on the cluttered mantelpiece. A picture of the two of them taken on their wedding day. He blew Sylvia a kiss. "Of course I forgive you," he muttered. "You silly, silly girl. I'd forgive you anything. You gave me strength and a will to live, and I'm gonna use that strength now to plod on."

And with that statement he left his living room, took his tray back to the kitchen, and went to look for the major and Molly.

Two days later, in the warmth of the spring sunshine, Jane was finally laid to rest in the village churchyard, near to the Inn and near to her home. Her grave, in the shadow of a mountain ash, was piled high with flowers from the locals, who had flocked into the little church, filling every pew, to say their last goodbye.

Later, after everyone had gone, Ned looked down on the flowers laid in tribute to someone he had known, not in life, but in death. Pensively he sat on a nearby bank, surrounded by daffodils, and crocus in shades of yellow, purple and white. Ned liked the churchyard. He liked the tranquility. It made him feel at ease and able to relax. He recalled Sylvia's sentiments regarding gardens. The churchyard, he considered, was much like a garden too.

Ned turned on hearing footsteps crunching along the gravel path. A young woman approached clutching a small, homemade wreath of primroses in her hands. She did not see him as she crossed to the grave where she knelt on the grass to lay her offering amongst the rest.

Ned watched, as she thoughtfully read the cards on the other wreaths. He could not see her face for her back was towards him, but she had pretty hair, light brown and wavy. Whilst pondering her identity, the peace was abruptly disturbed by the barking of a small dog.

"Freak," hissed the woman, laughing as she stood. "I told you to stay at home, you bad, bad boy."

Ned's jaw dropped in disbelief. "Rose," he gasped, rising to his feet. "I don't believe my eyes. I must be dreaming."

She hastily turned on hearing his voice.

"Christ! You startled me, Ned," she said, with a nervous laugh.

Ned was too dumbfounded to speak.

"Yes, as you can see, I've changed." She giggled, amused by the expression on his face. "And you're the first person to see the new me, or perhaps even, the real me."

Ned stepped forward and lifted her arms to admire the simple floral dress and pretty blue cardigan she was wearing. "Good God, so when did this transformation take place?"

Rose blushed. "This morning. Reg was really quite annoyed when I said I wouldn't be going to the funeral. I couldn't tell him why, though. I made the appointment with the hairdresser last week, you see, before the time and date of Jane's funeral was set. I'm quite scared. He's not seen me yet, so he's in for a bit of a shock."

"Shock! Surprise, I think would be a better word. You look terrific, Rose, you really do."

"Thank you. I feel it. After I'd had my hair done, I went straight to the shops and bought myself a new outfit. I left my old clothes there and asked the assistant to throw them away. I felt ten feet tall as I waited for the bus home."

Ned shook his head. "So what made you take such a drastic step?"

"Sylvia," answered Rose, promptly. "Sylvia spent two years trying to be someone else and look where it got her. I know there's no comparison, because Sylvia's character and that of Grace Bonnington were probably the same anyway. But it made me think how nice it would be, to be me again, if you see what I mean. And I also realised just how precious life is."

"So some good has come out of this. You really are a clot, Rose. Without all that dreadful make-up you're really very pretty, and you look younger too."

Rose laughed. "Pretty except for the freckles."

"There's nothing wrong with freckles," said Ned. "I have one or two myself."

A week later, as Friday dawned, Ned woke to the realisation it was his last full day in Cornwall. The following day he was due to return home to London and eventually to work. He was not sure how to spend his final day. There were so many places he wanted to visit and only, it seemed, a few hours in which so to do.

He looked from the window. The weather was fine. A few clouds drifted through the sky, but blue was more prevalent than grey.

After careful consideration, Ned decided to take a walk with his mother, if she could fit it in between her duties at the Inn. He resolved to ask her during breakfast.

Molly had agreed to stay at the Inn to help out Frank for a further two weeks after Ned's departure. But Ned knew she was also reluctant to leave the major.

Mother and son took their last walk along the cliff path. It had been difficult to choose which route to take as the area had so many delightful walks. They settled on the cliff path going west because of its significance. The Witches Broomstick had, after all, played a significant part in their being re-united.

Major Benjamin Smith, meanwhile, had an urgent trip to make of his own. Of late he had pondered long and hard about his relationship with Molly and had reached the only possible conclusion there was. That he loved her dearly and could not even begin to imagine how empty and dull his life would be should she ever return to Clacton. He realised, without doubt, she had filled the void which for so long had wounded him and he was not prepared to let her go.

The major parked his car with expert precision outside a jewellers with a first class reputation in Helston. After entering through the door, he removed his hat and shook hands with the elegantly dressed assistant, who greeted him warmly.

"May I," said the major, giving a little cough to clear his throat. "May I have a look, please, at a selection of your finest engagement rings?"

Friday night saw the Inn packed to full capacity. News of the major and Molly's engagement had travelled fast once Gertie and Betty had been told, and villagers, glad of something to celebrate, were delighted to show their approval by arriving in large numbers.

The sombre mood which had overshadowed the past few weeks, they hoped was changing for good. Fully aware, that it was not possible to turn back the clock and undo that which was done, they all agreed the only way was forward.

Half way through the evening, Ned left the revelry to seek Frank. He found him in his cluttered living room, sitting beside a glowing fire, smoking a pipe. On the mantelpiece stood an urn containing Sylvia's ashes, alongside the wedding picture and the photographs which Ned had found in Sylvia's red biscuit tin. Frank saw him look in their direction.

"Those pictures are all I have of Sylvia's past, so they're very precious to me. Molly's going to get them framed."

Ned half smiled. "That'll be nice." But he was not sure he liked the idea of Sylvia's ashes being on display like an ornament, although he very much doubted Frank would see it that way.

"I didn't know you smoked a pipe," said Ned, moving aside to avoid the cloud of smoke passing in his direction.

Frank laughed. "I only started yesterday. Sylvia always used to say how she liked to see a man smoke a pipe. I haven't quite got the hang of it yet, the ruddy thing keeps going out, but I shall persevere."

Ned smiled. It was good to hear Frank laughing again.

"Will you come up and join us for a drink? Everyone's keen to see you and it is my last night."

"Actually, I was thinking of popping up anyway. I might even pour a few pints, but I'll have to get changed first."

"Splendid," said Ned, "I'll get back then. You won't change your mind, will you?"

Frank grinned. "No, I won't, we'll be up shortly."

Ned paused in the doorway. "We?" he queried.

"Me and Sylvia," said Frank. "I feel she's still here with me, you see. I talk to her all the time. You don't think I'm crackers, do you?"

Ned shook his head. "No, no I don't."

Chapter Thirty-Two

In the quiet, still darkness of early morning, as Ned lay cosily tucked up in his bed, he heard the gentle, sweet voice of a woman singing. A familiar voice, tunefully singing of an enchanted evening.

"Jane," mumbled Ned, sleepily.

"I've come to bid you farewell and to say thank you," sang a happy voice in the darkness.

"Farewell?" said Ned, raising his head from the pillow. "Where are you and where are you going?"

"I'm moving on," whispered the voice, with an impish giggle. "I'm at rest now."

"What!" exclaimed Ned, now fully awake and sitting up in bed.

"Goodbye, Ned. Dear, kind, sweet Ned. Thank you for everything you have done for me."

He felt something soft brush tenderly against his face, like a kiss. It was followed by a gentle breeze, peacefully whistling, almost silent. And then all was quiet. She was gone. Vanished into thin air and the unknown.

"Jane," pleaded Ned. "Jane, please, please don't go."

But the room remained still and silent.

In the dark, Ned fumbled to put on his bedside lamp. He squinted, his vision blurred, as he looked at his watch. It was ten minutes past five. Rubbing his eyes, he mulled over Jane's words, her last words, and tried to decide whether she really had spoken to him or whether it had been a dream. He shook his head sorrowfully and sighed, realising he would never know.

Ned slid out of bed and walked down the passage to the bathroom where he took a bath and shaved before returning to his room to dress. The previous night, as he lay awake, before finally succumbing to sleep, his mind had been plagued by images of Sylvia's ashes trapped in the urn on Frank's cluttered mantelpiece. He knew this was not what Sylvia had wanted and it troubled him deeply.

As soon as the sky showed the first signs of daylight, he went downstairs to see if Frank was about. He found him in the cellar rolling barrels across the uneven, flagstone floor.

"Ned," he gasped. "You're up early. You gave me a scare."

"Sorry. I didn't mean to startle you, but there's something on my mind."

He then proceeded to tell Frank about the day he and Sylvia had ridden the horses to the old mine, and how she had told him of her love for that spot and her wish to have her ashes sprinkled there.

Frank listened intently to every word Ned uttered. "I'm glad you've told me," he said, thoughtfully. "Let's go up to the bar, because it's bloomin' cold down here and I've done all there is to be done."

They climbed the bare, stone steps which led to a trap door on the floor behind the bar, and then went into the snug which struck pleasantly warm in spite of the fire having long gone out.

"I've not been happy myself thinking of poor Sylvia cooped up in that ugly pot, but the truth is, I didn't know what else to do with her as we never talked of death when she was alive. But if she wanted to go to the old mine, then that's where she must go. Will you take her for me?"

"Me!" gasped Ned, surprised.

"Yes, if you'd be so kind. I'd much appreciate it, I really would, because I don't think I could face doing it myself."

"Oh, well, yes, alright then," mumbled Ned.

"Well, there's no time like the present," said Frank, rising from his seat. "And as you're off later you'd better go now. It would be best done early, anyway, before people are out and about, and Sylvia really liked early mornings."

Ned reluctantly agreed, and so the two men crept along the passage to the Newtons' living room, where Frank removed the urn from the mantelpiece.

"You'll not want to be seen carrying this cumbersome thing," he muttered, placing the urn on the table. "So we'd better find something more suitable."

He turned to the sideboard and from the top drawer took out a brown paper bag. "We'll tip her into this. It'll make things much easier."

Ned was aghast at the idea of Sylvia screwed up in a paper bag. Frank, however, found it amusing.

"You know, Ned," he laughed. "I'm pretty sure she's seeing the funny side of all this. My Sylvia had a great sense of humour."

Ned grinned, half-heartedly, as Frank pushed the bag into his hands.

"Now, off you go, and thanks ever so much. I'll make sure there's a nice cuppa tea waiting for you when you get back, and a slice of that lovely coffee cake your dear mum made."

Ned walked down the road to the foot of the cliff path and swiftly climbed to the top. Unlike the day of the storm, he walked with ease towards the old mine, enjoying the freshness of the new morning in spite of the bizarre task which lay ahead of him. He passed by the row of coastguard's cottages. There was no sign of life. The front gardens were overgrown and untidy. It crossed Ned's mind the houses were probably unoccupied.

A glorious day was dawning as he reached the old mine. Beneath the cliffs, the clear, crystal sea, rippled, leisurely and calm: the only sounds to be heard, its waves falling rhythmically onto the rocks and the welcome dawn chorus of birds in the vegetation.

Ned licked his finger and held it above his head to see from which direction the wind was blowing. It was south westerly. He turned with his back to the wind and carefully unscrewed the brown paper bag.

It seemed to him an irreverent act, as he gently tipped out the contents. But to his surprise, the ash did not fall straight to the ground, but rose instead with the wind. Ned watched, mesmerised, as the breeze lifted Sylvia's remains high above his head, where they danced and swirled in a perfect circle before finally drifting down and settling on the damp grass at the foot of the old mine wall.

Ned swallowed hard in an attempt to dispel the lump in his throat. He felt he should say something but could think of no appropriate words. Instead, he thoughtfully folded up the paper bag, pushed it into his pocket and headed back down the hill to the Inn.

After breakfast, Molly walked with Ned to the post office to collect his last newspaper.

"You will come back for the wedding, won't you?" she asked, gazing for the umpteenth time, at the clusters of diamonds on her new ring. "It'll only be a modest affair of course. We don't want a big fuss."

"I wouldn't miss it for the world and perhaps by then I might even have met Stella Hargreaves and she'll be able to accompany me."

Molly laughed. "You know I was only joking when I first brought up that name, although I do have faith in my other predictions, and I was right to get upset when I saw you crying."

Ned nodded. "Yes, I know. But what about the William Wagstaffe incident at Flo's party. What do you reckon that was all about?"

"You know, I've thought about that a lot, and I think it must have been Wagstaffe himself who spoke to me. I just remember hearing someone say his name, you see, so it must have been him saying who he was, not to whom he wished to speak. Does that make sense?"

"Hmm, I suppose so. In which case, I guess it was Sylvia he wanted to speak to."

"Most likely. I was a little drunk if you remember, which in retrospect was just as well. I dread to think how pandemonium would have broken out, had I got it right."

Ned sighed. "No wonder Sylvia fainted."

"Did she? I didn't realise that. Poor Sylvia, I hope history won't judge her too harshly, but I fear it will. She'll go down in history as an infamous murderer."

Ned grinned. "No, she won't. Grace Bonnington will."

They reached the post office and went inside.

"There's something I want to show you," said Molly, as Ned joined the short queue to pay for his paper. "It won't take long and I think you'll be quite impressed."

Ned was intrigued as they walked back down the road towards the Inn. Outside the village hall they stopped. On the opposite side of the road, next to Ivy Cottage and beside a tall, neglected hedge, Molly pointed to a gate on which the faded name Rose Cottage was engraved. Smiling, she lifted the latch.

"The old chap who lived here died recently, and he's left this to his only son who lives in Manchester, and the son has no wish to ever live here. The major said he'd like to buy it for us to live in, eventually. What do you think of it?"

They walked through the gate and stood on an overgrown path. Ned looked at the house with approval.

"You can go right up to it," said Molly. "There's no-one there."

Ned walked up to the house and peeped in the small, downstairs windows of the rooms where the curtains were pulled back sufficiently to catch a glimpse.

"It looks very nice from what I can see of it. And what an idyllic spot."

"From upstairs, you can even see the sea," said Molly, excitedly.

"You've been inside, then," said Ned.

"Yes I have. The major and I had a good look round yesterday after you and I came back from our walk. Fred and Annie have a key so they can keep an eye on the place. I didn't mention it last night in case it came to nothing, but when I said how much I liked it, the major phoned Manchester to negotiate a price with the agents handling it. It's all in his hands of course, but this morning he said there's no reason at all why it shouldn't go ahead."

"Wonderful. I'm so pleased for you both. You'll need to develop further your gardening skills though," said Ned, with a laugh, eyeing the flower borders knee high in weeds.

Molly smiled. "I've already spoken to Doris and she's going to give me a hand. She's only next door so it'll be perfect."

"Absolutely! A project to keep you both occupied, that's just what Doris needs."

He bent to pick two sprigs of white heather peeping through a patch of dandelion leaves and handed one to Molly. The other he put in his pocket. "For luck," he whispered, kissing her cheek.

Back in his room at the Inn, Ned pulled from beneath the bed, his brown leather suitcase and proceeded to pack his belongings. Whilst doing so, he paused to recollect just how tired and ill he had felt on his arrival in Cornwall. It seemed such a long time ago and so much had happened during his stay.

"I think I've probably grown up a lot," he said to old Fisherman Claude, hanging on the wall. "Wouldn't you agree?"

The old man's face retained its usual smile. "I'll miss you, you old bugger," he said, gently tapping the frame. With all his belongings, he then left the room for the very last time.

Frank had offered to run Ned to the station. He was eager to get out and about and keep himself occupied without being tied to the boundaries of the Inn. Ned's train was due at midday and so they planned to leave just after eleven o'clock.

As Ned put his suitcase into the boot of the car, Frank emerged from the front door of the Inn with a letter in his hand.

"I nearly forgot: this came for you this morning. Postmark says London."

Ned looked at the envelope and recognised the familiar handwriting of his school teaching friend.

"Brilliant, it's from George, no doubt filling me in with all the latest news and gossip. That's good, it'll be something to read on the train."

He opened his briefcase and dropped it inside.

With ten minutes still to spare before his departure, Ned went to the kitchen to find the girls to say goodbye. He found Betty peeling apples.

"Gertie's out the back, she's gone to cut a couple of caulis."

She blushed when he kissed her cheek.

Ned then walked through the backyard, past the well and into the vegetable garden. He looked around, Gertie was nowhere to be seen. Assuming she had already returned indoors, he turned to do likewise, but then he noticed Barley Wine lying beneath the apple tree, purring contentedly. Ned edged a little closer.

"Sylvia," he whispered, hoping and thinking her presence might be the reason for the cat's obvious happiness.

"Sylvia," he repeated, bending down towards the animal.

As he put forward his hand, the cat leapt in the air, hissing and spitting like an out of control Catherine wheel.

"I thought you didn't like cats," laughed Gertie, taking a large knife from the pocket of her pinafore.

"I don't," said Ned, embarrassed, as he turned to stand upright. "I came out here looking for you, but you weren't here."

"I went to spend a penny first," she grinned, bending and niftily sliced the heads off two cauliflowers.

He escorted her back to the kitchen and then kissed her cheek.

"I expect I'll see you in June, when I come back for Mum's wedding. But until then, goodbye, and behave."

She giggled. "We'll all still be here, I hope. And as for behaving, well, I always do."

Ned grinned, and as he turned towards the door, Gertie rushed forward, grabbed him by the arm and gave him a tight hug. "Have a good journey, Ned. We're all going to miss you ever so much."

Ned was touched. "I shall miss you all too."

Outside the front of the Inn, Ned kissed his weeping mother, and shook hands with the major, he then climbed into the car beside Frank.

Driving through the village, they saw Reg and Rose Briers leaving The School House together, with their bicycles. Frank tooted. They all waved.

"It's good to see everything well with them now," said Frank. "I always knew deep down Rose was alright and she never offended me with her rebellious ways."

Outside Helston Station, Ned bade farewell to Frank, who had a few errands to do in town before he returned to the village. He then wandered onto the platform and sat on a bench to wait the ten minutes until the branch line train was due.

On time, the train steamed into the station and collected its passengers. Ned disembarked at Gwinear Road, and then boarded the main line train for Paddington. To his delight, he found an empty compartment, for the train had only commenced its journey a few stops before in Penzance.

From his briefcase, he took his newspaper, unfolded it and read whilst he had peace and quiet. On the front page, it reported the funeral of William Wagstaffe had taken place. Ned read the article with heavy eyes and then lay the paper down on the seat. Having gone to bed late and risen early, he felt very tired. His eyes closed and opened intermittently, until finally the continuous sound of the rattling train lulled him off to sleep.

When Ned awoke, the train was nearing Plymouth. Hastily, he stood, pushed open the window and took in a deep breath. As they slowly steamed across Brunel's bridge, the fresh breeze rendered him wide awake.

Ned watched the River Tamar far below, and then glanced back to the rear of the train, beyond which, lay Cornwall. Thoughtfully, he closed the window and returned to his seat, knowing they would soon be arriving at Plymouth Station.

From the window, he observed rows and rows of houses and his thoughts turned to London, thus jogging his memory of the unread letter from George. He opened up his briefcase, took out the letter and slid his finger along the top of the blue envelope.

George had written several pages containing news of the party Ned had missed. He also told who was seeing who, and who was doing what. Ned laughed, realising how much he was looking forward to getting home and seeing everyone again.

As he folded the letter, he noticed a P.S. on the back of the last page.

It read: *Nearly forgot to tell you. We've a new English teacher starting school next term. She was introduced to us last week before we broke up for Easter. She's an absolute cracker. Slim, dark brown hair, greeny brown eyes and the most amazing straight teeth. Her name is Stella Hargreaves.*

THE END

Printed in Great Britain
by Amazon